Wonderfully Wicked

BOOK ONE OF THE VIRTUOUS VILLAINS SERIES

KAMY M. LAVIN

FAIRYTALES, FACTS & FABLES PUBLISHING

*For seventeen-year-old me mailing my first book off to publishers.
It took a minute, we learned a lot, and we did it, kid.*

I'm so proud of us!

Author's Note

Dear Reader,

While *Wonderfully Wicked* is a fictional story about fictional characters, it still contains topics of humanity that may be triggering, such as:

- Alcohol use
- Mild language
- Murder
- Physical, mental, sexual and emotional abuse
- Pregnancy complications/death

Please take care of yourself as you read.

Kamy M. Lavin

LEXLENT
The Sanctuary
Xeric Desert
YANZIE SEA
PHANNEL
TRANIK
WYSTFELLIA
MISTERIA
MONDGUE
THE KINGDOMS

CHAPTER
One

The ballroom was a sea of dancers twirling and bobbing across the black-and-white checkered floor, pulling Anna deeper into the current of colorful materials that washed her away from the ballroom doors.

"Ouch!" her dance partner grumbled, pulling her attention that had been glued on the arriving party guests, rather than her feet, which had a tendency to stray toward her partner's toes.

"Sorry," she said for the third or fourth time. She couldn't remember. The paper, which was the reason her eyes kept locking on to the ornately carved ballroom doors, was practically burning a hole in her dress pocket.

"It's fine, Lady Annalie," he said, smiling broadly at her. The *"gentlemanly"* thing to do in these situations. She wanted to sigh, but that wasn't *"ladylike"* according to her stepmother's grueling etiquette lessons.

"I'm sorry, I'm feeling flushed from all the dancing," she said, dropping their joined hands, halting their steps. She plastered on a sweet, soft smile like the good pawn she was taught to be and fanned herself with her hand. It was just half past noon, but Anna was done playing the game today, tired from the relentless line of strangers her oldest sister, Cyndra, sent her way for a turn on the dance floor.

"I need to take a moment to rest, and then I should be right as rain." She almost threw up in her mouth saying the words, but this was her life now that her eldest sister was a princess. Balls, tea parties, and cross-stitching. *The essentials to landing a fine husband.* Anna's father's message rang through her mind, drilled into her and her two sisters since birth. What she wouldn't give to escape the party for an hour or two to do something tolerable, like practicing archery at the castle's range.

"Absolutely. I'll get you some punch," he said, cutting into her wishful thinking of being a knight for a few hours versus a princess's pawn.

"Oh, that won't be necessary," Anna insisted.

"Nonsense," Lord whatever-his-name-was said. "Go sit over there, and I'll bring it to you." *Stars, he's a demanding one.* He pointed at the wall lined with plush golden chairs near where her sister and brother-in-law held court, talking and laughing with several guests. Anna nodded, waiting for him to turn, then shuffled to the opposite side of the ballroom, hoping it would buy her a few moments of peace while still in good view of the doors.

She smiled, nodding appropriately as she passed guests, who blessedly didn't engage in conversation. She exhaled, reaching her destination—no one within ten feet—and pulled out her letter. She scanned it for the dozenth time, hoping it would be enough to convince—

"Annalie," Cyndra trilled over the stringed music. She looked up. Her sister waved at her, bumping one of the thousands of gaudy blue-and-white decorations the attendants had put up for her son's birthday party. "Stay right there," she added and turned to the elderly woman she spoke to, smiling politely before heading her way. Anna quickly crumpled the paper and slid it back into her pocket. She couldn't risk her sister seeing the letter and telling their stepmother.

Cyndra gracefully navigated her way through the attendees, tiara gleaming in her perfect blonde updo, her fluffy robin-egg-blue dress taking far too much space as her mere presence forced aside the throng of game pieces. She left her husband, Prince Edgar, to deal with their wiggly son, the birthday boy, Prince Augustus, who was tugging at his suit collar.

A bit much for a one-year-old. The kid is miserable! Anna thought as she watched her nephew's futile attempts to get rid of his choking outfit. She glanced down at her pink monstrosity. Anna looked like she'd been swallowed by a birthday cake with the layers of taffeta draping down to the ballroom floor. Plus, she had to wear a corset, which dug into her chest and made her feel like a pin cushion, her ribs aching every time she moved too fast.

"Why are you hiding in the corner?" Cyndra asked, her perfect eyebrows pinched in confusion. Anna adjusted her corset, desperately trying to heave in a breath and give her oxygen-starved lungs some relief. She lowered her gaze to Cyndra, who was five inches shorter, only one of the many differences between them. Another was how Cyndra had no trouble breathing in her death contraption as apparent by how easily her chest rose and fell.

"Because it's just a one-year-old's birthday party," Anna answered, unable to fight the truth from pouring out of her. It was the magic she was born with, though often, it felt more like a curse. "I don't see why we have to get all dressed up! Or why you're making such a fuss when Augustus won't remember any of this." She pointed at the giant pink bow that Cyndra insisted Anna wear on her head. It stuck out like a sore thumb, covering most of her fiery red hair.

She preferred to wear her hair in a practical braid, out of her way, not piled on top of her head with a bow. *Why was Dru allowed to skip the party for one of Tinker's workshops? Isn't she Princess Cyndra's sister as well? Shouldn't she also be forced to suffer?*

Cyndra sighed heavily. "You could at least try. For Father's sake. You know how he enjoyed a good party. He would have loved to be here."

There it is. Cyndra used the father card, knowing it would stab Anna's heart. But no more. "Father has been dead for years, Cyn, because of that witch of a woman he married," Anna snapped back from the angst bubbling inside her. *Plus, it's the truth. The wicked woman poisoned him. I'm sure of it.*

Her father, Augustus Beck, was the picture of health, so to die suddenly from a heart attack weeks after marrying Elzbeth? Anna just needed proof. Proof that wouldn't be so hard to find if her father's autopsy report hadn't been destroyed when the royal city's documentation office burned down last month. That was why Anna was waiting for the *Fairytales, Facts, and Fables* newspaper reporter, Gertrude Penny, covering her nephew's party. She would give Gertrude the letter she'd written last night to publish to the entire kingdom so those not under Elzbeth's spell would believe her. Then the officials could get Elzbeth's past husbands' autopsy reports to prove—

"Don't you dare start that again!" Cyndra scolded, cutting off her thoughts. Her soft blue eyes, identical to Anna's and Dru's, narrowed to ice chips. "Stop this nonsense about Elzbeth."

"Did someone say my name?" Elzbeth said, appearing inside the ballroom doors, decked in a shimmering rose-gold gown. Embroidered flowers streamed from the bodice to the hem, creating dual sparkling waterfalls from the midday sunlight that glimmered through the tall windows and reflected off the beading. It was a gown fit for a queen who was wholly overdressed for a child's birthday party. All the guests turned their eyes on her, instant smiles beaming at her wicked stepmother as if *she* were the guest of honor. Anna rolled her eyes at their naivety.

Anna's magic allowed her to see what everyone else couldn't, that Elzbeth's spell masked her green skin that reminded Anna of pond scum. Just like Elzbeth's murderous heart.

Elzbeth waltzed into the ballroom, a small dog dancing around her flowing gown. Anna stared at the thing decorated in a large blue-and-white checkered bow around its collar. Her one-year-old nephew would get a dog for his birthday, but not her because Elzbeth's cat doesn't like dogs.

The dog's wiry black fur stuck out in all directions, like Dru's hair when she forgot to brush it for days. It pranced at the end of a golden leash ushered by Elzbeth's pea-green hand. She passed the leash to the closest royal guard, muttering something before getting in earshot of Anna.

"Stars help us all," Anna murmured as Cyndra left her side and shuffled over to embrace their stepmother. "Never mind, the Stars don't care," she added.

"Agree," a man whispered, causing Anna to jump out of her skin. Whoever the eavesdropper was, he was damn lucky her magic didn't wield the elements of fire or water, else he'd have been burned or drowned to death for startling her.

Anna's magical ability was to see through lies, which included spells, enchantments, illusions… any magic that deceived. *Bullshit*, as she liked to call it. At least in her step-mother's case, her bullshit spell she wielded to manipulate others into loving her—with no questions asked. Anna glanced over her shoulder for the source of the voice, finding a teenage boy who looked close to her age standing several feet behind her.

"Oh, Annalie, there you are." Elzbeth's words turned her attention back. The evil woman stalked across the ornate room, passing the dais as Cyndra followed on her heels. "I was so worried when you didn't come home last night," Elzbeth added, grabbing Anna by the shoulders and pulling her into a stiff, awkward hug.

"Where were you?" Cyndra asked in a low voice that wouldn't travel to the prying ears of their guests. Anna freed herself from Elzbeth's cold embrace. *Hugging a block of ice would be more enjoyable.*

"I was reading late at the library and fell asleep," Anna answered. Elzbeth's brow rose, her hazel eyes digging into hers.

"Daff needed to leave early—a family matter or something—so I closed up and took advantage of the quiet to read."

"Hmmm," Elzbeth said. "That was the third time this week." She pulled her silver makeup mirror from her dress pocket and checked her appearance. The top was decorated with small emerald chips. She dabbed the makeup sponge several times on her cheeks, clanging her ring-drenched fingers with the movement.

"Glad to know you can count that high," Anna clipped, wanting to be done with the interrogation. These situations were always the same: they would ask Anna a question; she told the truth; got ganged up on by her stepmother, Cyndra, and even Dru sometimes; and then she had to apologize for hurting Elzbeth's feelings. Anna was skipping ahead so she could possibly sneak away to shoot arrows at the castle's target range or maybe escape to the woods for some solitude.

As predicted, Elzbeth produced instant tears, dabbing at them with the makeup sponge and sniffling so loudly that a guard across the noisy ballroom took notice. Anna didn't miss the sharp glare the guard shot her way behind his hooded mask.

"Apologize now," Cyndra demanded in the same motherly tone she'd used on Anna her entire life, whenever she did something wrong. It had never bothered Anna before Elzbeth entered their lives, but during the last four years, it hit a nerve, making her want to scream to Cyndra, *You are not my mother!* She was her sister. She should be on her side. But Anna knew what that response would bring, and she didn't want to deal with Edgar swooshing in to save his damsel-in-distress wife. *Again.* Prince Edgar with his perfect hair, teeth, and charming personality. Anna sighed.

"I'm sorry," Anna started. The only loophole she had with her telling-the-truth magic was that she could get away with a half-truth if she wasn't asked a direct question. "I know you can count higher than three." She wasn't sorry, but she didn't have to admit that unless she was directly asked.

"Apology accepted. *Again*," Elzbeth replied, emphasizing the last word before snapping her makeup mirror shut. She turned, swooshing her rose-gold dress across Anna's pink skirt, then moved toward someone more interesting to bother. Cyndra followed like a trained dog on her heels.

"She's such a delight," the eavesdropper said. Anna turned. His back was to her as he walked to the wall lined with royal portraits and leaned against it. There was a portrait of Edgar hanging above him, next to one of Edgar's father, King Tyson, with his late identical twin brother, Prince Leo, and their younger brother, Prince Aaron, standing in front of them.

Her eyes widened as she noticed the family resemblance between the stranger and the royals hanging on the wall. The stranger's chestnut-colored hair was long and straight, brushing over his shoulders, where Edgar's and the royal brothers' was short and curly. Other than that, there was no denying the relation.

Her heart did a strange flip as she took him in. All of him. He was at least six feet tall and muscular given how his tunic sleeves hugged his upper arms. The stranger turned and pushed the wall paneling to reveal a secret passage. He ducked to step in. Worried he would disappear, Anna quickly stepped forward.

"Wait," she whispered, taking a hasty glance about her, relieved that no one was paying them any mind, and scurried toward the door. The young man froze halfway inside the passageway. "You look just like Edgar and his..." She pointed at the picture above his head as his eyes grew wide as saucers. "Sorry, I mean, Prince Edgar." She bit her lower lip for forgetting to use her brother-in-law's title. "Are you related? A cousin, perhaps? Prince Aaron's son? Is he here? Has he finally come home?"

"You can see me?" he asked, shocked. His voice was kept at a hushed whisper.

"Yes," Anna answered, unable to fight the honesty of her magic.

"No one has ever…" He stopped, his brow furrowing. "Come with me." He held his hand out to her. "So we can talk. You shouldn't be able to see me. I mean… please?"

"Oh, you're using enchant—" The horns echoed through the ballroom, drowning out her words. It was the trumpets announcing the king's arrival. Everyone turned, looking towards the doors in anticipation of the grand entrance. Anna took the opportunity to escape and darted past the stranger through the secret door.

CHAPTER
Two

"Good decision," the stranger said, shutting the door behind them. Anna blinked several times, adjusting to the dim light of the secret passage. "Fath—er… the king's speeches can last over an hour to just say happy birthday."

Anna stopped dead in her tracks and gave the intriguing boy an arched eyebrow. "Father? It sounded like you were about to say father." She leaned in, her eyes squinting, the passage lit faintly by lanterns housing lightning bugs. She gave him a closer look. "Who are—"

But before she could finish her question, he grabbed her hand and started to pull her behind him, his strong legs taking them further into the passage.

"Wait!" she protested, trying to pull her hand free. "Why haven't I seen you before? My sister is Cyndra. *Princess* Cyndra. Why don't I know about you?"

He stopped and turned, her hand still held within his vise grip. His voice was kind but low. "You of all people should know what it's like to be the younger sibling, Annalie. We're practically invisible to everyone else compared to our older siblings." He sighed, then added, "Well, in my case at least." He waved his free hand at himself.

"So you're using magic," Anna said.

He nodded. "Invisibility. And you're the first person who's ever been able to see me." He tugged on her hand, moving them down the passage again.

"Where are we going? And what is your name?" she asked as he turned to the left, going down a new passage. She couldn't believe it! Edgar had a younger brother no one knew about? But why? And where was he taking her? How many turns had they made? One left and two rights, or was it two lefts and one right?

"I'll tell you, but you have to promise not to laugh," he said.

"I can't promise that."

"Why?" He stopped, freeing her hand from his, and turned to face her.

She threw a hand out against the wall, catching herself before tumbling into him. "My magic doesn't allow me to." As usual, her magic forced her to answer honestly. "I can't lie. That is my magic. Well, part of it. So, if your name is…"

"You can't lie!" he whisper-exclaimed. "And I thought I had terrible magic."

"Being able to go invisible isn't terrible. Do you know how many times I wish I could pop out of sight and slip away to escape my stepmother?"

"No, invisibility wouldn't be terrible… if only I had other powers," he said.

His confession shocked her. Royals normally had several magical abilities due to their strong bloodline. Prince Edgar had three, and the fact that Cyndra was allowed to marry him with her one ability to communicate with animals was a miracle that only Fairy Godmother herself could orchestrate.

"So why didn't I know about you until today, um…?" she asked, hoping he would give her his name.

"Rupert."

Anna arched a brow at him.

"You don't like my name?" he asked.

"No, that's not it. It's just not… what I was expecting. Rupert is a name that belongs to an old man," she answered, and his face fell. "I'm sorry," she added. "Do you have a nickname that your friends call you?" she asked, hoping to recover from her magic's honest answer.

"I don't have friends." He looked down at his feet.

Stupid truth magic, she berated herself.

"Well then, as your first official friend…" she began.

His head lurched up, his slate-grey eyes making her heart flip in a strange way again. Her face must have given her away as the prince suddenly asked, "Why are you staring at me like that?"

"Because you have the most beautiful eyes." She bit her lower lip, embarrassed at what her magic made her confess, and leaned back.

"Wow. You really can't lie." He shook his head. His silky chestnut hair swished back and forth over his shoulders as an amused smile formed on his lips. "Alright, well, Annalie, as—"

"My friends call me Anna."

"Okay, Anna," he said, with a lopsided grin. "As my first friend, your ability to not lie is a quality I really like about you."

"Just wait until you ask me something you really care about and I can't lie to spare your feelings. You might rethink how you feel about it," she replied, but he just turned and continued moving down the tunnel. She scurried after him, yanking up the layers of her hideous dress, trying to keep up.

"Where are we going?" she asked, coughing from all the dust and cobwebs in the secret passages. "And when was the last time someone cleaned in here?" She waved the largest cobweb she'd ever seen from her face before tasting it. Perhaps she could call him Prince Rup? *Nope.* She giggled to herself. That nickname wouldn't work. She raced to keep up with him.

"I haven't been in these tunnels in ages, not since my magic appeared and became strong enough that I didn't need it to get around unnoticed." His shoulders sagged as he said the last words, but he kept the pace up, moving through the tunnels expertly.

"Why are you a secret?"

They took another left, going down a new passage.

"I… well… you see…" He stumbled over each word as he swatted at the air, wiping a large cobweb away. The motion swished his hair over his right shoulder, revealing part of a design below his right ear, wrapping around his neck.

The sight of it caught Anna by surprise. "You're cursed!" she blurted. He stopped dead in his tracks. "Ouch!" she said, her nose colliding against his muscular back. A wall would've been more forgiving.

She took a tentative step back as he turned to face her, his eyes wide, revealing the entire apple-sized mark. "You're Star Kissed!" she added breathlessly, reaching out to touch the six-pointed star that reminded her of two arrowheads stacked atop one another. She continued in a hushed, reverent voice, "You defied the Stars, and They cursed you."

"No. I was born with it because of what my parents did." He stepped closer. Only inches separated them. He blinked several times. Silver flecks shimmered in his dark grey eyes like a starry sky. How had she missed that before?

She threw a hand to her mouth. His eyes were the same unique color as… She leaned closer, ensuring she was correct before slowly removing her hand. "Your eyes," she said softly. "They're exact replicas of Princess Fern's."

"That's because I have my mother's eyes."

"Your mother is Princess Fern, not Queen Lily?"

He nodded.

Princess Fern was Queen Lily's younger sister, who'd moved into the castle following the death of her husband, Prince Leo, who died suddenly after falling from a castle balcony.

"I don't understand. Royals have affairs all the time. Even with their sisters-in-law." Her stomach churned at her last words, but she continued, "So why would you be cursed for being illegitimate?"

"Because I wasn't illegitimate," he said. "I was planned, and Queen Lily helped orchestrate it."

"Planned!" she exclaimed.

He threw his hand over her mouth. "Not so loud. These walls are thin."

She inhaled through the nose, detecting the scent of vanilla on his skin before she nodded that she understood.

He lifted his hand slowly from her mouth and continued, "Queen Lily had difficulty producing and bearing children. It took years for them to get pregnant with Edgar with a lot of help from healers." He grabbed her hand again, leading her, and kept talking. "When Edgar was two, he became greatly ill. My father believed they were going to lose him, his only heir who took years to produce." Anna opened her mouth, but he added quickly, "The kingdom of Tranik was also threatening war, putting my father under greater stress while still mourning his twin brother's death. So Queen Lily suggested he sleep with my mother to produce another heir who would look similar to Edgar since my uncle Aaron left the kingdom with no word on his whereabouts." He sighed. "They planned to enchant me to look exactly like Edgar. To take his place if he didn't survive or was too sickly to…"

"That's horrible," she hissed. "You were born to be your brother's double?"

"It's a sacrifice I would have willingly made for my kingdom."

"But then… why hide you away? I understand their horrible plan to be Edgar's doppelgänger failed, but that didn't mean they had to lock you up in your own home." She gritted her teeth. "Especially since Edgar isn't sickly."

"Because my Star Kiss mark can't be hidden by any enchantment, and they hoped to find a way to break the curse."

"Clearly they failed." She spat the words, waving her hand at his neck, stirring dust motes into flight.

"True, but my life hasn't been so bad," he countered. She wanted to scream at the Stars for putting their curse on an innocent child versus the responsible adults. "Once I had full control of my invisibility magic, I could go anywhere I wanted. And in the middle of the night, I don't even have to use my magic, most of the time."

She shook her head at how easily he brushed off her anger for what they did to him. "You're a prince. You shouldn't—" she started to say louder.

He threw his hand over her mouth again. "Quiet, please. If anyone was near these walls…"

She inhaled deeply, trying to calm her emotions and words before she nodded. "Sorry," she said softly once he freed her mouth. "So, who knows about you?"

"Only my father and Edgar since my mother and Queen Lily passed."

"Cyndra doesn't know about you?"

"No. Well, at least not that she remembers," he said and took a left, leading to a wooden door. He opened it and gestured for her to enter first. She stepped through, taking in the smaller space before he followed, closing the door softly. It was a circular room, brighter than the tunnels, lit by sunlight beaming in through high windows that went up along the spiral stone staircase.

"My father, he used his magic to make Cyndra forget me. She'd gotten lost, stumbled into my bedchamber, and saw me."

Anna's spine stiffened. What else had the king made her sister forget since Cyndra married Prince Edgar? He started ascending, Anna close on his heels, about to ask that very question.

"I know what you're thinking, and he only had to use his

magic on her that one time." He shook his head. "My brother and I haven't had much time together since he and your sister married. I was at the wedding, dressed as a royal guard, standing in the back."

Anna wondered how many royal events he'd been to over the years with no one truly aware who he was. And how many times his father had erased memories because someone accidentally caught a glimpse of the cursed prince.

"You're why the royal guard uniforms changed a few years back," she said, putting the pieces together. "The hood and mask only showing their eyes. It wasn't to protect the guards' identities. It was to protect you."

"Yes," he said. "It was my mother's idea. To give me more freedom." She opened her mouth to protest, but he said, "I'm okay with my life; it really isn't so bad."

"I doubt that," she scoffed. "Or you shouldn't be! No one should be okay being cursed for another's actions and then locked away in isolation from the world, or hidden behind a guard's mask because their plans failed. You're not a dirty little secret."

"I have my books to keep me company," he said. "And hopefully now you." He looked over his shoulder and smiled shyly. "And speaking of the first, I want to show you my personal library. After hearing that you sleep in one, I thought you would like to see mine."

"Well, that's because I work there," she said, aware he was changing the subject off himself. She'd drop it, for now. "I stay hours past my shift so I don't have to be around my stepmother any more than I have to."

"Yeah, I get that," he said, stepping onto the landing. Three doors, identical to the one at the bottom of the stairs, stood in a row a few feet from each other. "Your stepmother is a piece of work." He pushed against the middle door with his shoulder, using a bit of force. The door creaked open, and he gestured for her to step through. Her jaw fell to the floor.

When he said personal library, she was expecting a couple bookshelves, but a sob formed in her chest at the floor-to-ceiling bookshelves in the four-story tower, which held more books than the royal city's library. She turned in awe, trying to take it all in. The prince laughed softly as he shut the door. It was disguised on the backside with bookshelves, fitting perfectly with the book-lined walls.

"I take it you like it?" he asked, raising a brow.

She nodded with a sincerity so strong, it felt like magic, her compulsion to tell the truth unneeded as she soaked in the vastness of books. She wondered if he would let her borrow one, or a thousand, to read.

"My father's personal library is bigger than mine," he began, "but the castle library…"

She didn't hear the rest of what he said as she moved to the closest bookshelves, running her fingers over the spines, reading the titles. "You like romance?" she asked after reading a dozen titles.

He cleared his throat, walking up next to her. "Yes. But those were my mother's. She loved to read and would sit with me here for hours on end." He turned, looking at the chairs and couch by a large unlit fireplace. Several knocks echoed through the room, causing them both to freeze.

The prince's eyes went wide before he glanced at the large wooden door, then back at her. "Anna," he whispered. "In order for others not to see us together, I'm going to need to pull you close… May I?" he asked.

"Yes," she answered softly, her heart thundering against her ribcage.

He wrapped his arms around her waist and pulled her into his chest. "Stay quiet, stand still, and we'll both stay invisible." His whispered breath tickled softly against her ear. She suddenly became very aware of every place their bodies touched.

There was another brief rap on the door before it cracked

open, and Cyndra, with Edgar standing beside her, sheepishly leaned in to peek into the room.

"Hey, Rupert? It's me," Edgar called into the deceptively empty space. "I have some good news. Father says I can finally introduce you to Cyndra! And there's more!" Edgar paused, smiling broadly as he looked at Cyndra, then back again into the room, his eyes searching. "Father just proposed to Elzbeth Beck, and she accepted!"

CHAPTER
Three

Anna's heart lurched to her throat. *Engaged? Engaged! Elzbeth and the king?*

"It's okay, Rupert. You can show yourself," Edgar called into the room after his shocking announcement. "Elzbeth wants to meet you, and Fairy Godmother is here too!" He was gleeful, clearly expecting the revelation to entice the prince to stop using his magic. Instead, Rupert tightened his hold around her waist. "Father wants the ceremony to happen as soon as—"

"Edgar, darling," Elzbeth's voice cut in. Cyndra and Edgar turned, beaming like little children who'd gotten everything they wanted on winter solstice morning. "Sorry, dear. You didn't hear me calling to you?" Elzbeth added.

"Oh, I guess we didn't," Cyndra replied.

"Do you know where Annalie and Drury got off to? I want all our family present tonight when we announce our engagement to the kingdom." At Elzbeth's words Anna's heart squashed liked the pumpkin carriage Cyndra had taken to the ball.

"If Anna left the party, my guess would be she has snuck off to the archery range *again*." Cyndra emphasized the last word as Elzbeth sighed heavily in agreement.

It isn't proper for you to wield a bow, now that you are a lady of the court. Cyndra's words burned through Anna's mind the last time she was caught practicing at the range. "And Dru was going to miss the party for that workshop," Cyndra continued to explain.

"Yes, yes, that's right," Elzbeth said, waving her green-hued hand about, clanging her rings like she was already queen of the castle. She sighed heavily again. "In all the excitement, I'd forgotten about her workshop. Well, I guess we can wait a few days more and make our announcement when Drury has returned." Anna let out a soft breath. "So did you find your brother, Edgar?" Elzbeth asked, admiring the new almost acorn-sized ruby ring on her left hand. "It seems we'll have more time to chat now that Drury isn't here."

"No. If he isn't here, he's more than likely in the kitchen or the castle library. I'll check there next," Edgar answered. "If I can't find him before you leave, I'll come back here at dinner to let him know the good news." Edgar beamed at her with the last words. Elzbeth only nodded, jostling her inky-black hair. She turned, swishing her rose-gold skirt about as Edgar and Cyndra followed on her heels, closing the door behind them.

"I can't believe she's already weaseled her way into an engagement with my father," the prince seethed, releasing Anna now that they were alone.

"I can," she scoffed as she turned to face him. "I mean, I'm more shocked she didn't do it a year ago while Queen Lily's body was still warm in the catacombs." The prince grimaced, suddenly swaying on his feet. Anna threw her arm out to steady him. "Are you okay?"

"Yeah, I just need to sit." He stepped back toward one of the chairs by a low table stacked with books and sat down. "I haven't used my magic on two people in a long time."

"It was quick thinking. If you hadn't made us invisible, Elzbeth would've locked eyes, putting you under her spell." She shook her head at the thought of losing the prince to Elzbeth's spell when she'd just found him.

"Yes, but my magic doesn't last long. Edgar and I used to do it a lot, years ago, to sneak out of the castle past the guards."

"How long can your magic keep two people invisible?" Anna asked.

"Ten minutes."

Anna frowned.

"Like I said, my magic does one thing only, and not for very long." He heaved out a breath. "And that was when I was using it a lot on Edgar and me sneaking out, so it may take a bit to build it back up and keep us both hidden."

"Alright," she said and mustered up a smile for him. He really drew the short straw for a royal. She sat in the other chair, picking up a book from one of the stacks.

100 Ways to Cast a Curse.

"I've read pretty much every book in the castle that has to do with curses." He nodded at the book. "I was hoping to find a way to break mine. But every time I think I've found something, it leads to a dead end." Her heart cracked for him.

"I've been doing my own research on spells," she admitted. "Hoping I could find a way to break Elzbeth's."

"And?" He stood up, and Anna followed suit.

"Nothing." The prince nodded. She shook her head. She needed something to call him rather than prince. "What's your middle name?"

"Why?"

"Because it can't be as bad as Rupert," her magic compelled her to admit. He laughed at her honest answer and waved for her to follow him up.

"It's Phillip, my father's middle name, but no one ever uses it because, well." He stopped and turned to face her. He waved at his neck where his Star Kiss marked him.

"Okay, Phil," Anna said. His mouth quirked at the edges, his expression surprised yet pleased. "As your official first friend, I'm calling you by what should really be your first name, Phil."

His smile grew before he turned back and ascended the last few steps onto a lofted area at the top of the tower.

"It's the truth. The world should know whose son you are, rather than you being locked away like a dirty secret."

"Not anymore. At least for Cyndra and Elzbeth now."

"True. That's double the people who knew about you an hour ago," she deadpanned as she took in the loft that rounded a third of the tower. A massive bed sat between two windows with side tables beneath, a large wardrobe and changing screen taking up the rest of the space.

Phil walked to the wardrobe and opened the doors, revealing a collection of apparel that made Anna envious. She didn't wear even half the dresses Cyndra and Elzbeth provided, preferring pants and a tunic and drawing their ire in doing so. He rummaged through his shirts, then grabbed one and took it off the hanger. "I need to change before we leave the castle."

"Leave? To go where? And why?" she asked.

"I don't know where, but I know we can't stick around here. It's too risky. You don't want to take the chance of me bumping into that green grasshopper of a woman and ending up spelled like the rest of the castle. Do you?" He opened one of the drawers at the bottom of the wardrobe and pulled out a pair of pants.

"Yeah, we can't have that," Anna said, smiling at his description. It was true. Elzbeth was long-limbed and green like a grasshopper. *If a grasshopper had inky black hair and a murderous soul.*

"Plus, we need to find a way to break her spell. The solution has to be somewhere out there." He pointed to the windows, indicating the world outside the castle walls, before he stepped behind the changing screen.

"I hope so." She knit and unknit her fingers together, looking out the window casting in the warm summer sunlight. It felt like bees were swarming inside her stomach as she continued to weave her fingers in and out. She drew in a few breaths, trying to calm her nerves and reeling mind, focusing to formulate a plan. Phil stepped out, now dressed in a pair of black pants and matching boots with a forest-green tunic that hugged his chest, along with a leather bag slung across his back.

"What's in there?" She pointed at the bag.

"A disguise. It's one Edgar and I used when sneaking out of the castle… especially for long adventures. You know, in case my magic sputtered out," he explained, adjusting the bag strap on his shoulder and suddenly looking serious. "Listen, if we're getting out of here while the sun is up, you'll need to hold my hand once we are out of the tunnels in order to stay invisible, and we'll both need to be as quiet as we can." He leveled her with a warning look. "Even your footsteps need to be light. We don't want to alert the guards standing near the tunnel walls of our presence. Can you do that?"

"I can," she ensured him. "I've gotten pretty good at sneaking out at all hours of the night without Elzbeth knowing. Sneaking back in is the trickier part."

He approached her, then stopped, cocking his head as he took in her fluffy, pink layered mountain of a dress and frowned.

"Not quite the right garment for someone trying to be quick and quiet," he said. "And I'm too large for you to wear anything of mine."

"Give me a second." She reached toward him and grabbed the small dagger secured on his hip.

"What are…?"

Anna ignored him and slashed at the layers of her gown, ripping them free from her legs, exposing her knees.

"Oh yeah. That should help." Phil laughed, his eyes lingering on her legs, before extending his hand, silently asking for his dagger back. She returned his smile, but his washed away like a wave cleaning the sand, his eyes traveling down to her shoes. Pink slippers, with barely a sole. "Those might be a problem."

"At least they're not glass."

He laughed at her sad joke.

She continued, tossing the discarded dress fabric behind the changing screen. "We'll go to my house and get me decent clothes, boots, and provisions before we head out."

"Provisions?" He slid the dagger back on his hip, then started to lead them down the spiral staircase. "Did you formulate a plan that has us going on a long journey?" He waved for her to enter the secret door into the tunnels before him.

"Not long… but will take maybe four to five hours walking," she answered, blinking to adjust to the dim lantern light. "I don't think we can risk taking my father's horses because Elzbeth will know that I left the royal city," she said, waving her hand at a cobweb, continuing the plan she'd formulated. "I need to see Dru and create some excuse to delay her coming back to give us more time to search for how to break Elzbeth's spell. We can't let her marry, then kill your father, like she did mine."

"You think she killed your father?" he asked, leading them through the tunnels.

"Yes." Her magic had her answering swiftly as she wiped another cobweb from her face. "But my proof burned up in the documentation building fire last month." She sighed heavily.

"Won't your stepmother become suspicious if she can't find you?" He turned to the right, then stopped to look at her.

"No, you heard her earlier. She is used to me not coming home for a night and won't be suspicious about my absence until tomorrow afternoon."

He nodded, then continued walking down the tunnel, leaving boot prints in the layers of dust, leading them to a dead end. She coughed, waving a hand to clear the thicker dust, seeing a small metal ladder connected to the stone wall going up twenty to thirty feet. He grabbed a rung and started climbing. After a few seconds, she followed.

"Where does this lead to?" she whisper-called up.

"Outside." He balanced his legs on the second-to-last rung

while pushing both hands at the door above his head. Anna leaned back, holding both sides of the ladder, watching his arm muscles flex with the force he was using.

It seems the prince does more than just reading in his hidden tower, she thought, taking in the fine lines between his perfectly carved arms.

The door creaked open, flooding the tunnel with sunlight. She blinked feverishly at the sudden onslaught of light, bright stars swimming before her eyes. Once her vision cleared, she followed him up the last rungs. He put his hand out and grasped hers, his calluses scratching her palm, sending tingles through her body.

He leaned down, taking her with him as his other hand lowered the tunnel door shut. He brushed his boot bottom back and forth, covering the door with gravel to blend into the road. She squinted through the canopy of ash trees shading them from the midday summer heat, lining the road leading to the castle. Birds chirped merrily from their perches as her father's favorite carriage, led by six white horses, suddenly barreled around the corner, headed straight for them. Phil wrapped his free arm around her, pulling them off the road and rolling them over several times. He stopped on top of her just as the carriage passed them, her stepmother glaring out the window in their direction.

CHAPTER

Four

ANNA: 3 DAYS, 22 HOURS BEFORE THE CLOCK
STRIKES 12

nna let out a loud groan. "Another close call," Phil said, his body pressed against hers. Anna's heart thundered against her chest, and she wondered if he could feel it. "You alright?" he asked. Anna's magic had her nodding, rendering her speechless, his face so close to hers. "Sure?" he asked. His vanilla scent wrapped around her.

"Yes. I can't lie. Remember?" She brushed a loosed strand of her crimson hair and tucked it behind her ear, her eyes falling to his lips.

"Right… yeah, forgot." He stumbled over his words as he rolled off her only to fall to his back in the grassy field, their fingers still interlocked. He drew in a long breath and let it out slowly. "Looks as if going to your house is now out of the question."

"I know," she said, sitting up slowly, tugging him with her. "So let's go to the library." She surveyed the woods several dozen yards from where they sat. They could make their way to the library, concealed by the tall oak trees. "I have a set of clothes, boots, and one of my bows hidden away there."

"Anna, we can't go into the royal city during daylight." He

got to his feet and helped her up. "What if someone sees a bow floating in midair?"

"You can't make it invisible?" she asked, leading the way towards the woods, the thick timbers resting between the castle and city edge.

"I can, but the more items needing to stay concealed, the more magic I use. It could sputter out without notice."

"I wish my magic would sputter out," she grumbled, the oak leaves crunching beneath their feet as they drew closer to the woods. "Would make my life a lot easier." Phil halted abruptly, the unexpected motion jerking her arm and yanking her back a step. Anna hissed, Phil's grip suddenly tightening into a vise.

"Sorry," he said quickly, realizing his hold was too tight. "Anna… we can't go into the haunted woods!" He glanced between the thick canopy of oak trees and her like she'd lost her mind. "There are things, creatures that will—"

"The woods are perfectly safe," she said, cutting him off as her wrist thrummed, the pain turning to a dull ache. "Trust me." She switched hands with him, tugging, but he didn't budge.

"Safe?" His voice went two octaves higher. "There are creatures living in there that would make a feast of us."

"It's just an enchantment," she said, her heart clenching for the responsibility of the fear etched in his features. "Like I said, trust me."

"Trust you?" He flicked his eyes from her to the woods and then back. "You'll need to explain before I set a foot in there."

"I asked my friend Daff to place an enchantment on the woods," she said.

"Why would you ask him to do that?" His voice quivered.

"Well… after Cyndra married and my father died six weeks later, I needed a place to escape, somewhere away from everyone. Especially my stepmother. So I asked Daff, short for Daffodil, to empty the woods, and she did… by creating the enchanted monsters." She chuckled, realizing the absurdity of saying it out loud. Her smile suddenly dropped, another memory coming to mind. "And she'd done it just in time too. A day later, Elzbeth came to the library, unannounced, and poof! Daff was under her spell like everyone else."

"So no deadly creatures?" He pointed at the trees, his doubt obvious, making Anna wonder exactly what it was he saw.

In reality, the woods were a magical place. She spent hours there, eating from the blackberry bushes that grew along the small stream in the summertime and practicing her archery. The only animals that truly lived in them were small woodland creatures and deer.

"No. Stars' honest truth," she answered with a smile. She found his worry over the "scary" woods endearing.

He smiled softly back, then took a quick breath. "Okay, I'm ready."

She exhaled with relief and started to lead them into the woods. Once hidden from view of the guards on the castle roof, she let go of his hand.

"What are you doing?" he protested.

"It's alright. No one comes in here because of the enchantment. I figured we'd give your magic some time to rest until it's needed again," she explained.

"That's fine for you, but I can still see the enchantments. And they are not pleasant." His voice shook as his eyes darted around. "I'd appreciate a guide through. If you don't mind?" He flexed his hand, silently asking her to grasp hold.

"Yes, sorry, of course." She grabbed his hand again, a smile tugging at her lips.

"The growls I hear growing closer with each step we take are very convincing… too convincing."

"Daff may have gone overboard." She laughed, remembering how excited she was to help.

"Yeah." He gripped her hand tighter. "If the growling wasn't enough, there are steaming pits and…" He stopped, yanking Anna back a step. She turned to look at him, but he was frozen, eyes closed. "How about you just lead me through."

"Of course, and sorry again." She tugged on his hand and began to lead him down a worn deer path, the trails numerous as they weaved through the woods, the deer free to multiply without the interference of hunters.

She stole a glance at Phil's face, and seeing his eyes pinched together tight, she decided it might be best to give him something else to think about.

"When we get to the library, I want you to make me invisible," she started to explain, his grip tight. She picked up the pace. "We'll need to go through the back window. It leads to a storage room. Once inside, I'll go find Daff and let her know to cover for me."

"I don't know. What if Elzbeth comes to the library looking for you and she tells her the truth?"

"She won't," Anna's magic answered honestly and swiftly. "Elzbeth only came that one time... Since Daff's been spelled, she's never returned. She sends fire messages when she wants to summon me." She rolled her eyes, stopping when she realized his were closed.

"You're sure?" He sounded reluctant.

"Yes," she answered, halting their steps. "You can open your eyes. We're at the edge of the woods." She surveyed the back of the library, which was only twenty yards away.

"The window is boarded up," Phil said, staring intently at the building.

"Oh, that's another one of Daff's enchantments. Only she and I know of the window that still works." She stopped. An idea formed. "Why didn't I think of this before? Daff can enchant me to be invisible! That way, you don't have to use your magic on the two of us."

"Oh, I like that plan, especially after seeing what her enchantments can do." He shivered, keeping his back to the woods, and then took a bracing breath, inhaling through his nose and exhaling slowly through his mouth. "Alright," he said, his voice a tad stronger. "I'm using my magic, so when you're ready."

"Let's go then!" Anna grasped his hand tighter, and tugging him along, sprinted down the hill towards the window, dead leaves crunching beneath their feet as they charged towards the building. Never in her wildest dreams did she imagine she'd be sneaking a secret prince into the library! Crossing the distance to the back of the building, Anna could hear her heart pumping in her ears. With her free hand, she pulled the window key hanging around her neck out from under her dress.

"I'll need both hands now to lift the window," she whispered softly. "I'll push myself up and inside, then hold the window for you. Just follow what I do since you can't see past the enchantment." He nodded, letting go of her hand. She jolted when he pressed it at the small of her back.

"Just in case," he whispered.

She nodded, not daring to look back at him as her heart flipped at the contact.

Focus, she commanded and pulled the window out, pushed off the sill to boost herself up a couple feet, then wiggled inside on her stomach, headfirst. Phil lifted his hand from her back before the window knocked into it softly. Once inside, she crouched on an old library table, one that she and Daff had placed there just for this reason. She turned, pushed the window back open, and nodded for Phil to come through. He braced his hands on the windowsill, pushed up—flexing his arm muscles—and leaned in toward her. But his bag slipped down his shoulder, catching on the window.

"Sorry, I know it has to be tricky since you can't see past the enchantment," she whispered, reaching to unhook his bag. "Let me free it. Then push yourself the rest of the way in directly towards me." She lifted the strap off the window hinge where it caught. "You're good now."

"Who are you talking to, Anna?" Daff questioned from behind her. She turned quickly, finding her best friend standing a few feet away, holding a tall stack of books as the window fell with a loud *thunk* against Phil's back.

"It's my new friend, Phil," her magic made her answer.

Phil came up behind her, covering her mouth, causing Anna to disappear out of sight. Daff gasped, dropping all the books in her hands.

"Anna, what's going on?" Daff's words shook. Her eyes were as large as saucers behind her black-rimmed glasses.

"It's Phil," Anna tried to say, the words muffled with his hand over her mouth. She tapped his hand to release her, but before he did, he grabbed her arm, keeping them linked and invisible. She pointed at Daff, then paused. How could she convince him that he could trust Daff? She was the only person who believed Anna about her magic, even under her stepmother's spell. She still helped. Not only had she created enchantments for her to escape Elzbeth, but Daff was also trying to help her find spell books in the library. She hoped to find one that contained the way to break Elzbeth's spell.

"Trust me," she whispered, her blue eyes pleading with his. His hand tightened as his eyes shifted from her to Daff. She understood his fear, but he didn't know Daff like she did. "Please," she added.

"Anna, how are you invisible?" Daff asked, her foot rapidly tapping out a rhythm. Anna recognized it as Daff's favorite nervous tic, how she got energy out in high stress situations. Anna craned her neck. Daff's glasses fell down the bridge of her nose to the rhythm of her foot as her bun wobbled, sending several strands of her lavender hair free.

"Phil's magic," Anna's magic answered. Then she turned back to Phil, imploring. "Please. You can trust her."

He took in a long breath and exhaled it slowly, then let go of her hand.

"Thank you," she said, turning around and jumping from the table. The toe of her slipper landed on one of the books Daff had dropped, and she slipped into her best friend, sending her to the ground first with Anna on top.

"Sorry," Anna said, scrambling off Daff.

"Are you okay?" Phil asked, jumping off the table, hands extended.

Daff blinked her lavender eyes, the same color as her hair, at Phil before saying, "You look a lot like Edgar—I mean, Prince Edgar," she hastily corrected her mistake, shifting her eyes warily at Anna. They never used titles when referring to Edgar, Cyndra, or any of the other royals. At least, not when it was just the two of them.

"It's alright. I don't use his title either," Phil said and smiled softly.

Daff smiled back, taking one of his hands as Anna took the other, getting to her feet. "Why are you sneaking in?" Daff asked.

"Because Prince Phil is a secret."

Daff's eyes widened in surprise as Phil stiffened, Anna's magic revealing too much truth.

"I thought you looked a lot like Edgar, but I thought maybe a cousin? That Prince Aaron had possibly returned with a family." She eyed him for a second, then added, "Are you an illegit—"

Phil threw his hand over Anna's mouth, stopping Daff's question.

"Would you stop?" she said against his hand.

"Do not tell her about my mother," he said, so low that Anna strained to hear him. "Stop talking about me and ask her to enchant you so we can go." He released his hand from her mouth.

Daff jolted as she came back into view. "What exactly is going on, Anna?" she asked, hand to heart.

"Long story, but Elzbeth is engaged to the king." Daff's face lit up. *Stupid witch's spell.* "I met Phil at Augustus's party when he was lurking about, using his magic."

"I wasn't lurking!" Phil said. The silver flecks in his eyes burned brighter.

"Yes, you were! And I told you that you wouldn't like my truth magic at some point, but you were definitely lurking." He must've popped back into view because Daff turned to look at him.

"Fine, call it whatever you want." He crossed his arms in front of his chest.

"I understand you're frustrated," Daff said. "But Anna can't help her magic—"

"I said I was fine," he clipped.

Anna flinched at Phil's sharp words. Her magic had already put a crack in their newly formed friendship.

Maybe I should cut ties with him now. Go alone to get Dru before our friendship deepens and I lose him like I've lost everyone else to Elzbeth's spell.

"Sooooo," Daff said slowly to Phil, then turned to Anna. "You met at the party because you saw through his invisibility magic?"

"Yes, and Phil told me who he was, and then Edgar and Cyndra came and told Phil… well, stated… that the king had proposed to Elzbeth. They didn't know we were hiding right in front of them. The king wanted Elzbeth to meet Phil and then have us all announce to the kingdom about their engagement today, but Dru wasn't there."

"Another workshop," Daff guessed, and Anna nodded, thankful that she didn't have to explain every single detail. "Okay, so he's Edgar's younger brother?"

"Half brother."

"Understood," Daff said. "I'll stop asking questions so Anna's magic can keep your secrets." She gave Phil a look that made his shoulders soften a bit.

"We need your help to cover for me because we're going to delay Dru," Anna explained quickly. "Also, I need you to enchant me so we can walk out of town unseen."

"I can't," Daff said.

"Can't or won't?" Phil exclaimed, throwing his arms into the air. "I knew we couldn't trust her!"

CHAPTER
Five

"Wait," Daff said as Phil paced the cluttered space. "I didn't mean I won't cover for Anna. I meant I can't enchant her because I don't have access to my magic."

He halted, a flush creeping across his cheeks. "I'm sorry, I…" He cleared his throat. "I apologize for how I've been acting." He bowed his head, brushing his hair forward, revealing his Star Kiss. Daff's eyes widened at the sight of it.

Anna shook her head to not ask questions. They didn't have the time.

"We're good, Phil," she said to him, then asked Daff, "So, what did you do this time to get grounded?"

"Theo caught me enchanting Maggie yesterday, and he went straight home and told our mother." Daff huffed, clearly annoyed at her little brother. "I hadn't realized Theo was here," she continued. "It's why she sent the fire message for me to come home yesterday." Anna nodded. "So she restricted me from casting new enchantments until tomorrow."

Anna groaned that Daff couldn't help, but also because she wished for the thousandth time that her father was still alive to restrict her magic. It was something only parents could do until their children turned eighteen, to ensure they didn't use their magic wrongfully. Elzbeth could do it as well, being Anna's guardian, but that would require her wicked stepmother knowing the truth, and there was no way Anna was going to let on that she could see through Elzbeth's bullshit.

"Well, there goes that plan!" Phil gave his head a regretful shake and looked to Anna, who crossed her arms in front of her pink bodice, her face set in disappointment. "And I'm sorry again for accusing you, Daff. And for getting angry at you, Anna. I know you can't control your truth magic." He sighed heavily, raking his hand through his hair. "I've never had a reason to trust easily. I've… never had friends before."

"Well, now you do. Two of them," Daff said, smiling. "And as your friend, I wish I could help. And I'm sorry that I can't because my brother was an annoying tattletale." That got a grin out of Phil.

Suddenly, a book from the pile that Daff had dropped earlier popped up and began rotating in the air before dipping as if it were about to plummet back down to the floor. Anna quickly lurched forward and caught it.

"Whoa," Phil said, stepping closer, brushing his shoulder against hers, examining the book.

"You found a new spell book?" Anna asked, raising a brow.

"Um…" Daff stepped to her other side. "I don't know. A large donation box was dropped off this morning. It was too heavy to bring back, so I was carrying a stack at a time."

Anna read the title printed on the spine.

Marvelous Magical Maps Spell Book

She flipped to the cover, but nothing was written on the worn brown leather. She opened the book only to find the pages blank.

Phil leaned in closer. "Probably protected with a spell," he remarked as Anna pulled at the corner of the page, the sheet refusing to budge. She tried a different page but had the same result. "Here, let me try," he offered.

"Hello, is anyone here?" a woman's voice carried from the front of the library at the same time as Phil disappeared, causing Daff to startle and throw a hand to her heart.

"Oh, Stars!" Daff laughed. "It's going to take some time to get used to you popping in and out of sight."

"Hello?" the woman's voice called again, this time more insistent. "Anybody?"

Daff pushed the door open and yelled, "Coming!" Then she added over her shoulder to them, "I'll be right back," before dashing out the door.

Phil pointed at the mysterious book, his voice awed. "Look, Anna!"

She leaned in and read.

Marvelous Magical Maps Spell Book
  Table of Contents:
  Map of the Forgotten
  Map of the Heart
  Map of the Known
  Map of the Mind
  Map of Tomorrows
  Map of Truths
  Map of Yesterdays

"The words appeared when I went invisible," Phil explained, running a finger down the page.

"Can you flip to the spells?" Anna asked eagerly.

"No, the pages won't budge." Phil's shoulders slouched.

"Hmmm. Let me change out of this." She waved at her outfit. "Give ourselves a moment to think." He nodded. She maneuvered to the back of the cramped storage room, where a box sat nestled in a shadowed corner that only Anna and Daff could see because of an enchantment.

She opened it and grabbed her bag of clothes, boots, arrows, and her bow, then moved behind two towers of boxes next to each other to change. She kicked off her slippers, then froze as she realized she wouldn't be able to get out of the dress alone. She needed help unbuttoning the two dozen buttons down her back. She took in a quick breath, then darted her head around the box tower. "Can you help me get out of this?" she asked as her cheeks flamed.

"Oh yeah, sure," he clumsily replied, setting the open spell book on the table.

"Thank you." She chewed her lower lip as he approached slowly. "It took an attendant several minutes to close me up into it."

He motioned for her to turn around.

"So," she said, trying to sound casual and completely unaffected by the situation as he started unbuttoning her. "First time helping a lady out of her gown?" His hands stilled, causing her heart to flutter like pixie wings. "I'm sorry, I was just…"

"It's alright, and yes, you are my first," he said and continued with the task. "My first friend, and now the first lady I am helping…" He cleared his throat. "Undress."

"Guess we're going to have many firsts together." She laughed softly. *Why does he have such an effect on me?* She didn't fawn over the boys at school before she was removed for her lessons to become a lady of the court. It wasn't like she was oblivious to them, but there wasn't anyone who caught her attention until she'd met Phil earlier today, with his silver-flecked, slate-grey eyes and long silk hair that brushed the top of his shoulders. His vanilla scent wrapped around her.

"All done." His words yanked her from her thoughts. "Going to use my dagger on the corset because I have no idea what I'm doing there, and we don't have time to waste."

"Good decision." She held the dress against her chest as her body vibrated. Metal scraped against metal with the unsheathing of his dagger.

"It's going to be cold against your skin," he warned before pulling the corset back to get the dagger between it and her body. Goosebumps sprouted at the brush of his knuckles, leaving a trail as he worked up her spine, freeing her from the breathing contraption. "Finished."

Does his voice sound huskier?

He cleared his throat, then added, "I'll wait by the table." He dashed from the box towers to give her privacy.

"Thank you," she said, dropping the dress. The pink material pooled around her ankles. She tossed the corset on top of it, taking in a full breath for the first time in hours. She swiftly put on her black pants, then followed with her black boots. They were pretty beat-up with scuff marks—but they were way better than the slippers.

She pulled on a deep violet tunic, snagging it on the hideous pink bow she forgot was in her hair. She took a quick breath. *What do I do? I can't ask Phil to help me with this!* She patted her hands on top of her updo, trying to find the dozens of hair pins that were securing the bow in place and holding her captive. She worked quickly to remove them, releasing the bow, then lowered the tunic.

"All good?" Phil whispered.

"Yes, almost ready." She tossed the bow on top of the dress, then pulled her fingers through the long, wavy crimson strands a few times, relishing in the relief. She crouched to the dress, pulled out her crumpled letter for the newspaper, and transferred it to her pants pocket. She rummaged in her bag for her leather strap, then swiftly braided her hair over her shoulder. It wasn't the neatest job, but it would do. She walked back around the box towers, throwing her bag over her head and slinging it across her back.

Phil looked up from the book as she approached him.

"Any ideas on how to get the spells to show up?"

"No." He sighed. "*Map of the Forgotten*," he read from the table of contents. "*Map of the Heart. Map of the Known—*"

To Anna's surprise, the contents page suddenly disappeared and was replaced with instructions for the *Map of the Known* spell. "Well, then." He read the instructions.

"Hold tight and use your magic while saying the spell."

"Wait," Anna said. "Don't use your magic on it yet. Let's read the spell first."

"Alright," he said, then cleared his throat.

"Think of a place you have been, but focus your mind not to spin. Concentrate while closing your eyes, then open them up for a big surprise."

"Do you think this spell will take us to Dru?" she asked, hoping to see her sister.

"I think so, but have you been there?"

"Yes, several times."

"Are you willing to try the spell then?" he asked.

"Yes," she answered. It might be a bad idea, but they didn't have time to come up with a better plan. And if the book worked and took them directly to Dru, then she could delay her and be back at the town library in minutes versus hours. "But do you think it will work if you're the one using magic while I think about the place?"

"Only one way to find out," he said. "Alright, you think of the place, I'll use my magic and read the spell."

She nodded, read the directions two more times, then closed her eyes to focus on where Dru would be. She pictured the road that led to the tiny village.

"Anna, open your eyes," Phil said.

They were still in the library.

"Well… I guess that didn't work." She practically pouted, disappointment dripping from her lips. But then she noticed the book was glowing, the shine increasing.

And suddenly, it sucked them inside.

ELZBETH: 17 YEARS, 2 MONTHS, 5 DAYS, 23
HOURS BEFORE THE CLOCK STRIKES 12

"Thomas, are you in here?" Elzbeth called for what felt like the hundredth time in the past two hours. Nothing. Just the rattling of her lettuce-colored hand shaking the door handle. Thomas was always good at hide-and-seek, but now, Elzbeth thought as her frustration mounted, it was getting ridiculous. First, she was the one that agreed to play the childish game with him. A game they'd played since they were five years old, but now at sixteen, it seemed silly. But Thomas convinced her like he always did, with his pleading blue eyes and a smirk that she could never say no to.

She released the handle and took a timid step into the library, keeping a hand on the heavy mahogany door. "Thomas," she called wearily this time, eyes flicking about the space. She doubted he was hiding in here, but after hours of searching the estate, she couldn't think of where else he could be.

Normally, she wouldn't dare look in her father's personal library. But her father was off on another honeymoon with her latest stepmother, so if she were caught by one of the attendants, she knew she wouldn't be punished.

She turned to leave, annoyed that Thomas had taken up their entire afternoon playing this silly game, wasting hours they could've spent down by the pond or in town. All things she wasn't allowed to do when her father was home.

Without warning, a loud *pop* echoed through the room. A book suddenly appeared, open and levitating in the air, pages flipping rapidly back and forth. It abruptly stopped, opened right in the middle. Elzbeth's heart was beating a mile a minute. She took a cautious step forward.

Starlight burst from the pages, the magical dust dissolving like water droplets winking out of life on a blazing summer's day. Out came Thomas, his dirty-blonde hair disheveled, brushing across his eyes, his clothes covered in soot.

"Thomas!" Elzbeth exclaimed as he landed on the ground with a loud *thunk*. "You almost scared me to—Shit! You're on fire!" The hem of his tunic was burning up his right side. Elzbeth lurched forward and tossed him to the ground, hastily stomping out the flames.

"That was quick thinking!" Thomas staggered back to his feet.

"Not quick enough." Elzbeth scowled at his bright smile. Her finger pointed to her father's rug and a large hole scorched into its threading. "He's going to kill me," she said shakily.

"We can fix it," he offered, putting a gentle hand on her shoulder.

"How?" She pointed again at the hole, the size of a tomato, and wondered what her punishment would be this time. Living in the animal stalls for a month in the summer heat? She shivered at the thought. But she wouldn't put it past her father, who had threatened her with that very thing the last time she'd disappointed him. "You can't put a spell on it. If he found out that you did…" She shivered again. Her father might not stop at disciplining her. There were a number of things he could do to punish Thomas. Worst of all, he might throw him out on the streets.

"We'll use the book!" He pointed at it lying on the wooden floor near the large fireplace, reminding Elzbeth of its existence, the ruined rug having consumed her attention. "We can use the *Map of Yesterdays* to go back and fix my mistake with the dragon."

"The dragon den? It truly exists?" They had grown up hearing the story from Thomas's grandmother, Mrs. Hazel, about a dragon's den full of jewels and other treasures.

"Yes, Elz, it does!" His face beamed. "I used the map spell book to sneak a jewel from its hoard."

"Thomas, you know better than to use a spell book alone! Anything could have happened." Her scolding turned abruptly to frustration. "Wait…" She paused as the realization he'd been off having an adventure settled over her. "That's why I couldn't find you for the past two hours!" She crossed her arms.

"Two hours?" His voice went up an octave. "But I was only gone minutes."

"No, it was two hours. And you clearly didn't succeed, unless you're hiding a jewel somewhere I can't see." She uncrossed her arms, pointing at his burnt tunic hem, wiping the smile right off his face.

"Details," he retorted and grabbed the book. It opened on its own, falling perfectly in half, just as it had before Thomas launched from it. She peered over his shoulder at the book, the pages blank. She was about to say something when words gradually appeared, listing a title and table of contents.

Marvelous Magical Maps Spell Book
   Table of Contents:
   Map of the Forgotten
   Map of the Heart
   Map of the Known
   Map of the Mind
   Map of Tomorrows
   Map of Truths
   Map of Yesterdays

Elzbeth read the contents twice before looking at him. "Did you buy this?" If so, it had to have cost him a fortune.

"No," he said. "I stumbled upon it when I came in here to hide. It popped out of the bookcase over there." He pointed across the room. "But I wanted to ensure it was safe to use before I showed you and…"

She glared at him, her hazel eyes, sharp as emeralds, stopping his excuse.

"Fine," he continued. "I got excited and couldn't wait, but I was gone minutes. Well, I thought I was." He took a quick breath. "I'm sorry, I didn't realize I was gone for so long. But now we can use the book to go back and fix my mistake of using it in the first place, so this"—he nodded at the ruined rug—"never happens."

She looked at the rug, then back at the book's table of contents. "Which one did you use?"

"*Map of the Forgotten*." He smiled. "Went to the dragon's den near the border of Tranik and Phannel, like the story says, and, well…" He waved at his burnt tunic.

"I wonder what *Map of the Heart* is. That's such a strange name." She stopped as the table of contents page melted away, replaced by instructions and the *Map of the Heart* spell. He put his free hand around her waist, pulling her close to him. "What are you doing?" Her cheeks heated for how close they were in a room alone, her father's personal library at that.

He smiled his goofy grin. "It's how the book works," he said. "But it also allows me to do this." He leaned in slowly, and his lips lingered inches from hers, waiting for permission. She nodded. He smiled before closing the distance, pressing his lips into hers. Her heart flipped like it always did as she took in the softness of his mouth. Chills ran down her spine.

For a moment, she forgot about her father and the ruined rugs and what he might do to punish her when he found out about them. But then the book began to shake in Thomas's hand, jolting her back to reality and breaking the kiss.

He cleared his throat, turning his attention to the instructions as her heart tried to find a steady rhythm. He read,

"Hold tight and use your magic while saying the spell."

"What does that mean?"

"Put your hand on the book and see." He smirked. Normally, she'd elbow him in the ribs for his coyness, but curiosity had her wondering where the *Map of the Heart* would take them, so she did as he said. His smile broadened, and she read the spell.

"For two hearts to beat as one, you first must learn how love is truly won. Close your eyes, put your heart at rest, and think of a time when you were truly blessed."

As she said the last word, the book glowed brightly, sucking them inside. Light as feathers, they were suddenly flying through a translucent tube with every color imaginable rushing past. Thomas gripped her waist tighter, but just as swiftly as they entered, they were ejected right back to where they were standing before—her father's library.

"What the..." she barely got out as the library door flew open, freezing her heart with hoarfrost as her father stormed into the room. *Shit!* She'd not only ruined the rug, but she was in her father's personal library, uninvited, and alone with an attendant boy—a boy who dropped his arm quickly from her waist and took a side step away from her.

"Now, Teressa!" her father bellowed over his shoulder, ignoring Elzbeth. Her terrified heart leapt to her throat at the use of her mother's name. *Teressa.* Her mother walked into the library, followed by Elzbeth's half sister, Jaqueline. Elzbeth shook her head.

Maybe she was dreaming. Maybe she'd fallen asleep while waiting for Thomas to quit the silly kids' game. After all, she'd dreamt of her mother and half sister many times over the past three years after finding their portrait hidden in the storage room. She'd returned many times since that day to talk to their beautiful faces and imagine them talking back to her, encouraging her to be strong.

Her sister looked to be thirteen or fourteen in the portrait, making Elzbeth believe it was painted before Jaqueline's father died and their mother married Elzbeth's father. According to Mrs. Hazel, Elzbeth's mother was left with nothing after her first husband died due to his long and expensive illness. Nothing but a daughter with exceptional beauty. The portrait didn't do them justice because seeing her mother and sister now, they truly were the most beautiful creatures she'd laid eyes on.

"John, I told you. Jaqueline isn't to blame for—" *Smack!* The sound reverberated across the room, ringing Elzbeth's ears. She could only imagine how hard it rang her mother's as her father's handprint formed on her mother's cheek. Thomas gasped, but Jaqueline didn't make a sound, and Elzbeth knew why. *"Emotions are a sign of weakness."* One of her father's first lessons, and clearly, Jaqueline had learned it too. Unfortunately.

"The book," she whispered to Thomas, eyes glued on her mother and sister. "Why did it bring us here? To when my mother and sister were alive?"

"I don't know," he whispered back.

"Do not defend her!" Elzbeth's father spat at her mother, who stood frozen, holding her hand to her reddened cheek. The monster's handprint was fully on display now. "Take care of that, and I will speak to our daughter about her disobedience. Alone." He said the last word so calmly, Elzbeth wondered what punishment he would inflict on Jaqueline. He had made Elzbeth sleep an entire night outside in freezing temperatures once for just being late to dinner.

He'd gotten more creative with her punishments by the time she'd turned thirteen. Like cleaning the fireplace with her bare hands while the coals still cooled. She shivered at the memory, looking down at the faded scars on her fingertips and palms.

Thomas grabbed her hand, seeing what she was doing, and squeezed it tightly. He was the only one who truly saw her because it was his magic that created the beauty spell. The spell faded after thirty days, so her father made him use it on her each month to ensure her curse was always hidden.

Thomas had a rare magic that allowed him to create spells. When his magic appeared at ten, it surprised his family. No one for generations before him had been gifted with magic in their blood. This caused accusations of infidelity to arise from his father. And one night, on a drunken rampage, he took his wife's life, then his own. Several years later, Thomas's grandmother found a family ancestry book, and it turned out the magic was from his father's line, proving his mother's innocence too late.

"You okay, Elz?" Thomas asked, pulling her from her thoughts. She studied her mother and sister, trying to figure out when this was taking place before her birth. Before the day Elzbeth killed her mother and the pixie midwife cursed her.

"I hate this room," Elzbeth murmured. Thomas squeezed her hand tighter. It wasn't because of the thousands of books but because this was the one room her father always had her "lessons" in. It was soundproof, a spell Thomas was forced to create, which she didn't learn about until after her first lesson at age eleven, when her screams went unanswered from the attendants. Yet they knew what happened in this mahogany room and were ready with a healer when she returned to her bedchamber. No one spoke of what happened to Elzbeth, and apparently her mother and sister too. *Why did Mrs. Hazel not tell me that my father was cruel to my mother and sister?*

Someone cleared their throat near Elzbeth and Thomas, making them both jump.

"Lord Grayson." Her father sounded flustered as he turned toward the man, who looked close to Jaqueline's age, standing up from one of the overstuffed chairs in front of the large fireplace. *How did we miss him?* Elzbeth's heart slowed from the shock of someone else in the room, replaced by a bigger shock of seeing her father flustered in Lord Grayson's presence.

Lord Grayson moved toward her father. Elzbeth glanced at Jaqueline biting her lower lip as a faint blush came to her cheeks.

"I wasn't expecting you until tomorrow," her father added.

"Yes, I arrived early before the storm fully hit." Lord Grayson waved a hand at one of the floor-to-ceiling windows. Snowflakes danced from the sky, swirling with gusts of wind before they landed. "I asked to wait for you in here so I could enjoy the fire and some reading," he added, never taking his eyes from Elzbeth's father. The lord had a backbone, she would give him that. But if anyone acted like this toward her father today, well, they wouldn't do it again.

"Yes. My servants neglected to tell me you'd arrived. We were just discussing a private family matter." Her father still sounded flustered. She knew once Lord Grayson left the estate, the attendants would be getting an earful, and a cut in wages at the least, for this mistake.

"I see." Lord Grayson moved his eyes from her father to Jaqueline and then to their mother, who was still holding her cheek, either in pain or shock that they had an audience. Elzbeth couldn't tell. Their mother bowed her head, and Jaqueline followed suit.

"Well, it seems that your discussion is now over. Would this be a good time to speak on Jaqueline's dowry and my offer of proposal?" By the stunned stare of Jaqueline, this was clearly news to her.

"Yes, of course. My wife and daughter were just leaving."

"No, I would like them to stay for our meeting."

Elzbeth's jaw fell. She blinked several times, as did Jaqueline and their mother, who kept her head turned, trying to cover up what her father had done. It was ridiculous; Lord Grayson was in the room when it happened. But she knew why her mother did it. She didn't want further retribution against her later when the lord left.

That was the thing about her father: he was a monster within the walls of his estate, but outside them, to anyone else observing, he was just an overly protective father of his only beautiful daughter. It was utter bullshit, but she had learned her father had many connections in town, or more accurately, many men under his thumb. She learned that when she tried to ask for help once. She absentmindedly rubbed her free hand over the scar she got for that mistake on her right forearm, which her father forbade her to have healed. After all, with her beauty spell, the only people who saw it were her and Thomas.

"As you wish," her father agreed, bowing his head to Lord Grayson, who was half his age. This was both amazing and terrifying to witness. Amazing, because she'd never seen her father bend his will to another's. By the time she was nine, her father's wealth had moved him up the social ladder, never looking back, only down on those beneath his status.

Lord Grayson waved his hand at the small couch and two side chairs sitting perfectly centered in front of the fireplace. They were presently in this same position, never to be moved unless you wanted to pay the consequence. This was another reason why she hated this room, really every room, in her father's estate. Everything had to be perfect at all times. Perfectly placed, perfectly cleaned, perfectly removed from all human interaction. If her mother had been cut by his slap and blood trickled off her face to the floor, then an attendant would be scrubbing it for hours until all the evidence was gone. Or they would be fired and replaced by another desperate human with no magic.

Her father was a controller, and his home was the embodiment of his perfectionism. She used to believe it was how her father protected her. Until her tenth birthday, when her magic should've manifested, but instead she transformed. Her dewy pale skin took on a pond-green hue, and with the transformation went her father's love. His heart blackened toward her, and after some time she came to see that he'd always have a black heart.

The curse that appeared in place of her magic only served to darken it.

Once everyone settled into their seats, her mother and sister on the couch and Lord Grayson in a chair opposite her father, he rang the spelled bell for an attendant. The sound could be heard throughout the entire estate. The door opened, and a younger Mrs. Hazel, by maybe fifteen or twenty years, scurried in as fast as her short legs would let her.

"Grandma," Thomas said, exhaling, watching the only mother Elzbeth had ever really known approach her master with her head bowed. She hated how her father treated his attendants, barely paying them enough for the work they did to keep them reliant on his "charity" (as he called it) in giving them a roof over their head and food in their bellies. Her father thought those without magic were the lowest of creatures and treated them worse than the animals he housed in his expansive stalls. Mrs. Hazel bowed quickly to Lord Grayson, then to Elzbeth's father.

"Tea, for four," he commanded, not looking at her. She'd spent her entire life serving Elzbeth's father and his parents before him, and he couldn't even give her the courtesy of looking at her? Elzbeth balled her hands into fists. She wondered if she punched him now, would he feel it?

"Yes, my lord." Mrs. Hazel bowed again to Lord Grayson and Elzbeth's father, then scurried out the large room, closing the door behind her.

Once the door clicked shut, Lord Grayson said softly, "My infant sister's condition isn't improving from the influenza that took my parents." Elzbeth unfurled her fists at this news. There was heartache written all over his face. She didn't know much about Lord Grayson. Just that he had a baby sister nineteen years younger than him. Lord Grayson and Jaqueline died in a carriage accident a week after they were married, leaving Grayson's five-month-old sister orphaned.

"I'm sorry to hear this," Elzbeth's father replied. It was obvious that he didn't care.

"The healers informed me last week there isn't anything more they can do," Grayson said. Elzbeth's heart cracked at his obvious pain. "But I believe if she has a mother's love again, that she might, maybe..." He paused. Jaqueline's chest stopped moving, holding in a breath. "She might survive if she had deep love from me and my wife to help her pull through." He finished, blowing out a long, soft breath. Jaqueline followed suit, letting hers out too.

"I understand, but I wasn't planning on listening to new proposals until tomorrow," her father said.

"I know, and I am prepared to pay double what I offered last time if you allow us to leave tonight." He glanced to Jaqueline, then back at her father.

"I don't know," the monster replied, slowly looking him in the eyes for the first time since his arrival. All signs of his previous fluster were gone. "It's asking a lot of me to depart with my dear daughter earlier than my wife and I were planning."

Elzbeth's stomach lurched as her father used the lord's dying baby sister as leverage to get a higher price for Jaqueline. *Just chattel to be married off. That's all we are to him.*

"I understand, and as I'm the one asking you to let go of your dear daughter so quickly, I'll pay three times what I offered originally if you let Jaqueline wed me tonight and leave before the storm hits."

"But it's already snowing buckets out there," their mother started to protest, still keeping her bruising cheek turned from Lord Grayson's view.

"Four times, and it's a deal," her father said, turning Elzbeth's stomach.

"Deal." They both stood, clasping hands, their magic mixing in the air. Her father's, a deadly ash against Lord Grayson's white, sparkling diamond-shaped magic. They shook, binding their agreement.

ELZBETH: 17 YEARS, 2 MONTHS, 5 DAYS, 22
HOURS BEFORE THE CLOCK STRIKES 12

"This doesn't make sense," Elzbeth said as the magical agreement was made. "I was born the night my sister married, and my mother is rail thin. She doesn't look pregnant at allll…" Her words swooshed away, stomach flipping as the location shifted faster than a shooting star. She blinked as the world settled on a room, one she knew well, though it didn't appear in its usual state. They were clearly still in the past.

"Jaqueline," their mother said, hurrying into the bedchamber where her sister packed a travel trunk on top of the bed. "One of the attendants can do this."

Jaqueline shook her head. "It's fine, I'm almost done." Tears welled in their mother's eyes, squeezing Elzbeth's heart tightly, her own eyes stinging. "Come with me," her sister begged. "You know his cruelty won't stop now that he's sold me off."

"No, Jaq." Her mother said the nickname sweetly, clenching Elzbeth's heart further. "I made my choice."

"Choice? You had no choice, Mother!" she said curtly, making Elzbeth take a step forward, bringing Thomas along with her. "With neither of us having magic, you had no choice but to sell us." Their mother pulled Jaqueline into her arm, the other hand holding a pair of silver sparkling shoes as a soft cry escaped her lips. She buried her face into Jaqueline's collarbone, trying to muffle the sound. Jaqueline was the same height as her mother, six inches shorter than Elzbeth, who got her height from her father.

Jaqueline held their mother, and Elzbeth wished on every star in the night sky that she could embrace them. Jaqueline finally let go and put a tender hand to their mother's bruising cheek. "He apparently won't be letting you see a healer this time." She gritted her teeth while speaking.

"It's fine, don't fret."

"You need to come with me," Jaqueline demanded as a tear rolled down their mother's injured cheek. "Who knows what he'll do to you now that he has his money for selling me off!"

"I can't," their mother said, softer this time, lowering her eyes.

"Why?" Jaqueline spit back. "Why would you stay with him?"

"Because I'm pregnant."

Her sister startled a few steps back. "It makes so much sense now," Jaqueline began, "why after eight months of turning down bidders for me, he agreed to Lord Grayson's proposal tonight. He's going to have a true heir and no longer needs to hang on to me."

"It's a girl, and she's due in—"

"What?" Jaqueline took in their mother's slim frame. "How do you know? You're not even showing."

"He had me enchanted so no one knew but him. Though I suspect Mrs. Hazel knows after how sick I've been the entire pregnancy." Elzbeth shook her head. Mrs. Hazel never told her that her mother was sick carrying her, making her wonder what else Thomas's grandmother hadn't told her about her mother or her sister. "He didn't want anyone knowing he was having another daughter because he thought the price for you might be compromised."

"That low-life bastard! He made you hide your pregnancy

because he wanted more money for me!" Anger flared in Jaqueline's eyes as it burned in Elzbeth's veins.

"Yes, and I'm sorry. But he threatened that if I told you about the pregnancy that he would…" Her mother paused, taking in a quick breath. "Never mind that. He just informed me, now that he's agreed for you to marry Lord Grayson, we can reveal the pregnancy as your wedding gift."

Their mother's last words must have stabbed her heart, twisting the blade deeper with every breath, because Jaqueline faltered back a few more steps, hitting the side of the bed. She sat down, tears welling in her eyes, clenching her hands into fists. *The monster knew how to give a gift,* Elzbeth thought, watching her sister.

"It'll be okay," their mother said after a few moments. "And here is my gift." She extended the silver sparkling shoes to Jaqueline.

"Maybe she'll have magic," Jaqueline said.

"Of course she'll have magic. She's my daughter." Jaqueline got to her feet as Elzbeth's father stalked into the room, chest puffed out, surveying the bedchamber like he'd never seen it before. "This will make a lovely nursery for my daughter," he continued, surveying the space, knowing this declaration would cut deep.

No one spoke for a long time. Elzbeth mulled over all the ways she wished she could kill him. "Why is the book showing us this?" she asked. "The night I kill my mother."

"The spell said to 'think of a time when you were truly blessed,'" Thomas said and squeezed her hand. "And the day you were born was the day I was truly blessed." Elzbeth's face softened. She gazed into Thomas's warm eyes until her father's sharp voice called out into the hallway, slicing through the silence.

"Hurry up. We don't have all night," her father said sternly.

A man Elzbeth didn't know scurried into the room. He was sickly thin, but that wasn't what caught her attention—it was the flicker of hope in his eyes. She knew that look and wanted to scream at him not to touch her father and use his magic. Her father was an amplifier. He didn't have magic of his own to wield, but in a magical agreement with someone, he could amplify their magic to be more powerful. But only once.

Her father grasped his hand, and the man winced at the vise hold but still held the hopeful smile on his face. Elzbeth wondered what her father had promised this victim while omitting that the payment would never be received. When her father amplified the man's magic, it wouldn't only suck the victim's magic dry. It would also take his life, leaving her father to move on to his next "client" as he liked to call them.

The sickly man waved his hand, and golden dust fell onto Elzbeth's mother's abdomen, dissolving into her dress before revealing her true state. She wanted to close her eyes at what came next but stared at her mother as she began to rub her hand tenderly over her swollen stomach.

Jaqueline tossed the shoes into the trunk and reached toward their mother as the rail thin man released a bloodcurdling scream before collapsing to his death. Jaqueline's hand froze mid-reach, horror painted on her face. *Has she never seen her step-father use his magic?* She snapped out of her stupor as the monster grabbed her wrist, wrenching it back forcefully.

"No time for that. Lord Grayson and the officiant are waiting downstairs for you to make your union official and then be on your way," he said icily.

Their mother smiled at Jaqueline as several attendants came into the room. One kept their head bowed, grabbing the ankles of her father's latest victim to pull the corpse from the room as the other two closed the travel trunk and carried it out. Her father dropped Jaqueline's wrist before turning on his heels to follow the attendants out the door. Alone with their mother again, Jaqueline reached out, touching her stomach tenderly, whispering something too low for Elzbeth to hear.

The room melted away, shifting easier than it had before,

revealing a large black carriage as her sister and Lord Grayson climbed inside.

"You would think the book would warn us," Thomas said, exhaling and dropping her hand.

Elzbeth grabbed it back and tugged him towards the carriage, pushing him inside. They flopped down on the plush cushioned seat opposite her sister and her new husband. She blinked, adjusting to the dimmer orb lights floating in the corners (the kind only the wealthy could afford). With a jolt, the carriage began to move, and Elzbeth's stomach dropped, the feeling of weightlessness taking hold.

"Whoa!" Thomas said, his face practically glued to the windowpane. "Elz, we're flying!" He flopped back in his seat, beaming at her. "This guy has winged horses and powerful magic to make the carriage fly!" he added giddily.

Elzbeth looked out her window. Small clouds formed, then dissolved as the horses huffed and puffed, ascending higher, her heart lifting with them, as she'd never traveled like this before. She took a final glance back and smiled softly as their prison faded out of sight behind a curtain of snow flurries.

"This is amazing!" she exclaimed before catching a glimpse of her sister and Lord Grayson. The lord placed a thick blanket over his and Jacqueline's laps. With a smile, Elzbeth turned back to the window, still in awe of the fact that they were flying. The carriage suddenly dropped, making her weightless.

With the dip in altitude, Lord Grayson flung out his hand. White, sparkling diamonds sparked from his fingertips, settling the carriage as Elzbeth fell back into her seat, skirt hem tangled around her ankles.

"It's a protective shield," Lord Grayson said and placed the jostled blanket back over their legs as Elzbeth disentangled her feet to look out the window again. A slight film, like a soap bubble, surrounded the carriage and the winged horses pulling it. Snow pelted off the shield, bouncing away as the carriage seemed to warm from the protection of the icy wind.

"That's amazing... I... I haven't any magic. I don't know exactly what my stepfather told you, but I..." Jaqueline's words trailed off.

He took her gloved hand into his two large ones. "I know." He smiled shyly at her. "And I'm so sorry for how rushed this is, and I know you must have so many questions for me."

"Several, but if I can ask one... just for now?" she asked, and bit her lower lip.

"Yes, of course." He rubbed his thumb over her gloved hand.

"During our outings together, we never talked about, you know." Jaqueline bit her lip again and chewed on it for a few seconds. "I mean, we never discussed about tonight. Later. When we are..."

"Oh!" Lord Grayson said abruptly. "I expect nothing from you as a wife." He looked at their hands and let go quickly, clearing his throat.

"This just got awkward fast," Thomas said and laughed softly as they watched the newly married couple converse.

"I mean, not until you're ready." Lord Grayson stumbled over each word, his cheeks blushing bright pink.

"Thank you," Jaqueline said. They both went silent for several agonizing minutes.

"It's just..." He finally broke the silence. "My baby sister, she isn't sick."

Jaqueline's eyes widened, as did Elzbeth's. "But then why did you tell my stepfather she was?" she asked.

"It's the only way I thought he would take the bait for me to..." he paused. "Save you."

Jaqueline furrowed her brows. "He'll realize it's a lie when your sister—"

"He won't." He cut her off. "I mean..." He blew out a long breath. "He won't know about her because..." He paused again, flicking his eyes out the window, then back at her as if Elzbeth's father might somehow be eavesdropping. "Because of who my mother is."

"Was," Jaqueline said, then softly added, "I'm sorry for your loss. I can't imagine the pain of losing both parents just mere hours apart."

"My mother isn't dead."

Elzbeth's jaw dropped right alongside Jaqueline's as she wondered, as her elder sister must have, who this man really was. When they got back, Elzbeth had a lot of questions for Mrs. Hazel. "My father died almost fourteen months ago, days after my mother got pregnant." He paused taking a breath. "A few months after that, my mother, well, she thought it best for me to finally enter society to find a wife." He stumbled over each word. "The parents everyone believes to be mine and my sister's did pass last month from influenza, but my mother is very much alive. She travels a lot, you see, so we would be caring for my sister when she's away."

Jaqueline stayed quiet for a few moments as the carriage soared through the sky. Elzbeth was grateful for the silence. It was a lot to digest. "My mother, she's having a girl."

"I know. We're going to have two little sisters now." He smiled at her.

"He told you it's a girl?"

"He did. Said if I tired of you and wanted to wait sixteen years, then I could…" He didn't finish, making a disgusted face that Jaqueline mimicked.

"I'll kill him," Thomas murmured.

"So you know of his cruelty?" Jaqueline asked. The lord nodded. "And you married me to save me and help raise your sister?"

"No, not just…" He stumbled again over his words. "I married you…"

"Please, I promise you, I won't break. You can tell me, Lord Grayson."

"It's Gray," he corrected tenderly. She didn't respond so he continued. "I mean, unless you want me calling you Lady Jaqueline," he added, making Jaqueline laugh. The burst of laughter made Elzbeth wonder how long it had been since her sister last laughed. It was a beautiful sound, making Elzbeth wish she could've known her sister.

"It's just…" Jaqueline started, wringing her gloved hands together. "With all that has happened tonight…"

He lifted his hand to her cheek, sweetly caressing the very space the monster had struck their mother. "I'm sorry, Jaq."

She gasped. "My father and mother are the only ones who call me Jaq," she whispered upon recovery.

"Is it okay if I use it?" he asked. She nodded, staring at him intently. "I'm sorry I lied to you during our outings about my family, but I'm especially sorry I couldn't do much more tonight for your mother and sister." The carriage bumped, knocking Jaqueline toward him and pushing Elzbeth into Thomas, nearly hitting their heads together. "Sorry, landings can be bumpy, even with a shield, but we're here."

"That was fast," Thomas said, letting go of Elzbeth.

"Look out your window, Jaq." The lord pointed directly in front of Elzbeth's nose. She leaned forward, inches from her sister, at Lord Grayson's estate. "Castle" would have been a better word to describe the residence. There was a large main building, at least four times larger than her father's, with several outlying buildings the same size as her father's estate sprinkled about the grounds.

"Wow!" Jaqueline said. "Lord Gr—I mean, Gray," she corrected. "This place is…"

"It's protected so that only my mother and I know about it."

Elzbeth turned from the window to look at him.

"But your home? The one I went to, to meet your parents?"

"That was their home," he explained. "And I'm sorry again for all the lies. I didn't know how else to get your stepfather to agree."

"I understand." Jaqueline squeezed his hand. "And thank you for helping me. It's just my mother and soon my sister, well, they're now there without me."

"We will figure out a way to help them," he said. "I promise."

The carriage wheels hit the gravel path, bumping them all from their seats several times, separating Grayson and Jaqueline.

"Like I said." Grayson chuckled softly. "Landings can be bumpy." The carriage settled, and the door opened. Grayson stepped out first, then held his hand out to Jaqueline. "Mother is excited to finally meet you," he added, smiling broadly.

"Oh yes, I'd nearly forgotten," Jaqueline said, stepping out.

"I guess we're going too," Thomas said as Elzbeth waited for the book to take them away as before, but the scene held. She followed him out of the carriage before the coachman shut the door.

"She will be in the nursery. She tries to spend as much time with us as possible when she's home," Grayson explained. As they moved about the large grounds, they lit up with thousands of firefly lights that made Elzbeth's skin prickle with goosebumps. Her mind was reeling with so many questions. Starting with who was Grayson's mother?

Before she knew it, they were standing at a half-opened large mahogany door. Jaqueline clutched her hands in front of her as Grayson stepped aside to let her enter first. The room was beautiful. But nothing compared to the beauty of the baby cradled in the arms of the rocking woman as she lowly hummed. The sleeping babe looked to be just a few months old.

"Mother, we're back," Grayson said, stepping in next to Jaqueline, leaving just enough space for Thomas and Elzbeth to slide into the room next to them.

His mother lifted her head as Jaqueline unceremoniously pointed at her new mother-in-law and exclaimed, "Fairy Godmother!"

CHAPTER
Eight

Elzbeth barely had time to register what her sister said as the book appeared, floating in front of them. It opened swiftly, pages flipping with tiny sparkles shooting like stars as it sucked them inside. Like before, they flew through the tube, and all the colors under the sun blurred together as they rushed by. She and Thomas were ejected from the book, depositing them on their feet in her father's personal library.

"Again, a warning would be nice," Thomas said as the book snapped shut. He caught it before it fell to the ground, just as the door flung open. He put the book behind his back. Elzbeth went stiff as a board at the arrival of her father and newest stepmother standing in the doorway. *How long have we been gone inside the book? Father isn't expected home until tomorrow.*

"What are you doing in here?" her father demanded.

"Sir, we were…" Thomas started explaining, his voice cracking. Elzbeth glanced at him. He was standing over the hole they'd burned into the rug. They should've used the book to go back and fix it.

"We don't have time for this," Elzbeth's father said. He pushed his way past without acknowledging her. It was one of the two ways he treated her: either acting like she didn't exist or targeting her—especially during her lessons. Perfect posture, perfect manners, perfect everything. Because otherwise, how would she convince a man to marry *her?*

"Regina has much to do, as do you, Thomas," he continued, waving a hand at Elzbeth's newest stepmother, pulling her from her thoughts. "A ball is being held in three days for all noble ladies to meet the new king so he can finally select a wife." Elzbeth's stomach rolled, threatening to release her lunch. The new king of Tranik was fifteen years older than she was. What was he suggesting? "So I need a spell that'll have him falling in love with Elzbeth and proposing on the spot to marry her that night."

Elzbeth's heart froze. "Father, please…" she began.

His hand slapped across her face with a resounding *smack.* The sting of the blow made her eyes glisten with tears that she blinked away quickly. She knew better than to interrupt but couldn't stand silently in the face of what he was suggesting.

The last bit of hope that she'd foolishly held on to for her father's love burned away as anger boiled through her blood. Her father was a monster. He would only ever care for himself.

"Sir," Thomas said after a few heartbeats. She glanced at him. He was shaking like a leaf in the wind clinging to its branch. He'd never been present when her father "corrected" her. He only saw the aftermath before the healer arrived. Her father turned from her to look at him. "I don't think my magic is strong enough to create that type of spell. Covering Elzbeth's curse for a month has been hard enough."

"You have two days." He pointed his finger at Thomas like it was a weapon. And it was. "Two days to make it strong enough to create what I need, or else you and your grandmother are out on the streets." Regina gasped, bringing her father's dark hazel eyes on her, making her bow her head quickly. Apparently, she didn't know what kind of monster she'd married, but she would soon find out. It didn't take long for her father to show his true colors.

"All of you leave, now," he commanded, turning his back on the three of them, striding to a side table. He poured himself a glass of amber liquid, knuckles high, and threw it back in one gulp. They all rushed out before he finished pouring the second, Thomas closing the door softly behind them.

Without waiting to see Regina's reaction, Elzbeth grabbed Thomas's hand, yanking him towards the back door. They didn't say anything, not until they entered the gardens. She glanced around, ensuring they were alone.

"I have to leave," she whispered, just in case prying ears were around. Not all of the attendants sympathized with her. Some lined their pockets with extra gold snitching on her, and she couldn't risk one of them hearing her plans. He lightly put his fingers on her cheek. "I'm fine." She waved off his concern, but he murmured the healing spell anyway, causing the stinging to instantly dissolve from her cheek. "I can't marry the king," she continued. "He's as heartless as his father was."

"Stars rest his soul," Thomas said and mockingly rolled his eyes. Over the last month, the late king's death had been cele-brated by many within their kingdom, mostly by the poor and mostly in private. When word got around about his death, they'd snuck out to such a celebration at the nearby town where Elzbeth had drank, ate, and danced with Thomas deep into the early morning.

"If you go, I go," he declared, all mocking gone from his voice.

"But what about your grandmother?"

"Marry me," he said, sucking all the oxygen from her lungs. "Marry me. Then you're no longer eligible. We can do it in secret. Your father never has to know. He can just think that the king passed on you."

"But he'll blame you for your spell not working."

Thomas sighed heavily and began pacing. "Then we must

leave." She opened her mouth, but he held up his hand. "We take my grandmother with us. We find an officiant we can trust to marry us so your father can no longer control you, and then we create a new life for ourselves far away from him. In another kingdom if we have to."

"I don't know." She wrung her hands in front of her skirt. It made her think of her sister doing the same thing in front of Lord Grayson. Her sister who escaped this prison, whose mother-in-law was *the* Fairy Godmother.

"I know you're scared. I am too, but if we don't run now and get married, then you'll be engaged and married in two days to a cruel king." His words made her spine rattle. She couldn't do that. It would be the end of her.

"Okay." She stood up a little straighter. "Let's do it."

"Really?" he asked excitedly.

"Yes, but we leave tonight. Get married far away from here so word doesn't get to my father, at least for a few days." A plan started to formulate, one inspired by the spell book. "Then, once married, we use the book to find Fairy Godmother," she continued, words racing to keep pace with her thoughts. "We could ask her to let us live at her home that no one knows about. We could work for her, if that is what she requires… but she's the only one who can protect us if we do this."

Thomas smiled brightly, taking two large steps, closing the space between them. He reached for her, strong arms pulling her into his warmth and swinging her around in a circle. When he stopped, they were both dizzy. He held her until her feet found the ground, then moved his hands to tenderly grasp her face. "I promise you, I'll love you until the day I die, and beyond."

Her heart melted at his words. It wasn't the first time he'd said them to her, and she knew it wouldn't be the last. He planted a burning kiss upon her hungry lips, making her toes curl in her slippers. She ran her fingers through his locks, deepening the kiss, forgetting where they were. She could have kissed him just like this forever. Until the end of her days.

They broke apart, breathless, chests heaving. "I, too, promise to love you until the day I die, and beyond," she said, and his face lit up with the most beautiful smile. "We leave tonight. Once everyone is asleep."

"Alright. I'll create a spell on your doorknob that whoever touches it believes you are sick and staying in your room." He brushed a loose lock of her hair behind her ear. "It won't give us much of a head start, maybe a day, but better than nothing."

She nodded in agreement and kissed him one last time before dashing away through the garden, back to the estate, reveling in the butterflies fluttering in her stomach. It wasn't because she was scared to marry Thomas. She loved him. She had most of her life. No, the butterflies took flight in her stomach at the possibility they might not find Fairy Godmother in time—before her father caught up. Because John Thornton would never leave money he believes is his unclaimed.

CHAPTER
Nine

A whooshing filled Anna's ears as the map spell book sucked them inside. Scenery flashed by, all blurry shapes and colors, too chaotic for her to make anything out. Was this how all spell books worked? She'd never used one before. But just as quick as they were sucked in, they were thrown out, standing just as they were before. Instead of the library's dusty storage room, they found themselves outside, basking in the summer sun. Beads of sweat instantly formed on Anna's brow.

The book's glow diminished as it snapped shut and dropped with a thud onto the pine-needle carpeted ground. Birds sung from the canopy of pine trees above as she surveyed where they landed. She dropped Phil's hand, turned slowly, and exhaled. Thankfully, they were not in the middle of the village but in a thicket of trees beside the road leading to Tinker's shop. "That was wild," she finally said, turning to Phil. He knelt to grab the book, looking more or less recovered from the shock of their transportation.

"Please put this in your bag for safekeeping," he said.

"Me? Maybe you should keep it since you're going to be invisible," Anna countered.

"I'm out of magic. The book, it drained me, so it may be a while until I have enough to make myself invisible again."

"Oh." She chewed her lower lip.

"Yeah, I wasn't expecting it to drain me… and so fast."

"What if you don't have enough to use the book to get us back?" she asked.

"Would Dru help? Use her magic to take us—"

"She doesn't have magic," Anna interrupted. "That's why we were in school before Cyndra became a princess. And my magic isn't the type that could help us with the book." She rolled her eyes, frustrated at their situation.

"I didn't know you and Dru were in school before."

"We needed to learn a livable skill," she said. "But now"—she turned on the toe of her boots in a circle—"we get to be ladies of the court." She curtsied mockingly. "It's why Dru doesn't believe that I have magic, because she doesn't and Cyndra's isn't anything powerful." Anna thought of the many times she tried to convince Dru, but she was too far under Elzbeth's spell to believe her about their father's death or Anna having magic. She hated the wedge it'd put in their relationship the past years.

"It must be hard to have those you love not believe you," he said, raking his fingers through his hair.

"No harder than those who are supposed to love you locking you up your entire life," she deflected, not wanting to simmer in her own heartbreak.

"I know you don't agree with what my father did, Anna, but my life…"

"I'm sorry," she said, and looked at the ground. "It's… none of my business."

"It's alright. I like that you care," he said. She lifted her eyes to meet his as he went on, smiling softly. "Look. My life hasn't been ideal, but neither has yours. So let's change at least one of our circumstances. You go delay Dru, and I'll wait here."

"We're not splitting up!" Her heart fluttered like pixie wings.

"What if I lose you like…?" Her chest tightened at the thought. "No, we can't split up. I just found you." Fear raced down her spine, lungs working to pull in a full breath.

"Breathe," he said tenderly, placing a hand on her back. "You're not going to lose me." Feeling the weight of it, she took in a deep breath, then another. "Since I don't have my magic at the moment, and we're not splitting up, I guess it's time for me to put on my disguise," he said after she took several more breaths.

She straightened, his hand dropping from her back. "Oh! With everything that happened this past hour, I almost forgot that I have a surprise for you," she said. He arched a brow as she unslung her bag. She pulled out the wrinkled royal guard's uniform.

"How did you get that?" He pointed at the hooded black robe she'd stolen a few months prior. It was big on her even though she'd taken the smallest one she could find, but it should fit him. Muscles and all.

"I took it from the castle laundry bins," she answered, beaming, before pulling the black leather gloves out from the bottom of her bag to hold out to him. "I needed it for situations like this when I don't want to be seen because I have useless magic," she added of her own will.

"Your magic isn't useless. You're able to see through spells and enchantments! And yeah, I imagine having to speak honestly when questioned is tough, but at least I know with you I'm never getting any bullshit."

Anna laughed before shaking the uniform. "We're running out of time, so please put it on."

"Fine, but I'm putting my disguise on underneath it too," he said and took the hooded robe and gloves and motioned with his finger for her to turn around.

"Don't want me to see you get naked?"

"Stars, what, no!" His words rang two octaves higher. "I

never said I didn't want you to..." He cleared his throat. "I just want to see your reaction after I put the entire thing on."

"Right, yes." Her cheeks heated. *Why did I say that?* she wondered as she turned around, putting the book into her bag, waiting patiently for him to put his disguise on. His boots crunched the dry pine needles as he shuffled around.

"The gloves are a bit snug," he declared.

"You're not letting me see your disguise first?" She turned to face him as he shoved the last glove on. He was covered head to toe, only his silver-flecked, slate-grey eyes visible behind the guard's black masked hood. They shimmered like stars in the sunlight.

"Good things come to those who wait." He chuckled softly and winked. Anna's stomach fluttered.

"Fine," she grumbled, grabbing his bag and slinging it over her shoulder to join with hers before stepping out of the trees. Thankfully, the road into the village was quiet with no one around.

"What's your plan for delaying Dru?" he asked as they made their way over the last hill revealing Tinker's entire village. It wasn't big, maybe a dozen buildings, unlike the royal city, which stretched on as far as the eye could see around the castle. Less than a hundred people lived here, a half-dozen more during Tinker's workshops. Anna knew the inventors would all be at Tinker's shop with their heads down, absorbed in whatever new inventions they were working on.

"Well, I won't be able to talk to her. She'll ask too many pointed questions that I can't lie about. I was thinking of creating a problem—something that would delay her."

"Like?" he asked, softer now that they were walking behind the shops.

Anna glanced around, ensuring no one saw them. "A few stray cats live behind Tinker's shop. Dru talks about them all the time. I was thinking I could release a few through the backdoor."

"Cats? Your plan to delay your sister is cats?" he said, a bit louder than they were whispering before.

"Shh." She turned to him and pointed at the back door to Tinker's shop. "Trust me, it's a good plan. The cats will knock things over. And I know Dru. She won't be able to leave until all the inventions are fixed." He frowned, glancing at a few of the strays eating from dishes on top of various wooden barrels. "If you're worried about the cats, don't be. Dru loves cats. I promise, once she's done cleaning up after them, she'll be petting and consoling them for their troubles."

"I hope you're right." He sounded unconvinced as she reached for the door handle. He scooped up two strays, a grey tabby and calico curled up together on top of a barrel, and stepped next to her.

A high-pitched yowl had her practically jumping out of her skin. Phil stumbled back, his boot releasing a cat's tail he'd accidentally stepped on, knocking into the barrels, toppling porcelain bowls to the stone path with a loud crash. The hinges from the shop's back door squeaked. Phil clambered to his feet as Anna turned to the door just as Tinker crashed into her face.

CHAPTER

Ten

Anna clasped her eyes shut, gasping as Tinker bounced off her nose, inhaling a mouthful of her pixie dust. A coughing fit followed.

"Oh my!" Tinker's voice rang like a tiny bell. Anna attempted to clear her throat of the dust, but it only caused her to cough harder. Wiping her hands across her face, she slowly opened her eyes, the pixie coming into focus through the blurry haze.

What am I going to say? How can I explain why I'm back here?

"Lady Annalie, right?" Tinker asked. Her cyan dust bustled behind her translucent rainbow wings. "Lady Drury's younger sister," she added with a sweet smile.

"Yes, that's me. But just Anna, please." Her magic had her answering between the dry coughs. She hated the use of her full name because that was how Elzbeth addressed her. But also, she really hated the "lady" title that she and Dru had now that Cyndra married a prince. The etiquette lessons Elzbeth made her and Dru attend were grueling. Anna thought many a time of taking her butter knife or sewing needle and stabbing it into—

"And I'm her friend Phil," he said in a low, husky voice, stepping next to her. *What is he doing?*

"Nice to meet you, Phil," Tinker said.

Phil patted Anna on the back, helping to ease her coughing. She glanced at him, noticing he'd removed the royal guard uniform, revealing his disguise. Dark glasses and a bushy, long chestnut beard that blended into his hair completely, covering his Star Kiss mark. Anna almost burst into laughter, ramping up the coughing again.

"Here," he said and handed Anna the water bladder she kept in her bag with her few snacks. She removed the cap and drank quickly to get rid of the dust. "We're sorry to bother you, but we need to speak to Lady Dru for a moment. We didn't want to interrupt everyone, so we were trying to come in the back, but my clumsy feet found a cat's tail, resulting in…" He waved his hands at the discarded barrels and broken bowls on the ground. "We'll pay for the damages," he added.

"Oh, don't worry about that." She waved her tiny hand at the mess. "But Lady Drury isn't here." Anna nearly started coughing again from choking on her water. *Where is Dru? Did Elzbeth send a fire message for her to come back early?* She felt ill at the thought.

"Well," Phil interjected, "sorry for interrupting your workshop and also for making a big mess. It was lovely to meet you." He grasped Anna's arm and tugged to make their escape.

"Workshop? That's next month." Tinker's tiny golden brows, the same color as her hair, scrunched as she looked at Anna. "Why did you think—"

"Oh, wait, my mistake," Phil interrupted before Tinker could finish her question and unwittingly force Anna's magic to answer truthfully. "Dru didn't say she was going to a workshop, she said she was going to shop. Yes, for some of her items for her new invention." He threw his free hand to his forehead. "That's why she couldn't see me this week." He shook his head. "I need to remember to listen better."

"Oh, I understand." Tinker smiled softly. "And who knows what Lady Drury said to you, especially if she was absorbed in a project. Isn't that right, Anna?"

"Yes, when Dru is working on one of her inventions, it's hard to get a full coherent sentence out of her, let alone get her to stop for five minutes to eat." Her magic rushed to answer. Dru wasn't absent-minded; she just got so absorbed in her inventions that she lost track of time or anything outside of what she was working on.

A bell chimed from inside the store. "Be right with you," Tinker called over her shoulder. "Well, it was nice seeing you again, Anna, and wonderful meeting you, Phil." They both smiled back, and Tinker flew inside, the door snicking shut behind her.

Anna exhaled as Phil reached behind the toppled barrels and pulled the guard's uniform and gloves out. He opened his bag and shoved them inside as they made their way out, quickly navigating the path behind the shops. Neither one spoke until they were back on the road, heading for the thicket of trees they'd landed in. "That *is* some disguise," she finally said, laughing at the ridiculous beard.

"Well, it does the trick of covering my Star Kiss." The beard moved with each word he said.

"It does, so why did you put on the guard uniform if you had that?" she asked as they stepped off the road into the pine trees.

"You were so excited to show it to me, and I didn't want to disappoint you." He smiled shyly, making her heart flip. Dead pine needles crunched beneath their boots as he cleared his throat. "So, why do you think Dru lied about being at a workshop?"

"No clue," she answered. "But we need to figure out where she is and why she lied." A vise tightened around her heart at her sister's betrayal, but she ignored it—or tried to ignore it, at least.

Where is Dru, and what is she up to? I just hope she's okay.

Once they were back at the spot, Phil removed the beard and wiped his sweat-glistened chin with his hand before putting the disguise back into his bag.

"We should sit. It might be a bit until my magic is fully restored to use the book again," Phil suggested.

Anna didn't want to sit. She couldn't. Her evil stepmother was engaged to the king, and Dru was not at Tinker's, thus ruining their ability to use her to stall for time to find a way to break Elzbeth's spell.

"I can practically hear the wheels turning in your head."

"Because Dru is Stars knows where!" She threw her hands into the air. "Now how will we delay your father from becoming Elzbeth's next victim?" she added.

"Too bad you were unable to get your father's report before it was destroyed."

"That's it!" she squealed loudly, scaring a few birds from their perches above.

"Shh."

"Sorry, but I know how we get my father's autopsy report," she said in an excited whisper, stepping closer to him.

"How?" Phil's brows furrowed.

"The map book," she replied. "The *Map of Yesterdays.*"

"You think it can take us back in time?"

"I do." She almost squealed again. She finally had a way to pin her father's death on her wicked stepmother. "So once your magic is back, we can use the book to take us to the documentation office, before the fire, to steal my father's report so we can have our evidence." She wished she could use the book to go back and save her father from Elzbeth. But Anna knew what that would cost—no matter how much she wanted to. If she used the book to save her father from marrying Elzbeth, then Cyndra would never go to the ball to meet Edgar, then her nephew Augustus would never exist… Anna could never do that.

"Okay, but even with the report, do you think my father will believe us?" he asked, pulling her back to the present.

"I wasn't planning on giving it to your father. He won't believe the report. He and everyone else in the royal city is under her spell. I have a letter I wrote last night. I hoped to give it to

Gertrude Penny at *Fairytales, Facts, and Fables* newspaper to publish." She pulled the balled-up parchment from her pocket and flattened it out. "We can now put my father's report with the letter as evidence."

"That's brilliant! The newspaper goes out to the entire kingdom, so those who aren't bewitched will see it and know the truth."

"Exactly," she said clearing her throat before reading the letter.

"Dear Readers,

There is a murderer living amongst us. One who is marrying and killing her way up the ladder of society and wealth. One who I know is responsible for the death of my father and her previous husbands before him.

If you know whom I speak of, I suppose my accusation shocks you. So I'll start at the beginning and tell you all about the real Elzbeth Beck, my not so wonderful, wicked stepmother.

It began on the day of the royal ball. Drury, my middle sister, and I had come home from school to find that our father had been spelled into marrying a stranger, the union overseen by our oldest sister, Cyndra, and the Fairy Godmother, who had already moved the murderous creature into our home.

If I had been there, I would have called bibbidi, bobbidi, bullshit on the whole arrangement, but as I stated above, I was at school because I had no magic... until that day.

My sisters didn't believe me when I told them that

*my magic finally appeared and that it made me able
to see through Elzbeth's tricks. And almost four years
later, they still don't believe me. Hence why I am
writing this letter. People need to know the truth!
Elzbeth Beck is a murderer. And I can prove it, but
I need the officials to pull her past husbands' autopsy
reports."*

"Elzbeth was married before your father?" Phil chimed in.

"Yes," she answered, looking up from the letter. "Eight times." His eyes widened. She continued,

"I became suspicious of her after my father died suddenly, just like her last husband the year prior. So I snuck into her room when she was out shopping."

She took a quick breath.

"I found a small bag, I'm guessing spelled or enchanted not to be seen because it was sitting on her dresser top. It contained eight wedding rings, ranging from a band with diamond chips embedded in it to the large star-shaped diamond ring my father had given her."

Phil's eyes widened. "You need to add that to the letter. Why you suspected her of murder. It's a big accusation, so you may want to offer to let your magic be tested to prove you can see through enchantments and spells to make your accusation credible."

She rummaged through her bag, searching for her pencil, running her fingers over the apples she put in there yesterday. She grasped the pencil and scribbled down:

add why I suspect Elzbeth of murder.

She worried her lower lip, then added:

*offer to let my magic be tested in order to prove
I'm telling the truth. That I got my magic late on
my 13th birthday and can't be spelled or enchanted.*

She pulled the pencil back, biting on the end, quickly reading over the letter.

"I probably should take out the bibbidi, bobbidi, bullshit part too," she said. "If I want to be taken seriously."

"No, leave it in! That was my favorite part."

"Mine too." She laughed softly, putting the pencil back into her bag and folding the paper several times before sliding it back into her pocket. "Now, we just wait for your magic to come back and use the book to jump to the documentation office before the fire and get my father's autopsy report."

"About your plan… I think it's great except for one thing," he said.

She looked up from the letter. "Which is?"

"The wards on the building to keep people from stealing documents. How do we get past them?"

Anna tapped her finger to her chin. "Hmm…" Her eyes brightened. "I've got it! We'll use the book to get there the night of the fire. When Elzbeth has whoever was helping her start it."

"You think Elzbeth is behind the fire?"

"Yes," her magic had her answer. "So once her henchman brings down the wards to set the fire, I'll slip in quickly, grab the report, then slip back out."

"That's too risky." She opened her mouth, but he beat her to speak. "You could get caught by whoever is helping Elzbeth, and then she would know that you're not spelled." He stepped closer, only inches between them, eyes blazing. "Or worse."

"What's worse than being caught by Elzbeth?" Anna had been so careful to not let Elzbeth know she could see through her spell. If she knew the truth, what would become of Dru, herself, or even Cyndra?

"You getting trapped inside a burning building," he said.

"I won't."

"I know you're excited, but we have to be smart about how we do it. And your plan is too risky."

She huffed, knowing he was right. They both stood silent for a bit until she finally asked, "Do you have a better plan?"

"I think I do," he said and drew in a long breath, then let it out slowly, sending the loose hairs around her face dancing. "We use the book to get to the woods near the documentation building the night before the fire." She nodded. "You shoot an arrow at the back of the building, getting a guard to come and see what it is. I then use my magic to slip in the door unseen."

"That should work!" Excitement coursed through her.

"But once we get there, I'm going to have to rest for a bit before I can use my magic again."

"We can wait in the woods unseen?" Anna offered.

"Only if you hold my hand the entire time." He gave her a small smile. Her stomach flipped.

"Why?" she asked breathlessly.

"Because the enchantment on the woods is… scary," he said, with a lopsided grin.

"Right, yes, of course." She stumbled over each word. "That part of the woods isn't enchanted, just so you know," she added.

"Well." He stepped back. "If you feel like holding my hand as we walk through them, just to be safe, that's fine by me." He smirked, and Anna cursed her heart for squeezing. "Let's go then, my lady."

He doesn't like you. He is just a charming prince like his brother.

"Once we get there, I'll rest for a bit, we get the report, then we get back to today," he continued, snapping her from her thoughts to focus back on what they were doing.

She would finally have evidence that hopefully got her stepmother locked up, which would delay the engagement announcement or maybe even break it. *One can dream.* Either way, they would have more time to search for a way to break her spell. She pulled her bag off her shoulder and placed it on the ground.

"Ready?" she asked, pulling the book out and standing next to him.

"Yes." The book opened on its own to the middle like before. She held one half while he held the other. Phil grabbed her free hand, intertwining their fingers as the table of contents materialized upon the page.

"Map of Yesterdays"

She read as the contents page disappeared, replaced with the spell's instructions.

"Hold tight and use your magic while saying the spell."

Phil began to read as Anna closed her eyes, holding tight as the book instructed.

"Close your eyes and think of where and when you want to go
in your past, but don't lose focus because the path won't last,"

Anna thought of the night before the fire and the woods just off from the documentation building.

"Taking time from yesterday will come with a cost, so be careful
how long you dawdle before today's time is all lost."

CHAPTER
Eleven

The air swooshed, taking Anna's breath away, and lifting her off her feet. She opened her eyes as the book glowed brightly, sucking them in. Her vision swam, colors zooming past in a blur outside the translucent tunnel. Their journey stopped as swiftly as it started, the book ejecting them onto the ground. It closed on its own and dropped to the forest floor at their feet.

"I don't know if I'll ever get used to that!" she gasped as the world settled. It was dark, just a sliver of moonlight peeking out from above through the canopy of oak trees. She exhaled. They'd made it. Phil dropped her hand, sidestepped away from her, then proceeded to empty the contents of his stomach.

"Phil!" she whispered and leaned close to him. He was white as a winter's moon. She grabbed the book and quickly shoved it into her bag before rummaging around for her small light. It was a gift from Dru on Anna's ninth birthday, one of her earlier inventions. She switched it on, placing the bag on the ground so she could illuminate its interior. Her fingers grazed the apples and a couple of oat bars on their way to the water bladder.

"I'm okay. Just give me a moment," he croaked. "That was intense." She nodded, wishing she had healing magic like her father. He turned toward her, wiping his mouth with the back of his arm. "I guess it's to be expected though. Traveling through time."

"Here, drink." She handed him the bladder.

He rinsed his mouth, spitting several times before taking a slow sip, followed by several gulps.

"Apple?" she asked and pulled one from her bag.

"Yes. Please."

She handed it to him, accepting the bladder and putting the cap back on before returning it to the bag. "Let's move over there to sit and wait for your magic to return." She pointed the light toward a few large boulders about ten yards away.

"Sounds good. Lead the way." He waved his hand holding the apple. An owl hooted in the distance as something scampered on the forest floor, not too far from where they stood. Anna hoped the typical sounds of the night didn't conjure memories of the enchantment for Phil.

"What do you think of the spell's warning?" he asked, biting into his apple. The crisp sound silenced the woodland creatures for a few seconds as they reached the boulders.

"Honestly, I was so focused on picturing this place and time, I barely heard the last part of the spell," she answered, peering past the thick woods at the back of the documentation office about thirty yards away. She would have to get to the edge of the tree line to shoot her arrow at the door, then somehow manage to get out of sight before someone opened it to unknowingly let Phil in. "Something about taking time from the past," she added.

"That's right—the book said it comes with a cost. That the time we take here will be taken from our today," Phil agreed.

She wondered what time it might be back in their true today. *Does time move the same speed in both whens?* She kept her eyes trained on the back door.

"So," he continued, "since we have a few moments. What's something about you that no one else knows?" he asked before taking another bite.

She cringed as her magic had her confessing something that Daff and her sisters didn't even know. "I visit my mother's grave on her birthday."

"Oh, shit!" he exclaimed softly. "I didn't think this through! It slipped my mind that your magic makes you… I'm sorry, I didn't mean to force you…"

"It's fine." She kept her eyes locked on the door. "I was four when she died, and I don't really remember her, unfortunately. But ever since Elzbeth came into our lives, I just needed someone to talk to who would listen and believe me," she explained.

"That makes sense," he offered.

Neither spoke for several minutes, and the crickets' serenade grew louder as their silence lengthened. Anna shifted her weight back and forth like a clock's pendulum, thinking how to break the silence.

"What about you? Tell me something no one else knows about you." She interrupted the insects' song. "To make us even."

"Queen Lily adopted me." She glanced at him, then back at the door. "It was their first attempt to break my curse. They thought if she legally recognized me as her son, that the Stars might remove my curse."

"The Stars are hard to please," she said, then realizing she was being callous, added, "Sorry, all the same."

"Enough with the sad questions." He waved his free hand. "What do you like to do when you're not hunting down a solution to stop your—how did you put it? Wonderfully wicked stepmother?" He smirked.

"Sleep," she answered, matching his smile.

"Wow, and I thought I had a boring life," he teased.

"Haha," she replied dryly. "But it's the truth."

"What about before Elzbeth married your father? What did you like doing? What did you dream about?"

His last question surprised her. She hadn't thought about her dream of becoming the first woman archery guard in years. The first woman royal guard ever. He crunched another bite.

"Before Elzbeth, I practiced my archery every day." She patted the bow hanging over her shoulder. "I would go into the woods to practice before my sisters or father were awake."

"Why the woods?"

"Because my father never went in there."

"Oh, he didn't know you liked archery?"

"No, he knew. But he didn't take it seriously. He called it a hobby. Something I could practice twice a week for my tournaments but never more." She exhaled. "He didn't know it was my dream to become a royal guard in the archery division," she added, answering his previous question.

"Was?" he asked.

"It was a child's dream, and I was forced to grow up."

"But you're the three-time junior archery champion!" he protested. He must've read the newspaper article after her last win, a week before Cyndra became a princess. "You would make an excellent royal guard."

Her heart swelled, and a warm smile tugged at her lips. It was nice hearing Phil say those words. No one had ever told her she'd make an excellent royal guard before. "True. But I'm also Princess Cyndra's sister. A lady of the court who is now required to marry someone of noble breeding as soon as my stepmother finds one who will make her richer."

"I bet Father would make an exception for you." He stepped next to her. She turned to look at him. "Have you ever told Cyndra about your dream?"

"No, Cyndra wouldn't understand," she said. "She is elated with me marrying a man of the court. She fully supports my stepmother's grueling etiquette lessons, so much so that she has attended each one the past year to ensure Dru and I land noble husbands." He opened his mouth, and she raced to console him. "It's fine. At least when I marry, I'll be free of Elzbeth and—"

Footsteps crunched against rock. She jerked her head to the

door, scanning. *Shit!* She'd gotten distracted. A large cloaked figure moved along the shadows of the building toward the back door. The person knocked, glancing around as the door opened, revealing the night security guard. The cloaked person sent a swirling puff of green smoke at the guard, the same green shade as Elzbeth's skin. His face went from alarmed to pleased, opening the door widely for the hooded person to step in.

CHAPTER
Twelve

ELZBETH: 17 YEARS, 2 MONTHS, 1 DAY, 12 HOURS BEFORE THE CLOCK STRIKES 12

Elzbeth had never been one to pine over her wedding day much. It didn't matter to her that she was getting married in a courthouse in the middle of the night by a pixie judge, four towns over from her father's estate, with only Mrs. Hazel as their witness. All that mattered was that she was marrying Thomas.

And as she looked in Thomas's eyes, full of so much love, she had to remind herself this wasn't a dream. This was her own version of a fairytale—her happily ever after. She wouldn't change a thing—except, of course, in a perfect world, her mother and sister would be alive and present.

"You may kiss your bride," the pixie judge proclaimed as lilac dust fluttered about her busy wings. Thomas smiled broadly as he leaned in to seal their union. As their lips touched, Thomas's magic encircled them, binding their marriage. Mrs. Hazel sniffled, and the pixie clapped joyfully. Elzbeth lingered in their kiss, in her love for Thomas. She could have remained there forever.

A thundering boom rocked the ground beneath her, yanking her and Thomas apart. She blinked, debris falling on their heads and dust billowing about as the roof caught fire, followed by a bloodcurdling roar. Mrs. Hazel screamed, the pixie barely dodging a piece of rubble that was at least ten times her size as the center of the roof caved in.

"Dragon!" the pixie yelled as the beast landed in the wreckage, blue scales burning like fire, smoke puffing from its nose. Death gleamed in the blood-red eyes locked on the fairy. The dragon bared its dripping fangs.

The pixie fluttered her wings feverishly, darting like a shooting star for safety, but the dragon's fire was quicker. Her wings turned to ash, dropping her like a stone to the ground, dead before she landed.

Mrs. Hazel screamed again. Thomas moved to block Elzbeth with his body, the dragon's blazing eyes turning on them. It didn't attack but lowered to a crouch, revealing a far greater beast sliding off its back.

No, no, no! her mind and heart screamed.

Elzbeth's father marched toward them, finger pointed at Thomas, fire blazing in his hazel eyes. "Thought you could hide from me?" he barked, locking eyes with Elzbeth. "Thought that by missing the ball, the fool would get engaged to another?" He gritted his teeth. "Well, congratulations, he did just that. And married the princess from Lexlent that very night. You foolish, stupid girl!"

His anger turned to rage. "You married a penniless servant when you could have been queen!" Thomas extended his hand behind his back, reaching for her, but before she could take it, her father commanded the dragon, "Grab them!"

"No!" she screamed. The dragon lurched, a small puff of smoke releasing from its lips as it fell forward onto its belly.

"Weak shapeshifter," her father cursed. The creature transformed, leaving a naked, trembling older man gasping for breath, unaware like all those who came before him that this would be the result of the foolish deal he'd made with her father.

"Run!" Mrs. Hazel yelled.

They turned as one to flee, but Mrs. Hazel's bloodcurdling scream froze them. Thomas turned, falling to his knees, yanking Elzbeth with him. Her wail caught in her throat at seeing the only mother she'd ever known splayed on her back, throat split open. Thomas crawled on hands and knees to her lifeless body, gingerly lifting his grandmother from the rubble, her blood still dripping onto the stone floor.

"You monster!" Elzbeth screamed, getting to her feet. She rushed her father, fist ready. But he was faster. *"Ladies don't need to know how to wield weapons,"* his voice taunted in her mind as he grabbed her fist, twisting it with a crack, breaking it. Elzbeth's knees weakened with the pain of it. He turned her, holding the dagger dripping with Mrs. Hazel's blood to her throat.

"Please!" Thomas begged, gently moving his grandmother from his lap, and leapt to his feet.

"He won't kill me," Elzbeth said. "He may do a lot of things, but he won't kill me. I'm his next fortune to be made, even if I won't be queen."

"Not anymore," her father retorted. "Regina has twin daughters who turn sixteen in four months. They aren't as pretty as your spell. But there are two of them, so they'll get me more than a cursed daughter ever would." His words made her stomach drop. Her heart skipped a few beats as she groped for something that might save their lives.

He pushed the dagger harder, nicking her skin. A trickle of hot blood trailed down her throat. "You're no longer needed, *dear daughter."*

She lifted her good hand, yanking on his arm. The blade cut deeper, making the blood flow faster, soaking into the front of her dress. She yanked again, but his arm wouldn't budge. She elbowed her other arm into his ribs, then gurgled as the blade bit deeper. She didn't care. She wasn't going without a fight.

"Wait!" Thomas put his hand out. "What if I promise you my magic to use?"

"No," she choked out through a mouthful of blood.

"I'm listening," her father said, seething.

"If you amplify the spell, then you can make it stronger, permanent." He took a tentative step closer. She wanted to tell Thomas to stop, that she was okay dying, but the room was starting to dim and sway.

"You'd be willing to die for her?" her father scoffed.

"Yes," Thomas answered. He didn't even flinch. "But if I agree, then you have to agree to never lay a hand on or harm Elzbeth ever again."

"Deal." Her father removed the blade, letting her slump toward the floor. Thomas was there in an instant, catching her by the waist. He sat cradling her in his lap.

"No, please don't," she pleaded. The words were hard to get out as her throat filled with blood. He touched her wrist and waved the other hand over her throat, saying the three word spell he'd created to heal her when her father wouldn't let a healer do it. She felt her wounds knit as he spoke the last word, but the spell couldn't heal her broken heart. She couldn't imagine her life without him. "I'm sorry," she whispered, tears filling her eyes.

"I'm not." He leaned in to kiss her one last time.

"Time's up." Her father grabbed him by the collar of his tunic, yanking him to his feet before their lips could touch. The action sent her tumbling to the floor. She struggled to get onto all fours, still dizzy from blood loss, as her father and Thomas clasped hands. "I promise to amplify your magic to make Elzbeth, permanently, the most beautiful creature ever seen, in exchange for never laying a harming hand on her again."

"I promise," Thomas agreed. Her father's deadly ash magic and Thomas's sky-blue magic sparkled and mixed between their hands before she got to her knees.

"Thomas," she choked out. Tears streamed like twin waterfalls down her cheeks.

"I love you until the day I die, and beyond," he whispered to her, then said the spell. But it wasn't the one he'd used for the past five years. As he spoke the last word, her entire world went dark.

Thomas's spell, amplified by the cruelty of Elzbeth's father's magic, transformed her, permanently making her appear exactly as her father desired.

CHAPTER
Thirteen

The cloaked figure stepped inside the door that the security guard held open. An owl hooted from a nearby tree, making whomever it was turn and stare in their direction. Anna stiffened, holding her breath, hoping it was dark enough that they wouldn't be spotted. Thankfully, the guard said something, and the figure moved further inside the building, the door closing behind them.

"Did you see the color of the magic used on the security guard? It was identical to Elzbeth's skin," Anna whispered. "That has to be who is helping her."

"Why are they here tonight?" Phil sounded just as perplexed as her.

"No clue."

"We have to go back," he stated.

"But the report—"

"I know. And we can come back to a different night and bring Daff with us so we're not reliant just on my magic."

"But we're here now!"

"Who knows how long that person will be inside?"

"We're so close," she pleaded. "We can't just leave!"

"It's too risky. We need to..." Phil stopped as the security guard opened the door, letting the hooded person slip out with a nod of thanks. The figure moved quickly away from the building back into the shadows, out of sight. "That was fast."

She jumped from the boulder. "Change of plans. The guard uniform, please." She pointed at his bag.

"I know what you're thinking, and no!" He got to his feet.

"Please," she practically begged. "With the uniform I can go in through the front door."

"That's too risky."

"No riskier than our original plan," she countered. "I'm going to put on the uniform and knock on the front door." He opened his mouth, but she kept going. "I'll tell the security guard that a fire message was sent stating that several buildings were broken into tonight on the same street, so royal guards were sent to investigate. While I'm talking, you slip in with your magic, grab the report, and we can go back with evidence in hand."

"Unless whoever that was just took the report." He pointed in the direction that the hooded figure retreated.

"Why burn the building then?" Anna asked.

"To cover their tracks."

She huffed, crossing her arms. He was probably right. But just in case he wasn't… "Can we check, please?"

"What if you get caught? You know the punishment for impersonating a royal guard is severe, right?"

"I won't get caught. Trust me, I've done this before," she said, then quickly added, "And please don't ask me about it because we're wasting precious time."

"Fine. But I want to go on the record that I think this is a horrible idea." He inhaled deeply, raking his hand through his long silken hair, before exhaling. "But as your friend, I'll help you."

"Thank you." She wrapped her arms around him and squeezed before she realized what she was doing.

"Um. You're welcome." He chuckled softly, his warm breath tickling her ear.

Her cheeks heated, and she released him.

"Well, you better get dressed quickly so we can execute this flawless plan of yours," he said in a teasing tone.

"Your magic is back?" she asked, looking up.

"Yes." He opened his bag and pulled out the hooded robe and gloves, then handed them to her.

"It returned quicker than before," she said.

"Not really." He pushed her bag, then his between the rocks. "It was about the same time, but you were so captivated with my amazing ability to ask great questions that it seemed shorter."

"Yeah, that and the time it took for you to get sick." She smirked before throwing the hood over her head, covering her face.

"And that," he said, holding out his hand. She placed her gloved hand into his. "Let me do the talking since you can't lie and he can't see your mouth," he added softly, weaving them through the oak trees, jogging down the hill to the back of the building.

"Okay," she whispered as they neared the edge of the woods. "Ready?"

"Yes, let's do this, then get out of here." He squeezed her hand tighter. *Is he scared for what we're about to do or is it something else?*

They picked up their pace. Dead leaves crunched loudly beneath their boots as they passed the tree line. They slowed to a walk once on flat ground just a few yards from the building. Thankfully, the lush grass absorbed their footsteps as they approached, but they moved more cautiously when the grass turned to a stone path.

She glanced at the clocktower, both the small and big hand resting on the three: 3:15 a.m. She wondered what time it was in their today and hoped minutes here didn't take away hours. Magic spells were tricky things, but she couldn't think on that now. She didn't see anyone on the street at the early hour. She took in a deep breath and let go of Phil's hand before knocking on the glass door.

Phil stood behind her, his breaths warming the back of the hood. A security guard's boots clicked across the marble floor, approaching the double doors. He peered out the glass. Anna placed him in his mid-to-late fifties based on his grey hair and weather-worn skin. Seeing a royal guard at the doors, the man fumbled with something in his tunic pocket. Anna held her breath, hoping their plan would work. The wards' humming filled the night. The security guard pulled out a pin, which he used to prick his finger and produce a single drop of blood. He pressed it against the door and the wards' humming ceased, allowing him to open it.

"Sorry to bother you, but we received a fire message," Phil said. "Several buildings on this street were broken into earlier tonight."

"That's awful," the guard replied, putting the pin back into his pocket. Anna exhaled lowly.

"Yes," Phil said, clearing his throat. "The royal guard is checking all the other buildings to ensure none of them were breached."

"It's been quiet here, but thank you for checking." The guard smiled politely. Phil crouched and grabbed a small stone, throwing it over the guard's shoulder into the lobby, shattering something inside.

"What was that?" the guard exclaimed, turning to look behind him, pushing the door wide open.

Phil took the opportunity and slipped past him inside. *Good thinking*, Anna praised as Phil ran past the lobby desk and disappeared down a hall to the right.

"Stay here, and I'll check," Anna mimicked in Phil's voice.

"No, I'm coming too," the guard said.

"Fine, but no talking," she commanded.

She walked in slowly, took a step, then a breath, hoping to

give Phil enough time to search. She paused after several steps, looked around, then took another cautious, slow step as the security guard stayed glued to her side.

"There's no way—" he started to say. She turned and held her finger to her mask where her lips were to silence him. *What part of no talking did he not understand?* She couldn't risk him asking her anything that her magic would make her answer and blow their cover.

She crept past the lobby's receptionist desk and saw what Phil had hit. A small rock and broken porcelain cup were strewn across the marble floor.

"How did—" the security guard started to ask. A loud crash sounded from the back of the building. They both jumped, but thankfully, it cut his question short. Phil ran down the long hall toward them, waving his hands frantically for her to run.

"Stop!" a security guard yelled, chasing after Phil.

"Stop!" the guard next to Anna echoed. "Stop in the name of —" But his command was cut short as Phil punched him in the face, his body crumbling to the ground.

"What happened?" she asked. Phil grabbed her arm, yanking them past the desk and through the lobby toward the exit.

Phil tugged her through the door as the guard called out again. "Stop!"

They ran around the side of the building, the beat of her blood pulsing rapidly in her ears. "Take off the uniform," Phil said between breaths, letting go of her hand for her to do so.

"What happened?"

"I'll meet you back at the rocks." He turned, not answering her, and ran back toward the front of the building.

She wanted to protest, but she knew what he was doing. He was ensuring the other security guard couldn't contact the true royal guard until they were back in their time. She awkwardly pulled the hooded robe off her body, stumbling a few times as she ran up the hill into the woods. Her breath was labored from the sprint as she pulled their bags out, shoved the uniform into

Phil's bag, then slung her bag over her body. She pulled an arrow from it and readied her bow, moving back down the slope toward the building.

Why had Phil's magic sputtered out so fast? And what was he doing now? It shouldn't take him this long to knock the other guard out… unless he was caught.

Shit! her mind screamed. She had no idea what sort of an effect a situation like this would have on their today, all because of her insistence to go into the building. They should've waited. She should've stayed here and sent him as the guard so neither of their magic got them caught. That would've been a better plan. It was too late now.

The back door opened. She raised her bow, ready in case she needed to shoot. Phil popped his head out, looked around, then darted out the door and up the hill toward her. She stayed ready, scanning for anyone following.

"It's okay," he said softly upon reaching her. "I took care of the other guard. They'll be out for a bit, but we better move away from here while we wait for my magic to return."

"What happened?" Her heart raced as they moved toward the rocks to reclaim his bag.

"I didn't realize there was another security guard in the back." He grabbed his bag, slinging it over his shoulder without stopping. "He startled me, and I stumbled into a file cabinet and knocked over whatever was on top of it."

"I'm sorry, it's my fault," Anna said. "We should've done what you wanted in the first place to get Daff to help with her magic on another night."

"Yeah, probably, but I know how much you wanted the report." She opened her mouth to apologize again. But before she could, he said, "And we'll get it. We'll come back on another night before tonight to ensure it's still here, with Daff to help us."

"That's what took you so long? You went back for the report?"

"Yeah, but it was gone."

"It must've been Elzbeth's henchman."

"I think so," he said. "And whoever it was didn't just take your father's autopsy report. My adoption papers are also gone."

"What? Why? She didn't know about you until today! Well, our today, that is."

"Best guess is my father must've told her about me earlier. They'd been seeing each other what, four weeks by this night?"

"Maybe." She pulled her bag around to grab an oat bar. "Here, eat this." She handed it to him.

"Thank you, I'm starving." He tore the wrapper open and bit half the bar off. She grabbed the other apple from her bag and bit into it; the sweet juices ran down her chin. She wiped them away with the back of her hand, the symphony of chewing and crunching of leaves beneath their boots filling the silence. She tossed her apple core for a creature to find later and grabbed the water bladder. She took a few sips and passed it to him. He took a quick drink and handed it back. He pulled out the ridiculous beard and dark glasses, proceeding to put them on. "No more risks."

"Yeah, we've had too many close calls."

"I know. My magic has never depleted that quickly." He shook his head, swishing his hair, a few strands catching in the bushy beard. "But I've never depleted my magic multiple times in one day so… could be because of that."

She nodded, and they walked in silence for a few more moments. "So, you can knock grown men out with one punch?"

"Edgar taught me." He laughed softly. "It was after a night we snuck out and got caught. I saw Edgar do it and begged him to teach me."

"Oh, I wish I could've seen that."

"Why?"

"Because I can't imagine perfect Prince Edgar doing anything that would mess up his clothes or hair." Her magic made her answer honestly.

"Edgar isn't perfect."

"Could've fooled me and the entire kingdom. After all, his nickname is Prince Charming."

"Sadly, his perfect persona is part of the job as heir to the throne." He raked his hand through his hair. "You think my situation is bad? Imagine being on display from the moment you're born. Never being able to have a private moment beyond your own bedchamber. Always having to be on your best behavior even when having a bad day because you're next in line to become king." He took a quick breath. "Honestly, sneaking out created some of my favorite memories. We weren't princes. Just two brothers, not burdened with kingdom matters. Edgar could shed his charming mask, and I could be... me."

"I never thought about the burden for Edgar to have his life fully on display. That sounds... awful."

An owl hooted above.

"Not just for Edgar, but now your sister and Augustus too," he said. Anna mentally kicked herself for how much she'd assumed her sister and Edgar's life was perfect. She opened her mouth to apologize again, but Phil stopped walking. "I'm good to use the book."

"Thank the Stars."

"Yes, so let's get back so we can grab Daff," he said.

"I want to go to my house."

"That's too dangerous," Phil replied. "Elzbeth is there."

"She won't see us because the book will drop us in Dru's room, and her door is always closed." He opened his mouth, but she continued. "I need to see if I can find any clues in her room for where she may be. If we can still find and delay her, we'll have more time to get my father's autopsy report and maybe even find the way to break Elzbeth's spell."

He heaved out a large breath. "Alright. I trust you."

Her stomach fluttered at his words. "Thank you," she said, pulling the book from her bag. It opened halfway on its own, and the title and table of contents appeared. He put on the dark glasses, then grabbed her hand, squeezing softly. Anna scanned the contents. "Which map should we use to get back? *Map of Tomorrows, Map of Yesterdays,* or *Map of the Known.*" Before he could answer, the contents page disappeared and was replaced with instructions for *Map of the Known.*

"I'm guessing that one." He chuckled.

"Hold tight and use your magic while saying the spell."

He looked at her. "You ready?"
"Yes."

"Think of a place you have been, but focus your mind not to spin. Concentrate while closing your eyes, then open them up for a big surprise."

Anna closed her eyes, thinking of Dru's room and the orderly chaos it was always in.

Phil's hand tightened around hers as the swooshing of air filled her ears and the book sucked them inside. She opened her eyes, blinking to adjust to the blurring shapes and colors flying outside the tunnel, but before her sight could settle, the book ejected them.

It snapped shut, falling to their feet. But Anna was ready this time, grabbing it before it sounded against Dru's floor. She turned to check on Phil. He was statue still. She could faintly see his eyes behind the dark glasses shut tight. "It's over," she whispered. He opened his eyes slowly. "How do you feel?"

"Not as bad as before," he said and took in a long inhale through the nose, wiggling the beard, letting it out slowly through the mouth. "I think keeping my eyes shut helped."

She nodded and placed the book back in her bag.

"So, this is Dru's room?" he asked. It was hard to see with only the glow of the moon, so Anna rummaged in her bag for the light and flicked it on.

"Ah, that's better. Thank you." He turned around, taking in the space. "Her room is very interesting," he added after surveying.

She knew what he meant because Dru's room was just that. It was like getting to see the inner workings of her brilliant mind. At first glance you would think she was a slob. She was actually very organized but in a way that only Dru's mind truly understood. Anna learned at an early age to respect Dru's room, not touching anything unless first given permission.

"Where do we start?" he asked, looking at the various piles of "projects," as Dru called them, on her desk, floor, and shelves.

"Well." She tried to focus on all she knew about Dru and her unique system.

"Hey, this has your name on it." He held up a small box, the size a ring would be kept in.

"Really?" Anna asked. "Are you sure it—"

"Bellenda, I know you see this as an invasion of Drury's privacy," Elzbeth's voice shrilled outside Dru's door, halting Anna in her tracks. "But Annalie has never been gone for three days."

What in the Stars is Fairy Godmother doing here? With my wicked stepmother? And three days! The spell book took three days! Anna's mind screamed, missing Fairy Godmother's reply as the door handle rattled and began to turn.

ANNA: 15 HOURS, 30 MINUTES BEFORE THE
CLOCK STRIKES 12

Anna dropped Phil's hand, crouched to the floor, and slid under Dru's large bed. Phil wiggled in next to her as she thanked the Stars that the bed was high enough for her to slither under with her bag and bow in tow. Phil slid a pile of books near the outside edge of the bed to help block their faces. Anna flicked the light off as the door creaked open. She forced herself to breathe softly, her heart pounding between her chest and the wood planks.

"I need to figure out where Annalie is," Elzbeth said. "Where is that damn light thingy Drury created?" she cursed. "Ah, here it is," she added. The room lit up bright, like the sun was shining through the windows on a hot summer's day. Their heels clicked across the wood as they moved about the room.

"Elzbeth," Fairy Godmother said.

"I know what you're going to say. It's too late now to do anything about Drury and Annalie. I wanted to take care of them, and we should've done that immediately after their father's death. Just like the others."

Anna's heart lurched. Phil grabbed her hand, squeezing tightly. *Shit!* She'd always suspected Elzbeth's hand in the death of her late husbands' children, but this was proof.

"I know. I'm sorry I convinced you otherwise. But unfortunately, we can't change that now." Fairy Godmother sighed heavily. *Double shit!* Elzbeth's spell had Fairy Godmother helping the wicked woman with her scheming! Her stomach rolled with disgust. "Also, I agree with Will. Marrying the king is too risky. This isn't like before, not with what we have…"

"It isn't too risky, and you know it has to be done. You know there's no other way to get what I want."

"What we want," Fairy Godmother replied. Their heels clicked as they moved toward the west side of the room. Phil squeezed Anna's hand tighter as she held her breath. If the conniving women moved a few feet over, they would be right in front of them.

"True, what we want," Elzbeth said. "So we need to find out where Annalie is, and we need to do it quick because my patience is running thin."

Anna's heart beat faster, which was surprising considering it was already attempting to thump its way outside of her ribcage. What would Elzbeth do if she didn't come back soon? It seemed like the book's cost for going back took three days from their today. Could they risk using it again to get her father's autopsy report?

"What are you looking for?" Fairy Godmother asked, cutting into Anna's thoughts.

"For any clue on where Annalie could've gone. I searched her entire room and found nothing." Anna's blood pulsed in her ears. She thanked the Stars for Daff having enchanted the way she left and returned to her room a few months back. Elzbeth was none the wiser.

"Maybe she went to see Drury? Heard the news of your engagement and left the party to tell her sister?" Fairy Godmother said.

Damn! That was what she did. But if Elzbeth were to send an attendant to retrieve Dru and learned the truth about Tinker's workshop, what might she do? Would Dru be safe upon her inevitable return? It occurred to Anna that she truly had no idea where her sister was… and if her return was, in fact, inevitable.

Everything was spinning out of control, more than it was before. Horns blared, announcing the arrival of the king. Phil's hand tightened like a vise around hers. Elzbeth's and Fairy Godmother's shoes and the hems of their skirts came into view as they moved toward the windows overlooking the front entryway. Elzbeth let out an annoyed sound that Anna knew all too well. She stared at her green ankle as the evil woman tapped her sparkling silver slipper against the wood floor.

"What the hell is he doing here?" Elzbeth spit out sharply.

"Probably wanting to see his fiancée since it's been three days," Fairy Godmother replied, calm and cool. "But let's find out for sure what he wants."

Anna watched her pink slippers disappear, with Elzbeth close behind. The door hinges creaked, followed by a soft click of the door closing.

"I'm seriously beginning to think the Stars don't like us," Phil whispered.

"Really, you think?" she said. He tugged on her hand to stop her from climbing out from under the bed.

"I want to go hear why my father is here," he began. "But I don't think I have enough magic restored to keep us both invisible. Stay here and look for clues to where Dru could've gone. Then we need to get Daff and use the book fast."

"We can't use the book to go back and get the report," she whispered quickly. "It took three days from us, and if Dru returns while we're gone, or worse, Elzbeth discovers Dru lied…" She shivered at the thought of returning and Dru being gone permanently.

"Let me go listen," he said, rubbing small circles on the back of her hand with his thumb. "Then we'll get Daff and come up with a new plan."

She nodded, and he released her hand to wiggle free of their hiding spot. His boots thumped softly on the wood floor as he moved toward the door. It creaked open. She doubted anyone could hear it downstairs. *But what if they can?* She braced herself, but the only sound she heard was the door clicking shut.

She relaxed a fraction, forcing her mind to calm. Once free from the confines, she scanned the room, seeing the small ring box on Dru's desk.

Just as Phil said, there was a small piece of paper next to the box with Anna's name on it. Maybe it was her birthday gift? It was next month, after all. She debated opening it, not wanting to spoil the surprise, but curiosity won out. She could act surprised when Dru gave it to her.

She lifted the lid, revealing a blue-grey, plain-looking band. She pulled it from the box, examining it closely. It wasn't much to look at, but Anna knew what Dru was capable of. The band reflected the light as she turned it over, wondering what it might do. She slipped it onto her right ring finger.

Anna moved her hand around in a figure eight motion, then a circle, then up and down. Nothing happened. She tapped the ring, and still nothing changed. Horses trotting away with the king's carriage pulled Anna's attention from the ring, and knowing that Elzbeth and Fairy Godmother could be back any second, she shimmied back under the bed. The door creaked open. She held her breath.

"It's me," Phil said softly.

She let out her breath, crawling out to join him. But he wasn't there. She looked under the bed.

"What are you doing?" he asked, his voice inches from her ear. She practically jumped out of her skin at his closeness. And at not seeing him. "Are you okay?" His hands squeezed her shoulders.

"What in the Stars?" she gasped.

"What's going on? Why are you looking at me like that?" Phil's voice was heavy with concern.

She bit her lower lip, not compelled to answer out loud. Biting down on her lip was something she did as a child when her father or Cyndra asked her something and she needed time to come up with a good excuse. Her eyes widened with the memory. "The ring." She held her hand up and looked at it.

"What?" he asked, but she didn't answer. She didn't have to. *This feels amazing!* She couldn't believe it. Dru had invented a way to suppress magic? But why? She didn't think that Anna had magic. *She never believed me when I told her!* Maybe this wasn't meant for her. But there was a note with her name on it.

Even though Anna wasn't sure why Dru made her the ring, in that moment, she didn't really care. "The ring!" she said giddily, louder than before. She threw her hand over her mouth, hoping Elzbeth didn't hear. "What did your father want?" she asked, blinking because it was strange to talk to Phil without seeing him. "Should we hide again before Elzbeth comes back?"

"They left. Something about a picnic under the stars. They'll be gone for several hours."

She relaxed, knowing Elzbeth was gone for now. "And Fairy Godmother?"

"Also left," he answered. "Anna, why can't you see me using my magic? And why aren't you answering my questions?"

"The ring!" She held it up again and pointed at the small box on Dru's desk. "I put it on, but it didn't do anything, at least I didn't think it did. But you came in and I heard you but couldn't see you, and then when you asked me questions, I didn't have to answer." She paused for a moment as it all sunk in. "I think this ring suppresses magic. At least, that's my best guess."

He popped back into view, and she jumped. "Did you just stop using your magic?" She hoped it wasn't that the ring stopped working.

"Yes." He smiled broadly, squeezing her shoulders.

She pulled the ring off and handed it to him. "Ask me something."

"Uh…" He took the ring and placed it in his palm. "Please

don't hate me for asking this." He took in a quick breath. "What do you like most about me?" He waved a hand down his side, a sly smile sprouting on his lips.

"The color of your eyes." Her magic had her answering before she registered his question.

He chuckled, making her heart flutter. "What, not my sparkling personality?" he teased.

"I like that too, and the smell of your skin. But you asked me what I liked most and then gestured to yourself." *Stupid truth magic.* Her cheeks started to burn.

"You don't smell so bad yourself," he said softly, taking her hand. His calluses rubbed gently against her finger as he slipped the ring back on. "Jasmine is my favorite flower," he added, dropping her hand.

He took a step closer, inches separating their faces, their warm breaths mingling.

"And this is my favorite color." He reached for a loose strand of hair fluttering against her cheek.

There was a sudden crash, making them jolt apart, turning to see who'd caught them. She relaxed at the sight of the culprit.

"Lucifer, you mangy beast!" she said to the grey cat standing atop the pile he had just knocked from Dru's shelf.

"You have a cat?"

"No, my stepmother does," she answered and narrowed her eyes on the menacing creature. "Cyndra gave him to her as a wedding gift. He's a pesky thing. Loves everyone but me." The cat hissed at Anna as if to prove her point. "He must've snuck in with Elzbeth," she added, showing her teeth to the creature.

"I think the ring is made out of osmium," Phil said, pulling her attention away from the cat, who was now cleaning himself atop of whatever project he'd just broken.

"Osmium... like guards' swords and dungeon cell bars are made out of?"

"Yes, but how did Dru get osmium?" He shook his head as he stared at the ring.

"No clue," she said. "We can add it to our list of questions for later, but right now, we need to get going." She headed for the door. "Can you use your magic for both of us to get out of the house unseen by the attendants?"

"Yeah, I'm feeling normal, so I think we're good."

Anna pulled the ring off and slipped it into her pants pocket. She wanted to be able to see him while he used his magic to get them out of the estate.

"We'll take the woods all the way to the back of the library. Keep us hidden until we get into the trees." She swooped Lucifer up, keeping him at arm's length so his claws couldn't retaliate. "Open the door and I'll put him down, then grab your hand," she instructed.

Phil opened the creaking door slowly as Lucifer growled. She poked her head out and looked both ways. It was clear. She put the angsty cat onto the lush carpet, and he hissed at her the moment his feet touched the ground. She grabbed Phil's hand, the cat's protest fading as they vanished out of sight. Phil shut the door softly. They quickened their steps, passing an open door where an attendant dusted a guest room, completely unaware of their presence.

They slowed their pace at the top of the three-story landing and moved onto the toes of their boots, stepping lightly down the marble stairs. They paused as an attendant crossed the entryway in the opposite direction. She pulled his hand, leading them to the hallway with a hidden side entry. Elzbeth's bedchamber was the only room this direction, and attendants only came to this part of the house when summoned. No one would see them exit.

Anna pushed on a small piece of panel, sliding it to the side to reveal a latch. Elzbeth had renovated the entire estate except for Anna's and Dru's rooms, adding this secret door that Anna discovered by accident. She used it only when Elzbeth was away.

Once in the thickness of oak trees that edged two-thirds of

the estate, Anna let go of Phil's hand, pulling the light from her pocket and turning it on. "Okay, let's go get Daff."

"Um." His voice shook. "Can I hold your hand?"

"Oh, sorry, I forgot," she said and grabbed it again. "You can close your eyes if you want, like before."

"No, as long as I'm holding your hand, I'll be fine." He smiled, and her heart did a flip in her chest.

Was he going to kiss me before Lucifer interrupted us? Anna had never been kissed and wondered if Phil's declaration of not having friends before meant he'd also never been kissed. The toe of her boot caught on a tree root, making her lurch.

"Sorry," she said. She righted herself, refocusing on the worn deer path, casting the light a few feet in front of them. "So, it seems Fairy Godmother is helping Elzbeth."

"Yeah, I can't believe it either." He shook his head.

"It explains how Elzbeth knew about your adoption. Fairy Godmother must have told her. I don't know why your father didn't use his magic to make her forget about you after she signed your papers."

"Fairy Godmother can't be spelled, enchanted, or made to forget using magic."

"What?" Anna's heart sank. "She knows what Elzbeth truly looks like and that she kills innocent people?" If Fairy Godmother wasn't a victim of Elzbeth's scheming, it meant she was a willing participant.

He squeezed her hand. "A lot has happened in the past day, well, three days technically, since we used the book and borrowed time. Maybe you should let Daff and me handle looking for a way to break the spell so Elzbeth doesn't know about your involvement," Phil said.

"We're not splitting up. What if she finds you and spells you?" Her throat constricted as tears welled in her eyes. "I… I don't want to be alone again," she said, giving voice to her greatest fear.

"Anna." Phil tugged at her hand, bringing her to a halt. He turned, eyes wide and locked on her face. "We won't split up. I'm sorry I brought it up again." She dragged in a deep breath, then let it out slowly. "You know I know what it's like to be alone."

She wrapped her free arm around him and squeezed tightly. "Thank you," she said softly into the crook of his neck, inhaling his sweet vanilla scent. Anna didn't realize how lonely she'd been until she met Phil. She took in one more breath, then let him go and tugged on his hand to continue walking.

Neither said anything as they walked, the sound of their breaths filling the silence as they approached the edge of the woods at the back of the library.

She turned to face him. "Your beard is a bit crooked." She dropped his hand to adjust it. He ran his fingers over the ridiculous bushy thing, smoothing it against his upper lip and chin, making her smile. He offered his hand back to her. "Conserve your magic. The library is closed. Maggie has never worked a late shift, so Daff will be the only person there cleaning up."

She turned the light off, slipped it into her pocket, and led them down the small slope to the back of the library. She removed the key, then unlocked the window and replaced it around her neck. She braced her free hand on the sill and pushed up, like one would getting out of a bathing pool. Her breath hitched at Phil's hands grasping her hips and lifting her inside.

"Thank you," she said shakily, pulling her legs in and sliding onto the table. "Your turn," she said, moving to the side and holding the window open.

He pushed both hands onto the sill and slid next to her. She closed the window, slid off the table, and set her bag and bow on top. "I'm going to go get Daff." She moved toward the storage room door.

"Sounds good," he said.

She walked down the short hallway, passing a few stacked

boxes of books that didn't fit into the cramped storage room. The chair behind the front desk scraped across the floor, letting her know where Daff was.

"Hey, Daff, can you come…" She froze as she entered the large open space lined with mahogany shelves. Standing at the front desk were Cyndra, Edgar, Dru, and Fairy Godmother.

CHAPTER

Fifteen

ELZBETH: 15 YEARS, 6 MONTHS, 4 DAYS BEFORE
THE CLOCK STRIKES 12

"**G**irl, are you ready?" Gail squealed up the attic stairs.

"Almost!" Elzbeth called back to her newest stepmother, the most insufferable of them all. She pulled at the last buttons behind her neck, practically choking herself with the silk material, struggling to get the buttons to cooperate. She just wanted to get this day over with. Gail insisted on personally greeting the judge instead of sending her fifteen-year-old brat of a daughter (or literally anyone else), so there was no one to help her into her wedding dress.

Her father could've greeted the judge. He was a pro at giving her away to insufferable men now. Baron Tremaine was the fourth man in two years. But thankfully, it would be the last because tomorrow she would finally be eighteen. This time, when her newest husband took ill and died hours after the ceremony from the poison she slipped in his drink earlier, she'd be free. She would never have to marry in order to make her father richer again.

The thought sent a thrilling chill down her spine. She almost smiled into the mirror, but seeing her spelled reflection erased it from forming on her lips. She'd rather stare at the sun until she was too blind to look into another mirror as long as she lived. But there was no avoiding it today.

She needed to ensure her dress and hair were as perfect as the lie her father sold to each of her fiancés. She looked at the decaying green color her hands had become that only she and her father could see thanks to Thomas's spell. The spell that killed him and robbed her of the love of her life.

A pit formed in her stomach at the thought. She'd cried so much since that day that she didn't think she had any tears left to spare. Thomas had used her father's magic to amplify the spell, making her the most beautiful woman in all the kingdoms. But something about the way Thomas used her father's magic must've somehow tweaked it because he still saw Elzbeth as she truly was.

She had blacked out after the spell was placed on her. When she woke two days later, her father had already started taking offers for her hand in marriage. According to the story her father told her, he'd almost killed her because he thought the spell didn't work. He knelt before her unconscious body, held his dagger to her throat, catching Elzbeth's spelled face reflecting from the blade, and stopped. So instead of death, she was back on the market two days after he murdered Thomas.

But selling her off once wasn't enough. The bastard arranged for her husband to get sick days after they married, then die two months later. She never found proof it was her father, but after her next husband died "falling" from his horse, and a third was poisoned by a "jealous suitor," she was certain her father was behind it all.

Proving it would be a fruitless endeavor. She knew her father paid or threatened the right people to keep himself clear of any accusations. She thought she'd be labeled a black widow after her second husband's death, hopefully stopping the requests, but no. Her father's influence was far-reaching. Suitors came from the far edges of the kingdom of Tranik, some even from Mondgue, Misteria, and Wystfellia, begging to marry her, not knowing of her deceased husbands.

But today her father was marrying her off to a baron forty years her senior, and she knew he would finally rest. He'd leave her to suffer with him because she wouldn't be his property anymore. She'd be eighteen tomorrow, a free woman, inheriting all her husband's money and status, which was higher than her father's. So when the baron died from her poison in the early morning hours… *happy birthday to me.*

"Hurry up!" her stepsister squealed up the stairs. "It's time to start."

"No, it's time to finish this," she told her reflection, placing one more pin in her updo. She smiled cruelly, but her reflection smiled back, sweet as pie.

She turned from her mocking face, striding out the door and down the many stairs from the attic, which served as her room between marriages. While her father was magically bound to never physically harm her again, it didn't save her from the emotional and mental harm he inflicted whenever possible. He told her she had to earn her keep on account of him having to replace Mrs. Hazel's and Thomas's positions.

She stepped off the last stair, pulling up her skirt to navigate the bustling kitchen of attendants preparing her wedding meal. "Congratulations," several called to her. She smiled, thanking the Stars this would be the last time.

Never again would she have to put on a white dress. Never again would she have to play the part of the happy bride for another man who saw her as property. Never again would she be the thankful possession of a husband who demanded her body whenever he pleased—or so they thought.

It turned out, much to Elzbeth's surprise, that she *had* gotten magic on her tenth birthday. She hadn't realized—hadn't had an opportunity for it to manifest until after Thomas's death. She discovered on the night she married her first evil husband that she had a remarkable power.

She'd been cornered in his bedchamber, shaking like a leaf and swallowing against the rock forming in her throat as he sauntered closer, licking his lips. She felt like he was consuming her with his eyes. She'd never been intimate with anyone before. She and Thomas had only kissed. They'd never got the chance to do more thanks to her murderous father.

She closed her eyes and pinched them tight, wishing she had magic to stop this horrible moment. *No, no, no!* her mind screamed as her lips started to utter a spell of their own accord. Shock rolled over her as the words flowed from her tongue. At the last utterance, she opened her eyes, surprised as magic shaped like tiny emeralds leapt from her hands like a caged animal freed from its prison. Her husband went statue still midstep, his shirt pulled halfway over his torso and his eyes pinned on her, burning with lustful desire.

She stared at him, afraid to move and break the spell that she had somehow cast. Minutes ticked by before she dared take a cautious step forward. Then another, until she was close enough to see his chest moving.

What sort of spell was that? How did I just do that? I don't have magic!

She put her hand out, touching him lightly, then jumped. Her hand was a slightly darker shade of green. She lifted her eyes from her hand to her husband's face, startling. A huge smile formed on his lips, but he didn't move toward her. She stumbled back against the bed, almost falling onto her back, but she pushed off and dashed for the door. She escaped to her own room, locked herself inside, and pushed the dresser in front of the door.

It wasn't until after his death that she confirmed what her magic was. She was a leach, sucking her dead husbands' magical abilities from them and making them her own. And with each husband's death, she became more powerful, but she also became greener. *"I thought it impossible for you to get uglier, Elzbeth! But you never cease to amaze me."* Her father's sharp words cut the two halves of her heart each time he said them after she used her magic to escape consummating her unions to the monsters he forced her to marry.

She wouldn't give him the satisfaction of cutting a final time. She had more tricks up her sleeves than her magic. She would stop her new husband's heart the old-fashioned way—with the poison she'd slipped into his drink. She vowed to never use her magic again.

"You're the color of decay," her father had spat.

"Just like your heart!" she'd bit back just hours ago, finding the courage to speak back to him for the first time. In less than twelve hours, she'd be free.

"Finally!" her robust, silver-haired fiancé grumbled. His cane pointed at her as he leaned against the large parlor wall. It was covered floor-to-ceiling with mirrors her father installed after she'd been permanently spelled so he'd never have to look at her true face. After today, she'd never look in a mirror again.

For once, however, in this parlor of mirrors, it wasn't her reflection capturing her attention. A woman stood next to her future husband, hands clasped, in a moss-green dress.

"Fairy Godmother!" she said breathlessly.

What is she doing here? Why didn't my stepmother tell me that the *Fairy Godmother will be marrying us today?*

"Hello," Fairy Godmother said and smiled sweetly, just like she had two years prior, smiling at her sister when Thomas and Elzbeth used the book. The book had refused to take them to Fairy Godmother each time they'd tried, denying them their escape. Elzbeth had searched for the book after her father killed Thomas. It had been left at the inn and was long gone by the time she made her way back. She tried to track it down, but the innkeeper said there was no book among the belongings left behind.

"I didn't know you'd be orchestrating the union," Elzbeth said as her fifteen-year-old stepsister entered the room, her eyes closed, on her mother's arm.

"Doesn't my daughter look lovely in white?" Elzbeth's stepmother said sweetly to Fairy Godmother. "It goes perfectly with her complexion," she added, keeping her head averted from Elzbeth to not fall under her spell.

Elzbeth bit her tongue. It would be a waste of breath on her stepmother, knowing she'd dressed her daughter in white to get under her skin. Elzbeth couldn't care less. They could all wear white, and she wouldn't bat an eyelash.

"It really does," Elzbeth's father said to her stepmother as he sauntered into the room.

"Finally," the baron huffed again. She turned her attention to him. He was leaning on his cane due to an injury he claimed he'd gotten from a drunken tavern fight. But if rumors were true, he'd gotten it from his late wife after she caught him cheating.

"Alright, now that everyone is here…" Fairy Godmother started.

Elzbeth didn't hear anything else after that. She'd gotten used to blocking out the rest until she had to kiss her new wrinkled-face husband. She closed her eyes, picturing Thomas, feeling the tears push their way to the surface. She shoved them down, chanting in her mind, *This is the last time, the last time.*

She opened her eyes, her emerald-green magic swirling with the baron's orange, encircling them, binding their union, and sealing Elzbeth's newest magical ability: heightened senses.

As his wrinkled lips left hers, his body crumbled to the ground like stones falling from a mountainside. Fairy Godmother gasped. Elzbeth didn't need to check for a pulse. Her magic pumped stronger through her blood with her now late husband's magic. Her father's laughter rang out like a warning bell, causing her to whip her head up to look at him.

"Do you have no heart?" Fairy Godmother rebuked. "This man has just died!"

"I have no need for a heart, and it seems neither does my daughter." He smiled wickedly at her. "Well done, Elzbeth." He praised her for the first time in eight years. But why? This wasn't her doing, not yet, at least. He wasn't supposed to die until early tomorrow morning.

"What have you done?" Fairy Godmother asked, looking from her father to Elzbeth with pleading eyes.

"I just kissed him," Elzbeth choked out. Her father laughed again, making her skin crawl.

"A little birdie told me that isn't all you did, is it?" He glanced at her stepsister, her eyes tightly shut as his laughter subsided. He strolled like a proud bastard to the liquor hutch and poured himself a drink, then winked at her.

Did her stepsister see her poisoning the baron's drink? And did he also poison his drink, killing her husband sooner than she'd planned? Elzbeth wasn't surprised by her stepsister telling her father, but she was confused on why her father poisoned her husband.

"Good thing too. Gives us a few more days to prepare," he said, throwing the drink back and swallowing in one gulp.

"Prepare for what?" Her voice quivered as delight danced in her father's eyes.

"The Misteria royal ball for the crown prince's hand," he replied smugly. "I received the fire message this morning." He glanced at the dead man, then back at her. "Seems you're getting a second chance to become a royal."

"No!" she screeched. "I'm eighteen tomorrow and no longer your property!"

"Oh, didn't you hear the news?" The two parts of her broken heart leapt. "Last night, King Henry updated the law because of how many died in Tranik during the Dark Days plague." A sinister smile formed on his lips. "Girls are to remarry until they're twenty-five or produce three children, to ensure repopulation of our kingdom."

Elzbeth swayed as her vision began to blur. Icicles pierced the two parts of her broken heart, pinning them against her ribcage as all air whooshed from her lungs. Her knees weakened, and she collapsed to the ground.

"You're lying," she hissed.

"I'm not." His sinister smile grew larger. His eyes were dark, like a lion on the hunt. She wanted to scream at the Stars for never intervening. For standing by and just watching as she suffered.

She turned to Fairy Godmother, the one who was supposed to grant wishes that helped girls like her. But Fairy Godmother stood shocked, pointing her wand at her father for what he just declared. But her magic couldn't harm, so he didn't even acknowledge her.

"You only have yourself to blame," her father continued. "If you'd done as I wanted and married the Tranik king, then you'd be queen now. You'd be free to have all the lovers you wanted, even that servant boy."

Servant boy? Thomas was so much more than that! Her blood boiled hotter.

"I won't let you sell me off again!" she spat. "I'll find a way to remove this spell so the Misteria royals know the truth of my appearance." He didn't flinch at her threat.

"You and I both know there is no way to break it."

"Shut up!" Elzbeth screamed, jumping to her feet. She was at her breaking point—beyond it. She was done. Done with being his pawn in his disgusting game, moving wherever he wanted.

She felt the change before she understood it—an alchemizing of her pain and rage birthing a new power within her.

All her dead husbands' magic surged within, mixing together to something greater. A volcano ready to erupt as the words for a death spell popped into her mind. "Heart, mind, soul, death. Remove this body by taking its last breaths."

As she said the last word, a blast of her emerald magic ripped from her chest. It hit not just her father, but her stepmother and stepsister also, sending all three of them flying to the large mirror, shattering it. They crumbled to the floor like rag dolls, broken glass falling like stars over their bodies.

She labored for breath, trying to quell the searing pain in her heart, wondering if this would also be her end. The pain vanished as quick as it came on, allowing her to clamber to her feet. The room was in disarray, furniture shattered, splinter pieces lodged in the walls.

Her father rasped out shallow, bloody breaths next to her stepmother and stepsister, who didn't stir.

"You're a monster!" Even near death, her father's words were sharp enough to slash the two pieces of her heart. "And you're going to rot for murder." His cough was wet with blood.

She stared into his hateful eyes, denying the child within her the right to scream at the man who should have protected her from the cruelty of this world but instead became that cruelty. She wouldn't waste the energy for the man who put her on the altar for the world to devour.

"You're the monster." She clenched and unclenched her hands at her sides. He laughed, turning his head toward her dead stepmother and stepsister.

"It turns out the apple doesn't fall far from the tree, does it?" He emphasized each word, smiling cruelly, showing his bloody teeth.

She wanted to deny it, wanted to curse him. But then he lifted his hand and pointed past her stepmother and stepsister to the corner of the ruined room. Elzbeth's eyes grew wide. *Oh Stars!* Fairy Godmother lay unmoving, a large shard of glass lodged in her chest. "Like father, like daughter," he rasped. A gurgled laugh escaped his lips.

"No," she said sternly. She wouldn't believe it. She couldn't. She didn't want to hurt other people. Just him. And in that moment, she understood that he had managed to transform her into something, but not what he'd intended. "I'm not like you." She leaned close to ensure he heard her. She whispered into his face, "You might be cruel… but I'm wicked."

He gasped his last breath as Elzbeth took her first full one as a free woman.

"Elzbeth," Fairy Godmother whispered behind her. She

jumped to her feet, moving quickly. She wasn't dead. But her moss-green dress was darkening from the pool of blood, seeping around the glass lodged in her chest.

"Hold on!" Elzbeth cried as she went to her knees beside her. "I can create a spell to remove it and heal you."

"You can't," she said softly. "No one can rewrite the stars." She gasped in pain. "One hour after I pass, my magic will enter my daughter, Bellenda." Her words grew heavier as she labored for each breath. "She will become the next Fairy Godmother. She'll come for my body, and you, now that you are…" She pointed her wand at her father and then to the other corpses. Her hand fell as she rasped her last breath, her wand clanging onto the wood floor.

"A murderer." Elzbeth finished her sentence.

CHAPTER
Sixteen

Elzbeth couldn't help but think time was unkind. When she needed it to pass, it dragged its feet, but when she wanted it to slow down, it raced forward. Time was absolutely rushing forward as Elzbeth ran from her father's estate. She only had an hour to put as much distance between her and the evidence of what she'd done, certain the *new* Fairy Godmother would seek justice.

She was several miles into the forest, constantly glancing over her shoulder to check if she was being followed. Something crunched behind her. As she turned to see what it was, the toe of her slipper caught the hem of her dress. She fell flat on her face, eating pine needles, rocks, and dirt. She rolled over slowly, feeling every place where her body had met the ground, the taste of blood on her bottom lip.

Get up, her mind screamed, but her body protested. What was she thinking? She might be able to outrun the authorities, but Fairy Godmother? The skies were darkening above the canopy of sequoia trees. A winter storm was brewing, promising freezing rain or maybe even snow.

Slowly, she sat up and peered down at her soiled wedding dress, the hem dyed crimson from kneeling in the blood of her father and the late Fairy Godmother. She was painted with the evidence of her deeds. If she wanted even a chance of escaping, she needed to get rid of it. She scanned for a sharp rock, wiping the blood from her lip with the back of her hand. She eyed one that might work and reached for it. Using the edge as a makeshift blade, Elzbeth slashed the rock above the hemline, making a tear in the fabric until she was able to rip away the bloody material. *Now, what to do with it*? She needed to hide it to cover her trail. Or destroy it.

Her mind swirled. She could use her second husband's fire magic to burn the bloody material, but that would leave ash behind. She clutched the evidence to her chest, looking at her greener hands as they moved with each heaving breath.

"Are you okay?" a man called, startling her. She whipped her head up and saw him dismounting a black horse several yards from her. He shook his overgrown blue-black hair out of his eyes as he moved toward her.

"I'm…" She flicked her eyes down to the bloody material.

"Are you injured?" he asked with concern.

She blinked several times, craning her neck to look up at him.

"I was, but I'm fine now," she lied, holding the material tighter to her chest as he knelt beside her.

"Let me check, please."

She knew her spell was working, making him concerned for a beautiful, injured woman. *If he truly knew what I looked like, he'd be screaming and running*, Elzbeth thought. Instead, he was a puppet, falling at her feet as her spell pulled at his heart strings.

"Really, it's fine." She tried scooting back to put distance between them. "I tripped and cut my chest on a sharp rock. But I closed the wound already with my magic, so I'm fine, really." She lied again, attempting to push herself up, but the man offered his hand. She grasped it, feeling a few aches from her fall as he helped to steady her on her feet. He surveyed her from head to toe, his honey-colored eyes drinking in the illusion.

"I best be going," she said. Time was ticking, and she

couldn't waste another moment with this man trapped in her beauty spell.

"Wait, where are you going?" He tightened his grip on her hand. "Let me take you! I have a horse."

"That won't be necessary," she refused politely. But it seemed the Stars were angry with her for killing Fairy Godmother, showing Their fury by sending a thunderous crash, followed by a streak of lightning. Icy rain pummeled down, drenching them in a matter of seconds. Her hair fell from its updo, plastering down her back.

"Now with this weather, I can't possibly take no as an answer."

"I don't need you acting like a heroic prince to save me," she protested.

"Oh, believe me, beautiful, I'm definitely not that." The sky must've agreed with him, sending another crash of thunder, followed by a flash of lightning that sent birds scattering from their sheltered perches among the trees. "But I'm not leaving you in this storm. We need to get to somewhere safe."

Elzbeth nodded, and the stranger pulled her into his arms with startling ease, gripping her against his chest and darting for his horse. He tossed her into the saddle. She grabbed onto the horn as he jumped on behind her, wrapping his arms around her waist and locking their bodies together before he kicked the horse's sides.

"Where are you taking me?" Elzbeth asked as she tightly gripped the saddle.

"No clue," the man shouted over the storm. "I'm not familiar with this kingdom, as I've just arrived," he said, teeth chattering near her ear. "You see, I'm on the run. Away from my father, and I fear the storm is getting worse."

Lightning flashed, punctuating his last statement.

"Faster, Buttercup!" he yelled to his midnight-black horse. Elzbeth laughed at the horse's name as it charged through the maze of redwood trees, seeking shelter. "I know, but I was eight when I named her and—" Lightning cracked in front of them, raising every hair on her body as it hit a tree. Sparks burst, and the horse reared onto its hind legs, sending the stranger, then Elzbeth, from its saddle. White, blinding pain coursed through her head as the world went dark.

⚝ ⚝ ⚝ ⚝ ⚝

"Thank you so much." The stranger's voice broke into Elzbeth's dream softly.

"Remember, she needs to rest," a sweet sing-song voice replied.

"Yes, thank you. I'll ensure she does," the stranger replied before a door clicked shut. Elzbeth wanted to open her eyes to see where she was and who the stranger was speaking to, but the heaviness of sleep swept her away.

Light fluttered behind her closed lids. She slowly blinked them open before bolting upright. Her head spun from the action.

"Hey, not so fast," the stranger said on her right. She turned slowly as the room settled back into place. "The healer said you needed to rest so your pretty face could mend." He pointed at her forehead above her left eye, smiling, revealing a faint scar under his right eye.

"Who are you?" she croaked. A dry tickling sensation had her coughing before he could reply. He moved to her bedside, grabbing a glass of water from the table and handing it to her. She gulped it greedily, never taking her eyes off him.

He looked to be close to her age, maybe a bit older. But his tanned skin let her know he was not from the Tranik kingdom. She faintly remembered him saying he was new to the kingdom and on the run from his father. Maybe he was from the island kingdom of Lexlent, where the sun shined like a hot summer's day all year round. Once the glass was empty, she set it on the side table and asked again, "Who are you?"

"My friends call me Will." He smiled softly, scanning her with his honey-colored eyes. She was very familiar with the look. *Damn spell!* she cursed internally, then paused. Maybe her spelled beauty could convince Will to help her get away? He could take her to Lexlent, or maybe the kingdom of Phannel if they could sneak past the border. No one would find her there and hold her accountable for the blood on her hands.

"Okay, Will." She smiled sweetly, batting her lashes now that she had a plan. His smile grew, just as she knew it would. Part of her lessons the past two years involved seduction by various teachers, men and women, to help her trap her father's next victim. She leaned in slowly, closing the space between their faces, looking intently into his eyes. His breath hitched.

Gotcha!

"I need…" she crooned softly, moving her eyes to his lips as he ran his tongue over their surface, then back again, holding him captive in her spell.

"Anything," he said breathlessly.

She almost chuckled at how easy this would be. She brushed her lips lightly against his. "I need your help to…" He claimed her lips. They were soft. A welcoming surprise. His lips moved along with hers to their own rhythm. A beautiful song that only they knew. With each motion she fell deeper into the kiss.

She'd only experienced one toe-curling kiss like this, when Thomas proposed. The two halves of her heart thundered against her chest as her stomach growled viciously. Will broke the kiss, stepping back a couple feet from the bed, his face flushed.

"I'm sorry, I don't know what came over me. Please forgive me, my lady. I would never take advantage…" He stumbled over each word. Her stomach growled again. "You're hungry. As you should be—you've been asleep for over a day."

"What?" She threw the bedcovers off and noticed she was no longer in the ruined wedding dress but a pale-yellow sleeping gown.

He must have seen the horror on her face because he shook his head vigorously. "I didn't change you. The innkeeper's wife did!"

This snapped her back to where they were. The familiarity of the location. They were at the inn that she, Mrs. Hazel, and Thomas had stayed at once upon a time. But not just the inn; this was the very room they slept in the night before they were married. A tear threatened the corner of her eye, but she sucked in a breath, willing all emotions to silence.

"Emotions are a sign of weakness." Her father's words rang through her mind. *"They make one the prey rather than the hunter."*

"Would you be so kind as to get me something to eat?"

"Yes, I can do that," he said, moving for the door. "I bought you a dress. It's in the wardrobe. I'll give you time to change, and I'll be back in a few minutes." She nodded as he excused himself, taking his embarrassment with him.

Elzbeth rose from the bed, bare feet touching the cool wood floor as she moved to the wardrobe. She stopped when she passed a small table with two chairs, picking up the newspaper. On the front page was a drawing of her spelled face with the following words below:

Hefty reward for any information on her whereabouts.

Who put this in the paper? She read further. Had it been the new Fairy Godmother? Or maybe the authorities? But there was no name, just an address she didn't recognize to send a fire message to. Will knocked at the door, causing her to drop the paper on the table.

"Still changing. Give me a moment, please," Elzbeth called. Will didn't reply, but she heard his footsteps retreating. She opened the wardrobe, finding an expensive-looking dress hanging next to an equally expensive suit. *Who is Will? Didn't he say that he's new to my kingdom and fleeing his father? If so, then how does he have money to buy such expensive clothes?*

"Ouch," she hissed, cutting her finger on a corner of parchment paper barely sticking out from the suit breast pocket. She sucked her finger for a few moments, contemplating invading Will's privacy. She plucked the folded paper out and opened it.

Thank you for contacting me. I will cover all expenses incurred when I arrive with your second half of the payment.

What? No! She exhaled heavily. *Did Will contact the person who placed the article and sell my whereabouts to them?* She needed to get out of there fast.

Elzbeth ripped the dress from its hanger and quickly pulled off her nightgown, then replaced it with the dress she assumed Will bought with the reward money. "Scoundrel!" she said, seething, allowing herself this small indulgence before locking the anger down. She couldn't be distracted; she needed to leave. Now!

Once dressed, she put on the slippers. They weren't practical, but they would do until she got boots and better clothing for her journey. But that would require money. Money she didn't have. *Maybe Will hid the money somewhere in the room?* She opened the drawer in the bedside table, but it was empty.

Elzbeth surveyed the room. *Where did he hide it?* There was no other furniture with drawers but… she ducked down to look under the bed. She couldn't see anything. She put her hand under, feeling around. Her fingertips brushed something. A box, maybe? She slid it out just as the door opened.

She stood quickly, putting whatever it was behind her back. "Sorry, I dropped my…" Her excuse died on her tongue. Elzbeth's eyes grew as large as saucers at who stood in the doorway. Not Will, but her "dead" sister, Jaqueline.

CHAPTER
Seventeen

"Elzbeth, are you in here?" Jaqueline asked timidly, clasping her hands together while she stared at her. At least, she thought she was staring. She couldn't see Jaqueline's eyes behind the dark glasses she was wearing.

Elzbeth blinked several times. "You're dead… I mean, you're alive, but…"

"You sound just like Mother," her sister said. Elzbeth's heart pieces squeezed. *Mother.* "When she was flustered, she, too, would stumble over her words."

"I don't understand," Elzbeth said, her voice shaky. "We were told you died a week after you married."

Jaqueline stepped toward her, both hands stretched out, and pulled Elzbeth into a tight embrace. She didn't move, one hand still behind her back, holding the box.

"I'm so sorry," Jaqueline mumbled into her hair and neck. "I was so scared your father would come after me when we got the fire message that Mother and you had both died…" she choked out through tears, wetting Elzbeth's hair. "We staged the accident to keep me hidden."

"I don't understand." Elzbeth's brows furrowed. "Why would he tell you I was dead?"

"I don't know." Jaqueline took in a long breath, stepping back and dropping her hands to her sides. "But we acted rashly. I was terrified of him and wasn't sure if he would come after me after losing you."

"I understand," Elzbeth said. Her father was a monster.

"Of course *you* do," she said. "It wasn't until Callie—"

"Who?" Elzbeth interrupted.

"Sorry, my mother-in-law. The former Fairy Godmother."

Elzbeth froze as bile climbed up her throat. *Does she know I accidentally killed her too?*

Jaqueline continued, unable to see her reaction. "So it wasn't until Callie oversaw the union of the king of Tranik to the Lexlent princess that we knew your death was a lie." Jaqueline shook her head. "Callie overheard your father at the ball talking about his beautiful daughter, Elzbeth, to the Lexlent prince and how..." Her voice cracked. "And how you missed the ball because you were home helping a sick friend."

She took a quick breath. "We used a spell book immediately to go back and see your birth. The truth of that day, Mother and..." Tears streamed down her cheeks. She lifted the glasses enough to wipe the glistening streams with a handkerchief, keeping her eyes shut. "I'm so sorry we left you there. But that was why Callie was at your wedding."

Something clicked for Elzbeth as she watched her sister. "Your eyes are shut, and you're wearing the glasses because you know of my spell."

"Yes. Grayson, my husband, he made me promise to keep my eyes shut with the glasses on to ensure I don't fall under it." She fumbled with a small pouch hanging around her wrist. She pulled the bag open and put her hand inside, saying, "He can't wait to meet you. And the children too."

With that she flung a handful of light pink stardust above their heads, and the room melted away.

Elzbeth blinked to clear the stars from her vision, startled at the sudden onslaught of sunlight. She was stunned to find they were standing on a stone path, leading to the front doors of Fairy Godmother's estate.

"Mommy!" two girls squealed as they rushed toward them.

Elzbeth sidestepped, turning her face before the girls saw her and got locked in her spell. She stumbled over something and dropped the item she was still holding behind her back. She turned to pick it up but stopped at the sight of the *Marvelous Magical Maps Spell Book*.

"Oh, I haven't seen that in a few years," a woman said from behind her, making Elzbeth practically jump out of her skin. She turned, her breath catching in her throat. Standing perfectly straight, not a blonde curl out of place and wearing a pale pink dress, was the late Fairy Godmother's daughter.

"I'm Bellenda," she said, smiling as stars danced within her turquoise-colored eyes.

Elzbeth gaped.

"It's okay," Bellenda continued when Elzbeth didn't say anything. "I know this must be a lot. But you're safe here, and no one will harm you."

"Safe?" She turned her head and saw her sister crouched on the ground, embracing her two girls. "Safe." She said the word again as if trying a foreign language. It had to be a trick.

"Yes, you're safe here," Bellenda said again, causing Elzbeth to step back. Bellenda lowered her voice like she was talking to a wounded animal who might lash out at any wrong move. "You must have a million questions after everything that happened. But I'm sure you're hungry."

Elzbeth retreated another step.

Bellenda continued, undeterred. "I understand you don't trust us. After everything you've endured, it will take time."

Elzbeth cackled at this. *Is Bellenda joking?* Elzbeth didn't trust her one bit. This could easily be a ploy to get her arrested for her crimes.

"I'm no fool," Elzbeth spat.

"No one said you were." Bellenda took a step closer. Elzbeth retreated further. Bellenda flicked a pink wand Elzbeth had somehow missed earlier. Sparkling pale pink stardust shot from the wand onto Elzbeth's legs, freezing them in place.

She tried to lift them, only to find they wouldn't budge.

"What are you doing?" she shrieked.

"Taking control of the situation before it escalates further," Bellenda replied, grabbing the spell book from Elzbeth's arms. It opened on its own, perfectly in half. She tapped her wand, the pink stardust falling like snow onto the pages, revealing the title and table of contents page. She said quickly, *"Map of Truths."*

"What are you doing?" Elzbeth asked again.

"Showing you the truth." Bellenda grabbed Elzbeth's hand, slapped it on the book, held hers on top, then read,

"Close your eyes, breathe in deep, read the spell to uproot truth while you sleep."

"Wait!" Elzbeth protested.

"Ground at my feet, stars at my head, lead me to truth before more moments are shed."

Elzbeth tried yanking her hand free. But the book began to glow, gluing her hand to it before they were sucked inside.

There was no tunnel like there'd been with Thomas. There was only darkness and the squeeze of Bellenda's hand wrapped tightly around Elzbeth's own trembling hand. A blinding light flashed, melting away the darkness to a bedchamber Elzbeth knew.

Elzbeth's mother cried out from where she lay on the bed, drenched in sweat.

Elzbeth tried pulling her hand from Bellenda's, but she held fast. "If you break our connection, you'll wake up and won't know the truth you desperately need in order to trust us," Bellenda explained. "It's my magic that allowed us to use the book. So long as we are connected, you will stay asleep to see what truly happened."

Her mother screamed again, forcing Elzbeth's eyes back to her. She was pale as a sheet, red veins decorating the white of her eyes from bringing Elzbeth into the world. The pixie midwife fluttered about her mother's legs, mumbling something as her mother let out another agonizing scream. The fairy rushed to her face, saying something too low for Elzbeth to hear. Bellenda tugged them closer.

"I'm sorry. I can't save you both," the pixie said. "But there could be more children if you choose to let her die."

Elzbeth gasped, her heart beating fiercely in her chest.

"NO!" her mother commanded hoarsely. "Save her." She placed a tender hand on her swollen stomach.

"Are you sure?"

"Yes." She breathed harder as another contraction came on. "Save her, but promise me you will—" She breathed heavily through another contraction. "You will protect her from—" She clenched her teeth, hissing in pain. "From her father."

"I don't know if that will be possible."

"Promise me you will protect her from him using her beauty to—" She panted through several more breaths. "She has magic, I can feel it," she gasped out. "It's why I've been so ill with her. Magic and beauty together will tempt him to go too far." She hissed again. "Please protect her," she pleaded.

"I'll do what I can," the pixie said, and her mother nodded. "Open your mouth," she instructed. Her mother obeyed. The midwife sprinkled her green dust onto her mother's tongue, the same green as Elzbeth's skin when her curse appeared.

After a few moments, her features relaxed. "Thank you," she said and rubbed her hand in small circles over her abdomen. She stopped, her stomach lurching as Elzbeth shifted inside. Her mother let out a bloodcurdling scream. An arctic chill ran down Elzbeth's spine at the sound.

The pixie darted like a shooting star to her mother's legs, throwing her green dust out just in time to catch baby Elzbeth as she slipped out, wide-eyed, taking in the world for the first time. The dust landed on the baby, cleaning her and wrapping her in a blanket in one motion. The midwife waved her hand and floated baby Elzbeth like a feather to her mother's waiting arms.

"My beautiful Elzbeth," she whispered. Then her arms went limp, sliding the baby onto the mattress. Elzbeth lay contentedly in the crook of her mother's arm, sucking her fingers, unaware that her birth had killed her mother.

The door to the room banged open. Elzbeth's father strode in. "I couldn't save them both. The child, she was lodged and…" Her father ignored the pixie, not even glancing at his dead wife. He scooped the baby up, examining her.

"Finally," he said as he held baby Elzbeth. "Shame about your mother though. But at least she gave me a more beautiful child than your sister." He chuckled sinisterly, then glanced over his shoulder. "Hurry up!" he barked to someone outside the door. Baby Elzbeth began to cry at his thunderous words.

Mrs. Hazel scurried into the room, taking in the scene. "I'm sorry about your wife—"

"Take her." He shoved the baby into Mrs. Hazel's arms as she released another wail from his booming voice. "Send for a nurse-maid," he instructed.

"Sir, my daughter-in-law, she has enough milk to feed Thomas and Elzbeth," Mrs. Hazel said shakily, arms rocking the baby.

"Fine," he said, waving his hand and heading for the door. "I'll send a fire message to Jaqueline of her mother's and sister's deaths, and then I'll be leaving for a few months." Elzbeth gasped. Mrs. Hazel knew what her father did but never told Elzbeth? Had she been planning on telling Jaqueline the truth if she hadn't faked her death?

Her father strode out of the room, not giving his dead wife a single glance. Mrs. Hazel drew in a long breath. She cradled the baby closer to her chest and moved for the door.

"Wait," the midwife called. She flew over, stopping inches from the baby, and sprinkled her green dust onto Elzbeth's exposed skin.

"What was that for?" Mrs. Hazel asked.

"To protect her," the pixie replied.

Bellenda squeezed Elzbeth's hand. "Time to wake up."

"No, I want to..." Bellenda dropped her hand, Elzbeth's protest dying on her lips. The scene melted away to darkness, followed by a flash of light. She blinked against the onslaught, seeing stars until her eyes adjusted.

They were back at Bellenda's home, standing as they were before the book sucked them in. But her sister and her children were gone now, and the sun was lower. "So. Now you know the truth. Your mother had the midwife protect you." The book closed, but Bellenda caught it before it hit the ground.

"Protect me?" Elzbeth scoffed, fighting the whirlwind of emotions from what she'd just witnessed. Shock, fear, disbelief, and love fought for dominance in her tremulous heart pieces, warring like a four-headed beast. She shook her head, banishing them. "Never mind, you can't see past my spell. But I'm shocked, though, that you haven't apologized for your behavior. I would think that *the* Fairy Godmother wouldn't be so..."

"Pushy?" Bellenda offered.

"I was going to say rude." Elzbeth crossed her arms in front of her chest.

"Yes, Gray has called me that too. But as I've only been *the* Fairy Godmother for a couple days, I'm still getting used to all the magic."

"I'm sorry," Elzbeth said lowering her face. Guilt heated her cheeks and twisted her stomach. It was her fault Bellenda's mother was dead, and here she was, calling her rude.

"Why? My mother's death, and the others, weren't your

fault. You were defending yourself against your father," Bellenda said.

Elzbeth flung her head up, stunned.

Bellenda set the book on the ground, then took her hands into hers. "You're safe here," she said softly. "I know it will take time to believe it and trust us, but we know the truth. We know what happened on your wedding day."

Elzbeth yanked her hands free. "I'm not safe, I'm a monster! I turned green when I turned ten. I didn't get magic—I turned *green!* I thought it was a curse for killing my mother. But it turns out it was a pixie midwife's idea of protection." She shook her head, forcing the tears threatening to break free at her reality to dry up. "And it didn't even work. It made things so much worse, and then Thomas had to spell me so the world wouldn't see the ugly truth of my monstrosity."

"You're not a monster, nor are you ugly."

"That's because you're under my spell, but if you truly saw what I look like—"

"Elzbeth," she replied more sternly. "You're not ugly."

Elzbeth blew out a frustrated breath. She wished with all her heart that Bellenda could truly see the real her. "You see the product, what my father was selling to the highest bidder. Only I can see the truth now."

Bellenda flicked her wand. Pink stardust swirled out from it, producing a shimmering silver hand mirror embedded with pink rhinestones. She held it out to her and said, "Look at yourself."

Elzbeth crossed her arms. She didn't need another look at the permanently spelled face that killed the only man she'd ever loved. Bellenda thrust it at her, but she kept her arms in place.

"There you go again, being pushy," Elzbeth said as Bellenda tried to pry one of her arms free to force the mirror into her hand. "You really need to work on that now that you've taken on the role of *the* Fairy Godmother."

Bellenda turned the mirror around, shocking Elzbeth into

silence. She blinked several times, seeing her face, her *true* face, reflected back at her.

"You'll soon learn," Bellenda said as Elzbeth stared at her greenish skin. "Beauty is so much more than what many think it is. And I may be *the* Fairy Godmother now, but I'll be doing things differently than my mother."

CHAPTER
Eighteen

"**S**hit!" Anna threw a hand over her mouth at the sight of Cyndra, Edgar, Dru, and Fairy Godmother all standing in front of the library desk where Daff sat.

"Language," Cyndra said, rushing at her and almost knocking her over while wrapping her in a tight embrace. "We've been so worried." Cyndra's voice cracked.

"Thank the Stars," Fairy Godmother said.

Anna's stomach lurched. *The nerve of this woman!*

Anna reached her hand, sliding it as best as she could in Cyndra's vise hug into her pocket, placing the magic-suppressing ring around her finger and keeping her hand in her pocket to conceal it. "Elzbeth will be so relieved you've returned safely," Fairy Godmother added.

Sure she will.

"Where have you been?" Cyndra asked, but Anna didn't answer.

Thank you, ring.

Her sister pulled back and held Anna at arm's length to examine her. Tears glistened in her robin-blue eyes. Anna's heart squeezed. She hadn't meant to make her sister worry.

"Elzbeth has been worried sick and has hardly slept or eaten since you disappeared three days ago!" Cyndra added.

Anna knew the true reason Elzbeth was so worried, and it had nothing to do with her well-being.

"So… where were you?" Cyndra asked again.

Anna bit her lower lip, thinking. What could she say that would have them convinced? "I heard the news about Elzbeth and King Tyson," she started. Stars, it felt good to be able to lie again. "It made me sad, thinking about Father, so I needed some time. Alone."

"Oh, my dear child," Fairy Godmother said and shimmied between Anna and Cyndra. Anna's spine rose with hoarfrost as Cyndra graciously moved to the side, letting Fairy Godmother take her place. She placed her hands on Anna's cheeks. Anna fought back the urge to pull free. "We know you miss your father greatly, and I know Elzbeth wouldn't want you thinking that she was trying to replace him with King Tyson."

"My father wouldn't want you to think that either," Edgar said, stepping next to Cyndra and wrapping his arm around her waist. Concern etched his face. Anna's chest tightened at how much she'd misjudged him.

"Elzbeth will tell you the same thing about your mother, Edgar, and we'll also tell Rupert when they finally meet," Fairy Godmother said.

"Who's Rupert?" Anna tried to sound curious, contorting her face to sell the lie. It was a bit difficult with Fairy Godmother still palming her cheeks. Thankfully, she let go with the movements.

"Edgar's younger brother," Fairy Godmother answered. "We just told Drury about him." She smiled at Dru.

"Yes, it was quite a shock," Dru said, smiling back.

"Hold on." Anna held up her hand. "You have a younger brother?" She arched a brow at Edgar. She was one hundred percent committed to the I'm-shocked-to-hear-this-news act.

"Yes, and I can't wait to introduce you to him when he arrives."

"He doesn't live with you at the castle?" Dru asked.

"He does," Edgar replied. "But he went on a trip for a few days and should return soon, according to the fire message he sent me."

Fire message? Anna worked to keep her face blank as Daff shifted behind the library desk. She must have sent it when they didn't return quickly. *Thank the Stars for Daff and her magic.*

"And now that Anna and Dru are back, we can announce to the kingdom about the engagement tomorrow!" Cyndra said.

"Oh yes," Fairy Godmother said. "Elzbeth will be so pleased to finally be able to tell the kingdom."

"As will Father," Edgar added.

"Aren't you going to wait for Prince Rupert to return so he can be there too?" Anna asked. Her stomach twisted at the thought of the announcement happening tomorrow.

"No," Edgar said. "Unfortunately, even if he were here, the kingdom can't know about him."

"Why?" Anna and Dru asked in unison, side-glancing at each other.

"It's getting late, dears," Fairy Godmother chimed in. "We have much to do. The announcement is happening tomorrow at noon, and we can answer all your questions after."

"But what about Daff?" Anna pointed at her. Daff's lavender eyes widened, practically going into her hairline. She was sorry to put the focus on her, but her mind was reeling on how to delay the announcement. "Why does she get to know about Rupert but not the rest of the kingdom?"

"Oh, she won't remember," Edgar said. "After Father uses his magic on her."

Daff's face drained of all color. "My mother," she said shakily. "If I'm not home by curfew, she'll worry."

"I'll ensure you get home before curfew," Fairy Godmother offered like it was no big deal for King Tyson to wipe Daff's memory of Phil. "I'll also send a fire message to Elzbeth letting her know Annalie and Drury are back."

"Yes, and I'll send one to Father letting him know he's needed at the castle to utilize his magic," Edgar added.

"Oh, okay." Daff's lower lip wobbled.

"It'll be fine," Edgar said. "Doesn't hurt a bit. I've seen Father use it countless times."

Yeah, apparently on your own wife to forget Phil! Anna wanted to say. But she bit her tongue instead.

"Will I forget other things?" Daff asked, pushing her glasses up the bridge of her nose.

"No, just this entire conversation," Edgar answered, nodding his head.

"In that case," Cyndra said, looking at Edgar. Their eyes communicating something between them. "I wanted you two to be the first to know." She focused on Anna and Dru. "We're pregnant."

Anna's breath hitched in her throat. She was happy for her sister. Cyndra had always wanted a home full of children.

"Really?" Dru exclaimed before grabbing Cyndra and hugging her.

"Congratulations!" Anna said, flicking her eyes to Daff, then Fairy Godmother.

"Yes, congratulations, dear," Fairy Godmother said. "And I hate to cut the celebration short, but I should impress again that we need to get going. There is much to do in preparation for tomorrow, and the clock is ticking closer to midnight."

Dru released Cyndra, who giggled softly at their inside joke. A joke that her husband smiled at, not knowing the truth behind why he was so drawn to Cyndra at the ball or why he insisted they marry only a week later. Not to mention what Anna and Phil discovered about Fairy Godmother and Elzbeth working together. The night of the ball was just the first step of their mastermind plan—a plan that Anna had no clue how to stop.

"Please don't tell Elzbeth about the pregnancy," Cyndra said after the laughter subsided. "We'll tell her after the announcement. We don't want to overshadow her celebration." Fairy Godmother smiled softly and bowed her head in agreement.

"Be at the castle no later than 11:00 a.m.," Cyndra said to Dru, then turned her attention on Anna. "And be dressed in what has been chosen for you to wear." She eyed Anna's dirty tunic and pants. "And go home immediately and take a bath, Anna. You smell… well, you don't smell like a lady, I mean."

Anna rolled her eyes but didn't fight back. There wasn't time. They were taking Daff with them.

"I'll make sure she does," Dru said, walking over to loop her arm through Anna's.

"Sounds good." Cyndra smiled at them both before walking through the library door Edgar held open for her. Daff cast a weary look over her shoulder before exiting.

"So, you doing okay, Anna?" Dru asked once it was just the two of them.

"I'm fine," Anna said, stepping free of Dru's grasp and forcing her to face her. "How about you? Invent anything new this week at Tinker's?"

"Um, well…" Dru's blue eyes grew large before she looked away. "Not fully, but I made some progress on something I've been working on the past month."

"That's nice," Anna said, thumb grazing the ring around her finger. She was relieved she could have this conversation without having to answer Dru's questions truthfully.

"Shocking news about Edgar having a brother, isn't it?"

"Yes, very shocking," Anna lied again. "I wonder why he's been kept a secret," she added.

"No clue, but I can't wait to hear why tomorrow after the announcement," Dru said, yawning widely in the middle of her thought. "Sorry, I'm beat. Let's go home." She headed for the door.

"I'll catch up in a bit. I need to close up since Daff had to leave."

"No worries, I'll wait."

"Really, you don't have to—"

"It's fine, Anna. I can wait a few minutes." She ran her fingers over the cover of

100 Ways to Use Magical Beans

then picked up

Magical Equations for Dummies

and started flipping through it.

"Okay," Anna said. Dru's attention turned to the book in hand. "Let me go check the back room first, and then I'll be back."

Dru, already absorbed in the book, made a noise confirming that she heard her. Anna walked briskly for the storage room, hoping Phil was close behind. She closed the door and pulled her hand from her pocket, slipping the ring off to reveal him standing in front of her.

"This is bad," he whispered.

"You heard everything?"

"Yes."

"What do we do now?" Anna asked. "Daff is getting her memories erased, and Dru is back acting like she's been at Tinker's all week."

"I don't know." He raked his fingers through his hair.

"Can you follow us? Is your magic back?"

"It's good. I'll stay behind a few yards."

"Okay, once back at my house, we'll split up from Dru and sneak back out." She opened her bag and pulled the map book out for Phil to put into his bag. She quickly put her bag and bow back into the enchanted box. He eyed what she was doing so she explained, "You can't risk carrying more to stay hidden from Dru."

"Hey, Anna! You ready? I'm really tired and would also like to eat," Dru called down the hall.

"Yes, coming!" she blurted, her magic back to its old tricks without the help of the ring. She grabbed the spare key to lock up the library from the hook by the door. She smiled at Phil, who smiled back before she slid the ring on her finger and her hand back in her pocket. She didn't want Dru knowing she had it.

"Let's go," Dru said as Anna entered the main room. Anna followed her out the door, keeping it opened wide behind her for Phil to slip past. She closed and locked the door, turning to walk down the street, but froze as Dru climbed into one of their carriages. She hadn't realized Dru arrived in one.

The white horses whinnied softly as the coachman held the door open for her. She dropped the key, hoping to give Phil enough time to slip in before her. She slowly bent down and plucked the key from the ground, smiling at the coachman who was offering his hand to help her in.

Dru was seated to the left. Her head was back, eyes closed, possibly already asleep. She really did look very exhausted. *I wonder why?*

Anna sat directly across from Dru, hoping Phil was next to her and hanging on to something as the horses took off and jostled the carriage about. She grabbed her free hand on to the side to help her not bounce around.

"So…" Anna started. "You said you made progress on an invention you've been working on this past month?"

Dru didn't answer. Okay, so she'd fallen asleep or was faking to avoid confrontation.

Anna pulled the ring off to check on Phil. He was crouched, feet on top of the seat, holding on to the carriage frame with both hands. He smiled at Anna, then nodded at Dru. Her head bopped along with the carriage, causing some of her brown hair to fall on her face. Anna leaned forward, brushing it out of the way, as the carriage bounced over something and pushed her onto Dru.

"What in the Stars?" Dru exclaimed, eyes popping open.

"Sorry," Anna slid next to her, pushing Dru's dress out of the way. "The carriage hit something and threw me."

"It's fine." Dru pushed the hair from her face. It looked as though she hadn't brushed it in a week. The dark circles under her eyes suggested she hadn't slept much either. *What's going on with her?*

Anna put her hand back in her pocket, sliding her finger into the ring. Now that Dru was talking again, she didn't want her magic confessing what she'd truly been up to the past few days. Dru yawned, covering her hand over her mouth.

"Didn't sleep much this past week?" Anna asked.

"No." Dru yawned again. "Tinker and I were so absorbed that we barely ate, let alone slept." She lied so smoothly, keeping her blue eyes trained on Anna's face. An icicle pierced Anna's heart. Not because Dru was lying to her, but because Anna missed her sister. Dru was her closest confidant, next to Daff, before Elzbeth tore them apart.

The carriage slowed in front of their estate. The coachman had the door opened seconds later. "Well, I'm grabbing a snack from the kitchen, then going to bed," Dru said, exiting quickly.

"Okay." Anna stayed seated, hoping Phil was exiting on Dru's heels. "I'll see you in the morning then," she added as Dru took the dozen steps, two at a time, to the double doors.

"Lady Annalie," the footman said, pulling her gaze back to him, holding his hand out for her to exit.

"Yes, thank you." Once on the gravel, she pulled the ring off. Phil was waiting at the top of the steps. She went up quickly and nodded at the doorman as he opened the door for her. She paused, allowing Phil to step in first, then said, "Thank you."

Dru was going up the stairs, not to the kitchen but to her bedchamber. She stepped onto the third landing and rushed down the hall out of sight.

Why are you in such a hurry, Dru? Anna wondered, moving for the stairs with Phil next to her. She took the first step just as trumpets sounded, announcing that the king's carriage was approaching.

What are they doing here? Fairy Godmother said she'd have them join her at the castle to erase Daff's memories. Anna's thoughts swirled. She jumped down the stairs and darted to the side to hide. It was a tight space but dark enough that they could watch through the staircase spindles without being seen. Phil slid next to her and grabbed her hand.

"Don't deplete your magic. We can't be seen down here," she whispered. He nodded but didn't let go. She liked the feeling of his warm hand intertwined with hers. If they weren't in such a stressful situation, she'd be working overtime to hide a giddy smile.

The front door swung open, and Elzbeth's voice carried across the foyer. "Yes, darling," she purred as she and the king stood facing one another, a royal guard flanking them. "I just need to freshen up and check on my daughters, and then I'll join you at the castle." Anna's heart hammered, her breaths turning jagged. Phil squeezed her hand, and Anna was startled to realize that it helped.

"Don't take too long," King Tyson said, his eyes glistening with affection as he gazed upon Elzbeth. *Poor, foolish man.* Watching him drop Elzbeth's hand to caress her cheek made

Anna want to gag. She looked at Phil, but his face was turned the other direction. Clearly, he didn't want to see his father kiss Elzbeth. The king crushed his lips to his fiancée, closing his eyes, while Elzbeth's stayed wide open.

"I'll be an hour at the most," Elzbeth replied after she broke the kiss. She looked green behind the gills, at least more than she usually did to Anna. "Annalie may need some time to talk."

Tremors ran down Anna's spine. *Time to talk? Shit!* Phil squeezed her hand again and started rubbing small circles with his thumb on the back of her hand. It felt soothing, and Anna let out a long, quiet breath.

"Of course, my love. I'll take the time to freshen myself up after I use my magic on the library girl." He placed a quick peck on her lips before turning and walking down the stairs with his guard close behind. Elzbeth stepped inside, sighing heavily as the doors closed behind her.

She wiped the back of her hand across her mouth. "Kissing a fish would be a more pleasant experience," she murmured to herself, walking toward the hallway that led to her bedchamber. Before she disappeared fire crackled as a fire message popped up in front of her. Elzbeth plucked it from the air, breaking the seal to read it. "Thank the Stars," she said as the delivered message turned to ash.

Anna burned with curiosity. *Who was the fire message from? And what did it say?*

Elzbeth moved to the window next to the entry doors and peeked out. The sounds of the king's carriage traveling down the gravel drive grew fainter as it left their estate. Elzbeth pulled a flask from her dress pocket and took a large gulp, contradicting how she told Anna a "lady" drinks during her grueling lessons. Elzbeth returned the flask back to the pocket, rolling her neck in a small circle before pinching her cheeks the way Anna had seen others do to produce a blush. It was a strange thing for a woman with spelled beauty to do.

Elzbeth opened the front doors and stepped out, demanding, "Carriage, now!"

"Yes, my lady," the doorman said, followed by the sounds of his feet moving across the gravel toward the carriage house.

"Where do you think she's going?" Phil whispered.

"No clue, but it gives us more time." Anna was about to move out from their hiding place but stopped as footsteps hit the marble stairs, moving fast.

Dru jumped onto the landing, then jogged across the entryway to peek out through the small window.

"To The Devil's Tavern," Elzbeth called.

"I knew it!" Dru said softly after closing the window. She gathered her skirt into her hands and dashed up the stairs. Elzbeth's carriage departed, wheels crunching on the gravel as it went.

"What does she know?" Phil asked.

"I have no idea," Anna said.

"I'll follow Dru and find out what she's up to."

"Alright," she agreed.

The grandfather clock chimed ten times as Anna waited. Soft footsteps sounded down the stairs.

Is it Dru? Or Phil? she wondered as he darted back into the cramped corner.

"She had her door closed by the time I got there. All I could hear was her mumbling to herself," he explained.

"Let's go to my room." Anna grabbed Phil's bag and handed it to him. "If I lean out of my window, I can see into her bedroom."

"She could see you," he whispered as they moved up the stairs to the third floor. "I'll do it."

"I'm not letting you peep on my sister," Anna said, leading him down the hall to her room.

"Right. Sorry. I didn't think that through." He stumbled over his words as she opened her bedchamber door and hurried for the window.

"I'll hold your hand so she won't see me while I lean out," Anna said as she unlatched her window. Something moved outside the paned glass. She dropped to the floor below the windowsill and motioned with her hand for him to come over. "Are you still invisible?"

"Yes."

"Good." She grabbed his hand, and once invisible herself, stood up to look out. She watched Dru, who was now dressed in pants and a tunic, balancing on her window ledge. Dru tapped the top of her ring, and a large soap bubble inflated from it, enveloping her inside it. She put the hand with the ring out, and the bubble glided from the ledge until it landed gently on the grass, popping to release her. Anna wasn't sure if she was more shocked to see Dru's latest invention or her dressed in pants.

Dru doesn't wear pants! What's going on?

"She really is a genius." Phil's words yanked her from her thoughts.

She dropped his hand and moved to her bed, reaching under it for the enchanted rope she'd tied securely to the bottom of her bed frame. The other end was secured to a spelled arrow.

Anna grabbed the pair of gloves meant for chopping wood, offering them to Phil. "Put these on so you don't get rope burn."

"Rope?" he questioned, scrunching his brows together.

She grabbed her quiver from under her bed, slinging it over her body before she pulled her bow free. Gear in place, she lifted her window. She spotted Dru disappearing into the woods. *What is she doing?* Ever since Daff enchanted the woods, Anna had never seen her sister go into them.

"Not just any rope, an enchanted rope! You'll have to trust me," she said. She got into position, aiming for the large oak tree's trunk, about ten feet from the ground.

"Anna, I know you're a good archer. But the arrow won't hit hard enough to hold our weight."

"The arrow is spelled." She pulled back the string, taking in a long breath, trying to calm her nerves. She exhaled and released it. "Bullseye," she said as the arrow embedded itself deeply. Anna searched her room, eyeing a pillowcase. "Stand behind me and put your hands like this on the rope," she instructed Phil, wrapping her hands around to demonstrate.

He glanced from her to the window, then back.

"No one will see us leave on this side of the house," she insisted, climbing onto the windowsill. She placed the pillowcase over the top of the rope and tugged. The rope moved, but she was confident the arrow's spell was strong enough to hold Phil's weight like it had hers countless times before. His breath tickled the back of her neck, sending tingles down her spine as he leaned out the window, gloved hands grasping the rope. "Ready?" she asked.

He exhaled. "Yes."

"Follow as soon as I jump off." She pushed her feet off, her hands and arms vibrating as she slid toward the tree. Anna let go of the pillowcase before her boots touched the tree trunk, moving to give Phil space to land. Seconds later, he followed, his eyes wide and an enormous smile plastered on his face as he slid toward her. Once he landed, she yanked on the arrow, but it wouldn't budge.

"Here," Phil offered, wiggling the arrow. His muscles were on full display, making Anna's cheeks burn. The arrow came free under his manipulation. He handed it to her. She untied the rope from the arrow and put it in her quiver before placing everything in the bushes against the estate as Phil tossed the gloves on top.

He grabbed her hand, and they ran toward the woods, following the same path as Dru, who had previously been scared of the enchanted woods. Anna was now wondering if it had all been an act. It seemed Dru had a lot of secrets.

Phil stumbled as they ran.

"Sorry, we can't use the light unless we want her to notice us," she said softly between breaths.

"It's fine," he said. "I'm trying to imagine the woods as you see them."

Anna navigated them through the trees and onto the deer path she'd memorized over the years. After taking a sharp turn, Anna spotted Dru ahead of them and slowed their pace.

Dru moved with purpose, not looking the least bit frightened. Anna wondered if she, too, could see the truth of the unhindered path.

She stopped suddenly. Anna froze as well, tripping Phil with the sudden halt. He fell, pulling Anna down with him.

"Why did you stop?" he asked as several birds flew from the trees near where Dru stood.

"Dru," Anna answered in a low whisper. "I think she might have heard us."

"I didn't see her. She must have a way to make herself invisible."

"Interesting. I think she can also see past the enchantment on the woods." She got to her feet and put out her hand for Phil. She didn't want Dru to get too far ahead.

Anna followed at a distance as Dru darted out of the woods toward the back of the library. She walked down the side of the building and onto the main street of the royal city.

"She's on the street now," Anna said, yanking on his hand as they ran down the slope past the library. Once around the building, she scanned for Dru. The street wasn't overly busy this time of night after curfew, but there were still plenty of adults out dining or drinking. Anna feared she'd never spot Dru in the crowds.

"Do you see her?"

"No," Anna replied.

She tugged on his hand, leading them out into the middle of the street, away from others making their way to and fro on the sidewalks.

"Where are we going?" Phil whispered.

"To the tavern." She quickened their pace. "I bet Dru's going there to spy on Elzbeth," she explained. "I would love to know why she's spying on Elzbeth and lying about what she's been up to this past week."

"She's brilliant. Do you think she's figured out what Elzbeth's been up to?" he asked. They dodged a couple carriages moving down the street.

"Possibly," her magic had her answering, cutting off his gushing. She got it. He seemed to like girls with brains. But why did she care? She told herself she didn't. Even if she did, she needed to focus.

"I mean, the ring you found... maybe Dru invented a way to see past spells like you," Phil added.

"Or how to break them," she said as they neared the street that ended at The Devil's Tavern.

"Damn it!" Phil cursed. "My magic is depleted." He yanked her hand, breaking into a run down the middle of the street. She pulled them to the right, weaving around a couple of empty carts in front of a store, then between the buildings.

"Did anyone see us?" she asked, letting go of his hand. Phil bent over his knees, sucking in a long breath through his nose. "Are you going to be sick?"

"No, it isn't so bad when it depletes slowly. Not like how the book drains my magic in seconds," he said, taking in a few more breaths.

"There's Dru," she whispered, pointing to where Dru ran out from the woods bordering the three sides of The Devil's Tavern. She made a beeline for the closest side of the building, then climbed through one of the open windows. "She went inside through a window."

"Too bad my magic is too depleted for us to do that."

"I have another way we can watch," Anna said, her face brightening. She urged Phil to follow her between the buildings to the tree line behind them, jogging up the small slope and weaving around the trees.

"How?" Phil asked.

"The roof. We can climb onto it and watch from the skylight," she explained, nearing the back of the tavern.

"How do you plan on getting onto the roof? And how do you know no one will see us up there?"

"A ladder, and if they don't look directly up, they won't see us," Anna answered.

Phil opened his mouth, but she cut him off. "Trust me, I've done this before."

He smirked. "At some point you are going to have to tell me about all your escapades."

"They're nowhere near as brilliant as Dru's bubble ring." Her words tasted sour.

"I doubt that," he said, his smirk turning into a smile. "You have a spelled arrow and enchanted rope to escape your third-story window. Next time we find ourselves sitting around waiting for my magic to return, I'd like to hear more about your capers." He said the last word softer than the rest, making the hairs on the back of her neck stand up.

"Alright," she said breathlessly, then cleared her throat as she led him to where she knew the ladder would be. "We can share sneaking out stories next time you need a break," she teased. He laughed softly, and her heart flipped at the sound. She cleared her throat again. "Help me lift it against the roof." She grabbed one side of the twelve-foot ladder. He grabbed the other, helping ease it against the gutter on the roof's edge. Once in place Anna scurried up, then crawled on all fours across the roof to the skylight.

Halfway across, Anna froze at the sound of dead leaves crunching in the woods behind them. A horse whinnied, dashing her hopes it might be nothing more than a woodland creature and making her blood run cold. *Shit!* She turned slowly to face the woods. Phil was a couple feet behind her, lying flat on his back.

"Do you think the rider saw us?" she whispered. But he didn't respond. The horse neighed, closer to the tavern now. She could faintly make out the silhouette of the horse and rider as they exited the woods. She begged the Stars for the rider not to notice the ladder against the building. Phil rolled to his stomach and turned to look out at the woods.

Anna pulled her bow and an arrow and readied it. She couldn't risk getting caught spying on her stepmother. She lifted to her knees, trying to see the rider better, but she couldn't from this angle. She took in a deep breath and got to her feet. Anna slowly took each step. The rider came closer, but she still couldn't make out who it was in the darkness.

She wondered if the rider was the one who sent the fire message to Elzbeth. Anna took another step, trying to get a better look, but slipped and fell backwards, releasing her nocked arrow into the trees, waking the birds perched within and sending them scattering and shrieking in all directions.

CHAPTER
Twenty

ELZBETH: 15 YEARS, 6 MONTHS, 2 DAYS, 16
HOURS BEFORE THE CLOCK STRIKES 12

lzbeth stared into the hand mirror resting in Bellenda's hand, blinking feverishly at her reflection. "How?" she asked breathlessly, staring at her true reflection for the first time in years. She wanted to cry. Or scream. Or rejoice? She didn't know how to describe the emotions welling up from staring at her green skin. "How did you break the spell?"

"I didn't break it," Bellenda said. "My magic, it—"

"It's still holding me captive." Elzbeth pointed at her feet firmly planted on the stone pathway.

"Sorry, I was probably being rash." Bellenda waved her wand, making pink stardust fall onto Elzbeth's feet.

"I'll add it to the list of things I'm learning about you." Elzbeth shook out each foot as it tingled back to life.

Bellenda smiled softly. "But as I was saying, my magic lets me hear and grant wishes made from the heart."

"Yes, when wished upon stars," Elzbeth said, eyeing the sky. There were no stars to wish upon. Just the brilliant sun dipping toward the horizon.

"That *is* true. Normally. But you wished in front of me, and my magic answered, granting your wish for me to truly see you."

"But my reflection. I can truly see myself too." Elzbeth frowned, and her reflection did the same.

"I know. I may have fiddled with your wish. Like my mother, I could already truly see you. One of the perks of being Fairy Godmother is immunity to spells and enchantments. I can't be deceived." She smiled, her pale pink lipstick sparkling.

"Oh," Elzbeth said.

"So, since I could already see you, I was able to tweak your wish so that you could also see your true self. And that meant healing your scars." She pointed to Elzbeth's forearm.

Elzbeth marveled at her smooth green skin. She held her hand up. Her fingertips and palm were also scar-free. It seemed she had another thing to add to her list about Bellenda. She wasn't just rash and pushy; she also fiddled with wishes. She wasn't anything like she'd imagined Fairy Godmother to be.

"You don't see the spell? You don't see me as the beautiful creature that my father created?"

"No. Well, I mean, yes," Bellenda said. Elzbeth shook her head, confused. "What I mean is that I do see the beautiful you, the true you—"

"If you can see me, how can you call me beautiful? I'm the color of decay," Elzbeth interrupted. She held her scar-free but still green hand out.

"You are beautiful," Bellenda said, stepping closer. "Green is the color of trees and grass."

"Thanks, that sounds much better," Elzbeth deadpanned.

"You are the color of growth. Abundance. Beauty. Green is the color of life, not death. But until you stop believing the *lies* that your father poisoned you with, you will never be able to embrace your beauty."

"How can you call it lies? You know what my magic does! When I use it, it makes me even uglier." She fought back tears at the memories of her father not looking at her after the pixie's "protection" made her ugly. Memories of that year, isolated and locked away in her room, flooded her system, making her quake.

"I answered your wish to see yourself as you truly are, but I can't convince you of your beauty. That is up to you." Bellenda flicked her wand, pink stardust swirling around the mirror, vanishing it from Elzbeth's hand. She turned on her heel, swooshing her pale pink dress and platinum blonde curls around her shoulders. She headed up the stairs into the estate, leaving Elzbeth standing alone.

Three children popped out from behind a nearby shrub, nearly making her heart jump. "Timothy, Theodore, and James," a woman called from the front entryway. "Playtime is over. Get in here to clean up for dinner." *Jaqueline has five children?* Elzbeth shuddered. She didn't care for children, how they stared at her spelled beauty with great awe, like an acolyte to the Stars. It made her skin crawl.

"Hello," one of the boys said, smiling at her softly as they passed. He was a foot shorter than the other two and seemed to favor his right side, limping slightly as they hurried up the stairs to the estate doors.

"My apologies, Lady Elzbeth. They were playing hide-and-seek," the same woman called to her. "But please, do come in so you can eat and get settled."

Elzbeth's stomach growled fiercely at the mention of food. She moved up the stairs quickly to enter the estate, looking for the woman but not finding her. "Right this way," the woman said, but Elzbeth couldn't see her. She turned in a small circle.

"Oh. My apologies again," the woman said, appearing a few feet in front of her. "I forgot that I was using my magic while playing hide-and-seek with the children."

"Isn't that cheating?" She looked the woman over. She was much shorter than Elzbeth, maybe an inch or two over five feet, and had more curves than Elzbeth's lanky true build. The spell took care of "that little problem," as her father liked to call it. She blew out a breath, trying to forget him and focus on where she was. "What's your name?" she asked, realizing she was being rude for staring at the woman, who had several streaks of gray going through her auburn hair, which she had pulled back into a tight bun.

"Yes, it's cheating," the woman said. "But sometimes cheating is necessary to win a game. And my name is Hattie." She winked and bowed her head.

"Please, don't do that." Elzbeth waved a hand. "I mean, unless my sister and Lord Grayson require their attendants to bow. Because in that case, I wouldn't want to get you in trouble."

"Oh gracious, no." Hattie smiled and started down the hall. "There is no such protocol for the attendants, and we really don't even use that term because Jaqueline, Grayson, and Bellenda treat us all like family, aside from the salary, that is. But when someone first arrives, we do our best to help them feel comfortable." She smiled broadly before turning left, leading Elzbeth down another long hall.

"I don't understand," Elzbeth said as they passed several doors on each side of the hallway. She could hear voices, many coming from one room talking over each other, and… was that children singing in another room? "I thought this place was a secret."

"Oh, it is. But since the plague, our home has grown quite a bit. And very quickly in the past few years. So many children were orphaned." Hattie turned down another hallway, identical to the one they'd just come through.

"This is an orphanage?" Elzbeth gasped. She wondered if she truly was being punished by the Stars for what she'd done to her stepmother, stepsister, and Bellenda's mother. Being around one small child staring at her beauty spell would give her a rash, but dozens? That would be unbearable.

"No, this is their home," Hattie said. "Mine too since I lost my husband to the plague. The streets aren't kind to a woman like me."

"Oh Stars. I'm so sorry for your loss," Elzbeth offered.

The Dark Days plague had started in the kingdom of Tranik, sweeping through the bordering kingdoms of Phannel, Misteria, and Wystfellia before striking Mondgue, killing hundreds of thousands in the five kingdoms. It mostly took the poor, who didn't have access to healers over the course of two years before a cure was discovered.

"Thank you," Hattie said sweetly. "There are fifty-three children and twelve adults who call the Sanctuary their home. Thirteen adults if you decide to stay." She smiled at Elzbeth.

"Decide?" Elzbeth's brow furrowed as they turned down yet another long hallway. "I can leave?"

"Of course! No one is held here against their will. Well, the children do have to stay until they're adults, able to make their own way. To ensure they're not taken advantage of. But yes, it's your choice." They turned another corner, and someone crashed into Elzbeth, dropping several books onto the plush carpet.

"I'm sorry," Elzbeth said, bending down to help pick the books up. She paused, staring at the girl who looked to be a few years younger than her. There was a large birthmark covering half her face, but that wasn't what had Elzbeth frozen in place. It was the scar on her opposite cheek. There was a word carved down her skin. *UGLY*.

"I'm sorry," Elzbeth said again, blinking feverishly.

"It's alright," the girl replied before gently picking up one of the books. Elzbeth's stomach rolled at the thought of her reaction.

"No, I'm *truly* sorry," Elzbeth said. "I of all people should know what it feels like to have someone judge what I look like."

The girl's face scrunched. "But you're beautiful." Elzbeth had learned it was futile to explain that it was a spell. She was never able to convince anyone, and they always assumed she was just being humble.

"Tonya, this is Baroness Elzbeth," Hattie stated helpfully.

"Just Elzbeth," she corrected.

"This is Elzbeth, Jaqueline's sister," Hattie amended, smiling warmly. "She just arrived and must be very hungry. Would you mind taking her to the dining hall to get dinner while I go check on some of the children?"

"Absolutely," Tonya replied, eyes dancing with delight.

"Thank you," Hattie said to Tonya, then turned to Elzbeth. "I'll come find you after you eat to show you to your room."

"Thank you," Elzbeth replied. She wanted to ask if she would see her sister tonight. She had a lot of questions for her. But instead, she just watched Hattie walk away.

"This way," Tonya said, motioning down the hall. Neither spoke. Elzbeth didn't know what to say. She'd never been good with small talk. The awkward silence seemed to grow with each step.

"I was born with it. It's called a birthmark," Tonya said, breaking the silence.

"Yes, I'm familiar," Elzbeth replied, unsure what else to say.

"It never bothered me, having it. My parents always told me it made me unique." Elzbeth cracked a small smile. *How wonderful Tonya had parents who cared for her beyond her beauty.* "But when the plague came, I lost my mother and siblings, and then my father got sick." She paused for a couple of heartbeats. Elzbeth could imagine her gathering herself like she had done so many times in her youth. "We needed money, so I used my enchantment magic to remove my birthmark." She waved her hand at her face and turned to Elzbeth. The birthmark was gone, but the scar remained.

"Your scar. It was set." It wasn't a question.

"Yes. It was carved with an osmium blade, then set with black salt," Tonya agreed.

Osmium metal was the material the royal guards' swords were made of—the only kind that could wound someone with magic. She knew royal guards also carried osmium cuffs and that the bars of cells were made of it to prevent prisoners from using their magic. She'd even heard rumors of the Lexlent kingdom having osmium-tipped arrows for their royal archers.

"A royal guard did this to you?" Elzbeth asked, rage pumping through her body.

"My father was very weak and sickly from getting the plague, and we needed money. I enchanted myself and sold my body for coins. One night, after I serviced a royal guard, my magic must have been weakened from overuse, and my birthmark appeared. He cuffed me to the bed, then carved my skin with his osmium dagger, telling me I would never deceive another with my magic."

Elzbeth's stomach churned. She felt sick for what Tonya went through.

"When it was over, after he set the wound," she continued, "I ran home to find my father dead, so I kept running. I met Fairy Godmother a few weeks later, and she brought me here."

"How long ago was that?"

"Two years."

Elzbeth clinched her teeth. "You were, what, fourteen?" she seethed. Tonya nodded. "Why didn't Fairy Godmother help you before? I would guess that you wished for your father to be healed."

"Do you know how many wishes of the heart my mother had to sort through each night?" Elzbeth turned at Bellenda's voice. *How long has she been listening?*

Bellenda had changed and was now wearing a pale pink tunic over cream-colored pants. She looked less tense than earlier.

Elzbeth grimaced at the dress she was still wearing, hoping she could change into something similar soon. She yearned to dress for comfort and functionality—something she'd never been allowed to wear under her father's tyranny because *"ladies don't wear pants."*

"Thank you, Tonya. I'll show Elzbeth to her room," Bellenda said. Tonya nodded, then smiled brightly at Elzbeth as she hurried on down the hall.

"She was taking me to the dining hall. I haven't eaten in

days," Elzbeth said, unsure how to proceed given their circumstances.

"I know. And I figured you would prefer the meal I had sent to your private chambers. Unless you're up to eating with fifty children in the dining hall?"

"Thank you. That was thoughtful," Elzbeth said, letting out a relieved breath. The day had been quite the whirlwind, from Will selling her whereabouts, discovering her sister was alive, meeting Bellenda, and her using the book... After it all and considering everything, it seemed that she was safe here, somehow.

"Let's get you to your room. You must be practically starving," Bellenda said, pointing her wand at Elzbeth.

"What are you—" was all Elzbeth got out as the pale pink stardust swirled around them, melting away the hallway and replacing it with the grandest room she'd ever seen. It glowed with a soft, otherworldly light, its golden walls painted with patterns of blooming flowers and large windows framed by purple curtains. At the center stood a vast canopy bed, the headboard carved with flowers to match the walls. A fireplace crackled gently, filling the air with a welcoming scent. She turned around slowly, taking in the breathtaking accommodations.

"I figured you were tired of walking," Bellenda said, moving to the bedchamber table, where a feast of roast chicken, potatoes, carrots, and freshly baked bread was laid out.

"Are those chocolate strawberries?" Elzbeth exclaimed, moving toward the table and forgetting every etiquette lesson she'd ever had. She plucked one from the tray and bit down, moaning at the sweetness of the berry mixed with the richness of chocolate. Her mouth watered for more.

She'd never been allowed sweets, at least not when her father was around. Mrs. Hazel would sneak some to her from time to time. But once her father learned she had a sweet tooth, he became even more strict, only allowing her to have sweets if she earned them. Another way of controlling her.

"Okay, we're going to be quick friends," Bellenda said, popping a whole berry in her mouth as Elzbeth grabbed a second.

"I've never had a friend," Elzbeth said through a full mouth. "I wasn't allowed to have friends. Except for Thomas, but my father didn't know about him. He killed him after we ran away to get married. He wanted me to marry the king of Tranik." She shook her head as tears threatened her eyes and the sweet berry turned sour in her mouth.

Bellenda stepped closer, putting a hand on her arm. "I'm so sorry."

Elzbeth took in a long breath. "I'm sorry too. But this is why you shouldn't befriend an ugly monster like me. Sooner or later, you will get hurt. Or worse."

"Elzbeth, do you think Tonya is ugly?" Bellenda asked, her voice sharp. Her icy blue eyes pierced the two parts of her heart, freezing them in place along with her tongue. Elzbeth shook her head. "Exactly, and neither are you. But so long as you continue to think you're an ugly monster, you'll be letting your abusive father control you from beyond his well-deserved grave. That's not only awful for you, but it will also be horrible for our plans."

Her tongue thawed, allowing her to speak. "Our plans?"

"Yes," Bellenda answered. "So when you're ready, come find me and we can get started." She held her wand up.

"With what?" Elzbeth asked before Bellenda could disappear.

"Exactly what you asked Tonya about."

Elzbeth scrunched her face, puzzled.

"I can see your confusion. And while I can't grant every wish of the heart, we can be strategic in who we do answer to help the most."

"Why would you need me? My magic doesn't help like yours. And I've vowed to never use mine again." Elzbeth pointed at Bellenda's wand.

"Oh, we won't be using your magic. But you will be using your beauty spell and the skills you've honed over the years as a weapon."

Elzbeth opened her mouth to argue that Bellenda's plan was exactly like her father's, but Bellenda rushed to stop her. "As a weapon for good. For helping girls before their fathers marry them to evil, highly influential, powerful husbands. You are going to marry these men instead and use your skills to help them. You can influence the right people to make changes before you…" She trailed off, holding her wand to her throat and making a slash across it.

Elzbeth's mouth dropped.

"You proved at your last wedding that you are capable of doing so without using your magic," Bellenda continued, pulling a small glass vile from her dress pocket that looked very similar to the one Elzbeth had purchased to poison her last husband. "We'll figure out a way for you to not leave evidence behind. We can talk more tomorrow. You need to eat, bathe, and rest."

Elzbeth's eyes widened. How was it that Bellenda was speaking so casually about murder? She was *the* Fairy Godmother, after all!

Bellenda laughed softly at her expression. "I told you I wasn't going to do things like my mother." She waved her wand and was gone, leaving only a trail of light pink stardust behind.

Twenty-One

ANNA: 13 HOURS, 20 MINUTES BEFORE THE CLOCK STRIKES 12

nna held her breath, waiting to be caught. The rider must have seen them. Her stepmother surely heard the thump on the roof when she fell back.

"It's okay, girl, just birds," the rider said in a deep voice as his horse neighed loudly again. Anna rolled to her stomach and turned around to see the rider jumping off a black horse, patting its neck to calm it. "Once I change, I'll tie you up with a sweet treat out front while I meet with Elz." He yanked off a royal guard's uniform and put it into one of the saddle bags. "Alright, let's go," he said kindly to his horse. He led it around the tavern to the front.

"You okay?" Phil whispered.

"I'm fine. I slipped," she said, sitting up slowly, her mind racing. "But Elzbeth is working with a royal guard!"

"That or she, like you, stole—" He abruptly stopped his thought as he stared at the translucent sphere moving toward them. Dru stood within a floating soap bubble, approaching from the back of the tavern and staring directly at Anna.

They'd been caught.

"Shit!" Anna whispered as Dru maneuvered the bubble toward them. She landed next to Anna with a faint pop.

"Language," Dru said once freed from her bubble. She was always getting on Anna about her cursing. But Dru didn't look like she was scolding her. She was smiling.

Anna pushed herself up. "That's a pretty cool invention," she said, pointing at the ring.

"It is," Dru replied. "It's my third ring invention. But you already know that, don't you?"

"Yes," her magic had her answering.

"And you have the ring?"

Anna nodded, pulling it from her pocket, her fingers lightly brushing the letter she'd written for the newspaper.

"And it worked? Was it strong enough to suppress your magic?" Dru asked.

"Yes." She put the ring on her finger. "It works, Dru. You're a genius for thinking of using osmium metal." Anna's eyes widened, realization dawning on what Dru just said. "Wait. You believe me about my magic?"

"I do." Dru smiled, but it instantly faded. "I'm sorry, Anna. I should've believed you the whole time."

Anna grabbed Dru, pulling her into a tight hug. She didn't know why or how, but Dru believed her. Her sister believed her. "I missed you," she managed to get out as tears rained down her cheeks.

"I'm sorry it took me so long to believe you." Dru's voice cracked. Anna squeezed her tighter. The first true hug they'd had in years.

Phil cleared his throat. Anna released her sister. "Dru, this is Phil, well, I mean, Prince Rupert," Anna said as she and Dru wiped their tears away.

"I figured." Dru smiled at him. "You look like your brother and father. It's nice to meet you."

"And you." Phil took Dru's hand and bowed his head.

"Alright, enough pleasantries. I have questions," Anna said, taking Dru's hand from Phil's. Phil was staring at Dru and her bubble ring with a disconcerting amount of awe. "Where were you this past week?"

"So you figured out I lied about being at Tinker's?" Dru asked, raising a brow.

"Yes, we went there to delay you, only to discover that Tinker's workshop isn't until next month."

"Yeah, it was my cover," Dru admitted. "I needed time to find evidence on Elzbeth."

Anna's jaw dropped, but Dru must have not noticed.

She continued, "I knew we wouldn't find any evidence here, so I went looking for evidence of Elzbeth killing her past husbands."

"When did you figure it out?" Anna was in awe of her sister, who didn't just believe her about her magic but also about Elzbeth killing their father. Tears pricked her eyes again, but she took a quick breath to halt them, needing to focus.

"A couple weeks back, after the fire that burned Father's autopsy report. It got me thinking about all that you had said about Elzbeth killing Father and her being spelled. I started working on a way to see past spells, like what you told me your magic did," Dru explained.

Anna's heart squeezed.

"Did you find evidence?" Phil asked.

"Sadly, no. The death report for her last husband before our father had also gone missing."

"We need to use the book to get the proof of her murders. Then we can publish my letter," Anna chimed in.

"Letter?" Dru asked. Muffled voices loomed from the tavern, pulling them all from their huddle, reminding them why they were on the roof. "Take off the ring," Dru said.

"Oh, sorry. Here you go." She pulled it off, but Dru waved at her.

"Keep it. I made it for you."

Anna grinned. She felt a relief she hadn't felt in as long as she could remember. Dru believed her about Elzbeth having murdered their father. She believed Anna about having magic and made a ring to help her suppress it.

"But you can't wear the ring while I'm using this one on all three of us," Dru said before tapping the black opal ring that made her soap bubbles. "This will keep us invisible, but we can still be heard," she explained as the ring turned aquamarine.

"Like my magic," Phil said lowly as Anna slid her osmium ring into her right pocket. Dru reached for her and Phil's hands. Phil hesitantly took Dru's, blushing when their fingers interlocked. Anna's eyes narrowed, but she turned before either of them could ask why. She didn't want her magic making her confess her jealousy over how Phil looked at Dru or how brilliant he thought she was. *Stay focused.*

"Now let's see what our wicked stepmother is up to," Dru added, evaporating Anna's jealous streak. They moved toward the skylight and kneeled together around it to peer in.

Elzbeth was sitting in the corner of the tavern in a high-back booth, glaring toward the open door. The guard, now dressed in black pants and a matching tunic, walked in, glancing around before spotting Elzbeth. Anna wondered what had taken him so long as the tavern owner, who Anna recognized from her previous spying vigils, set two large pints of ale in front of the man and Elzbeth, who were now seated across from one another.

The owner said something, but Anna couldn't hear him. She turned to Dru and pointed at her ear, then shrugged. Dru tapped her ring's stone once. The stone swirled with all the colors of the rainbow, solidifying on tortoise-shell green.

"Did you take care of my coachmen?" Elzbeth asked, her voice emanating from the ring like she was standing in front of them. Phil and Dru exchanged satisfied and excited smiles before returning their focus to the scene below.

You are not jealous, Anna told herself, snapping her head back to the skylight. The sight of the tavern owner lying on the floor, eyes closed, next to Elzbeth's table sent Anna's heartbeat racing. *Did they kill him?*

"Yes, they are sleeping comfortably, just like him," the man across from Elzbeth replied, nodding to the tavern owner. Anna relaxed a bit, knowing he was alive. They picked up their ales for a mutual long drink.

"Thank you for coming so quickly," he said.

"Well, you called," Elzbeth replied, her tone raspy.

The man smiled seductively before standing and gesturing for Elzbeth to move over so he could sit next to her. *He must be spelled like the rest,* Anna thought.

"What are you…?" Elzbeth started to ask, but he leaned in, eyes full of lust. Elzbeth lifted her sickly green hand to the man's chest, allowing him to clasp it. His smile grew wide as he moved a loose strand of hair from her face, making Elzbeth's cheeks blush a deeper shade of green. "I'm engaged," she said.

"Don't marry him," he said and tapped the huge ruby on the ring King Tyson had given her.

"Jealous?" She cackled softly, sending a shudder down Anna's spine. It was like watching a cat play with a mouse. Taunting its prey before going in for the kill.

"No, Elz," he said softly. "I'm not jealous." He leaned in, his lips an inch from hers. "I'm green with envy," he added before Elzbeth crushed her lips into his, making Anna's stomach churn. The man grabbed her around the neck, deepening the kiss. *Thunk!* Something hit the roof. Dru yanked Anna's hand, pulling them both to their backs.

CHAPTER
Twenty~Two

"Would you trust me for once?" Elzbeth snapped, holding her candle out in front of her as she sloshed through the smelly brown waste. The thick liquid splashed and lapped at her legs with every step.

"I trust you all the time, and look where it's gotten us!" Bellenda snapped back. Her voice had a nasal quality on account of the clothespin pinched on her nose. "Like when we were knee-deep in dragon shit, and that was a good day!" She waved her hand, flickering her candlelight to illuminate Elzbeth's latest brilliant plan. Walking through the underground waste tunnels wasn't hygienic, but it was the safest way to ensure they were not detected.

"I've apologized for that a hundred times, Bell," Elzbeth said, emphasizing her nickname. "And I told you it was a dirty job this time. It isn't like the liquid is going to melt our skin off. Just cake every nook and cranny." She laughed at her joke.

"Not funny," Bellenda clipped. Elzbeth bit her lower lip, trying to contain her amusement at her friend's misery.

"I wish we still had the map spell book to get inside without having to wade through shit," Bellenda moaned.

"Too bad you can't grant your own wishes," Elzbeth said.

"Yeah, being Fairy Godmother sucks! Mother never told me the limitations to our magic," Bellenda griped as they continued to slosh through the foul liquid.

Elzbeth was beginning to regret not putting a clothespin on her nose.

"I have to be in the kingdom to hear the people's wishes," Bellenda started, ticking off the rules to her magic. "I can only grant one wish of the heart per family line for two generations."

Elzbeth knew this limitation frustrated her the most. She didn't discover it until Jaqueline tried to wish for Bellenda to break Elzbeth's spell and couldn't act. Then one of her nieces tried wishing, and the spell still held.

"And I can only use my magic for good," Bellenda concluded.

"You knew the last one. Everyone knows that about *the* Fairy Godmother."

"True, but I still hate it." They moved in silence for a few minutes. "I'll need to bathe for an entire month to get this filth off my skin. Not to mention the stench clinging to my hair." Bellenda shuddered.

"Shh," Elzbeth warned, holding her hand up. "Do you hear that?"

There was some clapping and an eruption of men's laughter above their heads. Elzbeth turned to look at her best friend, a huge smile on her face.

"Fine, you were right, this was clearly the way to sneak in undetected, but you owe me a new dress!" Bellenda replied.

"Let me guess," Elzbeth whispered so their voices didn't carry to the meeting above. "Pale pink."

"Is there any other color?"

"Yes, Bell, there are so many more."

Elzbeth held the candle higher, searching for the access ladder to the kitchen. She knew from the little details she was able to glean the past week that the meeting would be taking place in the dining hall, next to the kitchen, so that was her access point. She'd need to be careful, sneaking in through the garbage and waste access, but it was worth the risk. They'd tried for months to get an inside look at the inner workings of the Link and were finally going to see what this chapter of the illegal underground group was up to.

Bellenda moved next to her, holding her candle up, illuminating the brown crusted stone wall. They moved slowly, searching for the kitchen access until Elzbeth finally spotted the ladder. She handed her candle to Bellenda.

"Please be careful," Bellenda whispered as Elzbeth climbed the iron rungs, mindful that the soles of her shoes were slippery.

"I always am," she whispered, finishing the last dozen rungs to the door above her head. She turned the circular handle with one hand while gripping the ladder with the other. She made a mental note to ensure Gray and Jaq tripled the pay for anyone who had the nasty job at the Sanctuary of fixing or managing the waste system. She finally got the wheel to turn. There was a click as the trapdoor opened. She pushed up slowly, listening. Men's laughter erupted over the bustling kitchen where attendants prepared the meal.

She imagined the estate layout one more time before she slipped inside. The garbage door was in the back near the pantry and hopefully near where attendants kept extra uniforms. She wished on the Stars for an attendant close to her size to be working in the kitchen. There was no way to know for certain.

Elzbeth took in a long breath and pushed the door up.

She stepped on the last two rungs, poking her head out to ensure she was alone before using the potion she'd bought. It was supposed to dissolve her clothes, including her shoes, and was why she had an extra pair hanging over her neck. It was also supposed to temporarily clean her skin and hair. She would have twenty minutes.

The coast was clear as far as Elzbeth could see. She crawled onto the stone floor, closing the door softly behind her. She scanned quickly, spotting the extra uniforms hanging about ten feet away in the corner of the room.

Elzbeth pulled the potion from her tunic's front pocket and laid her shoes on a nearby shelf. The small glass of egg-yolk-colored liquid was plugged with a cork stopper, which she pulled free with her teeth before pouring the contents over her head.

A tingling sensation began at the top of her head, dripping down like the yolk of a very large egg. She closed her eyes and mouth, demanding her body to stay still as the potion covered her face and neck. When the sensation reached her shoulders, she opened her eyes, glancing toward the kitchen. She was still alone. *Come on*, she mentally begged the potion, feeling it reach her chest. She peered down. Half of her tunic was gone, exposing the green of her breasts. The potion continued to eat up the rest of her tunic, then the top of her pants.

Faster, she pleaded, wondering how much time had passed. Someone would surely come back to the pantry at some point. Pots and pans clanged loudly as the potion ate away the material over her knees. She strained to hear anything beyond the attendants preparing the meal. She hoped that dinner hadn't started yet because what she needed to do would be easier with her twenty-minute time constraint without a meal being served. The potion was almost done, dissolving the tips of her boots.

"What in the Stars?" a woman squealed.

Elzbeth covered up as best as she could with her arms. "I'm sorry. I was trying to change quickly," she said, leaning into the excuse that she and Bellenda had thought most believable.

"What happened? Why are you naked?" the older woman asked, propping her hands on her hips.

"I singed my uniform badly while stoking the oven fire." She continued her practiced lie.

"Clumsy girl," the attendant said, clicking her tongue.

Elzbeth looked up, locking eyes with the woman. Time was

ticking by, and she needed to get dressed before more attendants came back. The older woman blinked, then smiled broadly.

"I'm sor… sorry." She faltered over her words, then cleared her throat. "I mean, do you need my help to get a new uniform on? It's almost time to start serving the first course."

"No, thank you, I'm fine."

The attendant stepped closer. *Shit!* She didn't have time for this. Grabbing her shoes, she slipped out her necklace of rings and unclasped the chain before sliding them on her fingers. "Actually, yes, some help would be appreciated." She smiled at the poor soul trapped in her spelled web as she clanged the sides of her rings together to produce a small pin, quarter the length of a sewing needle, from her oval-shaped ring. The attendant stepped up, beaming now. Elzbeth grazed the pointed tip across the side of the woman's neck.

"Ow," the woman said before crumbling to the ground.

"Sorry," Elzbeth whispered, pressing her ring into the floor to retract the pin before grabbing the attendant's arms and dragging her to the corner. The woman would only be unconscious for five minutes, waking with a bad headache but their encounter forgotten.

She turned to the uniforms, snatching one close to her size and pulling the dress over her tight bun. She shoved her feet into her shoes and pulled her three rings off, then strung them back around the necklace and tucked them under the uniform. She yanked on the white gloves required for serving attendants.

She moved into the bustling kitchen, making her way towards a platter of empty flutes. People swirled around her, busy with their own tasks. All as she would expect it to be with Lord Byron hosting the Link's meeting. Elzbeth had counted on there being extra help on the premises. She'd needed it to slip in, unnoticed and unquestioned.

Once the flutes were full, she pulled the necklace out and flipped the heart-shaped, silver locket ring open. She tapped it once on the inside rim of the center glass. Several clear drops of truth serum dribbled in for Lord Byron to ingest and loosen his lips for when she seduced him into a secluded room. She lifted the tray expertly, thanks to the two years she was forced to be an attendant in her father's home between her marriages.

She gritted her teeth, forcing the unpleasant memory aside. Elzbeth took a cleansing breath before stepping out of the kitchen and down the short hallway separating the dining room from the kitchen. She pushed the door open with her hip, giving her body a gentle sway as she stepped out into the lion's den.

Thirty or so well-dressed men, from the ages of twenty to seventy, milled about the set table in groups of three or more. One particular group of five had their heads close and bowed away from the others in the room, making her wonder what secrets they were sharing. Three men next to them laughed loudly, patting each other on the back, sloshing their drinks.

Elzbeth moved about the room, head bowed as the guests grabbed glasses from her tray. She kept turning the tray for others to grab non-laced drinks as she moved about the room, closing in on her target. He was standing, arms folded, talking to a man who had his back to her. With each step she got closer to Lord Byron, her stomach knotted. She hated her father's lessons, but Bellenda was right when she said Elzbeth could use them as a weapon to help others. So she was doing just that—being the good hunter, with her eyes set on her evil prey.

Lord Byron oversaw the illegal auctions and sale of beautiful underage girls as brides to the highest bidder for his Link chapter. He was the final nail in their coffin, dooming them to wed corrupt, rich bastards against their will. Like they were nothing more than property. Just like she and Jaq had been to her father. The thought of such evil made Elzbeth sick. She thanked the Stars the Link hadn't existed when they were children. Elzbeth stopped a foot from her mark, who was engrossed in a conversation with another man. Before offering up the last two flutes, she lifted her head, needing to lock eyes with Lord Byron in order to trap him in her spell.

"Hello, beautiful." The words of flattery she'd heard countless times from hundreds of men were not spoken by Lord Byron but by his companion. Startled, she turned and took the stranger in, almost dropping her tray in utter surprise. Her smile dropped into a grimace as she bit back curses of shock and anger.

Lord Byron reached out and grabbed a glass, not even glancing at her. "Thank you, Lord William. We'll talk details further tomorrow." And with that, he strolled out of Elzbeth's web.

"You," Elzbeth said, seething.

"Me?" Will said, innocently holding a hand to his chest, batting his honey-colored eyes at her. He grabbed the last flute, never breaking eye contact, and threw it back in one quick motion.

"Wait, no," Elzbeth said, but she was too late as he swallowed the glass laced with the truth serum.

"What are you doing here?" he asked, taking in the splendor of her spelled beauty.

"I was going to ask you the same thing, Lord William," she said, pronouncing his name and title like a curse. "I would've thought you made enough money selling my whereabouts to avoid sinking so low."

He put his hand on her arm, gently pulling her toward a door a few feet from them. She glanced around, but no one was paying them any attention.

"Unhand me," she hissed with venom once the door shut behind them. He didn't answer, nor let go, but proceeded to pull her through the estate. "Where are you taking me?"

He grabbed the tray from her and leaned it against the wall without slowing his stride. "Away from them," he whispered, nodding his head in the direction of the dining hall.

"I don't need you to rescue me, Lord William. I didn't need you three years ago, and I don't need you now." Heavy footsteps sounded on the marble floor. Will pressed her against the wall and covered her entire body with his as the steps grew closer. The two halves of her heart beat rapidly at his proximity.

"Trust me?" he asked lowly.

"Like hell!"

A man's voice hissed, cutting the rest of her retort short. "Stop fussing with your gown. No one wants a fidgety wife, no matter how beautiful you are."

"Sorry, Father," a girl replied.

Elzbeth's body went rigid.

"Remember to do as I instructed. You do not speak unless spoken to, and do not refuse anyone who—"

Their voices were closer now. Elzbeth's magic bubbled insider her, begging to burst free, but Will's lips crashed into hers.

"See?" the horrible man said. "She knows how to behave. When you're done, I would like a taste of her," he said, stopping next to them. "You can sample my daughter. She's also for sale tonight."

Will broke their kiss, keeping her body covered with his as he lifted his head to the monster of a man. He looked to be in his sixties. His daughter, who was maybe fifteen, shook like a leaf caught in a winter storm, her auburn curls bouncing off her shoulders. *Shit!* This wasn't just a meeting for planning their next auction; this was an auction of underage girls!

"Sorry, this one is not on tonight's menu." Will tightened his hold on Elzbeth's arm. She wanted to scream that she was not a piece of meat. She refused to ever be treated as such again. But she had a role to play. She needed to get rid of Will and get back to Lord Byron to get information on the head of the Link in Tranik. It was only a matter of time before her cleaning potion ran out. And there were the girls to consider, this monster's daughter and whoever else was here.

Maybe she could take her back to the Sanctuary? Elzbeth turned her head and locked eyes with the daughter first. The girl's fear melted away, and she ceased shaking as a smile sprouted on her lips. *Damn spell!* Elzbeth hated that it manipulated emotions. She looked at the bastard father, locking hers with his. A wicked smile formed on her lips that would look nothing but wonderful on her spelled face. She felt no remorse for toying with him.

"I'm sorry," he said. He was breathless now, caught in her spell. "She is so beautiful. I assumed you were sampling the goods before the auction. But I can see you've already claimed her." Elzbeth didn't hear the rest of his words. She was busy contemplating drugging him and giving him a slow, agonizing exit from this world.

"Indeed! This beauty is mine," Will said, pressing his lips back to hers. He waved one of his hands, dismissing the bastard and vanishing her thoughts of murder. For now.

Once the father and daughter were out of earshot, Elzbeth pushed Will off her, but he didn't budge. He stepped back, putting a few inches between them.

"So, you're one of them," she hissed, forgetting her role again.

"Stars, no!" Will said. "Listen, we don't have time for explanations, beautiful. This is no place—"

"Stop calling me that!" Elzbeth snapped, cutting him off. She hated that her spell was manipulating him too. "If you truly knew what I looked like, believe me, you wouldn't have kissed me, let alone told that bastard I was yours."

"Oh, really?" He gave her a cocky smile. "Tell me then, what do you truly look like?"

She waved a hand over the length of her body. "Not like this!" She took a deep breath and straightened, raising her head. "Which is irrelevant. I have a job to do. So if you would kindly step aside, I need to get back to the kitchen before someone realizes I'm missing."

"Sorry, can't, beautiful," he said. She clenched her jaw. "I can't stay by your side tonight, enchanting every bastard who approaches you."

"I can handle myself just fine." She crossed her arms.

"Really, is that what you're calling it when I found you sitting in the woods, wounded, in a ruined wedding dress? You were *handling* it?" He smirked, his crooked smile infuriating her.

"*You…*" She gave a quick shove to his chest. "You sold my whereabouts while pretending to be my friend! If you think I'm going to give you an ounce of trust—"

"Whoa, beautiful." He put his hands up. She rolled her eyes at his pet name, but his smile widened. "I never sold your whereabouts. You disappeared on *me*." He stepped closer, closing the distance her shoves had gained. "When I came back to our room, you were gone. And when I inquired of the innkeeper, I caught his wife hiding behind the counter counting several stacks of coins. If I were a betting man, my money would be on them ratting you out. Not me." He gave his shoulders a shrug. "I'm sure the bloody wedding dress was a tip-off."

What? She'd always assumed it was Will who sold her whereabouts. She'd never asked Jaq or Bell about it because she thought she already knew the truth. "But the article… Why didn't you make contact for the money if you knew who I was?" Elzbeth asked, simmering on the newfound information. *And the note I found in his suit jacket…*

"To be honest, I didn't know you were the girl pictured in the article," he said. She shook her head, confused, as he continued, "My magic. I cast enchantments." He waved his hand. A puff of blood-red smoke left his fingertips, producing a rose the same color. He held it out to her. She crossed her arms again, not wanting to play his games. He waved the rose in front of her, but she didn't budge. He growled lowly, like she was being unreasonable, then flicked his fingers, making the rose disappear. "I can also see through enchantments, spells, and illusions."

"Wait… you can see me? What I truly look like?"

"Yes."

"But why then would you call me beauti…" She shook her head. "You're lying." She tried to sidestep him, but he grabbed her arm. His grip was gentle as he leaned in. *Is he going to kiss me again?*

Her stomach flipped as her heart pieces started beating like twin drums. His finger slipped under the chain around her neck, the silver rings clinking together. "You know I'm not lying, beautiful." He stepped back; her necklace dropped against her chest. Will turned on his heel and strode towards the dining room, leaving her staring after him.

Twenty~Three

ELZBETH: 12 YEARS, 4 MONTHS, 13 DAYS, 14
HOURS BEFORE THE CLOCK STRIKES 12

"Hold on," Bell said. "Will? He drank the truth serum meant for Lord Byron?"

"Yes," Elzbeth replied.

Bellenda's light laughter filled the air as they walked the Sanctuary grounds. It was the one place that Elzbeth could escape to from the world. "The Will, I mean, Lord William. The man who rescued you in the woods," Bell added, feigning to swoon.

"He didn't rescue me."

"Of course he didn't." Bellenda playfully elbowed her in the ribs.

"You're hopeless." Elzbeth swatted her best friend's elbow away.

"What, because I believe in the type of love my parents had?" Bellenda asked.

"No," Elzbeth said. "Because you believe in perfect princes who save damsels in distress."

"What about Gray? He isn't a prince, but he did rescue Jaq."

"Gray is a rare gem. How many times do I need to tell you that the bubble you were raised in isn't reality? Life isn't all wishes and happy endings," Elzbeth said.

"I would disagree." Bellenda raised her brows. "And it could be argued that Will, while not a prince, did save you while you were in a distressed situation."

"No, he put his nose in my business three years ago, and again tonight," Elzbeth said, cracking her neck to the side, stretching it. "Because of him I was forced to hide in a tiny closet and listen through the vent for over three hours until everyone left. Smelling like shit." She scrunched her nose as Bellenda giggled at the picture she painted.

"I'm glad he intervened three years ago," Bellenda said after her giggling subsided. "And we got the information we needed. We know when and where the Link is holding their next auction."

Elzbeth's magic bubbled within. She could've gotten that information in ten minutes, likely more, if Will hadn't distracted her. And the poor girl was sold to a man triple her age. Elzbeth could only sit and watch through the vent, unable to save her.

"So, *the* Will," Bellenda continued, and Elzbeth groaned. "You said they made him a junior member tonight?"

"Yes, something about him having to prove his worth. Putting his money where his enchantment magic is," Elzbeth replied as they walked up the three steps to their cottage on the outskirts of the Sanctuary grounds. She grabbed the handle, happy to be home. Elzbeth needed a long bath and a strong drink after the night she'd had. She turned the door handle, struggling to articulate her thoughts. "There's something else about Will. He could, I mean, he can—" She pushed the door open, freezing mid-sentence.

"Hello, beautiful," Will said, smiling and standing next to a not-so-happy Grayson, whose eyes were shut to keep from falling under Elzbeth's spell.

"What the hell?" Elzbeth and Bellenda said in unison.

"Language, ladies," Grayson corrected.

"What's going on, Gray?" Bellenda asked.

"I was going to ask you two the same thing," he said back

but waved his right hand at Will and added, "but first let me introduce you both to my new associate who discovered some interesting things for me tonight." He crossed his arms in front of his chest while trying to give them a stern look with his eyes shut. It would've been funny if it weren't for the situation.

"Associate?" Elzbeth asked.

"For what?" Bellenda added.

"Well, for tonight to confirm that my *little sisters* weren't as foolish as I'd heard from others." Gray's words were sharp. A slight smirk appeared on Will's lips. "Some of my associates heard murmurings about a breathtaking raven-haired beauty who'd been asking questions about tonight's Link meeting location."

Elzbeth's heart pieces lurched into her throat, cutting off her ability to speak.

"You thought they were talking about Elzbeth?" Bellenda asked two octaves higher than normal. Her cheeks turned pink, the same color of her dress where it was still clean. If her voice hadn't given away their lie, their smell certainly had.

"Fine, you caught us. But we didn't do anything foolish," Elzbeth said.

"Not according to Lord William," Grayson said.

"Gray, do you know who Lord William is?" Bellenda asked.

"Uh…" He sounded unsure.

"Clearly, you don't, so let me bring you up to speed, dear brother," she replied, using the sweet voice she reserved for displeasure with Gray. Leave it to a meddlesome brother to send Will to spy on them. Will, who could see past Elzbeth's spell.

"This is the man who rescued Elzbeth in the woods," Bellenda continued.

"He didn't rescue me," Elzbeth exclaimed, giving Bellenda a look to silence even the most hopeless romantic. Now was not the time.

"I most certainly did," Will said with a smirk.

Elzbeth turned to him with the speed and anger of a striking viper.

"I didn't know," Grayson said before Elzbeth could sink her fangs into the arrogant man.

"What do you mean you didn't know?" Elzbeth said turning to Grayson.

"I mean, I didn't know that Lord William was the same person who rescued you," he said.

"Would everyone stop saying he rescued me!" She threw her hands in the air, walking past Will and Grayson to the front room. She fell backward into the couch only to have a gust of wind filled with tiny pink stardust push her up, making her stumble forward and almost fall onto the rug. Will caught her before she fell, holding her steady.

"Sorry," Bellenda said. "But there's no way you're sitting on the furniture before you bathe." She scrunched her nose. Elzbeth rolled her eyes and pushed herself free from Will's grasp. "Actually, we both need to," she added, looking down at her ruined dress.

"You're welcome," Will said with a devilish grin. "For saving you again." If looks could kill, Elzbeth's glare would have put Will six feet under.

Grayson cleared his throat. "Clearly, you two have some things… to discuss. I'm going to leave you all and say goodnight." He moved toward the door, arms out fumbling a few feet until Will, ever the annoyingly present hero, grabbed his arm and led him to the door. Grayson paused on the threshold as Will held the door open for him. "Tomorrow, I want a meeting with the three of you. Lord William and I must be brought up to speed on your activities."

"Just Will."

"Alright, Will." Grayson nodded in his direction.

"Our activities are none of your business," Elzbeth protested.

Grayson held his hand up. "Once I know all the scheming you two have been doing, we can work out a way for us all to work together to bring down the Link before it spreads further." He smiled over his shoulder, then moved out the door. Will shut the door behind him, sealing Elzbeth, Bellenda, and himself in an awkward silence.

"It seems you two have a lot of catching up to do, so I'm bathing first," Bellenda said, bolting down the hallway. Elzbeth wanted desperately to stop her, but that would only serve to make things more awkward.

Before she disappeared completely down the hall, Bellenda called back, "Don't forget, Elz, you owe me a new dress."

"You better go after Grayson so he can show his new associate to his room," Elzbeth said, moving to follow Bellenda down the hall, fully intending to wait in her room with several glasses—or perhaps bottles—of wine until it was her turn to soak in a long bath.

"Hey." Will stepped in front of her, grabbing her hand to halt her escape.

"I'm tired. Can we do this tomorrow?" she groaned.

"The next auction is taking place at the harbor in two weeks."

"I know," she snapped. He dropped her hand. "I was in a very cramped closet on the other side of the dining hall, listening to you and your fellow jackasses droning on for three hours, smelling like what I waded through to get there."

"I'm not one of them."

"You could have fooled me. You fit right in." She waved her hand at his suit and slicked back blue-black hair.

"It's called a disguise," he said, pointing at her uniform, taking a step toward her.

"Well, there were only two ways I was getting in there to get the information I needed tonight," she countered. "And as unpleasant as tonight was, I vastly prefer it to being ogled by those bastards as they bid on me."

"You can't do this."

"How dare you tell me what I can and can't do!"

"What I mean is you need a man." She opened her mouth to

tell him exactly what she thought about that statement, but he continued, "A man on the inside, I mean. Who can get close to the Link's inner workings."

"I'm listening," she said, crossing her arms in front of her chest.

"Did you hear my cover? What the Link thinks I'm there for? What I can offer them?" he asked.

"Yes, but you can't use your magic to enchant underage girls' birth documents and…" Her stomach dropped. She gritted her teeth to hold back her emotions. She forced herself to finish the statement. "Enchant girls to be beautiful so their fathers get more for them when they're auctioned off."

"I know what you're thinking."

"You have no clue what I'm thinking!" she said, stepping closer, pressing her finger into his chest. "I was spelled against my will because my father thought I was ugly when my skin turned green on my tenth birthday. He locked me away in my room until…" She stopped. Beyond Jaq and Bell, she hadn't told anyone else about her and Thomas marrying. She knew Gray knew; she gave Jaq permission to tell him. But this man standing before her now? He had no clue the game he was getting himself tangled in. "You need to get out. You have no clue what men like Lord Byron are capable of."

He grasped her hand between his, lifting her finger off his chest.

"I know all about men like Lord Byron." The coldness of his words made her shiver. "I was raised by a man far worse and more influential than Lord Byron. I was meant to become just like him. To marry a woman for her beauty and strong magic bloodline. To give me heirs who would make me rich." He drew in a deep breath, his honey eyes piercing into hers. "I was able to get free of the monster who raised me. But not before he sold my sister into a marriage." He stopped. She waited for what he would say next, her body rigid. "By the time I learned the truth of who my father sold her to, it was too late for my sister. But it's not too late to help others before they're sold to evil men to produce children and keep the cycle going."

He released her hand, taking a step back. Neither said anything for a moment.

"But the girl tonight," she whispered. "You stood there as she was sold to the highest bidder."

"I did."

"How can you say that you want to stop the cycle but let that innocent girl—"

"I enchanted the bastard who bought her," he cut her off. "By the time he got to his carriage, he'd forgotten the whole night. And I enchanted her father to forget he'd ever had a daughter. The girl is here."

"Oh" was all she could muster. Will clearly had powerful enchantment magic if he could make someone forget their own child.

"Oh, indeed." Will sighed. "I'm not like them. I want to help the girls before they're sold to cruel men."

"Do you understand that Bellenda and I won't just be saving the girls and bringing them here to the Sanctuary?" He lifted a brow, and the scar by his eye moved almost imperceptibly. "We'll be disposing of the evil men in places of power within the Link, like Lord Byron, so they can't continue to harm anyone else."

"You're going to kill them." It wasn't a question, but she nodded. "And do you think Grayson will agree with you and Fairy Godmother disposing of these men?" She knew he used Bellenda's title on purpose. Not to judge but to remind her how risky their work was.

"Grayson doesn't believe in the glorification of murder," she said. "But he does believe in the empowerment of women."

"As do I."

"Good," she said. "And as for Bellenda, her hands will stay clean."

He started to pull one of his hands through his thick hair but stopped with a disappointed groan when his hand encountered the slicked-back mass. She didn't like it styled this way either, remembering his long, shaggy hair from three years prior.

"So, what's your plan?" he asked.

"Using this." She waved her hand at her face. "To seduce the powerful men within the Link." He grimaced, and she rushed to silence his expression. "I know you think I'm wicked for using my beauty spell to seduce men to their deaths, but they're monsters."

"No, beautiful," he said and stepped closer. "I think it's wicked that you're under a spell that hides your true beauty." He grabbed a piece of her hair that had fallen from the bun, placing it behind her ear.

"You're joking." Elzbeth shuffled back a step. She needed space between them because the pieces of her heart were beating rapidly, even faster when he touched her. He shook his head. "Alright then, Will. Tell me. What does my hand look like?" She held it out to him.

"I see your true colors." His honey eyes blazed into hers, like they were trying to melt the frozen wall she'd built around her heart pieces.

"Don't you mean color?" Elzbeth teased, trying to deflect because the room had suddenly grown warm.

"Did you know that green is my favorite color?" He flicked his fingers, producing a green puff of his enchantment smoke— the same color green as her skin. A green rose appeared, and he motioned it to her with a seductive grin.

"I know what you're doing." She crossed her arms, refusing the rose. "You're using your enchantment magic to make your-self charming so I'll fall for you."

"Well… is it working, beautiful?" he asked, raising his brows.

She rolled her eyes, annoyed at his use of the word.

"I'm just using my magic to show you how stunning you are." He waved the rose at her, but she shook her head, keeping her arms crossed. "But I like the idea of you thinking me charming."

"In your dreams," she said as the bathing chamber door opened, announcing Bellenda was done and Elzbeth could finally have her turn.

"Every night since we met," he said, his smirk making her traitorous cheeks heat.

"Well, speaking of dreams." Her tongue tripped over each word. "I'm tired and in desperate need of a bath." She side-stepped him, retreating down the hall before he could see the true color of her flushed face.

"See you tomorrow," he called out, but she didn't look back. Keeping her eyes directly on Bellenda, who was standing in a pale pink nightgown by the bathing chamber door, she tried to appear unmoved.

"Beautiful," Will added just before Elzbeth disappeared from his sight, making Bellenda smile widely at her, eyes dancing with delight.

"Not a word," Elzbeth said, holding her finger up to her best friend, who zipped her lips, locking her mouth with an invisible key. Elzbeth shut the bathing chamber door, forcing herself to take in a long breath. "He's just an associate."

"Keep telling yourself that," Bellenda sang sweetly from the other side of the door. Elzbeth shook her head, knowing she'd be getting an earful once she washed the filth of the day off her skin.

Anna's stomach churned as she watched the poor spelled man in the tavern below kiss her wicked stepmother like she was a gift from the Stars. There was a loud *thunk* as something hit the roof, startling Dru, who yanked Anna's hand, pulling them both to their backs.

"That low-life piece of shit!" Phil seethed. Anna sat up, taking Dru with her, and looked at him. His teeth were clenched. She imagined smoke puffing out of his ears with how red his face was.

"What the hell, Phil?" Anna hissed, realization dawning upon seeing his bloody knuckles about who and what had given away their presence. *He punched the roof?* She scrambled to her knees, not letting go of Dru's hand to look back into the tavern. Elzbeth and the man were on their feet, looking around.

"Time to go," Dru said, getting to her feet and pulling them up with her before she tapped her chin on her ring. The stone turned aquamarine before releasing a soap bubble. It grew, expanding around them until they were enclosed inside.

Thank the Stars for Dru.

"Move to the roof's edge and step off. I'll take care of the rest to get us out of here," Dru instructed.

"I'm sorry," Phil said softly as they were enveloped inside the bubble.

"What's done is done," Dru said.

What, no! Anna's mind screamed, but Dru continued, "Let's get out of here quick. I haven't used the ring on three people doing two things, so I'm not sure how long we have to make our escape." Anna nodded, unable to speak as anger boiled through her veins at what Phil had done.

A few drops of Phil's blood trickled from his knuckles and landed on the bubble floor. *Why did he do that? Why punch the roof when he knew it would give us away?* Anna slowly walked to the roof's edge, trying to mimic Dru before stepping off. *What was Phil thinking? We haven't learned anything that we could use against Elzbeth.*

Horns sounded, announcing the arrival of the king's carriage and pulling Anna away from her swirling thoughts. She understood none of this was easy for Phil, but seriously, what did he expect from Elzbeth? Of course she was meeting up with other men! She probably had a whole dozen men spelled to come whenever she beckoned. *What part of wicked does he not understand?*

"Where are we going?" Phil questioned. They were floating above the buildings, down the road to the main street of town. "Wouldn't the woods be a better place to float above in case your magic ring can't hold on?"

"Trust me, landing on a rooftop is much softer than landing in a tree or falling several dozen feet to the ground," Dru answered, eyes focused ahead. "But let's hope it holds up until we get back to the library."

"I'm really sorry," Phil apologized again. They floated over several more buildings, Dru moving their joined hands and navigating them down the main road. They only had to make it a quarter mile to reach the library. "It's just, Elzbeth has no heart," he said, seething.

"No kidding. She's a wicked witch!" Anna spat, looking him

directly in the face for the first time since they entered the bubble.

"She spelled my father to marry her so she can… what?" Phil retorted. "Kill him and keep his power and title? What will she do with that kind of power?"

"Hmm, I don't know, maybe rule a kingdom," she deadpanned, not needing her magic to force her answer. "But in case you forgot, she killed our father." Anna bit out each word. "She has killed who knows how many men before and will continue to kill. That's what she does." She drew in a ragged breath. "I know you don't have much experience being out of the cage they put you in, Prince Rupert, but—"

"Annalie," Dru chastised.

"What?" she snapped. "Don't defend him because you like him." Her anger and jealousy swirled into one. "I was finally getting somewhere. After years I…" Hot tears blurred her vision as she choked on her last words.

"She's right," Phil said. "I screwed up… royally." The sad joke dissolved Anna's anger, and her shoulders slumped. He continued, "I get it. You're the only person who has been trying to convince people about her killing your father, and I can't handle watching her spell my father to love her while kissing another man."

"I'm sorry too, Anna," Dru said tenderly. "For abandoning you the past years."

"You didn't abandon me. You were spelled."

"Well, I'm not spelled anymore. So we need to come up with a plan to stop Elzbeth before she marries King Tyson," Dru said, floating them up and over the library building toward the back. She landed the bubble next to the window. The bubble popped the second it touched the ground.

Anna dropped Dru's hand, then pulled her into a tight hug. "I love you," she whispered into Dru's mess of hair. "And I'm sorry for what I said about you defending Phil because you like him."

"It's fine," Dru replied. "Phil is nice, but I don't like him like that. Like how you—"

"You said you made three rings," Anna interrupted.

Dru laughed softly before she answered, "Yes." Anna stepped up to the window and pulled the key from around her neck as Dru continued, "The one you have that suppresses magic. This one…." Dru held up her right hand, then pulled off the ring that saved them with the soap bubble. She slid it into her pocket and pulled out a black band with a small white stone in the center of it. "And this one. It freed me from Elzbeth's spell, really from all spells and enchantments." Dru handed the ring to Phil. He slid it onto his pinkie finger and blinked several times.

"That's amazing!" he said. "Daff's window enchantment just dissolved before my eyes."

"Exactly." Dru smiled at him. Anna's heart ached. Dru said she didn't like Phil like that, and she trusted her sister. *But does Phil like Dru like that? And why does it even matter if he does?*

"That's why Anna said you weren't afraid in the woods," Phil said.

"Yes, and why I wasn't shocked to see you tagging along in the carriage." Anna's mouth dropped. Dru laughed softly. "Let's continue this conversation inside," she said once her laughter subsided. Anna unlocked the window. Phil held it open for Dru to go first.

"Thanks," Dru said before she crawled onto the table. She turned around, grabbing the window from Phil. He stepped back and gestured for Anna to go next. She put both hands on the sill but froze, his hands landing softly on her waist.

"I got you." His warm breath tickled her ear as her heart flipped.

"Your hand is injured," she said, more breath than words. Her skin tingled where his hands held her.

"I'm fine. And I'm sorry again," he said and lifted her with surprising ease.

"Thank you." Anna stumbled over the words as her heart

skipped a few beats. She was starting to realize she'd closed herself off from everyone because of her stepmother's spell. She'd been hurt too many times by her sisters not believing her. She had built a protective wall around her heart—a wall that was starting to crack because of a prince who…

Phil cleared his throat.

"Oh, sorry." She crawled off the table past Dru.

Phil put both hands flat on the sill, pushing up and sliding onto the table, then landing next to Anna before saying, "So, Dru, you said this ring"—he held his hand up as Anna closed the window—"broke Elzbeth's spell on you?"

Dru nodded.

"And now when not wearing it, you can still see past it?" he asked.

"No, I would be spelled again if I wasn't wearing the ring," Dru explained. "That's how I learned about the spell. When you lock eyes with her, it clicks into place."

"Yes, we also figured that out," Anna said, moving to the back of the room, hoping Daff hadn't thrown out her discarded gown. She opened the enchanted box and smiled at the pale pink cloth on top. She pulled it out and moved back to where they stood. "But something about the spell doesn't make sense to me." Anna stepped towards Phil and pulled his dagger from its sheath.

"What?" Dru asked. Phil's eyebrows scrunched together as he watched what she was doing.

"If the spell is on Elzbeth, wouldn't everyone see her as I do before they were put under it?" Anna asked, slashing the material and handing the dagger back to Phil.

"I tested this theory out several times. I took the ring off and was able to see Elzbeth as she truly is. But as soon as she looked into my eyes, the spell snapped back into place. I had no memory of what she looked like before the spell until I put the ring back on."

"Whoa, that's a complex spell," Phil said as Anna tore off a strip of material.

"How did you know if you forgot each time?" Anna asked, grabbing Phil's injured hand gingerly. Dru pulled something from her pocket and held it out, clearly unaware that Anna's hands were busy wrapping Phil's bloody knuckles.

"Thank you," he said softly as she finished the wrap. He grabbed her hand as she finished and kissed her fingertips. Her entire body tingled. Her heated cheeks were only one of many signs over the last several hours that she was falling for him. He raised his gaze, his silver-flecked, slate-grey eyes locking on to hers.

"I didn't only test it on myself. I have enough sense to get more data," Dru said, knocking Anna out of Phil's intense stare. *Seriously?* Dru waved the notebook between their faces. Anna snatched it as Phil chuckled lowly at Dru's obliviousness. "I recorded my learnings in there when my test subject used the ring."

Anna scanned several pages, then stopped on one. "You tested the ring on Daff and didn't tell me!" She looked from the notebook to her sister.

"Yes. And I didn't tell you because Daff doesn't remember. I was hoping to make more progress on the ring before I told you and got your hopes up. I had Daff put the ring on for the first time a couple weeks ago when I overheard that Elzbeth was coming here looking for you," Dru said.

"What? She never comes to the library! She always sends a fire message!"

"I know. I was shocked, but I wasn't going to miss my opportunity to test out the ring," Dru explained. "I knew you weren't here. I saw you sneaking into the woods to practice your archery. So I used my bubble to get here before Elzbeth and gave Daff the ring, then hid in the stacks to watch."

"Can we use it on Daff again so she can help us too?" Anna asked, hopeful to have her best friend back.

"That was why I was here earlier tonight. She put the ring on right before Cyndra, Edgar, and Fairy Godmother arrived."

"Why were they here?" Phil asked.

"I sent a fire message to Cyndra that I was back and coming here to see Anna," Dru answered.

"You were going to use the ring on Cyndra and Edgar too?" Anna asked.

"Yes, but I was shocked when they showed up with Fairy Godmother, nulling that plan."

"Can Daff still see past Elzbeth's spell?" Phil asked.

"As long as she hasn't seen Elzbeth and fallen under it again. For now, we need to focus on how to tweak the ring to permanently break Elzbeth's spell. Then have King Tyson put it on, see the truth, and arrest Elzbeth for her crimes."

Easier said than done.

"I've done some research," Dru continued and put her hand out to Phil. He placed the ring in her palm. She held it up between her thumb and forefinger, pointing at the stone. "I'm going to need a much larger opal than this one, and the only place I know where those exist is the Tranik kingdom." She sighed, and Anna knew why. The border between Phannel and Tranik had been closed for two decades.

"How did you get the one you used?" Phil asked.

"Tinker had it."

"If we get a bigger opal, could you make it work to break Elzbeth's spell permanently?" he asked.

"I believe so, but the fact is we can't get one—"

"Actually, we can," Phil interrupted. "With the map spell book."

"Oh, right!" Anna exclaimed.

Phil pulled the book from his bag and held it out to Dru. She opened it but frowned at the blank pages. Phil placed his good hand on the book, using his magic to make the title and table of contents appear. Dru's frown reversed.

"Which one do you think we should use?" Anna asked as

Dru hungrily took in their options. "We can't use the *Map of the Known* because none of us have been there."

"I've been to the border," Phil offered. "We could use it to get there, then cross over with my magic and Dru's rings."

"That'll take too long," Dru said, still staring at the table of contents. "Even if we found a large enough opal, I would still need time to work on it. Took me a week to figure out the ratio for this ring, so something larger would…" She stopped. "We could use the *Map of the Forgotten*," she said excitedly. The table of contents page melted away as the instructions and spell for the *Map of the Forgotten* appeared.

"Hold tight and use your magic while saying the spell,"

Phil read the instructions.

"To truly find what has been lost, you must share something that will cost. Close your eyes, think of what you need to find, then speak your truth, freeing it from your heart and mind."

"Um, why this map, Dru?" Anna asked, brows furrowed.

"Because as I said earlier, Tranik is the only place I know of that has larger opals, but Tinker and I have done some research the past month and found—"

"Wait. Tinker knows?" Anna questioned then added, "No wonder she didn't give us any grief."

"Yes, she knows. She's been helping me," Dru answered. "We did some research, and we think there might be a way to permanently break Elzbeth's spell. For everyone. But the stone I require —its location is probably more legend than truth. This could be a lost cause. But if it does exist, this map spell could take us to it. If we had that stone and could get Elzbeth to put the ring on in front of the entire kingdom, we could permanently break the spell."

"Tomorrow's engagement announcement," Phil said.

"If the legends are real and we can get our hands on that stone, Daff can enchant the ring to look like Elzbeth's engagement ring. Phil can switch them before his father places it back on Elzbeth's finger in front of the kingdom, and then... Dru, you're brilliant!" Anna exclaimed.

"Agreed!" Phil said, and Dru's cheeks flushed. "We better be going because we only have hours until the ceremony," he added. Anna moved to his other side, placing her hand on the book. "Loop your free hands through my arms, while still touching the book with the other," he instructed. "We're going to have to work together. Anna, please say the spell. I'll share a secret about my father that would cost a lot, while Dru closes her eyes and thinks about the stone."

Everyone nodded. Dru closed her eyes, her face contorting with concentration. *Please let this work*, Anna begged the Stars as she read the spell.

Phil closed his eyes, drawing in a deep breath before sharing his truth. "My father isn't Edgar's father. The man that we all believe to be King Tyson is his identical twin brother, my father, Prince Leo, who took his place after King Tyson died."

Dru gasped as the book glowed and sucked them inside.

"Alice, please pass me the pumpernickel jam," Elzbeth requested in an octave lower than normal.

"Yes, of course." Alice, Elzbeth's latest step-daughter, beamed at Elzbeth like she was the sun and Alice was blessed to be in her presence. She wanted to roll her eyes but commanded herself to stay in character. Just a few more minutes until someone discovered Alice's father.

"Thank you." Elzbeth smiled, taking the jam from the girl who turned fifteen just last week, the day after Elzbeth married her father. Alice hadn't been put out one bit to have her birthday overshadowed by her father's wedding. Elzbeth knew this was because of the spell but still wished the girl had put up some kind of fuss about her birthday being forgotten.

"My lady, my lady!" the head housekeeper called from outside the dining room. *Finally.* Elzbeth put her toast down. Alice jerked her head up as the frantic woman ran in.

"Yes?" Elzbeth said.

The woman stopped a few feet from the table, bending over to catch her breath. Elzbeth didn't scoff at her. After all, she was close to seventy and shouldn't be running. No, she should be retired, enjoying her four grandchildren rather than serving her latest evil husband. *And soon that can be reality for her if she and her family decide to move to the Sanctuary.*

"Lord Staffords, he's…" the housekeeper wheezed out, shifting her eyes from Elzbeth to Alice. "I'm sorry, my ladies, but he's… dead."

Alice gasped. Elzbeth threw a hand to her heart, stepping into her performance. The grieving newlywed. She'd done this seven… no, this was eight times now. Eight times in nine years, and yet they were no closer to finding out who was truly behind the Link. Plus, with every man and chapter of the Link they removed, it seemed a new one popped up across the four bordering kingdoms. And recently, Lexlent—an island kingdom northwest of the continent. Elzbeth suggested they go there next since the Link was new to Lexlent and they could possibly uproot it before it spread across the entire kingdom. But Will said he couldn't. The risk of his father finding out he'd come back home was too great. Elzbeth volunteered to go alone, but Bellenda shut that down quickly, marking the first time Will had ever agreed with Bellenda.

Alice let out a soft cry, pulling Elzbeth back to the present. "What happened?" Alice choked out.

"We aren't sure," the head housekeeper replied, still wheezing. "Trudy found him when she went in to clean his office. His head was down on a stack of papers, and an empty bottle of brandy was turned over next to him."

"He was complaining of chest pains when we went to bed last night," Elzbeth said, rising from her seat to comfort Alice. "I thought it was heartburn from all the food and…" She cut her words short, pulling Alice from her chair into an embrace.

She held Alice, tears and probably snot soaking the front of her gown. She hated this part—having to comfort the child until Bellenda arrived.

"I'm so sorry," the head housekeeper said, backing out of the room to give them space. Elzbeth nodded, still crying. She'd gotten good at producing tears on the spot. But for this final performance, she needed lots of them. Elzbeth turned the silver circle-shaped ring on her finger, knocking it against her other rings, producing a small pin she pressed into her palm. It wasn't a strong potion, but it was enough to make the waterworks flow.

"Would you like me to contact the coroner and the authorities for you, my lady?" the housekeeper asked.

"Oh, there's no need for that." Bellenda's sweet voice rang through the room, making Elzbeth's heart pieces flip with relief.

"Fairy Godmother!" Alice gasped.

"Yes, dear," Bellenda replied, practically floating toward Alice. Elzbeth released her, glad to be handing the child off. "And I'm so sorry about your father," Bellenda added, taking Alice into her arms and hugging her tightly. It wasn't that Elzbeth didn't care. She cared very much. Bellenda was just way better with the children than her.

The first time she married a man with children, she told them they would be going with her to live at the Sanctuary, and the whole thing turned into a disaster. So the next time, they had Bellenda show up to handle the children and their affairs.

They also learned fairly quickly that Bellenda's celebrity status made things a lot easier to orchestrate once the evil man was no longer in the picture.

"Alice," Bellenda said. Alice sniffled and let go of her, stepping back with red, puffy eyes. "Please go and pack a trunk." Alice's eyes widened, but Elzbeth knew by the time Bellenda finished explaining, Alice would be ready to pack and go.

Bellenda would tell Alice that she and Elzbeth should leave while the investigation was taking place. They'd go to the country for a bit, where they could mourn in peace until things were settled. It was a lie but a good one, which allowed Elzbeth to leave with Alice, no questions asked. And that's where Will came in.

He'd arrive with the authorities, pointing them to the financial documents that Lord Staffords, the local Link's accountant, had died upon. Documents that were proof of the buying and selling underage girls into marriage. The illegal act would have the Link chapter shut down in days, and hopefully, more after once the authorities became aware of the underground group.

Will would tell the authorities that he would question Elzbeth and Alice alone. He'd then enchant the authorities following the questioning, telling them that Elzbeth and Alice are innocent and of no concern, granting them the freedom to leave and never come back. The home, along with all other assets, would be sold to pay Lord Staffords's debts, and eventually, those who knew them would forget about the poor widowed newlywed and her stepdaughter, allowing Elzbeth to move on to her next alias and target.

"Yes, Fairy Godmother," Alice replied once Bellenda explained everything.

"Good. We'll leave after you're questioned. Pack quickly, dear, before the authorities arrive." Alice nodded and hurried from the room. Once the door closed, Elzbeth exhaled loudly and pressed the circle-shaped ring into the table to retract the pin.

"Don't relax yet," Bellenda said, handing her a piece of paper.

"What's this?" Elzbeth unfolded it.

"Our next target."

Elzbeth read the newspaper article from *Fairytales, Facts, and Fables* from the kingdom of Phannel. "You want me to marry Prince Edgar of Phannel?" The article announced a royal ball for all eligible ladies of Phannel to attend in order for the prince to pick a wife.

"No, he's half your age," Bellenda scoffed.

"No, he isn't!" Elzbeth argued back. "He's eighteen, and I turned thirty just last winter... five months after you did."

"Fine, he's still way too young for you," Bellenda said. "But you'll be marrying Prince Edgar's future father-in-law." Bellenda's eyes twinkled. "Becoming the prince's mother-in-law."

"Hold on." Elzbeth held her hand up. "This ball is in three days."

"I know. And I'm sorry for the quick turnaround, but the girl…" Bellenda paused, pulling a small pink notebook out of her pocket. It was the same color as her dress. She flipped through the pages. "Cyndra," she read. "She made a wish last night to be chosen by the prince at the ball."

"I would wager a lot of girls of Phannel have made that same wish since this was announced." Elzbeth held up the article.

"True," Bellenda replied with a yawn. She must've been up all night listening to the wishes, trying to decide whose was most worthy to fulfill for the good of the kingdom of Phannel. Elzbeth couldn't imagine the pressure to grant the right wish, knowing it could go sideways. That it could corrupt rather than help the person requesting it. "But it was the second part of her wish that stood out to me," Bellenda added.

"Which was?" Elzbeth glanced at the grandfather clock. Will and the authorities would be arriving at any moment.

"That if her wish were granted to become princess, that I would also provide a mother to care for her younger sisters while their father was away working."

"You're joking?"

"No. I'm not."

Elzbeth balled the article into a clenched fist, ready to fight Bellenda on her wild proposal.

"But just… hear me out," Bellenda said quickly. "After hearing her heartfelt wish for not just herself but her sisters, I decided to do some digging to find out more about her and the family. The girl's father isn't a good man."

"They never are."

"True. But I still believe there are some good ones out there," Bellenda replied. Elzbeth nodded, thinking of Gray and Will and a handful of other kind men who worked with them at the Sanctuary.

"But what this evil man does for the Link…" Bellenda paused, shuddering.

"Please tell me this one's in a place of influence over more than one chapter?"

"He's not in a place of influence for just one chapter…" Bellenda's eyes brightened. "He's in a place of influence for the entire kingdom of Phannel."

"Finally!" Elzbeth cackled, clapping her hands.

"Yes," Bellenda said, softer in case prying ears were close to the dining room doors. "Everyone, including his three daughters, believes that their father travels for his thriving business. But the truth is, it's a front for the Link to move the underage girls around to different towns within the kingdom of Phannel."

Elzbeth's magic bubbled at the thought of finishing the evil man. But she commanded it to be quiet so she could concentrate. "This could be it," Bellenda said, sounding just as eager. "This could be how we finally take the Link down. Once you marry…" She paused, going back to her notebook. It was something that Will and Elzbeth made her keep because Bellenda was horrible with names and details. "Lord Augustus Beck, then Cyndra will marry Prince Edgar. We will dispose of Lord Beck after their wedding. Then, when his boss starts looking for a replacement, we can have Will—"

"Hold on," Elzbeth interjected. "You can't ask Will to take that position."

"I know." Bellenda waved her hand at her. "He won't be applying for that job. He will, however, find out who gets chosen so he can tail him. I'm not sure how long it'll take to figure out who is behind the Link in Phannel. But once Will knows, you'll be able to tell the king because you will be…" She returned to her notebook. "Cyndra's stepmother."

"Sounds easy enough," Elzbeth joked, looking at the clock again. "We can talk details later. I need a few hours of quiet, away from people fawning over my endless beauty." What she truly needed was a month, but that kind of recovery would have to wait.

"Sorry, but there's no time to waste." Several loud knocks sounded from the front estate doors. "I sent Will a fire message with instructions to enchant the authorities of your innocence and take the girl to the Sanctuary," Bellenda said. She pulled her wand out and waved it about.

"Bell, wait!" was all Elzbeth got out before the tiny pink stardust melted away the late Lord Staffords's dining room.

"What are we doing in a forest?" Elzbeth asked once the world solidified again. She was used to moving about, using Bellenda's magic. But what she'd never gotten used to in all their years of friendship was Bellenda's absolute lack of manners in taking Elzbeth along for the ride without ever asking her permission.

There was an eruption of cheers and applause from behind Elzbeth. She furrowed her brows at Bellenda before turning around to what looked like a competition.

"Next up, we have last year's junior archery champion, Annalie Beck," an announcer's voice boomed as Elzbeth took in the scene. Beyond the thick forest was a vast valley. Redwood trees lined the valley, making way to an enormous mountain. It was beautiful. Bellenda moved about the brush to the edge of the tree line.

"That's Lord Beck's youngest daughter," she said, nose glued to her notebook. "Annalie, or Anna to her friends and sisters. She's almost thirteen." Bellenda flipped a page, then flipped back. "Actually, her birthday is the same day as the ball." Bellenda smiled widely. "It's a sign."

Bellenda loved these little synchronicities, saying it was the Stars approving of what they did. Elzbeth didn't need the deities' approval, nor did she think the synchronicities were notable. But if it helped Bellenda sleep better, she wouldn't argue.

The girl walked out, waving at the crowd, smiling broadly.

She was tall, with long limbs and no curves. She reminded Elzbeth of herself at that age—minus the green skin. "She doesn't have magic." Bellenda flipped through her notes. "Nor does her middle sister, Drury, age fifteen."

"And Cyndra?" Elzbeth asked.

"She can communicate with animals."

Annalie walked up to her first target, the sunlight reflecting off her fiery red braid as she lined up her shot. This wasn't the first archery tournament Elzbeth had attended. In fact, Lord Staffords had taken her to one only three days prior, where he lost a lot of money. Not wanting to be in further debt, he made plans to sell his underage daughter at the next Link auction. Elzbeth poisoned him before he had the chance.

Unlike the tournament Elzbeth had been to in the Mondgue kingdom, it appeared the Phannel kingdom allowed girls to participate. Elzbeth smiled at this as Annalie loosed her arrow at the target.

"Bullseye!" the announcer boomed. The crowd cheered.

"She's good," Bellenda remarked.

"Seems so," Elzbeth said as Annalie lined up for her next target twenty yards further back than before. "She'll get along well with Robyn," Elzbeth added as Annalie hit another bullseye, knowing her niece, Jaqueline and Grayson's oldest daughter, would be thrilled to finally have a worthy opponent.

"She's not going to the Sanctuary," Bellenda said after the crowd quieted for Annalie to concentrate on her next target.

"What do you mean she's not going?" She turned towards Bellenda, crossing her arms.

"I know, it's not ideal for you. But we can't have the princess's younger sisters and stepmother disappearing even for a long holiday after her father's death," Bellenda started to explain as Elzbeth shook her head. "I know children aren't your thing."

"No, they're not." Elzbeth's heart pieces beat rapidly. A cold sweat formed on her brow.

"I'm sorry, but you can't disappear this time," Bellenda said. "You have to stay and fulfill the second half of the wish. At least for a couple of months, Elz."

"I didn't sign up to be a mother!" Elzbeth spat.

"No, you didn't sign up for any of this," Will said from behind them. *How long has he been here listening?*

"Now is not the time, William," Bellenda bit out, pointing her wand at him. She couldn't do anything harmful, but she did this when they argued… which was all the time.

"Well, I think now is actually a great time before you send her into a situation that's way over our heads, Bellenda," he retorted. Will stepped closer, brushing the light pink stardust he used to travel from his hair.

"She can handle this," Bellenda said, her eyes narrowing.

"I didn't say she couldn't handle it, but what will it cost her?" Will asked.

"You mean, what will it cost you?" Bellenda said, putting her hands on her hips. It was her usual stance when readying for another verbal duel. Clearly, they'd both forgotten she was there.

Will mockingly threw a hand to his chest.

"You get all mopey whenever Elzbeth is gone on a mission. Don't deny it," Bellenda continued.

"Stop calling them that," he snarled. "They're not missions. They're men she has to seduce to marry her."

"Alright, you two," Elzbeth cut in. Their faces were inches apart, and if someone caught *the* Fairy Godmother having a fight, they'd have lots more on their plate. Elzbeth placed a hand on their shoulders, pushing them away from one another.

"While I appreciate your concerns, Will, Bellenda is right."

Bellenda smiled, her pink lipstick shimmering in the sunlight.

"And Will is also right," Elzbeth added, wiping Bellenda's smile clean as Will's face lit up. "Seriously, you two!" She threw her hands up, exasperated.

"Sorry," they said in unison.

Elzbeth shook her head at them.

"Who's handling the authorities at Lord Staffords's estate and taking the girl to the Sanctuary?" Bellenda asked after a few moments.

"Lucas," Will answered, not taking his eyes off Elzbeth.

"Lucas. Really, William?" Bellenda chided. "You know he can barely enchant!"

"He can handle it. Stop being a control freak, Bell-en-da." He emphasized each syllable of her name.

"I'm not a control freak. You're a pompous—"

"Stop! Just stop bickering for once," Elzbeth growled. "Is the situation ideal? Me having to ensure the welfare of two girls for months?" She laughed. "Of course not. There are so many things I would rather do."

"Like walk over hot coals, drink dragon piss, and…" Will started listing, but she gave him a withering look.

"But this could be it," Elzbeth said. "This could be the key to dissolving the Link." Her heart pieces fluttered with hope as the crowd cheered, turning their attention back to the tournament.

"This year's junior archery champion, for the third time, is Annalie Beck!" the announcer boomed.

"Well, if you're doing this, you'll need to watch your back with that one," Will said, pointing at Annalie.

Three girls charged Annalie. Elzbeth suspected two to be Drury and Cyndra, enveloping her into a group hug and nearly toppling them all over onto the grass.

"Ahhh," Bellenda cooed. "She's harmless."

"So, where's their evil father?" Will asked.

"Shh." Bellenda elbowed him in the ribs. No one could hear them over the chatter of spectators milling about, coming and going from the various tents around the archery tournament.

"Fine." Will cleared his throat. "Where, pray tell, is the father of the reigning junior archery champion? Lord Beck, you said it was?"

Elzbeth laughed. Bellenda gave Will a sour look, which only

made Elzbeth laugh harder. Though her friends were as different as night and day, she truly loved them both. Bell was the light to Elzbeth's darkness, seeing the positive in everything and believing in a better world. Will, on the other hand, was ever protective, scrutinizing every detail of their plan before she married their next target. *You know why he is that way. He wants to be with you,* the small voice in the back of her head whispered, but she pushed it aside. Now was not the time to examine her complicated relationship with Will. A relationship that teetered the line between friendship and something more.

"That's for you to find out since you left Lucas to wrap up the last mission," Bellenda said, pulling Elzbeth from her thoughts. She held her hand out to Elzbeth. "We'll be in our rooms at the inn, working on Elzbeth's new cover. Once you know where Lord Beck is, come find us in rooms three and four," she added as Elzbeth took her hand.

She waved her wand. Pink stardust transported them from the forest to the inn, where they would begin scheming for the final time (hopefully) for Elzbeth having to marry an evil man.

Twenty~Six

"Are you ready?" Bellenda called through Elzbeth's inn door.

"Almost. Come in." Elzbeth slid on her final ring, checking her dress and hair one more time in the mirror, before turning to Bellenda, who was already gliding into the room.

"Isn't that a bit overkill?" Bellenda pointed at Elzbeth's hands bearing multiple silver rings.

"It's called being prepared," Elzbeth said, clasping her earrings and necklace into place.

"For what? Will is going to be there so you don't need…" Bellenda stepped forward, grabbing her hand. She lifted it up, examining the rings. "Sleep serum, truth serum, and…" Bellenda dropped Elzbeth's hand and grabbed the other. Her face scrunched as she examined the new ring. "What does this one do?"

Elzbeth pulled her hand back with a sly smile. "It's just there to look pretty… like me. At least, until I add our newest potion. I'm just waiting for Gray to figure it out," she added with a twirl, showing off the elegant gown Bellenda had chosen for her to wear tonight.

Bellenda smiled with approval. "And the necklace, is it also just pretty like you?"

"It's like you don't know me after all these years." She winked at her best friend and moved for the door. It was already 11:00 p.m. Will should have Lord Beck several mugs into his ale at The Devil's Tavern, priming him for when Elzbeth would stumble in, playing her damsel-in-distress act.

"It's a shame your dress will be ruined after tonight," Bell said as they exited Elzbeth's room and headed down the inn's hallway toward the front doors.

"Yes, what a shame," she deadpanned, knowing this was going to be her life now. For several months, at least, until they finally ended the Link in Phannel. The thought made Elzbeth's heart pieces beat a little quicker. She could do this. She could do several months of being the overseer of two teenage girls, wearing ridiculous gowns, and acting like a gift from the Stars if it meant saving countless girls from being sold into marriages to cruel men. That was what she told herself before she had stripped out of her tunic and pants and put on the ridiculous thing that was already cutting into her ribs and oxygen supply. It was going to be a long night.

She glanced at the front desk, spotting the innkeeper sleeping. *Thank you, Will.* Bellenda waved her wand. A stream of pink stardust unlocked and opened the doors for their exit. A banged-up black carriage with two muddy-legged white horses waited for them.

"What did you use this time?" Elzbeth asked, climbing into the carriage.

"The horses are white mice, the coachman is a dog, and the carriage is…" She made a face. "Well, let's just say it's something we don't want to be inside of when the spell wears off. I highly doubt either of us wants to be lying inside a coffin with the remains of whomever was buried inside it."

Elzbeth shivered.

Bellenda closed the curtains and flicked her wand at

Elzbeth's dress, her magical stardust tearing and muddying it instantly. Elzbeth pulled her silver makeup mirror, a gift from Will on her thirtieth birthday, from her dress pocket and read the inscription on the bottom that was enchanted for only her to see.

So you don't forget how beautiful you are.

She smiled, opening the mirror and running the sharp-cut jewel on her necklace down her cheek. She bit back a hiss, reminding herself, *Pain is part of the job.*

They had thought up the perfect story for their plan. Elzbeth would stumble into The Devil's Tavern, distraught and injured because her horses were spooked. The coachman had been knocked unconscious, leaving Elzbeth jostling around inside the carriage. The horses had eventually settled enough for her to jump out a mile outside the royal city. Her coachman, having woken to find her missing, rushed back for her, and once he'd recovered her, drove to the tavern, seeking help and a room at the inn so she could rest and recover.

Altogether, it was the perfect explanation for why she was now exiting the muddy, banged-up carriage (before it became a coffin again) and darting up the stairs toward the tavern. She slid the mirror back into her dress pocket before pulling the door open, keeping her head down to scan the room for Will.

She didn't want anyone but Lord Beck to see her face first. Her spell would pull them in, and they were on a time crunch. She spotted Will in a far corner booth. He tilted his head slightly, acknowledging her but never taking his eyes off the man sitting across from him. Her heart pieces started to thump loudly in her chest. *Stop it,* she mentally scolded, but they thumped harder with each step she took towards the table. Towards Lord Beck, her next husband.

"Excuse me," she said at the table, her eyes moving from Will to Lord Beck.

"Go away," Lord Beck snapped, not looking at her. "Can't you see, woman? We're busy!" He waved his hand in dismissal. Will gritted his teeth, but Elzbeth could handle men like Lord Beck. She'd done it plenty of times. But never with Will watching.

"I'm sorry to bother you, but the healers' office was closed," she said sheepishly. "I was told you could help me, that your magic—"

"It'll cost you," he cut her off, still not looking at her. "Fifty gold pieces." Elzbeth forced herself not to ball up her fists. "Or a night in my bed if you're pretty enough," he added, finally facing her. He choked on the last word as Elzbeth pulled her hood back, eyes now locked with the evil man.

Gotcha.

Lord Beck blinked several times like he was looking at something too magical to be of this world. Elzbeth waited patiently for him to get a full look as Will continued to grit his teeth. She ignored him. She couldn't be distracted by his jealousy. But she also couldn't deny that she liked it. "My apologies. I'm drunk."

"It's fine." She smiled. "I have the gold. So if you're willing to heal my wounds, I would appreciate it."

"No." He jumped to his feet, nearly pushing her over. "I mean, no cost," he added, stumbling over his words. "Please, sit." He motioned to her. "Three ales and some soup for the lady," he yelled at the man behind the bar, who was filling a couple glasses with a purple drink that bubbled as it hit the glass.

"Actually." She put a hand on his arm. "I would love a glass of that." She pointed at the purple liquid, intrigued by how it smoked slightly at the top. Hopefully it tasted better than ale.

"That's not a drink fit for a lady," Will said. She wanted to cut him a look, but she stayed in character, turning sweetly toward him. "Oh, I didn't know. I just don't prefer the taste of ale."

"If the lady wants it, then the lady gets it," Lord Beck said over his shoulder, moving toward the bar and leaving them alone. She slid into the booth, hugging the wall to make room for Lord Beck when he returned. The dirt-stained, fluffy dress took up at least half the sitting space. Will leaned forward, grazing his knees against hers. He glanced over at the bar, then back at her.

"I don't like this," he growled.

"You don't have to stay and watch," she replied cooly. "Your part is done, thank you." She smiled. Truth was, it would be easier for her if he weren't here.

"You know what I mean, Elz." He tightened his jaw. "I don't like you having to be this. And for months." Will's hands clenched into fists.

"I know. Which is why I insisted on using my name this time." She glanced around to ensure no one was in earshot of them before continuing, "But if we pull this off, then the months will be worth it. And then…"

She paused before the words leapt off her tongue. She promised herself she wouldn't voice what she wanted for her future when this was all over. She wouldn't say it. She couldn't say it. Because she knew how foolish it would be to hope. So she shoved the thought way down to the place of her dreams. The only place where she could escape her life of marrying evil men.

She flicked her eyes to Will's. They blazed into hers. And for just a brief moment, she forgot why she was there at the tavern, working on getting her next husband. She wished in that briefest of moments to be anywhere else. With Will.

Lord Beck suddenly returned, holding a smoking glass of the purple liquid out to her.

"So, let me take a look at your face, Lady…" Lord Beck smiled from ear to ear at her. Right, then. She knew this would be an easy night.

"Lady Elzbeth," she answered, moving her gaze from Will's smoldering eyes to Lord Beck. She ignored the flutters in her stomach. *Just a few months, and this will all be over.*

ELZBETH: 3 YEARS, 11 MONTHS, 25 DAYS, 21 HOURS BEFORE THE CLOCK STRIKES 12

"You may now kiss your wife," Bellenda said cheerfully after Lord Augustus Beck slid the ridiculously huge, star-shaped diamond ring onto her finger. Elzbeth held herself. She forced her body to lock down, to not flee from the evil man she just tied herself to. As his lips touched hers, a swirl of their magic—hers a shower of tiny green emeralds and his raindrops as grey as a stormy day—encircled them, bonding their union.

Bellenda clapped vigorously, as did Lord Beck's eldest daughter, Cyndra, the only witness to their union. The other two girls, lacking magic of their own, were at school learning a "useful skill," as their father put it. They couldn't wait for the other daughters to witness their union. The ball was tonight, and Bellenda had much to do to get Cyndra ready to trap Prince Edgar.

Elzbeth had never seen Bellenda so nervous. She was practicing her spells into the early morning hours, changing odd things into carriages behind the inn. The longest one lasted was two hours. But Bellenda was determined they succeed. She was certain this was their opportunity, the game-changing move that would finally put an end to the Link.

"Congratulations!" Cyndra said. Elzbeth broke the kiss and plastered a fake smile on her real face, knowing that it would look angelic on her spelled one. "I just can't believe it," Cyndra said, smiling broadly.

"What, dear?" Bellenda asked.

"That you're here." Cyndra turned her smile from Elzbeth to Bellenda. "That my sisters will have someone other than me to care for them." Lord Beck cut her a look, but Cyndra didn't see it, as she was caught up in the presence of Elzbeth's beauty spell and *the* Fairy Godmother.

"Hey, Cyndra, we're home," a girl's voice called out.

"Oh, that's Anna and Dru. They'll be so excited to hear the news!" Cyndra said. "In the parlor," she called over her shoulder. Lord Beck grabbed Elzbeth's hand, intertwining their fingers as the footsteps approached. *You can do this. They're just children. Without magic. So how much trouble can they be?*

The question was still rattling in her mind when the two girls walked into the parlor. Drury was dressed like Cyndra, in an elegant gown, but Annalie was dressed in pants and a tunic. Elzbeth's shoulders relaxed at the sight of Annalie's outfit. *My kind of kid.*

"What are you wearing, Annalie?" Lord Beck questioned.

"A tunic and pants," Annalie answered quickly.

"Please tell me you didn't go to school dressed like a boy." He seethed.

"I did, but Cyndra said I could," Annalie answered.

"Fine. There are more important matters to discuss today." He dropped Elzbeth's hand, putting it to the small of her back. She wanted to arch away, a scowl crossing her true face. Drury's face lit bright as the sun as she gazed at Elzbeth, and Annalie blinked several times as she, too, came under her spell. "Meet your new mother."

"What?" Annalie squeaked.

"Isn't it wonderful?" Bellenda exclaimed.

"Fairy Godmother," Drury and Annalie said in unison, their

eyes wide. They'd missed Bellenda when they got trapped in Elzbeth's spell.

"Yes." Bellenda smiled graciously. Elzbeth knew this part wasn't an act. Bellenda was wonderful with children and talked about how many she would have when she found her perfect person. "And not only was I blessed to officiate your father's marriage, but I'm also here to help your sister." She turned to Cyndra, who beamed brightly.

"I'm confused," Drury said.

"That's a first," Annalie quipped.

"True, but can you tell me what's going on?" Drury asked Bellenda. "What does Cyndra need help with?"

"The ball." Bellenda practically sang the words, her eyes sparkling. She knew that look. It was the one she had when she talked about fairytale dreams and perfect princes. Elzbeth watched Bellenda, wondering if she was getting too wrapped up in the emotions of this particular job.

"Your sister is going to be a princess," Lord Beck said to Drury. "Isn't it a splendid day? First, I marry the woman of my dreams." He looked at Elzbeth. "And now, my most beautiful Cyndra will become a princess. I couldn't dream of anything else to make this day better." He wrapped his arm around Elzbeth's waist, tugging her along toward Cyndra, and pulled them into a hug.

"I can," Annalie said under the laughter and chatter. Her words were unnoticed by everyone but Elzbeth, who also was the only one who noticed her leaving the room. *That's different*, Elzbeth thought about Annalie's lack of happiness. Drury joined in on the chatter that Elzbeth was forced to endure thanks to her new husband having her locked into his side.

"Cyndra, I can't believe it!" Drury said to her sister, then turned to Elzbeth. "Congratulations, Father and..." She stared quizzically at her. "Mother?" She smiled shyly. She knew the spell was working its tricks, making the girl want to please the beautiful woman who was now married to her father.

"Elzbeth is just fine," she answered. Drury's face fell. *Damn it!* She was so bad at this.

"She doesn't want to replace your mother," Bellenda chimed in sweetly, swooping in for the save. Again. This brought the smile back to Drury's face. "Right, Elzbeth?" Bellenda added and turned to her.

"Yes," Elzbeth replied with a warm smile. She most certainly didn't want to do that.

I can do this, Elzbeth told herself, sitting on the bathing chamber floor after several hours of planning for Cyndra to be ready for the ball. It was the only way she could get away from Lord Beck for a few minutes. She turned the silver, poppy-shaped locket ring over and over on her right middle finger. It held Gray's latest potion to be used later tonight when Lord Beck wanted to consummate their marriage. The potion would make him believe they had, but in reality, he would be out cold, sleeping the entire night.

"What about a pumpkin?" Drury said, walking down the hall outside the bathing chamber.

"A pumpkin?" Bellenda questioned.

"Yes, its shape is unlike any other carriage, setting Cyndra apart," Drury replied. "Plus, I've been working on something that may help your magic last longer on it."

Elzbeth's ears perked at this. Could it also help with the enchantment glasses Gray and Will had been working on the past eight years to see past her spell? So far, the glasses only worked for a few seconds.

"Oh please, do show me, dear," Bellenda said.

Elzbeth could hear the excitement in her friend's voice as their footsteps moved away. She listened a moment longer, ensuring no one else was coming. She couldn't hide in the bathing chamber all night, no matter how much she wished she could. Maybe she could slip out and go exploring the woods next to the estate grounds for a few hours and say she got lost?

Elzbeth cracked open the door and looked each way before dashing down the long hall. If she remembered correctly, it would take her to the kitchen. She took several wrong turns but eventually found the kitchen and was about to escape out the door when Annalie's voice stopped her.

"It's not fair."

Elzbeth darted to a dark corner in the back of the room, hoping Annalie hadn't seen her. She needed a break from her spell and didn't need the girl fawning all over her.

"I know," an older woman said back, speckles of flour coating her hands and face. "But with your father getting married with no notice, I didn't have time to bake two cakes."

"So you took my birthday cake and made it their wedding cake?"

"Yes," the woman said. She turned her back on Annalie, busying herself at one of the worktables.

Annalie stood for a few moments, glancing around, then swiped her hand into the bottom tier of the cake and grabbed a handful. She stormed from the kitchen, leaving a trail of icing behind her.

Elzbeth sighed. She hated that their plans ruined Annalie's birthday. She made a mental note to tell Jaq to go all out on Annalic's next birthday when she and Drury were at the Sanctuary.

"Like I said…" Will's voice echoed behind her, making her practically jump out of her skin. After all these years, she still wasn't used to him popping up without any warning. Bellenda kept him well supplied with her stardust to travel about unseen and gather information for them. "Watch your back with that one," he added with a smirk.

"What?" Anna exclaimed once the book ejected them. She blinked several times, adjusting to the darkness they'd landed in, not paying attention to her surroundings because Phil's confession was at the top of her mind. "King Tyson died falling from the balcony, not Prince Leo?" Anna asked.

Dru flicked her portable light on right as the book closed and proceeded to fall. Phil grabbed it quickly, putting it into his bag. In the back of her mind, Anna wondered where they were. But the shocking news that Phil just dropped? Well, that took precedence.

"Yes. It was an accident. But my father blames himself for his twin brother's death." He took a few deep breaths. "They were having a late celebration together for Edgar's birth. They were both very drunk. And when they were up on the balcony, Tyson tripped." He paused. "He fell the six stories onto cobblestones."

At least that much of the story is true.

But what about the rest of the story? Had their youngest brother, Prince Aaron, truly left the kingdom, heartbroken over his brother's death? Or was he in on the lies that Prince Leo had cast? Or worse, was he locked away somewhere, silenced?

"Wow." Dru exhaled, pulling Anna from her swirling thoughts.

"My father feared what would happen to the kingdom. Rumors were already swirling of Tranik threatening to go to war with us. To absorb our kingdom into Tranik as they had done to the Danoli kingdom. If they knew who'd truly died…" He puffed out a long breath. "My father feared the kingdom would think he orchestrated it all. That he pushed his brother to his death to take the throne. And then he'd have a civil war on his hands. So he made everyone believe that it was him who fell off the balcony and took his brother's place."

"He used his magic to wipe their memories," Anna said.

"Yes. But only on the one person who was there and witnessed the truth."

"Prince Aaron," Dru offered.

"So that much of the story *is* true?" Anna asked, wondering what kind of person Phil's father truly was to cover up his twin's death and hide his son his entire life.

"How it happened and who was there is all true. Just not who died," Phil answered, shaking his head. "My father erased that part of Aaron's memory. Of him calling out Tyson's name as he fell."

"How did you learn the truth?" Anna asked.

"I had always suspected something because of this." He pulled his hair back and pointed at his mark by the Stars below his right ear.

"Your curse isn't because your father tried creating a double for Edgar," Anna said. "It's because of what your father did. Faking his own death, then… wait, you said your father only changed your uncle Aaron's memory, but what about Queen Lily? You can't tell me she didn't know the difference between her husband and—"

"Queen Lily and my mother knew the truth," Phil cut her off. *And I thought I have a complicated family life.* But it seemed the royals took it to a whole new level. "My parents were married, and my father knew he couldn't fool her or Queen Lily, nor did he want to. He loved my mother, his twin, Queen Lily, and Edgar dearly. So the three of them kept it all a secret. But when Edgar got sick…"

"That part was true?" Anna questioned.

"Yes."

"You were truly born to cover up your father's deceit?" Anna seethed.

"No. I was born because my parents loved one another," he bit out. "And their kingdom. They were willing to do whatever was needed."

"I'm sorry," Anna interrupted. "I didn't mean it like that."

He nodded, nostrils flaring. She could tell he was working hard to compose himself. That she hit a nerve. She opened her mouth to apologize again, but then Dru asked, "How did you learn the truth?"

"I overheard my parents a couple nights before my mother passed, just after Queen Lily died, discussing it all. My father was blaming himself for his brother's death, for the curse on me, and begging my mother to forgive him for keeping the truth from Edgar and me," he explained.

"What about your uncle Aaron? Did he truly leave the kingdom, heartbroken?" Anna asked, not daring to voice what she feared. If Prince Aaron were still living, they could search for him. They could use the book to show him the truth of what happened, and then he could expose King Tyson. *Prince Leo.* And maybe that would break Phil's curse? Anna would keep that plan to herself for now, but it was a good plan.

"Yes. He hasn't been back since my uncle's funeral. The last fire message he sent my father he said he was going to the Lexlent kingdom," Phil answered.

Anna exhaled. At least if Prince Aaron were still alive, there might be hope for breaking Phil's curse.

"Does Edgar know the truth? That he is your cousin, not your brother?" Dru asked.

"No." Phil let out a long sigh. "But now that my father is going to let Elzbeth, Cyndra, and you two officially meet me, I wonder if he'll ever tell us the truth about who he really is."

"That's why Elzbeth wants to marry your father!" Anna said. "She must already know the truth. Maybe Fairy Godmother told her about Queen Lily adopting you!" Phil's eyes widened but she continued, "The adoption papers, they have your parents' true names for giving you up for adoption. All royal adoption papers need Fairy Godmother's signature to seal the document, to make you a rightful heir when they tried to break your curse."

"You're right! That's why she sent her henchman to the document office!" Phil exclaimed. "She knows who my father truly is and that Edgar's the rightful king. But if the proof is gone—"

A deep growl cut Phil's words short. Anna quickly pulled her bow from her quiver as another growl rumbled, closer than before.

"What is that?" Phil whispered. They formed a circle, backs to each other, and began to move. Dru put her light above her head, but it only illuminated the space a few feet in front of them. Anna had never heard anything so bone-chilling in her life and cursed herself for not investigating their surroundings better.

"No clue," Anna answered. She readied an arrow, pulling the string taut as they kept circling.

Dru tapped her portable light, making it brighter and illuminating the space another ten feet around them. They were inside a cavern at least twenty feet high. The light bounced off a rock wall with large scratch marks—like a creature used it to sharpen its claws.

"I think we may have landed in someone's home," Anna said.

"A large someone if those piles of bones are any indication," Phil said in a shaky voice as he pointed at an unsettling accumulation of bones. Another growl sounded directly in front of

Anna. They all froze as Dru tapped her light once more to illuminate more of the cavern.

Standing before them, with smoke puffing from its nostrils, was the most beautiful and horrifying creature Anna had ever seen. "Dragon," she whispered as her hands quivered. Her heart pounded in her ears. The beast growled lowly.

"Phil, please tell me your magic is back so we can use the book," she pleaded as she slowly raised her bow.

"No, Anna don't harm it," Dru said. "We need the dragon's help to get the stone."

"You knew the book would drop us in a dragon's den?" Phil whispered.

Dru took a step toward the beast. A low rumble from the dragon followed, making Anna's stomach churn.

"What are you doing?" Anna hissed.

The dragon's golden eyes zeroed in on Dru, who lowered her light so that it wasn't pointing directly into the beast's eyes. Its blood-red scales glimmered like jewels in the warm white glow.

"Beautiful," Dru said with awe. The dragon shifted, rumbling at Dru, smoke puffing from its nostrils in warning. But Dru took another slow step forward. "We aren't here to hurt you," she said.

"Seriously, Dru, get back here," Anna warned. She surveyed the creature, calculating where she could shoot to give them a chance to escape and use the book before it recovered enough to pounce on them. If Phil's magic returned in time, that was.

The dragon's body was exactly how the stories described. Thick scales overlapping each other like armor that moved as the creature lumbered closer. Its golden eyes sized Dru up, likely as its next meal. Anna pointed her bow up at the dragon's right golden eye. That seemed to be the best option.

"It's alright," Dru said, never taking her eyes off the dragon. "You need to put your bow down."

"Absolutely not!" Anna exclaimed at Dru's back. She wasn't lowering her weapon. She kept her arrow aimed at its golden eye, zeroing in on the bullseye of its black pupil. The dragon moved closer, flicking its wings and lifting off the ground. It landed ten feet from Dru, shaking the cavern and raining small debris on top of them.

"It won't give us what we need if it thinks we're a threat," Dru explained far too calmly for someone standing ten feet from a fire-breathing dragon.

"Breaking Elzbeth's spell is not worth your life, Dru. Step back, and let's get out of here," Anna pleaded. The dragon opened its mouth, showing two rows of razor-sharp teeth. "Please," Anna begged.

Dru ignored Anna's plea, putting her hand slowly into her pocket. When she withdrew it, she held the small opal ring in the air.

"We need your help," she began.

The dragon took another step forward. It was now practically towering over Dru. Its body had to be at least twenty feet high as it craned its neck down, keeping its teeth on display. The smoke, however, had stopped flowing from his nostrils. *Is that a good or bad sign?* Anna didn't know. She kept her arrow aimed at its right eye.

"Please," Dru said to the dragon. It beat its wings, sending a gush of wind that made Anna falter back, temporarily losing her aim.

"Get the book, Phil," Anna said. "We need to be ready when your magic—"

"Put the bow down, Anna," Dru whispered, glancing over her shoulder at Anna. "It won't trade with us until you put the bow down."

Everything in Anna screamed that putting her weapon down would seal their doom.

"Trust me," Dru pleaded.

Those two words silenced the screaming in her head. Dru was asking for her trust, even when Anna couldn't see it. Anna drew in a deep breath, then exhaled it slowly and lowered her bow.

She returned the arrow to her quiver with a shaky hand. Her mind and body screamed that this was foolish, but her heart was trusting Dru. Once Anna's bow and arrow were put away, the dragon moved closer to Dru, who was still holding the ring up toward its face.

"Your ring, Anna," Dru said, holding her hand out. "I need it to trade."

Anna slid her hand into her pants' right pocket. It was empty. The ring and letter were both gone.

"What is it?" Phil asked, seeing her go statue still.

Anna unfroze, shoving her hand into the left pocket. But it only contained the light. "Can we trade my light instead of the ring?" Her voice quivered.

"Dragons have no need for a light. They breathe fire," Dru said. The dragon nodded, shifting its feet. *Does it understand us?* "It's okay. I have more osmium to make you another ring," Dru added, mistaking why Anna asked about the light.

"I lost the ring," Anna admitted. "I'm so sorry."

"It's fine." Dru put her free hand into her pocket and pulled out the ring she created to make her floating bubbles. "I made this." She held the ring up next to the other one. The dragon blinked. "It's one of a kind. And it can do several things."

Dru slowly slid the ring on her finger and tapped it. Anna assumed Dru made herself go invisible because the dragon beat its wings. Dru tapped the ring again and came back into view. This time the dragon puffed a small cloud of smoke out of its nostrils. "It's yours in exchange for making this ring powerful enough to break a spell," Dru said. The dragon snatched the ring from her hand.

"I hope that's a yes," Phil said as the dragon eyed the ring dangling from its talon.

"I believe so," Dru answered. "Thank you," she added to the dragon. She held her right hand higher, showing the other ring.

The dragon moved its gaze from its new treasure. It breathed out a large puff of smoke, pushing its hot breath onto Dru and making her disappear into a cloud.

Anna gasped at the hot temperature of the dragon's breath from behind Dru. She reached for her bow, but Phil stopped her. "Look." The smoke was clearing, and Dru was standing in the same position, unharmed. And the ring she held…

"It's a dragon's breath stone," Dru said. The ring now housed a red stone that looked like dragon scales and blazed like fire. The stone was four times larger than the previous opal, and the band had changed from silver to black. "Thank you." Dru bowed her head. The dragon lowered its head, then pulled its ring close to its chest before lumbering out of sight.

"That was…" Phil started to say as Dru moved back toward them. "Well, I don't know what it was. But one thing's for sure. No one will believe us when we say we traded with a dragon."

"Don't be so sure," Dru said. "After we put the ring on Elzbeth, everyone will finally believe us."

Anna pulled her into a tight embrace. "Don't scare me like that again." Anna tightened her hug as her heart thundered.

"I promise," Dru said. "But we need to get going."

Anna squeezed Dru one more time.

"As long as Phil's magic is back?" Dru inquired.

"It is," he said, pulling the book from Anna's bag. Anna and Dru looped an arm through his and put their hands on the book as the title and table of contents appeared. *"Map of the Known,"* he said as the table of contents melted away, revealing the instructions and spell.

"I'll think about Daff's room as Phil uses his magic," Anna said. They both nodded.

"Think of a place you have been, but focus your mind not to spin. Concentrate while closing your eyes, then open them up for a big surprise,"

Dru read the spell aloud.

The *whoosh* sound of the book pulling them in had Anna opening her eyes. She looked over at her travel partners. Phil's eyes were clamped shut, but Dru's were wide open. There was a huge smile on her face. The book ejected them right on Daff's braided rug at the foot of her bed, then closed with a snap. Anna and Dru pulled their arms quickly from Phil's as he opened his eyes and caught the book before it slammed to the ground.

"Good catch," she whispered, grateful their arrival hadn't woken the household.

She moved to the side of Daff's tiny twin bed only to find it empty.

"Where is she?" Phil asked.

"No clue," Anna answered. "What time is it?" She turned from Daff's bed to the small clock on the wall. Anna gasped, throwing her hand over her mouth to muffle the sound. Phil and Dru turned quickly, both going rigid. Sitting in the worn wooden rocker, illuminated by the full moon casting in from the window, was none other than Fairy Godmother.

"I loved him so much," Cyndra cried into Elzbeth's shoulder. She glanced at Drury and Annalie, who were huddled together in a tight ball on one of the large, over-stuffed armchairs, sobbing.

"I know, dear." Elzbeth said the last word hesitantly, hoping it would work for her as it did for Bellenda. She knew Bellenda used the word because she couldn't keep names straight. Regardless, the endearing term seemed to work for her for the past decade, so Elzbeth thought it was worth a try. "I loved him too. Even if I only knew him for a short time."

One of the royal guards who'd come with Prince Edgar and Princess Cyndra coughed loudly. Elzbeth knew that cough. *Will.* Her body relaxed a fraction. It seemed she didn't have to do this completely alone.

Bellenda was up the entire night listening to wishes in the kingdoms of Wystfellia and Misteria. Elzbeth sent her home just moments after she arrived in her bedchamber, as Bellenda was practically dead on her feet after being up for over thirty-six hours.

Lord Beck had died in his sleep. Heart failure, according to the autopsy report that Gray created and Will would file at the documentation building. It was true. Augustus Beck's heart did fail. But the reason why? No one would ever know. Elzbeth had been poisoning his drinks for the past six weeks. Just a little each time, slowing his heart a bit more each day, until after months, it finally stopped.

However, when Augustus informed her yesterday that he'd found a husband who would double his wealth for fifteen-year-old Drury, three years before the legal Phannel marriage age, Elzbeth poured the entire bottle into his drink. It may have not been her best decision, but she couldn't let Drury be sold off to a man in his sixties.

It was by the grace of the Stars that Elzbeth didn't use her magic on him when he told her the news. But Drury and Annalie were safe now from their evil father. And hopefully, in a few months, living at the Sanctuary, where they could grow into adults who could choose if they want to marry. In taking their father, she was giving them their lives.

To keep with her story, Elzbeth waited until early morning to send a fire message to Princess Cyndra, who arrived immediately. Cyndra had only returned from her month-long honeymoon the night prior. Cyndra and Edgar had come with several guards, minutes before Drury and Annalie had woken. And now, they all were gathered in the parlor, where Cyndra clung to Elzbeth.

Prince Edgar stood, staring into the unlit fireplace. He seemed as uncomfortable as Elzbeth was, at a loss for how to comfort his new wife. Elzbeth gently patted the back of Cyndra's head. It was something she'd seen Bellenda do in the past that seemed to comfort the children. Cyndra stopped crying and pulled back, blinking away tears.

Elzbeth dabbed a handkerchief at her own tears. They were flowing freely, thanks to the trusted potion from her ring.

"May I get you anything, my love?" Prince Edgar asked.

"No," Cyndra answered, her voice slightly hoarse. "But Dru and Anna, do you need anything?" She turned to her sisters, who were clinging to one another. They pulled back, wiping their eyes with the back of their hands.

"No," Drury said softly. Her eyes were red and puffy, highlighted by dark half circles underneath them. Elzbeth wondered if she'd been up working on one of her inventions all night. Dru must've noticed Elzbeth staring. She smiled softly, nervously running her fingers through her hair, trying to tame the curls springing in all directions.

"Can I speak with you?" Annalie asked her oldest sister.

"Absolutely," Cyndra said, pushing a strand of her blonde hair from her face.

"Both of you," Annalie added, looking to Drury.

"Yes," Drury answered, still combing her fingers through her tangled hair.

"In private, please?" Annalie's tone shifted lower.

"Yes, of course we can—" Cyndra started.

"Sorry, my love, but you can't," Edgar cut Cyndra off. "You're a princess now, and your safety is priority, so you need to have a guard or myself with you at all times."

"But it's just my sisters—"

"I know." Edgar strode over and clutched her hand. "And we haven't discussed much how your life will be different now. But you are not to be alone with anyone except for me."

"Oh, okay," Cyndra looked from him to her sisters. "Anna, which would you prefer, a guard or Prince Edgar?"

"Prince Edgar," Annalie answered quickly.

"Alright," Cyndra said.

"Just you three," Annalie said softly, motioning to Drury, Cyndra, and Prince Edgar. But not Elzbeth. *Stupid spell, making the poor girl worry about hurting my feelings.* But Elzbeth couldn't care less. She welcomed the excuse to get out of the stuffy room and take a few breaths of the summer morning air.

"Do you mind?" Cyndra asked Elzbeth. The worry plastered on Cyndra's face made Elzbeth believe she was torn between her sister's request and trying to please her.

"Of course not. I need some fresh air. I'll take a walk."

Cyndra sighed with relief, a smile forming on her face. She gave Elzbeth a quick hug before saying, "We won't be long."

Elzbeth headed for the door, where Will stood dressed in a guard's uniform covering all of his face except his honey eyes. She heard the door shut behind her as she headed for the gardens. She needed a moment of peace. It was only eight in the morning, but the day already felt long.

"I'll accompany you, Lady Elzbeth," Will said, making her heart pieces flip. "You two, stay posted outside this door," he added to the other guards.

Steady, she warned herself. *We have months to go and still don't know who is behind the Link in Phannel.*

Elzbeth and Will stayed silent until they arrived in the gardens. She broke the quiet by saying, "So you're a royal guard now?" She spoke softly, just in case one of the gardeners who wasn't from the Sanctuary was out and about. She'd asked Augustus if she could hire a few more attendants as a wedding gift for herself. He'd agreed, and the next day, five associates from the Sanctuary were hired.

"What? You don't like the uniform, beautiful?" he teased, pulling his hooded mask back so she could see his face.

She rolled her eyes, but her heart pieces flipped again. *Stop that!* she inwardly scolded.

"I know I don't look beautiful beyond the spell. Not after an hour of nonstop tears. My eyes are aching," Elzbeth said.

He grabbed her hand, and her stomach somersaulted.

"What are you doing?" she hissed, looking around for prying eyes.

"How many times do I have to tell you?" he scolded, gently squeezing her hand. He leaned in close, and her heart pieces beat so rapidly she suddenly felt flooded with heat.

"You are the most stunning creature I've ever seen," Will insisted.

She rolled her eyes.

"If words won't work, then I'll show you." He leaned closer. Elzbeth found herself slowly inching forward.

They both jumped at horns blasting, announcing the arrival of the king and queen. The sound yanked Elzbeth's mind and heart from the green magical fog that puffed out of existence as suddenly as it had appeared.

"You were enchanting me to… to… kiss you!" she said, taking a step back, crossing her arms.

"No, Elz, I wasn't." He pulled his hand through his hair. "I mean, I was using it. But to keep us concealed. I would never compel you! I'm not like *him*. You have to know I'd never use my magic on you without your permission."

Elzbeth ran her hands down her skirt, straightening it. "King Tyson and Queen Lily have arrived. They'll expect me to greet them," she said.

He pulled the guard's hooded mask down, hiding his face, and she did the same with her heart, hiding what she was feeling and stepping back into the role of a grieving wife.

"Going somewhere, Annalie?" Elzbeth asked calmly. She had spotted Annalie opening the estate's front door on her way back from the kitchen. She'd not been able to sleep and had decided to make a snack, but Drury's latest invention had taken over the kitchen, making her instantly change her mind.

"Yes," Annalie replied, looking anywhere but at her. Elzbeth groaned internally. She hated being the villain, but Annalie gave her no choice. It was past curfew.

"Hmm." Elzbeth tapped the toe of her slipper, stalling until she could think of a suitable consequence. "Where were you sneaking out to at this late hour?"

"To Daff's," Annalie said, still refusing to look at her. Probably because of the shame her beauty spell was making her feel for displeasing her. She hated that it manipulated other's emotions. That it took away their free will.

"Well, you know, if you wanted to go to your friend's house, you should've asked me for permission."

"I didn't think I needed permission to go to Daff's. You let me go over all the time," Annalie said.

"True, but at a reasonable hour," Elzbeth stated. "Are you

aware what it might mean for us if you were caught out after curfew? Especially being the princess's sister." She shook her head. Elzbeth didn't need this headache on top of everything else her life had become in the past years. If Annalie were caught out after curfew, it would cause quite the stir. She could see the headline now from the busybody reporter at the *Fairytales, Facts, and Fables* newspaper: "Royal's Sleepless Knight for Roaming Sister." Or something ridiculous like that.

"Yes, I'm aware," Annalie answered.

There was a terrible bang, and something crashed in the kitchen. They both jumped at the explosive sounds.

"Drury!" Elzbeth called, gathering her skirt and running. Annalie got there first, maneuvering easily in her pants and boots. Elzbeth clenched her jaw. Oh, how she missed pants.

"I'm fine, Anna, honest," Drury was saying as Elzbeth entered the kitchen—or what she could see of the kitchen—which was now almost entirely covered by oozing orange slime.

"I was trying something new," Drury said, her voice calm until she spotted Elzbeth. "Oh, I'm sorry. I truly am." Drury held up her hands dripping with the orange substance. "I'll have it all cleaned up before breakfast preparations tomorrow. You have my word."

Elzbeth crossed her arms over her chest, taking in Drury's state to ensure she wasn't harmed. She couldn't care less about the condition of the kitchen. A kitchen could be replaced, but not Drury. Elzbeth let out a sigh of relief and nodded. "Yes, that's acceptable." She tried to sound like a proper parent. "And Annalie can help you clean up for her punishment of trying to sneak out after curfew."

"What?" Annalie protested.

The crackling of a fire message filled the room before the note popped out of thin air in front of Elzbeth. She snatched it, broke the seal, and read quickly.

High-ranking Link meeting happening at midnight. Catch you up tomorrow. W.

Her pulse quickened, forcing her to work overtime to stay composed.

"You heard me, Annalie," Elzbeth said after reading the message. "Help your sister clean this up, then straight to bed."

Annalie huffed.

"Either help Drury or a week of no going out besides working at the library. Your choice," Elzbeth added, trying to speed the encounter along so she could change and meet Will. She crossed her arms, waiting for Annalie to answer. Time was ticking.

"Fine," she said. "I'll help Dru."

"Good." Elzbeth turned on the toes of her slippers and exited the destroyed kitchen, which would keep the girls busy for hours and allow her the freedom to sneak out instead of Annalie.

⊠ ⊠ ⊠ ⊠ ⊠

When Elzbeth came back to her bedchamber, she found Bellenda sitting in one of her plush chairs, drinking from a wine bottle. "I thought after all these years, we were done sneaking into Link meetings," Bellenda said, gulping down a drink. "Will doesn't need us. He has it covered."

Bellenda petted Lucifer, who was curled in her lap, purring softly. Cyndra had given the cat to her and Augustus as a wedding gift. Elzbeth wasn't a cat person. Perhaps if Lucifer had been a puppy…

Growing up she'd always wanted a dog. A furry baby to love and cuddle. But she couldn't tell Cyndra. She'd been absolutely beaming upon gifting them the kitten. So she tolerated Lucifer, and he occasionally let her pet him. But he never cuddled with her like he did Bellenda.

"Desperate times call for desperate measures," Elzbeth said. She tore off her nightgown and put on a black tunic and pants, reaching for her matching boots.

"I'm not desperate," Bellenda said, taking another long draw from the bottle. "You and Will are." She pointed the bottle at Elzbeth. The cat's ears flicked as if in agreement.

"It's been years, Bell," she hissed. "Years of ensuring that Drury doesn't blow up anything or anyone, including herself." She exhaled, thinking of how her heart stopped when she'd heard the explosion. Drury was a brilliant girl who belonged at the Sanctuary. There, she could work with Grayson and his associates to get her inventions out into the world and help those with no magic. The Sanctuary, where Elzbeth didn't have to ensure Drury ate three times a day because she was so wrapped up in her current project that she forgot. The Sanctuary, where Drury wouldn't be forced to marry now that she was eighteen.

The last thought made Elzbeth's blood boil. She was sick and tired of the "potential callers" that filled her parlor these past months. She was running out of excuses to give Cyndra for not having chosen anyone suitable. She wished she could tell the princess the truth: she wasn't sure if Drury was being amicable due to her spell manipulating her emotions or if Drury truly wanted to be married.

"Well, if it weren't for her, the pumpkin would have burst before Cyndra made it to the ball," Bellenda countered with a giggle.

"You've had enough." Elzbeth snatched the wine bottle from her.

The pumpkin wouldn't have burst that quickly, but things certainly would've been harder if Bellenda hadn't had Drury's help that night.

"I don't understand what's gotten into you," Bell said. She stood, placing Lucifer on the ground, and snatched the bottle back.

"Annalie has gotten into me, that's what! The girl is *difficult*."

"She's a teenager."

"Who tests me every chance she can," Elzbeth countered. "I sleep in late each morning, missing her and Drury at breakfast, because I'm up the entire night, watching out my window to catch her sneaking out after curfew. Or returning! It's exhausting!"

Lucifer stretched out and jumped onto her bed, scratching the blanket before curling up.

"I told you to put a ward on her windows and doors," Bellenda offered.

"No!" Elzbeth said, harsher than intended. She plucked the cat from her bed and placed him into his ridiculously oversized cat bed. She took in a long breath and let it out slowly. "I will never lock a child in their room," she said more calmly. "But would it kill Annalie to ask my permission to go out or at least send me a fire message to let me know where she is, what she is doing, so I could sleep instead of pacing all night?"

"It appears you've taken a liking to them." Bellenda smirked before taking another long drink.

"No, I don't like them," Elzbeth said with a huff. "I tolerate them."

"Keep lying to yourself about that, just like you've been lying to yourself about Will for the past ten years," Bellenda said and took another big gulp. Red dribbles ran down her chin, soaking into her pink bodice.

"Okay, you're cut off." Elzbeth took the bottle again and downed the last gulp of wine before Bellenda could get it back. "And," she added, "you're grounded because you're drunk. I'm going alone."

"What?" Bellenda shouted.

"Shh. I don't need the girls hearing us. And why are you drinking so much, anyway?"

Bellenda fell back into her seat, flopping like a fish out of water as her pale pink skirt floated into place around her. "No particular reason. Just had my first night off in…" She held up a hand, trying to count on her fingers, but she kept losing count after three. Elzbeth had never seen her this drunk, and she knew it wasn't because she had a night off.

"What happened?" Elzbeth knelt before her best friend.

Bellenda looked away from her, plucking the small pouch of rings from the side table. She pulled it open, pouring them into her hand.

"I don't understand why you keep these," she said, looking up from the various wedding rings Elzbeth had received over the years.

"To remind me on the hard days that we're making a difference," she answered, swiping the rings from Bellenda's palm before pouring them back into the pouch. "But you're deflecting. What's going on? Did another wish go bad?"

"No," she said, flicking her eyes at the pouch of rings, then bursting into tears.

"Shit, Bell! Please, tell me what's wrong?" she asked more tenderly this time.

"James… he stood me up," she said between cries. "Last week, I answered his wish, and we were meeting up tonight to celebrate. But he…" She hiccupped. "He never came."

"I'll kill him." Elzbeth stood. "I knew he was only using you. Buttering you up with flowery promises of the life you'll have together after you answered his wish." She clenched her hands into fists. Her magic boiled to be released on the man who'd broken her best friend's heart. Like the others before him.

"No. I love him," Bellenda protested. "He was probably scared tonight because of my title, and—" The sound of crackling fire cut off her words as a fire message popped in front of Elzbeth.

She grabbed it before it floated to the floor and singed her rug. She had spent months redecorating the estate, making it brighter and cheerier than the dark woods and depressing colors that Augustus had used. Plus, it gave her a chance to add her secret door to meet up with Will or Bellenda without the girls knowing. She opened the message, thinking it was from Will, only to find it was from Prince Edgar.

"Cyndra's in labor."

"Finally!" Bellenda clapped. A smile formed on her face as if all signs of her broken heart had washed away. Until the next time someone used her for her magic and shattered her heart all over again.

"You're too drunk to deliver the baby. I'll send for a midwife."

"Nonsense! You know the Stars won't allow that," Bellenda exclaimed, jumping to her feet. "Royals are only delivered by *the* Fairy Godmother." She pulled her wand from her dress pocket and pointed it at her temple. "Sober, sense, and a cup of stew," she said. But no stardust fell from her wand. She frowned.

"Notebook," Elzbeth said, knowing Bellenda was right. Even if she were drunk, the Stars would yank her to deliver the Phannel royal baby when the time came for Cyndra to push. Bellenda had already been yanked multiple times from Elzbeth's sight in the past years to deliver children for the royal families across the various kingdoms.

"Right." Bellenda pulled the pink notebook from her dress pocket, flipping through it. She'd gotten a lot better at remembering details, but she still kept magic spells that she didn't use very often written down in it. "Here it is." She held her wand to her temple with her right hand as she read from the notebook. "Sober, sense, and stability too." The pale pink stardust danced from her wand, landing on her, cleaning her dress and fixing her hair in a blink of an eye.

"Does it also clear up hangovers?" Elzbeth asked as the

magic fizzled from sight, pulling Bellenda from her drunken state.

"Don't know. But we must go."

"Fine, but don't think we're done talking about why you were drinking tonight," Elzbeth said. Bellenda waved her wand, changing Elzbeth's comfortable dark clothing into a gown of pale yellow. "Permission," Elzbeth added, crossing her arms in front of her chest, the tiny beadwork cutting into her sensitive skin. "You're supposed to ask permission."

"No time to waste," Bellenda countered and waved her wand again, melting away Elzbeth's bedchamber and landing them inside the castle hallway outside Cyndra and Edgar's suite. Several guards turned on them, swords drawn. But once they saw that it was Fairy Godmother and the beautifully spelled Elzbeth, they relaxed and put their swords away.

"Good, you're here," King Tyson said behind Elzbeth, making her quickly whirl around. "Edgar and I aren't much help. We thought Queen…" He stopped his words, shaking his head slightly. "We thought my wife would be here." He exhaled a long breath as tears pricked the corners of his eyes.

"I know, Your Majesty," Bellenda said sweetly. "But all will be well. Let me go check on Princess Cyndra, and I'll come out in a moment to give you an update."

He nodded, and Bellenda slipped into the room, leaving Elzbeth alone with him and several guards.

"I'm sorry you must see me in this state," he addressed her, and she bowed lowly. "Please don't do that." He waved his hand at her. "We're about to share a grandchild. Unless we have a public audience, there is no need to bow before me."

"Yes, Your Majesty." She forced herself to not shudder from his words. *Grandchild*. She was too young to be a grandmother at thirty-three.

"And it's Tyson." He smiled.

"Okay, Tyson." She smiled back.

"Well, I could really use a drink," he said after a few moments of silence. "Care to join me?"

"Yes, please," she agreed quickly, thankful for the excuse to not linger outside the room where her very young twenty-one-year-old stepdaughter was birthing a child. A baby that she'd now be required to hold, coo over, and say so many ridiculous things about. "I could really use a drink too."

"Wake up, beautiful," Will said softly.

Elzbeth slowly opened her eyes. Will was kneeling before her, dressed in a royal guard's uniform with the hooded mask pulled back. She blinked, trying to recall why she fell asleep in the oversized chair in the king's personal library.

The baby, she remembered. "Has it arrived?" She sat up, stretching out the kinks in her back from sleeping in a tight ball.

"Yes, it has. But you probably should call him Prince Augustus." He chuckled softly.

She nodded knowingly, even though she hated it all. Several months had turned into several years, and now Cyndra had named her son after her evil father because she didn't know the truth.

"But I'm not here to tell you about the baby," Will continued as she stretched out her arms. Dresses were the most ridiculous things to wear. But to sleep in them? That was even worse. She could feel where the beads dented into her ribs and rubbed at the sore spots. "How much did you drink last night?" he added, looking her over.

"Don't know. Lost count after Tyson started telling me stories."

"Tyson, is it?" he clipped.

"Yes, and he's actually quite nice," she said. "He also has no clue what to do with a baby, so he invited me here for drinks and we ended up talking." She yawned. "Well, he did most of the talking, especially once the drinks were flowing. But he isn't so bad."

Will's jaw clenched.

"*And,*" she added on account of his reaction, "he doesn't fall all over me like others do when under my spell. I think it's because he's grieving his wife's passing," she said, referring to the passing of the king's wife of almost thirty years only four months prior. "Which is a good thing. Not her death, of course. But him being nice," she corrected. "What I mean is… that I'm glad he was comfortable with me. When we finally know who's behind the Link in Phannel, I'll be able to tell him."

"It's him."

"What's him?" She stood, stretching out further.

"The king. Tyson, that is." He gave her a look of disgust. "He's behind the Link in Phannel."

"What?" she blurted. Her eyes widened. Will couldn't possibly mean what he was saying.

"Last night at the Link's meeting, there were documents circulating with Phannel's royal seal approving the sale of fifteen underage girls from Phannel to Lexlent."

"No," she said on a long breath. "Maybe you were mistaken. There's just no way—"

"It's not a mistake," he said and pulled a piece of parchment paper from his pocket and handed it to her. She scanned the document. King Tyson's royal seal and signature were at the bottom of the contract.

Shit.

"The bastards were celebrating bringing Lexlent's royals into the underground like it was the victory of the century." Will clenched his teeth.

"This doesn't make sense! It has to be a fake." Her face scrunched. "You know the Link has men with many talents. And forging the royal seal and signature is within the realm of possibility."

"I know. I thought that could be a possibility, too. So I did some digging and found past documents for the selling of underage girls from Phannel to Tranik, six months ago, that also bear his royal seal," he said.

"How? The borders are closed." Her mind spun, trying to put it all together. The kind, broken-hearted man she had drinks with last night who was devastated over his wife's death was actually a cold-hearted king, endorsing the sale of underage girls?

"Closed for commoners, but apparently not for royals to make deals." Will seethed, anger flashing in his eyes.

"What do we do now?" she asked, unsure what to make of it all. "Our entire plan hinged on telling Tyson about the Link! But if he's a part of it?" *Have the last years been a waste?*

"You're doing nothing." Will slipped the contract from her fingers, putting it back in his pocket. "I, on the other hand, will be going with the girls for the trade."

"No, that's too risky!" she argued. "You can't go to Lexlent! What about your father? You said he was powerful and had eyes and ears all over the kingdom!"

"It's a risk I have to take. I need to find out who the girls are being sold to, get them to the Sanctuary, and end this thing."

"No, absolutely not." She stepped closer to him.

"Worried about me, beautiful?" He dipped his head, his honey eyes blazing into hers, only inches separating their faces. Her stomach somersaulted.

"Of course I am. You and Bell are my best friends."

Will laughed.

"What's so funny?" she asked, not seeing any humor in the risky situation he was proposing.

"You," he answered, taking a step back.

"Me?" Elzbeth questioned. "How am I possibly being funny?"

"Never mind. I should know by now that there will be no convincing you." He exhaled and waved his hand at his face. A light blue puff of his magical smoke hit it, changing his features before he pulled the hooded mask down. "We need to go so I can escort you to your new grandson," he said coldly, making her shiver.

It wasn't his words; it was his magic. He hadn't used anything but the green of her skin these past years. Her heart pieces squeezed.

"Will, we need to talk." She stepped toward him. She needed to fix this. She needed to make him understand. But he didn't stop.

He made it to the door. When he opened it, two guards were standing just outside, and she forced herself into the role of the princess's stepmother. But as she passed him, she spoke softly, for his ears only.

"Later."

"You've been quiet," Bellenda said once she shut the door to Elzbeth's room.

"The girls?" Elzbeth asked, looking at the clock on her wall. The hands pointed at 9:30 a.m.

"On their way to the castle to meet their nephew," Bellenda said. "Isn't he the most handsome thing?" she added, beaming with delight. Elzbeth knew how much she loved children, but she had more pressing issues to discuss than how cute a newborn baby was.

"Will discovered a contract last night with Tyson's royal seal on it for the Link." The words scrambled off her tongue, laced with the relief of sharing the news with Bellenda. "He thinks King Tyson is the leader of the Link in Phannel."

"I know. He spoke to me before he went to get you," Bellenda said, moving to the small table where breakfast was laid out for them. She plucked a strawberry and began devouring a piece of toast.

"Why aren't you concerned?"

"Why would I be?" Bellenda asked between bites.

"Because Will is going on the trade." *Why do I have to spell this out for her?*

"I know," Bellenda said again, giving Elzbeth a confused look.

"And you don't care about Will's safety?" she asked, her voice rising.

"Of course I do. But Will has been on several of these trips now."

"Yes, but never to Lexlent!" Elzbeth spat.

Bellenda froze mid-bite, dropping the half-eaten piece of toast onto the table.

"You didn't know," Elzbeth said.

Bellenda shook her head.

"Well, now you do. So please back me up when we see him next and tell him it's too dangerous to go."

"I can't," Bellenda said, swallowing hard.

"Bell, you have to—"

"He's already left," Bellenda said, slumping into one of the chairs by the table.

Elzbeth was at a loss for words. She reeled, wracking her brain and trying to remember what she'd read on the document. "The contract said the ship was leaving tonight," she said.

"Will told me the ship was leaving two hours ago," Bellenda countered.

"He lied." Elzbeth's voice cracked. "Enchanted the document to deceive me!"

Bellenda stood, stepped toward her, and grabbed her into a tight hug.

"He'll be fine," she whispered softly into Elzbeth's hair. "It's Will, he'll be…" She paused as Elzbeth let out a broken cry. For the first time in years, she was shedding real tears. Will had lied to her.

You know that's not why you're crying, a small voice said in the back of her mind. But she ignored it, letting the tears fall and telling herself they were angry tears for Will's deception. Not because she might never see him again to tell him how she truly felt.

"**D**amn it!" Dru exclaimed.

"Language, Lady Drury," Fairy Godmother said. She stood up from Daff's rocking chair and pointed her wand at the three of them.

"What are you doing here?" Anna demanded. "And where's Daff?"

"I think I'll be the one asking the questions, Annalie," Fairy Godmother said with a soft smile.

No, no, no! Anna's mind screamed. She didn't have the ring. Her magic was going to ruin everything.

"I see you've been busy popping about in the map spell book." It was a statement, thankfully. She pointed her wand at the book in Phil's hands. "The question is—"

"I don't think we've been properly introduced," Phil interrupted in a regal tone. He passed the book to Dru and extended his good hand to Fairy Godmother. *Should I run? Is Phil giving me a chance to escape before Fairy Godmother asks me more questions?*

"Yes, Prince Rupert, I believe we have not." She smiled sweetly at him, lowering her wand and extending her other hand. He lifted it as he lowered his head. But before his lips touched her skin, he yanked her arm. She tripped forward, losing her grasp on her wand. It clanged against the wood near Anna's feet.

"What in the Stars?" Fairy Godmother protested. Phil twisted her around, her thin, pale pink skirt swooshing with the motion, not settling before he brought his dagger to rest against her throat. "Prince Rupert, you need to—"

"It's Prince Phil. And you need to stop talking before I am forced to make you." His icy words licked a chill down Anna's spine as her heart fluttered like a caged bird. She liked this side of the prince. He was commanding and assured, not hiding who he truly was. He was also protective, ensuring Anna's magic didn't force her to answer Fairy Godmother's questions.

"Phil, maybe we should talk," Dru said. "We don't want to do anything rash."

"Where is Daff?" Phil demanded, ignoring Dru.

"The castle," Fairy Godmother answered, glancing between Anna and Dru.

"Why?" Anna asked, glancing at Daff's clock, whose hands rested at 12:30 a.m.

"Because something happened when King Tyson used his magic on her."

"What happened?" Anna commanded, grabbing Fairy Godmother's wand and pointing it at her like a sword.

"A deep sleep," she said, eyes widening at her wand wielded against her. Anna didn't know if she could use it. She didn't care so long as the woman who'd been helping her wicked step-mother answered their questions and didn't ask any of her own.

"We don't know why," she continued to explain. "Daffodil crumpled to the floor when King Tyson used his magic on her. I tried to wake her, but I couldn't. Cyndra sent word to her mother that she was staying with you to celebrate the engagement tomorrow, well, today that is, so she doesn't worry."

"Then why are you here?" Anna eyed her suspiciously. She didn't trust Fairy Godmother one bit. It could all be a story or a trap and they were holding Daff now.

"Because Elzbeth sent me to let you girls know about Daffodil. But when you weren't home, I checked the library next. When you weren't there, I came here and was taking a moment to sit and think where else you might be. And then, you popped out of the book." She waved at the tome in Dru's hands. "I haven't seen it in years, and I am curious. What have you—"

No! Anna's mind screamed again, waiting for her magic to force her to answer Fairy Godmother's question.

"Why didn't Elzbeth come herself?" Dru cut the question short, saving Anna from confessing what they'd been up to.

"Because she's consoling King Tyson," Fairy Godmother explained. "He feels responsible for Daffodil's condition. I sent for a healer who is strong in magic, but he won't arrive from the Wystfellia kingdom until after the engagement announcement."

Anna looked at Dru, wondering what she thought. Her sister was shaking her head, a furious furrow etched on her face. Anna's eyes grew. She was unaccustomed to an angry Dru since she fell under Elzbeth's spell.

"A word, Dru." Anna grabbed her arm with her free hand, tugging her toward Daff's door and out of Fairy Godmother's hearing. "What do we do now?"

"My ring. I think..." Dru stumbled over each word. She drew in a deep breath and continued more smoothly, "Daff is in a deep sleep because *I* had her use my ring. It must have been too much for her, using the ring and then having King Tyson use his magic on her." She balled her hands into fists, her anger washing away, replaced with a look of guilt.

"This isn't your fault," Anna whispered. "Even if that *is* what happened." She wasn't entirely convinced it was. "This is all Elzbeth's doing. But we need to figure out if it's true, and if so, then we need to figure out a way to wake Daff before the ceremony or find another way to enchant the ring."

Anna hated the last option, putting her best friend second. But if Daff really was in a deep sleep, then they'd need another way to enchant the ring and expose Elzbeth first before focusing on waking Daff.

"Fairy Godmother is telling the truth," Dru said. Anna opened her mouth to argue, but Dru said quicker, "Trust me. Tinker and I have done a lot of research on double magic, or invention and magic in this case, when used on someone. And we even started working on an elixir, but we don't have any yet, so it will take me some time to create it."

"How much time?" Anna asked.

Dru's face grew serious. Anna waited while she ran calculations in her head for all she needed to do.

"Nine hours, give or take," she said after a few moments.

Anna's shoulders slumped. "That's cutting it close."

"I know," Dru agreed with a heavy sigh. There were dark circles under her eyes. She looked weary. They were all running on little to no sleep

"We need to get home fast so you can start working. But what do we do with Fairy Godmother?" Anna glanced over her shoulder. Phil still held his dagger to her throat with one arm while the other held her tightly around the waist. "Never mind, it looks like Phil can handle watching her just fine," she said moving back towards them. "Is there somewhere you can take her that no one will find you while Dru works on a way to wake Daff?" Anna asked Phil.

"Oh, do you think you can, Lady Drury?" Fairy Godmother asked in a hopeful tone, her eyes suddenly twinkling.

"Quiet!" Phil barked. Fairy Godmother stiffened as tingles ran down Anna's spine. She liked this side of him. No longer the victim, Phil was a far cry from the prince locked away in his tower.

"Yes, I'll use the book to get us there undetected," he said softer to Anna, nodding at Dru, who was still holding the book. "Hand it to Fairy Godmother."

"No, I—"

"I said, quiet," he growled by her ear. Fairy Godmother swallowed hard. The gesture put the slightest nick in her skin, releasing tiny blood droplets that ran down her throat. "Hand her the book," Phil said calmly to Dru. She nodded and placed the book in Fairy Godmother's hands.

"You children don't understand…" Fairy Godmother started.

Phil pressed the blade deeper, turning the droplets to a trickle and darkening the bodice of her dress. "Unless you want to confess responsibility for helping your wicked friend," he threatened.

Her eyes widened, but she said nothing. "Thought so," he said after a few heartbeats. He lifted his hand from her waist and touched the book. It opened, and Phil said quickly, *Map of the Known.* " The spell appeared.

He read it and shut his eyes before they were sucked into the glowing book, disappearing in the next blink of an eye.

"Please put this in my quiver." Anna held Fairy Godmother's wand out to Dru.

"Sure, but can I have it to examine later?"

"Absolutely," Anna said and handed it to her. "Grab Daff's sheet, and we'll tie it to something to help us climb out the window."

Dru started to strip the bed as Anna surveyed her best friend's room for what would hold them to tie it to. Nothing seemed like it would work except for Daff's bed, and that was too far from the window to be of any use.

"I really wish you still had that bubble ring," Anna grumbled, taking the top sheet from Dru.

Dru started putting the blanket back on the bed, ensuring they wouldn't leave a trail. "How do you feel about swinging out the window?" Anna asked, setting the sheet down and pulling the spelled arrow out of her bag.

"Fine."

"Really?" Anna questioned. "You normally aren't one for daring ventures."

"I trust you, Anna." She felt her entire body soften at Dru's declaration. The words were like a balm to her wounded heart. She blinked away a couple tears.

"Alright, then," she said and pulled another arrow from her quiver, which she used to make several slashes into the sheet. That done, she replaced the regular arrow before tearing the sheet into three foot-wide strips.

"I should have told you about the ring and told you about Daff using it sooner," Dru said as she tied each strip to the arrow, one behind the other.

"I understand why you didn't," Anna said, braiding the pieces together. "But I'm not sure why Daff didn't tell me when she was free of Elzbeth's spell." She mentally kicked herself for inviting Daff over last week, who then saw Elzbeth and fell under it again. "I wonder why Daff didn't make up an excuse to not come over and fall back underneath Elzbeth's spell?"

"She wanted to tell you," Dru said. Anna knotted the end of the braid. "But I was still figuring the ring out, so I asked her to come."

"Oh," Anna replied. "That makes sense. But I wish I could've been a part of the experiment."

"I'm sorry, Anna. You should've been. But I let my fear win out." Dru sighed. "I was afraid of you knowing and then…"

"My magic spilling the truth."

"Yes. And I'm sorry," Dru apologized again. "It's why I started working on the ring for you."

"It's okay. You were wise to keep it a secret." Anna worked overtime to make her voice sound normal as her heart squeezed. Before Elzbeth entered their lives and Anna's truth-telling magic appeared, they had told each other everything. She missed that.

"Look. It will all be different after tomorrow," Dru said. "Once we break Elzbeth's spell and I make you a new ring, I promise no more secrets."

"I like the sound of all of that," Anna replied, smiling at Dru, who smiled in return.

"So, I'm guessing your arrow is spelled," Dru said.

"Yes."

Anna opened the window slowly, trying not to make any more noise than they already had. An oak tree grew near the window, several of its limbs reaching up and over. She surveyed the branches, trying to find her best target based off the length of the sheet, which looked to be maybe six feet long. She crawled out the window onto the short ledge, which couldn't be more than a foot deep. Dru gave her the arrow. She held it for a second, feeling the weight of the braided sheet. She slid the tied pieces toward the arrow's tip, then readied it in her bow. Dru climbed out, bringing the end of the sheet with her and holding tight at the knotted end with both hands.

"Ready?" Anna asked.

"Yes."

"Alright, on the count of three, I'm going to shoot the limb, then grab onto you."

"Got it," Dru said, white-knuckling the sheet knot.

Anna turned back to the limb. *Breathe in, breathe out.* "One." She angled her bow a bit higher. *Breathe in, breathe out.* "Two." She focused on her target. And… "Three."

She released the arrow, which landed in the center of the limb. The braided sheet tumbled behind. Anna grabbed Dru's waist just as she was yanked from the ledge, sending them both careening toward the trunk. *Snap!* Blinding pain seized Anna's head and back as she collided into the unforgiving ground before she was crushed by Dru, who landed on her chest, knocking the air from her lungs. Dru rolled off quickly as Anna fought to pull in a wheezed breath.

"Are you okay?" Dru asked, dropping the sheet that fell with them when the limb broke.

Her magic had her nodding because she couldn't speak. Dru put her hands out to help her sit up slowly. She managed to pull in a couple ragged breaths, each one easing the pain. "I'm fine."

"Are you sure?" Dru looked Anna over again.

"Yes," Anna said, moving slowly to her feet. "Sure, I'll have bruises all over my body for a few weeks, but I'm fine."

"Unfortunately, we can't say the same about your arrows," Dru said before pulling Fairy Godmother's wand from the quiver and turning it over. Thankfully, it looked unharmed.

"The good news is the wand is unharmed. I've got more arrows at home," Anna replied, slinging the bow over her shoulder and grabbing the spelled arrow that was still stuck in the broken limb. She yanked and wiggled it a few times until it finally came free. "I guess that wasn't my best escape plan." She untied the last knot. Dru pulled the rest of the braided sheet into her arms as Anna put the spelled arrow into the quiver. They moved quickly into the woods, which were about fifty yards behind Daff's house.

"We didn't have time to come up with a better one," Dru said as they stepped into the woods. "Plus, it worked." She gave Anna a smile of approval that practically made her float.

"What can I do to help with the elixir?" Anna asked. Her stomach growled fiercely, and she tried to recall when she last ate. "I probably should eat something first."

They picked up their pace. Anna held her light out to ensure they didn't trip on the deer path that led to their estate grounds.

"I think the last time I ate was technically a day ago, and it wasn't much."

"Mm-hmm," Dru replied. Anna knew Dru wasn't listening. Her mind was calculating what she needed to do to wake Daff.

Her stomach growled again, right before they turned the corner leading to their estate. They jogged down the slope. They made it all the way to below Anna's bedchamber window when carriage wheels crunching on the gravel drive stopped them in their tracks. Anna grabbed Dru's hand and yanked her toward the front of the estate. They peeked around the corner's edge.

"No!" Anna whispered at the carriage barreling up the drive. She let go of Dru's hand and turned to run toward her window. She scrambled behind the bushes, grabbing the rope that hung there. "Climb," she commanded, grabbing the sheet Dru still clutched and tossing it behind the bushes. Dru shoved the wand into Anna's quiver and started up the rope. Anna waited for Dru to get a few feet up before following, ignoring the screaming protest of her abused muscles.

"Faster," she whispered as the carriage wheels crunched at the front of the estate. They were just past the first level and needed to climb two more.

Anna's heart raced as Dru moved slowly up the rope. *Pick up the pace!* She knew Dru wasn't as accustomed to climbing ropes, but she silently pleaded with her sister to go faster as they passed the second story.

Nine more feet and a quick dash under the covers, and Anna would be in her bed, and Dru would dart into her bedroom window. She knew Elzbeth would check on them. Luckily, she would go to Anna's room first, since her door was closest to the top of the stairs. Plus, she was the one who made a habit of sneaking out.

Dru finally reached Anna's window and stepped onto the ledge. She let go of the rope and started to shuffle the last few feet to her window as Anna maneuvered onto the ledge. She didn't pause before diving through her window, trusting Dru would make it.

Anna jumped on top of her bed, which she thankfully never made, and threw the covers over her body just as she heard the sound of Elzbeth's footsteps passing by outside her door. Dru's door opened with a slight creak, then shut loudly, followed by Elzbeth's footsteps marching back to her room.

What am I going to do if Elzbeth decides to wake me and asks questions?

Something thudded on the floor behind her. *Has Lucifer gotten into my room again through the open window?* The handle jiggled as the latch clicked. The covers lifted behind her, then fell quickly as Dru curled in beside her, holding the comforter just below their chins.

Thirty~Three

ELZBETH: 4 DAYS, 16 HOURS BEFORE THE CLOCK STRIKES 12

"Sleep tight, dear," Elzbeth said, using Bellenda's go-to word. She reached into the crib and brushed the silver diamond-shaped ring over Prince Augustus's lips. The ring was laced with several drops of sleep serum that coated his lips. The almost one-year-old jutted his tiny tongue out to lick the sweet serum clean. Seconds later he yawned widely, falling into a deep sleep.

"You're a natural," King Tyson, Elzbeth's new target, said from the nursery doorway.

She knew exactly when he'd slipped in. She timed her putting the prince to bed just like she had the other nights when she volunteered to watch him these past weeks. Tonight's excuse to get some alone time with the king? Elzbeth offered Cyndra and Edgar an evening away from the castle before the tiny prince's first birthday party.

This served a double purpose. Though Elzbeth would probably deny it, she saw how exhausted Cyndra was lately. Watching a child wasn't Elzbeth's ideal situation to get time alone with the king, but it was what she'd decided to do to take matters into her own hands.

"He's an easy babe," Elzbeth said, turning to face Tyson with a seductive smile. *Especially when you have Gray and his all-natural remedies he created for the children at the Sanctuary to help Augustus sleep,* she told herself to ease the guilt of using the sleep serum on the prince. Again.

"He is. For certain people with the magic touch." He matched her smile. "My wife, she also had the touch with…" He paused. "With Edgar." He let out a long breath and held out his arm to escort her from the nursery. She looped her arm through his and shut the door quietly, nodding at the two guards standing outside the little prince's room before heading down the hall. "A drink in my library while you wait for Edgar and Cyndra?" Tyson offered.

"Yes, that would be lovely," Elzbeth said. Her lips twitched at how easy this was going to be. Between her beauty spell and the mended broken heart potion she finally created, she'd have Tyson proposing before Cyndra and Edgar were back.

She'd hoped by now he'd be over his broken heart, but apparently he loved his wife dearly. The man was committed to Queen Lily. She'd give him that much credit, even if he was supposedly behind the Link in Phannel. She hadn't been able to get any information out of him about that over the last weeks. She needed to up her game. Her beauty spell alone couldn't conquer his heartbreak, which was why she'd started working on the mending potion.

They entered his private library, nodding at the two guards stationed outside the doors as they entered before closing themselves in for some privacy. She forced herself to breathe in through her nose and out her mouth, not letting Tyson see how much the mahogany room affected her.

"Stupid girl." Her father's words rang in her ears. *"If you can't master your emotions, then I'll have the servant boy spell them into submission."*

She could easily avoid the royal city library by sending fire messages for Annalie whenever she needed her. But not this one. Tyson always insisted they have their drinks and chats in it.

She ran her finger across a few leather spines, pushing her father's words away and focusing on her task while Tyson poured their drinks. She would pour a second. That way she could put the potion in his drink, undetected.

Elzbeth pulled a book off the shelf and flipped through the pages. It was a silly fairytale about a prince rescuing, yet again, a woman in distress. Why were there no books about a princess saving a man in distress? Or better yet, why couldn't the man and woman be equals, fighting together for a better world?

"That's one of my favorite stories," Tyson said behind her, making her jump. She hadn't heard him approach. Elzbeth closed the book and slid it back onto the shelf, turning to face him. She took the glass of amber liquid that he held out to her.

"Yes, I like that one too," she said, forcing a smile she knew would appear sweet as pie on her spelled face. "How the prince saves her, and they fall in love." She batted her lashes before taking a small sip. She wouldn't be drinking much; she needed to keep her wits tonight. Tyson's eyes tracked the glass and stopped on her lips as she licked them after taking the small taste.

"Me too," he replied with a sad sigh. "Sometimes I wish I could use my own magic on myself." He walked over to the sofa and sat down with his drink. She followed, taking another sip but not too much. She hoped it would help to ease her pain if she had to listen to another hour of how much he loved his wife before she could drug him. "You know, to forget the pain of losing… her," he added.

Oh, how she knew. The two parts of her heart clenched as he threw back the amber liquid and swallowed in one gulp.

"Here, let me get you some more." She took the glass, brushing her fingers over his knuckles.

"Thank you," he said, his words slurring.

"Tyson, are you okay?" she asked as his eyes shut. Her words weighed heavy on her tongue as she reached for him, and the room began to spin, sending her tumbling. "Ty…"

"Elzbeth," Will said in her dream. He visited her there most nights. When she managed to sleep and wasn't up worrying about Annalie, Drury, or the king who wouldn't fall under her spell, that was.

"Wake up, beautiful," he prodded. She ignored him. She didn't want to wake. She wanted five more minutes away from being responsible for two adolescent girls and an entire kingdom that was depending on her because Will had left and… Something sour hit her nostrils, sending her into a coughing fit and yanking her from her dream.

She looked around and froze. She had no memory of leaving the castle and coming to her home. A home she hadn't seen in almost four years because it was too risky to come to the Sanctuary.

But that wasn't even the biggest shock.

Will.

He was cradling her in his arms.

"What's going on?" she asked groggily, clearing her throat. "Where's Tyson?"

"He's fine," Will said, brushing a strand of hair from her face. "But he'll be out for the rest of the night, so I brought you here."

"What?" she gasped and pushed at his arms. "Why?"

She was angry. She had plans for the king tonight, and Will had interfered. Will, who she hadn't touched in the flesh all year. Will, who sent fire messages maybe every other month to let them know he was still alive but not much more than that, and nothing in the past three months. She was livid.

"Seems Bellenda was right," he said.

"About what?" She practically spit fire at him.

"That you are cozying up with the king." He released her, letting her stand as he followed suit.

"I'm not cozying up with Tyson." It was a half-truth. She hadn't gotten that far.

"Liar." He smiled his stupid smirk and held up the small bottle of amber potion that she'd created to put in Tyson's drink. Elzbeth swiped it from his hand, putting it back in her dress pocket.

"Well, I'm not the only liar in this room," she said. The veins on her neck pulsed, emphasizing each word.

"I had to. There was no way you would've let me go to Lexlent."

"Exactly!" She nearly erupted with all the anger she'd built up over the last year with his absence. "You knew we'd stop you because it was a foolish idea."

"No risk, no reward," he said and took a step closer.

"Well, there you go." She stepped back, flipped her skirts, and turned for the hall. Elzbeth couldn't do this now. She had more important matters to attend to, like thinking of a new plan to get the potion into Tyson's drink so he would propose to her. She needed a plan that neither Will nor Bell could intercept.

He gently grabbed her arm and turned her around to face him. "I'm sorry. It killed me to lie to you," he said softly. "But I had to because I knew if you didn't let me go…" He shook his head.

"I would volunteer myself to cozy up to the king," she said.

Will nodded. Their eyes lingered on each other as their silence enveloped them.

"So, instead of me getting close to Tyson to find out if he's behind the Link in Phannel, you decided to put your life at risk?"

"Yes," he growled, letting go of her and throwing a hand through his jostled hair. "You have no idea what it's like to watch you with those *monsters*." He spat the last word, drawing in a breath before saying more calmly, "I'm not here to argue with you."

"Really, you could've fooled me," she said cooly, knowing he was trying to diffuse the conversation. She still had a lot she wanted to say to him.

"Later." Will smirked. "Later, you can berate me with how much heartache you suffered in my absence."

"You're insufferable." She crossed her arms in front of her chest to guard against him knowing how right he was, seeing him here now, alive. The wall she'd built around her heart pieces the past year began to crack.

"Who, me?" He put a hand to his chest, feigning surprise, knowing he'd gotten her to back off, for now. "But we do need to talk because I've discovered some things that you need to know if we're going to continue with your plan," he added in a more serious tone and waved at the pocket that held her potion.

"You're going to help me?" she asked, unraveling her arms.

"Yes, although it's against my better judgement." He shook his head, making his blue-black hair flop back and forth. He was weeks past needing a cut, meaning his hair fell perfectly across his face, accentuating his cheekbones. Exactly how she liked it.

"Stop that!" Elzbeth said, knowing what he was doing.

"What?" he asked innocently, his honey eyes blazing.

She said nothing, holding his gaze.

"Fine," he said after a few heartbeats. "I can see you are not in a teasing mood."

"What was your first clue?" she deadpanned. Oh, how easily they fell back into their normal banter.

He took a cleansing breath; all jokes washed from his face as he said, "There are a few things you need to know before we start down the dangerous path of seducing the king."

"Alright," she said, moving to the couch.

He sat next to her. "I'm sorry I haven't been in contact much. But when I went to Lexlent, I heard some murmurs from those within the Link about a beautiful woman taking on a different alias to marry wealthy men across several kingdoms, only to kill them for their money and titles."

Her eyes widened as he continued.

"So, I spent a few weeks following a few of the members only for it to all lead to nothing. I was hoping to find out who was behind the rumors and silence them. But I never tracked down who was spreading the rumors. I ended up retracing the steps of our past *missions.*" He said the last word sourly. "Nothing stood out, at least from what I could see. Until one night I overheard a side conversation between two members at a Link meeting. They were talking about making birth certificates disappear for the underage girls."

She sat, stunned by this revelation. Will raked his hands through his hair as he continued.

"I followed them to their contact and discovered that the Link has been paying off documentation officials to create new papers. They replace the documents for those not kept in high security offices and make documents from high security offices disappear."

"Not sure what this has to do with the underage girls' documents being altered or disappearing. We knew they did this type of thing," Elzbeth said, feeling as though she was missing something.

"Because of the rumors about you," he said, "I went to the documentation office that we filed our first mission's report at."

"Oh," she said, connecting the dots. "You went to see if the autopsy report was still there?"

"Yes," he answered. "And it was, but not the one we created." Her eyes widened. "I took it and checked all the others. They were the same as the first. Someone has been replacing the ones we planted."

Her jaw dropped.

"I've been trying for the last several months to figure out who replaced them but had no luck until last month, when I pulled Lord Beck's report." He pulled a paper from his tunic pocket and handed it to her. "It's the one we planted." Her brows scrunched together. "Exactly. I, too, was confused. I went back the next day to enchant the security guards and get some answers, only to discover someone else had come uninvited into the documentation office the night prior, just after I left."

"You'd beaten whoever was replacing the false reports?" Elzbeth asked as the paper trembled in her hand.

"I'm not sure." He cleared his throat. "The security guards told me a royal guard had come and said that several buildings had been broken into that night, and they wanted to check out the building. But the royal guard wasn't alone. He had an accomplice, using invisibility magic to go into the filing rooms. But his magic sputtered out. They both fled, but not before one of the security guards caught a glimpse of the person using the invisibility magic. He said he looked a lot like Prince Edgar."

"Edgar doesn't have invisibility magic."

Will stood and began to pace. "Exactly. I went back that night and searched through the royals' files and discovered this." He pulled another paper from his pocket and handed it to her. "It was enchanted to not be seen," he added.

She unfolded it quickly. "Adoption papers?"

"Yes. Look at the names on it." He pointed at the child's name first.

"Rupert Phillip," she read aloud. "Doesn't ring a bell."

"Read the next line." He pointed at the line naming the individuals surrendering the child for adoption.

"Princess Fern and Prince Leo." She scrunched her brows, reading the child's birthdate, doing the math quickly. "This doesn't make sense. According to his birthdate, Rupert is seventeen, and Prince Leo died over twenty years ago."

"Look at who adopted him." Will pointed at the bottom of the document.

"Queen Lily."

"Just Queen Lily. Not the king." She flicked her eyes up at him. "Why do you think King Tyson didn't adopt his identical twin brother's son?" Will asked.

She flicked her eyes back to the birthdate. Three years after Leo died. But why, then, was his name on… Elzbeth gasped, drawing a conclusion. Before the idea completely solidified, she asked, "Why would the royals enchant this document to not be seen?"

"Why indeed?" Will replied arching a brow. "Could it be they were trying to cover up something? Possibly a king's death?"

"What if King Tyson died falling from the balcony instead of Prince Leo? Leo could take the king's place, and no one would be the wiser," she said, voicing the conclusion she was nearly certain of.

"That is what I think happened," Will said. "To lose Prince Leo would be devastating to his family and friends, but to lose the king would impact not just his inner circle but the entire kingdom. Remember what was happening between the kingdoms of Tranik and Phannel when Prince Leo died?"

She nodded, remembering the newspaper articles that Thomas snuck to her to read. The king of Tranik had conquered the kingdom of Danoli the year prior and had set his eyes on going to war with the Phannel kingdom next. The king of Tranik's expansion-lust was the reason King Tyson had the wall built between the two kingdoms.

"They were identical twins. Down to their magic. It would have been an easy switch," Will said.

"This could be a fake," she offered.

He tapped the bottom of the paper where the notifier signed to seal the magical certificate. For royalty it had to be Fairy Godmother, and sure enough, *Fairy Godmother* was scrolled on the line. But it wasn't Bell's handwriting—it was her mother's. The one signature that couldn't be forged. She looked up from the document.

"Queen Lily knew the truth," Elzbeth said. She shook her head, trying to piece together why she'd go along with covering up her husband's death. What would possess her to act like Leo was king? "Why is Tyson—I mean, Leo"—she corrected—"so heartbroken over Queen Lily's death that my spell hasn't worked on him?"

"Because he's not actually heartbroken over Queen Lily's

death. Princess Fern, his true wife, died of influenza a week after her sister," Will explained.

Elzbeth had forgotten that Princess Fern had also died. She tried to fit the pieces together.

"So Prince Leo takes King Tyson's place and moves Princess Fern into the castle to keep his wife close under the guise that he is caring for a mourning relative."

"That explains almost everything, but why does no one know about Rupert? And why did Queen Lily adopt him?" she asked.

"I have no clue. We can work on that next. But there's more."

"More than a fake king and a prince no one knows about? How can there be more?"

"It's on the back of both the documents," he said. "Take a look for yourself."

She flipped them over, sending her heart into the pit of her stomach. There was a message on the back of Augustus Beck's autopsy report, as well as on Rupert's adoption papers, written in the same handwriting:

I know what you did.

You can do this, Elzbeth told herself for the dozenth time as her dead husband's prized carriage bumped along the road. She hated the thing but thought it was cruel to the girls to get rid of it. She knew how much their father loved it. *If they only knew who he really was.* She desperately wished she could replace it with a carriage that didn't smell of his evil escapades.

Elzbeth shook her head. She had better things to think about on her way to a child's birthday party to seduce a king who really wasn't a king. A party where Will would need to slip the mending heartbreak potion into the fake king's goblet before his traditional toast.

The carriage pulled to a stop in front of the castle. She took a quick sip from her flask and returned it to her dress pocket before the footman opened the carriage door. "Thank you." She smiled politely as he handed her the leash to her birthday gift for the young prince. In all her planning to seduce the king, she'd forgotten to get a gift, but Will found a solution by enchanting a stray dog.

Will had held the enchanted dog close to his chest, stroking her head. She was wearing a ridiculously huge blue-and-white checkered bow tied around its fluffy neck. "She is now a white poof-ball," Will had said, describing the dog for Bellenda's benefit. Elzbeth had rolled her eyes at his ridiculous smile as Will dropped the dog into her lap.

"I liked it better before," Elzbeth said, giving the too-cute-for-its-own-good snow-white puppy a scratch behind her ears.

"Me too," Will agreed.

"If we had more time, girl," Elzbeth said to the droopy-eyed pup, "I would've gotten your fur tamed so you didn't have to be enchanted."

"I thought you hated animals, Elz," Bellenda said and raised a brow.

She shook her head, still scratching the pup, who had more in common with Elzbeth than it knew. "Not all animals, just Lucifer," she added, making Will chuckle.

"When this is all over and we're back here together again"—Bellenda waved her hand around their living room—"I'll get you your own pretty puppy to love."

"No, I want this little muffin," Elzbeth said. "When all of this is over, I want her. Not enchanted, but just as she is. Perfect."

Bellenda had teared up at her words as the most dazzling smile had formed on Will's face.

Elzbeth liked the idea. No more marriages to evil men. A life with a dog and…

The coachman cleared his throat and held his hand out to her. She took it and exited the carriage, holding the golden leash in her other hand. She led the prancing puppy, wagging its puffy tail, up the front steps of the castle. Elzbeth held the leash out from herself to keep the dog from getting tangled in her ridiculous skirt. It was just a one-year-old's party, but Bellenda insisted she dress the part of a future queen to help lure the king into her trap.

She strolled through the entryway and down the great hall toward the ballroom where the party was being held. *Ridiculous.* Lavish decorations hung from the castle ceiling every five feet.

She wondered how long the attendants had been up last night decorating. *The guest of honor won't even notice them.*

Several party guests nodded at her as she strolled by, and some even oohed and ahhed over the dog. *Here we go.* She turned toward the double doors, casting a quick glance around the room before entering. She instantly spotted Edgar holding the wiggly birthday boy, who was overdressed and tugging at his collar. *I don't blame him,* she thought. Edgar caught her eye, but she quickly averted hers so he wouldn't ask her to hold the prince.

"Stop this nonsense about Elzbeth." Cyndra's voice floated over the string music, catching Elzbeth's attention. She glanced over to find Cyndra speaking to Annalie.

"Did someone say my name?" she called to them as some of the guests turned their eyes on her, instant smiles beaming on their faces. Cyndra made a beeline for her. Elzbeth handed the leash to the closest guard. "The prince's birthday gift." The guard nodded and an attendant scurried over, then took the spelled dog from the guard and ushered it somewhere out of sight.

Elzbeth moved towards Annalie before Edgar maneuvered over to her, and Cyndra, now close on her heels, followed her step for step. "Oh, Annalie, there you are," she said once they were closer. "I was so worried when you didn't come home last night." Elzbeth grabbed her shoulders and pulled her in for a hug. It was stiff and awkward with how tense Annalie was standing, likely on account of her admonishment.

"Where were you?" Cyndra cut in, sounding like a scolding mother. *Damn it!* She wasn't upset about Annalie being out. It was just an excuse to come over. She freed herself from the awkward embrace and straightened her gown.

"I was reading late at the library and fell asleep. Daff needed to leave early—a family matter or something—so I closed up and took advantage of the quiet to read."

"Hmmm," Elzbeth said, hoping Cyndra would continue. She

didn't. Elzbeth groaned internally before saying, "That was the third time this week." She pulled her small round makeup mirror from her dress pocket, checking her face was like Cyndra's when the princess had interrogated Annalie in the past.

She understood that Cyndra scolded her sister out of love, but no one was perfect, and Bellenda was right: Annalie was just a teenager thrown into this world. While Drury loved her etiquette lessons, Elzbeth could see how Annalie was struggling to fit into court. After she failed at the flute and singing lessons, Elzbeth tried to go easier on her. But Cyndra started to attend last year for moral support, so they were back to suffering through Annalie trying to master the flute and singing, hitting notes that practically made Elzbeth's ears bleed.

Once this was all over, she'd whisk Annalie away to the Sanctuary. Annalie could practice her archery and Drury could invent, both completely free.

"Glad to know you can count that high," Annalie bit back, snapping Elzbeth to the present and making her groan internally again. Now she'd have to produce instant tears, acting like an almost seventeen-year-old's words actually wounded her. Truth was, she liked Annalie's fire. She was the only one who pushed back, even under her spell.

She dabbed her sponge again, clanging her rings together to produce the pin with the tears potion to prick her cheek as she dabbed the makeup sponge several more times. Once the tears ran freely, she sniffled dramatically. So loudly, in fact, that Will, who was twenty feet away and dressed like a royal guard, took notice.

"Apologize now," Cyndra demanded, taking the motherly reins. Annalie sighed, and Elzbeth exhaled.

"I'm sorry," Annalie said. "I know you can count higher than three." Elzbeth almost laughed. Annalie was a sass, and who could blame her? She was a teenager who'd lost both parents only to be raised by a stranger, while her older sister was a princess living out her dream.

"Apology accepted. *Again.*" She emphasized the last word, snapping her mirror shut. *Two can play at the game of sass.* She turned, swishing her rose-gold dress about her legs. Elzbeth moved toward the other side of the room, knowing that the fake king would arrive soon to give his speech.

⧓ ⧓ ⧓ ⧓ ⧓

"Like his father and mother, Augustus is an exceptional child," the fake king Tyson droned on from the dais in front of the golden throne that was rightfully Edgar's. *How long is this speech going to be?* The birthday boy, who was practically screaming his head off, had been taken out by one of the attendants.

"Thank you, Father," Edgar said. He stepped next to him, pulling Cyndra along. Apparently, Elzbeth wasn't the only one done with the long-winded speech. Several guests perked up at Edgar and Cyndra joining him, knowing the torture was almost over.

"Such a lovely speech, King Tyson," Cyndra said, beaming.

"To my son. Prince Augustus," Edgar said, holding up his goblet. The fake king followed suit. Elzbeth shook her head. She had to stop referring to him as "fake" or she might let it slip that she knew the truth. She wondered for the dozenth time if Edgar knew. Elzbeth hoped she'd get the answer to that and many more questions soon.

"Yes, to my grandson, Prince Augustus," Tyson echoed.

"Happy birthday!" all the guests echoed in reply.

Finally! she thought, sipping the fizzing champagne and moving toward Cyndra to put herself close to Tyson once he was done. But he kept drinking. Apparently, his long-winded speech made him thirsty. Once he drained the goblet, he turned it over and frowned.

"I would like another," he said to the nearest attendant as Elzbeth approached.

"What a lovely speech, King Tyson," she said. Guests began to mill about the ballroom, chatting amongst themselves, eating, drinking, and dancing.

"Yes… a… fantastic…" Tyson slurred each word. "Speech."

"Are you alright, Father?" Edgar asked lowly.

"Yes… quite… fine." He smiled drunkenly as concern painted Edgar's face.

"How about King Tyson and I take a short stroll while you tend to your guests?" Elzbeth suggested.

"Yes, thank you," Edgar said, and Cyndra smiled gratefully. Elzbeth looped her arm through his and led them out a side door, just as Will had instructed when they made their plan last night.

"Such… a… nice… day," he slurred, beaming at Elzbeth as she led him down the hall and toward the private stairs to his personal library. The footsteps of several guards sounded behind them. One of those guards was Will.

"Yes" was all she said as she wracked her brain to figure out why the potion made him drunk. *Maybe I messed it up? Or maybe it sat too long in the wine during his speech?* She led them down the hall, and once in front of the door, nodded at the two guards stationed, who opened it for her and the king.

"Would one of you get us some refreshments?" she asked of the six guards standing outside the door now.

"Yes, my lady," Will replied before a guard closed the door to give them some privacy.

"Let's sit while we wait." She led him to the small couch. A dreamy look had overtaken his face. *Maybe I made the potion too strong?*

"You!" he gasped. She froze midstep before the couch. "You're the most breathtaking creature I've ever seen." His words were smoother now.

"Thank you." She smiled.

"Oh, I'm not worthy of being in your presence." He fell to one knee, bowing his head to her. She had clearly made the potion too potent, and now, with her beauty spell working, he was…

"Marry me!" he practically shouted, startling her. He whipped his head up, his brown eyes burning into hers. "Marry me, and I will make you the happiest woman in the kingdom."

"Yes," she said. He jumped to his feet and grabbed her waist. He twirled her around, reminding her of when Thomas proposed. Her stomach soured. She shut the painful memory out. Locking the trauma away was the only way she knew to endure. She needed to focus.

His blazing lips collided into hers. He kept one hand around her waist and put the other in her hair, deepening the kiss. Will cleared his throat very loudly, causing Tyson to pull back and break their kiss, but his hands remained in place.

"Oh yes!" He smiled and nodded at Will, standing several feet away and holding a tray of fruit, cheeses, bread, and a pitcher that hopefully contained water because Tyson clearly needed some.

Elzbeth could feel his honey eyes searing her flesh. She couldn't see Will's face, but she could imagine his disgust. He knew the plan. She couldn't let his reaction bother her.

"But first," Tyson said, scurrying over to his large desk in the corner of the library. As much as she hated this room, Elzbeth had always liked how it overlooked the castle gardens.

Will placed the tray on the small table in front of the couch and asked lowly, "What happened?"

Before she could answer, Tyson appeared at her elbow, holding a small box. "Your ring." He opened it, revealing the largest ruby ring she'd ever received. He took it out, slid it on her left finger, and grabbed her again to kiss her deeply. She'd always been aware of Will's disapproval, but feeling his scorching gaze from five feet away was almost unbearable.

CHAPTER
Thirty-Five

"You must've made it too potent. It sounds like it worked *too well* and made him drunk on love." Bellenda giggled. Leave it to her best friend to think the whole situation was funny. So many things could've gone wrong if Elzbeth hadn't been the first woman the king had seen after drinking the potion.

"Hopefully it subsides quickly," Elzbeth said, pacing back and forth in the bathing chamber.

Moments after King Tyson had slipped the ring on her hand, Bellenda, Edgar, and Cyndra had all joined them to share the news of their engagement. To her surprise, Tyson also told Elzbeth, Cyndra, and Bellenda about Prince Rupert, shocking only Cyndra, but she and Bellenda had acted like it was the first time they'd heard the news. Edgar seemed to have no qualms about his half brother and gushed about how he'd been adopted by his mother. Elzbeth couldn't help but wonder if it was all an act. Could Edgar possibly be the one who left the threatening message on the back of Prince Rupert's adoption papers? Did knowing about Rupert mean he knew about Prince Leo taking his father's place?

"Are you in there, my love?" Her fiancé's voice rang from the other side of the door. She groaned softly.

"You can't hide in here all afternoon," Bellenda whispered. Elzbeth made a face. She took in a cleansing breath, readying herself for the king's excessive affection, and opened the door.

"Yes, I'm here. And now I'm going to find Annalie to tell her the wonderful news," she said, coming up with a quick excuse to have a few more minutes of freedom from the lovesick man. "I won't be long," she added as he opened his mouth, probably to volunteer to accompany her. She moved down the hall quickly, leaving Bellenda to handle him. Elzbeth needed some time to breathe.

Everything was moving too fast. King Tyson was actually his twin brother, Leo. Rupert was Leo's son and a hidden prince. And on top of it all, Tyson's heartbreak was now fixed so thoroughly, on account of the accidentally too potent potion, that he was drunk on love. And now they were engaged.

He wanted to wed today!

Thankfully, Bellenda was there to remind the king that there were royal formalities to follow, the first being an announcement of their engagement to the kingdom. Unfortunately, Tyson suggested they announce their engagement today since half the royal city was at the party, thus giving them the ability to marry tomorrow. That was when Elzbeth made an excuse to hide in the bathing chamber.

She turned down another hall, and, her mind swirling, she almost missed Cyndra and Edgar, who were walking hand in hand down the hall right in front of her. She was about to make her escape, but Edgar put his hand on the floral-papered wall, revealing a secret door. He held his hand out for Cyndra to go through first.

Elzbeth dashed for the door, slower than she liked on account of the hideous gown and corset digging into her ribs. The door was inches from closing, but she threw her left hand out, stopping it just in time. Elzbeth slid through, taking a few heaving breaths and cursing the contraption restricting her lungs from a full breath. She pulled her flask from her dress pocket and stood it upright against the door frame to keep the door ajar. She wasn't sure if the enchantment security was on both sides, and she didn't want to risk being trapped in a secret corridor.

Elzbeth took in her surroundings. She was at the bottom of a circular stone stairwell. *A tower*, she thought, as Cyndra's and Edgar's voices echoed from above. "I can't believe you didn't tell me you have a brother," Cyndra said, sounding hurt.

"I was planning on telling you," Edgar said

"Really… when?" Cyndra asked, her voice clipped. It was the curtest Elzbeth had ever heard her speak to Edgar. "On our fifth anniversary!" Her words dripped with sarcasm. Elzbeth grinned. She liked this side of the princess. She started quietly up the stone stairs behind them, holding up the many layers of her dress.

"No… I was going to tell you after our honeymoon. Once you settled into your new role. But then your father died—"

Cyndra let out a soft cry that made Elzbeth's blood boil. If she only knew the truth of who her father was, she wouldn't shed a tear or have named her son after him. The rhythmic sound of their footsteps ceased, making her freeze lest she be caught

"I'm sorry. I waited, thinking I would tell you after some time. But then you got pregnant. I'm so sorry, love. I should've told you. I have no good excuse for keeping Rupert a secret from you this long."

"I don't understand, though," Cyndra said between sniffles. "Why is he even a secret?"

"Well, because… Actually, let me introduce you two first. Then we can tell you why together," Edgar said. His suggestion was followed by several knocks that reverberated off the stones. Elzbeth used the racket to cover several quick steps, getting her close enough to see without being seen. Cyndra and Edgar stood, backs to her, before a large wooden door.

"Okay," Cyndra said, sounding like her usual cheerful self. She let out a breath and pinched her cheeks before she looped her arm with Edgar's. Elzbeth's heart clenched, seeing Cyndra put her "perfect princess" mask back on.

Edgar knocked again, the sound echoing around Elzbeth. Cyndra shifted on her feet as several heartbeats passed with no answer. "Maybe he isn't here?" Cyndra questioned softly.

"I'll check to be sure," Edgar replied and opened the door. "Hey, Rupert? It's me," he called into the room. "I have some good news. Father says I can finally introduce you to Cyndra! And there's more!" He paused, turning to smile broadly at his wife. "Father just proposed to Elzbeth Beck, and she accepted!"

Elzbeth held her breath, listening for Rupert's reply, but nothing.

"It's okay, Rupert. You can show yourself," he called. "Elzbeth wants to meet you, and Fairy Godmother is here too! Father wants the ceremony to happen as soon as—"

"Edgar, darling," Elzbeth interrupted before he told his brother about the king's quick wedding plans. Edgar and Cyndra turned to face her. "Sorry, dear. You didn't hear me calling to you?" she lied.

"Oh, I guess we didn't." Cyndra smiled broadly. *Damn spell!* Elzbeth mentally cursed.

"Do you know where Annalie and Drury got off to? I want all our family present tonight when we announce our engagement to the kingdom," she said, changing the subject before Edgar questioned why she'd followed them. But more importantly, to remind them that Drury was gone at another workshop. They couldn't announce their engagement tonight, which meant she didn't have to marry the king tomorrow. *Thank you, Drury.*

"If Anna left the party, my guess would be she has snuck off to the archery range *again*." Cyndra said the last word sourly.

Elzbeth sighed at the princess's judgement of her youngest sister. A judgement she had because of Elzbeth's spell, manipulating her emotions and making her believe she was pleasing Elzbeth by being against such *unladylike* things. Elzbeth wished for the thousandth time she could've taken Drury and Annalie to the Sanctuary years ago. Before her spell transformed Cyndra from the supportive older sister who saw no wrong in Annalie's archery to a royal pain in the…

"And Dru was going to miss the party for that workshop," Cyndra added.

"Yes, yes, that's right." Elzbeth waved her hand like she'd just remembered. She let out a heavy sigh, feigning disappointment. "In all the excitement, I'd forgotten about her workshop. Well, I guess we can wait a few days more and make our announcement when Drury has returned." She sighed again for good measure.

"So did you find your brother, Edgar?" She pretended to admire her new ruby engagement ring. "It seems we'll have more time to chat now that Drury isn't here." Elzbeth had a lot of questions for the secret prince. Starting with: why did Queen Lily adopt him?

"No. If he isn't here, he's more than likely in the kitchen or the castle library. I'll check there next," Edgar answered. "If I can't find him before you leave, I'll come back here at dinner to let him know the good news."

Elzbeth nodded and turned quickly to get down the stairs before Edgar and Cyndra. She practically jumped off the final stair, Cyndra and Edgar close behind. She bent down and yanked the flask from the door. It closed on a soft click just as she slid the flask into her dress pocket. Edgar and Cyndra rounded the last steps, beaming at her.

Edgar put his hand on the door handle, opening it to let her and Cyndra exit first, as Elzbeth worked to keep her breathing even.

"Edgar," she began her interrogation, hopefully to learn if he was the one who left the threatening message on Rupert's adoption papers. She paused for a moment. *If that's true, then he'd also be behind the message on Lord Beck's autopsy report.* She looked the prince over, wondering if his charming personality were a mask. *Is Edgar behind the Link in Phannel?* He did have access to the royal seal…

"Yes," Edgar replied, closing the door and grabbing Cyndra's hand before leading them down the hall.

"Why did your parents not want anyone to know about Rupert?" Elzbeth asked.

"Well, um, because…" He tripped over his words. She looked at him and smiled, letting her spell do the work to make him want to please her by telling her the truth. He smiled back, clearing his throat. "For my mother's sake," he said, steadier. "It wasn't a love match, my father and Princess Fern—it was a necessity."

"Necessity?" Elzbeth tilted her head and raised a brow, prodding for more details. *Maybe he doesn't know the truth about his father and Prince Leo's switch?*

"I had grown ill from the Dark Days plague, and my father was afraid for what would happen if there was no heir on account of his youngest brother, Aaron, having left the kingdom. He was heartbroken after my uncle Leo died, you see. It took my mother years to get pregnant with me and a lot of magical help. My father feared they couldn't wait that long."

Elzbeth weighed each word, wondering if they were true. *Maybe I can get some truth serum into Edgar's next drink?* She needed to make sure she was getting accurate information.

"Oh, I didn't know that," Cyndra said, clearly shocked by the revelation, but Elzbeth caught how she squeezed Edgar's hand tighter. She was certain Edgar would be getting an earful about all the secrets he'd kept from his wife once they were alone.

"It wasn't something that was widely known." Edgar half smiled, then cleared his throat. "Since it took years for my parents to have me, they made an arrangement with my aunt Fern. They'd hoped the child would look like theirs and they'd be able to enchant him to look exactly like me if I passed."

"He was meant to replace you?" Cyndra asked, putting her free hand to her heart.

"Yes. Or, if I was too sickly to perform my public duties, he would do them for me."

"So what happened?" Elzbeth asked, slowing her pace. She needed the full story before they got back to the king's personal library and her lovesick fiancé.

"When Rupert was born, he did look like me, except he had his mother's unique eyes. They normally would be easy to enchant if he didn't have…" He cleared his throat. "A mark, on the right side of his jawline and neck that couldn't be covered up by magic."

"He's Star Kissed," Elzbeth chimed in, knowing there was only one kind of mark that magic couldn't disguise, thanks to her best friend. Bellenda had heard countless wishes over the years to remove Star Kisses. Some were rightfully earned… and some, like in the case of Prince Rupert, were not earned by the person but their parents.

"Yes. My father believes it was the Stars judging him and my mother for how they wanted to deceive the kingdom." He heaved out a long breath. "They had my mother adopt Rupert, believing the Stars would approve and break Rupert's curse. But it didn't work." *This explains why Queen Lily adopted Prince Rupert*, Elzbeth thought as a piece of the puzzle snapped into place. "The Star Kiss remained after the adoption, so my father had Rupert moved into the tower."

"He's been living here in the castle his entire life?" Elzbeth asked. "How has it never leaked out?"

"Father had a network of secret tunnels built around the castle for Rupert to get around unseen. And if anyone learned of him who shouldn't have, Father used his magic to make them forget."

Snap. Another piece of the puzzle.

"But when Rupert's magic appeared, he didn't need the tunnels anymore."

"Why?" Cyndra asked.

"Because Rupert has invisibility magic and can walk around unseen."

Snap. Snap. Several more puzzle pieces connected.

"Which is why I thought he might be in his tower, hiding with his magic, because he isn't supposed to let anyone see him except for family," Edgar explained.

Elzbeth gritted her teeth. A prince locked away from all but four people? Her magic burned in her veins. Flashbacks of the year her father locked her in her bedchamber when her beauty dissolved flipped through her mind. But your entire life? Locked away? Like a dirty little secret? Her bubbling magic begged to erupt. The worst of it was the poor boy was lied to his entire life for why he was born. She took a cleansing breath to focus.

"So that's why my parents decided it best for Rupert to not be known by the public, because his Star Kiss would reveal their deceit to the kingdom," Edgar said, putting an end to their conversation. Edgar guided Cyndra forward a few steps, then paused once he realized Elzbeth wasn't with them.

"I'm sorry," she said, clicking her rings together, producing a pin from the square-shaped locket ring. Elzbeth held her hand to her cheek and pressed the pin to administer a little bit of the potion. A few beads of sweat formed on her brow. "I don't feel so well."

"Oh dear," Cyndra said, dropping Edgar's hand, moving back to Elzbeth. "You do look flushed."

"Yes," Edgar agreed. "Shall I get my father?"

"No, please don't worry him. But would you call for my carriage? It's probably just all the excitement of the day with the party and the engagement," Elzbeth said and smiled softly. "I just need to go home and lie down for a bit. I'll send a fire message to Tyson that I've left and will see him tomorrow."

"Absolutely." Edgar turned on his heel, moving quickly down the hall and around the corner.

"Cyndra, would you let Fairy Godmother know I wasn't

feeling well, and I am sorry for leaving without saying goodbye."

"Yes," Cyndra said and gave her a quick hug and hurried down the hall, leaving Elzbeth with her swirling thoughts and boiling magic.

She knew neither would settle until she could tell Bellenda and Will that Prince Rupert was Star Kissed. But more importantly, she believed she'd figured out who wrote the threatening messages on the back of the adoption paper and Lord Beck's autopsy report. Rupert had invisibility magic. He was very likely the culprit who broke into the documentation office. The one with invisibility magic lurking around unseen, learning secrets and possibly the truth about his father. There was one other thing she knew to be true about Rupert. He hadn't been seen by Elzbeth. That meant he wasn't under her spell.

Anna closed her eyes, willing her racing heart to settle as the door softly squeaked open. "Hmm," Elzbeth said at the sight of the two of them curled up in Anna's bed. There was a beat of nothing before the door clicked shut. Anna stayed still, listening for Elzbeth's footsteps to retreat down the hall, but heard nothing.

Was Elzbeth waiting outside her door, listening? Did she suspect they were up to something? They clearly were. Anna couldn't help but imagine Elzbeth waiting for them to make a sound or come out the door and catch them.

There was a light tap on her shoulder as Dru stirred, pulling Anna from her racing thoughts. She rolled over awkwardly, the bow and quiver strapped to her back clanking softly as she faced Dru. Anna couldn't see her well. She pulled her portal light from her pocket and clicked it on just as Dru pulled the comforter fully over their heads.

She blinked, her eyes adjusting to the light and focusing on Dru's face. *We need to wait*, Anna mouthed. She yawned, her body relaxing with the comfort of her bed. It had been more than twenty-four hours since she'd fallen asleep in the library on top of the book she'd been reading for research. Her eyes drooped, heavy with exhaustion. They still hadn't heard Elzbeth's retreat.

Anna yawned again. She was physically and mentally exhausted. She let her eyes fully close. *Just for a few moments.*

Anna flung her eyes open. The summer sun beat hot through her windows, informing her she'd slept not for minutes but hours. Anna rolled over to wake Dru, only to find her gone. So were her bow and quiver.

She leapt off the bed, glancing at her clock. The small hand pointed halfway past eleven and the big hand at six. *11:30 a.m.!* The room filled with the crackling of ignition as a fire message popped in front of her. She grabbed it and broke the seal. A bluish-white string, the thickness of sewing thread, fluttered from the page. She caught it before it landed on her rug, palming it before reading the message:

Anna, tie this around your finger.

It was in Dru's handwriting.

Anna sat the message on her side table, wrapped the string around her finger several times, tied it at the top the best as she could, and picked the message back up.

When you need your magic to be silenced, break the thread to release the osmium. It won't last long, maybe a minute at best. You can only use it once. But just in case you run into Elzbeth before the announcement, break the string to stop your magic.

Dru is a genius, she thought and continued reading.

> *Clean up and put on the dress Elzbeth put out for you. Transportation will arrive soon.*

The message caught fire and burned away.

Anna turned around, spotting the dress. It was atrocious. Burnt gold with layers upon layers of tulle pushing the skirt out so far that no one would be able to stand close to her. Normally, she'd like that idea. But how was she supposed to walk in it, let alone sit?

She grimaced at the hideous thing but began stripping out of her dirty pants and tunic, tossing them to the floor. There wasn't time for a full bath. She grabbed a cloth from her personal bathing chamber and did a quick wipe down before stepping into the dress. Thankfully, the dozen buttons that would close her inside the monstrosity were in the front. She gathered fistfuls of the material, holding the hem up to slip on the matching slippers. "You could hide an entire family under this ridiculous thing," she muttered. That gave her an idea.

She shuffled to her bed, crouched down, and slid her hand under for a quiver. Anna felt around for few seconds until she grazed one with her fingertips. She pulled the spelled arrow and bow out, not seeing Fairy Godmother's wand. *Dru must have taken it.* She slid the quiver back under, reaching for one with unbroken arrows. After a few heartbeats, she found a suitable quiver and laid it atop the bed.

Once upright, she slid the bow and spelled arrow inside the quiver. Hiking her skirt up past her knees, she secured the quiver straps around her waist. She turned slowly, gathering her skirt in the front again, and moved to her full-length mirror. Anna smiled at her reflection. Nothing looked amiss. She turned toward the door, which began to open before she could reach it, making her jump.

"Are you dressed?" Phil whispered, hand over his eyes.

"Yes." She exhaled at the sight of him. "What are you doing here?"

"I'm your ride to the castle, my lady." He bowed teasingly with a smirk that turned sour when he opened his eyes. "That *is* some dress."

"Tell me about it." She rolled her eyes. "It makes me look like…"

"The most beautiful girl I've ever known," he said, closing the distance between them. "No matter what you're wearing."

Goosebumps trailed down her spine at his words.

"I'm not sure if that's a compliment, Prince. You've only known three girls," she teased.

He took her hand and used it to pull her into his arms, his vanilla scent wrapping around her. "Anna, let me make this very clear. I like you. Only you. No one else," he said as the silver flecks flamed in his slate eyes.

Her cheeks burned red as her hair. It felt like butterflies were taking flight inside her stomach.

"I like you too," she said, wrapping her arms around his waist.

"Good." Phil leaned down, holding his mouth a breath from hers, waiting for permission. The moment felt suspended, like the world had paused just for them. Her heart raced so loudly she was sure that he could hear it.

Anna closed the distance, her mouth melting into his. Phil's lips were soft. Everything seemed to dissolve, leaving only them. Though the kiss was gentle, it sent sparks racing down her spine, making her feel as though she might float away.

Anna had never given much thought to her first kiss, but if she had, she would've been way off. Kissing Phil was so much better than she could've imagined.

Her stomach growled. She ignored it. Food would have to wait. She was experiencing a different kind of hunger—one she hadn't realized she had until Phil's lips touched hers. She was ravenous.

Phil smiled against her mouth and slowly pulled back, landing her back on solid ground. *Damn it!* she internally cursed.

"I forgot," he said as her heart found a steady rhythm again. She let go of his waist as he reached for his bag. "Dru told me you fell asleep before eating." He rummaged around and pulled out a loaf of bread and the map spell book.

The rich, yeasty aroma of the bread wafting in the air nearly made her weak. He handed the loaf to her, and she took it, tearing a chunk from the end as her stomach roared. "Thank the Stars. I was afraid we would be walking to the castle," she said through a full mouth, tapping the book with the remainder of the loaf.

"Yeah, that would be quite the feat in that outfit." Phil chuckled.

"True, but you'd never guess I was hiding a quiver under here, would you?" she said. His eyes sparkled with amazement. She shoved another bite into her mouth, salivating around the tangy taste. Phil stepped next to her and held the book out between them. It fell open halfway as he scooted as close as the dress would allow. She grabbed it with her right hand as he wrapped his left arm around her wrist. The title and table of contents appeared before them.

"Map of the Known," he said. The words melted away, replaced by the map spell. He read it and closed his eyes. The book began to glow before it sucked them inside and ejected them at their destination in a blink of an eye.

Anna shook her head, taking in the room. They were in the castle in one of the guest bedchambers, standing in front of a large unlit fireplace. Anna turned, spotting the large bed in the center of the room where Daff lay, eyes closed. Next to her Dru sat on the edge of the bed, holding Daff's hand.

"Were you able to make it?" Anna asked Dru.

"Yes, and I gave her the elixir," Dru answered, not looking up from Daff's face. "She should wake at any moment." Anna handed Phil the book, placed the remainder of the bread in her mouth, and moved as quickly as she could to the bed.

"Daff, can you hear me? It's time to wake up," Dru whispered.

Anna leaned over Daff's face as she moaned, blinking. Her heart had been in a vise since hearing of Daff's condition. Seeing her stir, she could feel herself relax. *Thank the Stars for Dru's brilliant mind.*

Daff blinked again, adjusting to the light. "What happened?" she asked groggily.

"The king's magic put you to sleep," Dru started to explain.

Daff sat up slowly. Anna reached for the glass of water on the side table and handed it to her.

"Do you remember anything about last night?" Dru asked.

"Yes. I—"

A loud knock sounded at the door before Cyndra and Edgar burst through. In a panic, Anna looked toward Phil, hoping he was using his magic, only to find him gone.

"Thank the Stars!" Cyndra exhaled, seeing Daff awake. "How do you feel, Daffodil?" she asked once she reached the bed, putting the back of her hand to Daff's face.

She rubbed her temples. "I have a slight headache."

"Oh dear. You did hit your head quite hard when you fell." Cyndra lied so smoothly that Anna wanted to gawk, but she stayed focused. Edgar and Cyndra needed to leave, and Daff needed to enchant the ring. Daff glanced to Dru and Anna, then settled back on Cyndra.

"That makes sense," Daff said and rubbed at the side of her head, playing along with the lie.

"Elzbeth will be so relieved that you've woken," Cyndra said with a pleased smile. Anna knew Cyndra couldn't wait to deliver the news. *Just a few more minutes… then Cyndra and the entire kingdom will know the truth about Elzbeth.*

"We need to send a fire message to Fairy Godmother to inform her that Drury's elixir worked and there's no need for the healer. Just in time for the ceremony too," Edgar said, smiling broadly and yanking Anna from her thoughts. Had Phil lost Fairy Godmother? She was so focused on Phil's declaration, and their kiss, that she didn't even ask him about Fairy Godmother's whereabouts.

"I'll do it," Dru volunteered, getting to her feet and shifting the mattress. Anna had no clue how she moved so gracefully in the moss-green dress that was stylistically identical to hers.

"Thank you, Drury," Edgar replied, putting his arm out to Cyndra. She took it, smiling warmly in return. Anna hoped that when Edgar knew the truth about how and why he'd married Cyndra, it wouldn't damage his love for her. "We better go let Elzbeth and Father know Daffodil is awake. It's nearly time to tell the kingdom of their engagement," Edgar said, leading Cyndra to the door.

"We'll catch up after helping Daff get ready," Dru answered as Edgar and Cyndra stepped out the door.

"Alright, but don't take too long. It's nearly noon," Cyndra added over her shoulder as a guard closed the door behind them. Anna looked at the clock: fifteen minutes until noon.

"What did I miss?" Daff asked, throwing the covers back.

"No time to explain it all," Phil said as he slid out from under the bed. Daff threw a hand to her heart, startled. "Sorry. You weren't awake when I arrived. I had to hide when Edgar came in," he explained.

"Where's Fairy Godmother? Did you lose her?" Anna asked quickly.

"No, she's locked up in the dungeon." She opened her mouth to ask if the guards saw her, but he added, "The guards are all taking a long nap." He winked, making her smile. "And everyone else is busy preparing for the announcement, so no one knows she's down there."

A thrill zinged down her spine. Just a few more minutes until they exposed Elzbeth, and Anna would get her friends, family, and kingdom back. She'd been dreaming about this moment for years, and it was finally coming true.

"I had Fairy Godmother send a fire message that she was going for the healer herself," Phil added.

"Brilliant," Anna said and smiled. He brushed the back of his knuckles against hers.

"Yes, and now we need you to enchant this ring to look like Elzbeth's engagement ring," Dru said to Daff, holding the ring with the dragon's breath stone on it.

"What's that?" Daff asked, grabbing the ring to examine it more closely.

"Dragon's breath. We believe it'll break Elzbeth's spell permanently once the king puts it on her finger," Dru explained. "We need you to make it look exactly like Elzbeth's ruby engagement ring."

Daff nodded and closed her eyes, holding the ring tightly in her fist. No one moved or dared to even breathe as she concentrated. Anna counted her heartbeats. Nothing happened. Not a single spark of Daff's tiny, flower-shaped lavender magic sparkled. She opened her palm, staring at the ring with a frown.

"My magic feels…" Daff paused to search for the right descriptor. "Sluggish."

Anna glanced at the clock nervously. Fifteen minutes to twelve. They were running out of time.

"It must be from the king's magic and me using my ring on you," Dru explained. "Your magic must've also fallen asleep and hasn't fully woken. Like when your mom grounds your magic. The longer you're grounded, the longer it takes to come back."

"How long do you think it will take?" Phil asked, glancing at the clock.

"It took fifteen minutes for her to wake once I administered the elixir, so I would guess probably about the same time," Dru answered.

"Fifteen minutes from now?" Anna let out a huff.

"Ten," Dru answered. "She's been awake for five minutes."

"We don't have ten minutes!" Anna exclaimed. "We barely have five! Daff needs to enchant the ring, Phil needs to switch the rings, and all this needs to happen before the guards bring it out for the announcement!"

A thick silence filled the room.

"I'm sorry," Daff said softly.

"There's no need to be sorry, Daff," Anna said. "None of this is your fault." She turned to Dru. "Or yours."

"Alright," Phil said. "Here's what we're going to do." He intertwined his fingers with Anna's and squeezed gently. She saw Daff take notice before he continued, "Dru and Anna will go to the announcement. I'll stay with Daff and have her enchant the ring once her magic is back, then switch them out as planned."

"What about the time?" Daff asked.

"Delay the ceremony," he answered, looking at Dru.

"How?" Anna asked, her mind spinning into a frenzy. They couldn't get this close only to fail! Phil's hand tightened around hers, as if he knew what she was thinking.

"Say you want to make a toast to my father and Elzbeth before he presents her the ring," Phil offered. "He loves toasts. It will be the perfect way to stall!"

"I can't," Dru replied. "Once I see Elzbeth, I'm under her spell again, and I won't remember any of this."

"Any of it?" Anna asked, wondering if they were risking letting Dru near Elzbeth. *Maybe we should say she fell ill?*

"Pretty much," Dru replied. "I'll be back under her spell, thinking she is the most wonderful person in the world. I won't remember anything related to me thinking negatively toward her, so I won't remember any of this." She waved her hand. "I won't remember the past month of searching and working with Tinker."

Tears lined Anna's eyes. The thought of Dru falling under Elzbeth's spell again had her heart clenching.

"Hey," Dru said reaching for Anna's hand. "It'll be alright.

Once Elzbeth's spell is permanently broken, I'll remember it all again."

Anna nodded. She looked at the ring cradled in Daff's palm. The red stone danced like fire in the sunlight cascading through the windows. *Please, Stars, let this work*, she begged of the deities.

"Since I won't remember, I think you should make the toast, Anna," Dru added, rubbing her thumb gently across the bluish-white string tied around Anna's finger.

"But what if you're asked why you want to make the toast?" Daff asked Anna.

Anna held up her hand, showing the bluish-white string to Daff and Phil. "If I break this string, I won't have to answer honestly," her magic answered for her. "Dru made it for me. It will only work for a minute, but we have no other choice," Anna added of her own free will.

"Okay, but that doesn't give you ten minutes," Daff countered.

"It will once Anna has finished her toast," Phil said. "Trust me, if someone gives a toast, my father won't be able to resist giving one himself. And you know how he is about toasts… He goes on and on."

Everyone nodded knowingly.

"You need to go." He squeezed Anna's hand. "I'll be there as soon as I can," Phil added, dropping her hand. She turned, but he caught her, placing his hands on either side of her face, caressing it tenderly. He leaned in, careful to not smoosh her dress, and pressed a tender kiss to her lips.

She went lightheaded as her spirit took flight again, her lips lingering on his. A chill ran down her entire body.

"Finally!" Dru exclaimed.

Phil pulled back, dropping his hands.

Anna's cheeks flushed. She turned from Phil to a smiling Dru and then to Daff, who matched Dru's smile. "The way you two look at each other," Daff said. "I can't wait for that day."

"Same," Dru added. "And I'm not trying to spoil the

moment, but we need to get going before someone comes for us."

"You can do this. You're the bravest person I know," Phil whispered softly into Anna's ear.

"You only know—"

He kissed her quickly, cutting off her retort. "Go," he said and stepped back. "I'll be there soon."

She smiled and turned for the door.

"You've got this," Daff called as Anna made her way awkwardly across the room.

"So do you," she called over her shoulder to Daff but looked at Phil, sending him one last smile before following Dru out the door.

She had no clue how Dru could maneuver with such ease. But who cared about elegance at this point?

Six guards stood in the hall, waiting to escort them to the announcement.

"Everyone has already assembled near the balcony and is waiting for you to join them, my ladies," one of the guards said over his shoulder.

"Yes, sorry for the delay," Dru replied as they turned down the next hall. "Please tell the king that Daffodil sends her apologies, but her head still hurts so she's going to continue to rest," Dru added.

Good thinking, Dru, Anna thought. Dru was letting them know about Daff before she got under Elzbeth's spell. It gave Anna an idea. She leaned over as best as she could in the hideous dress and said to the guard on her right. "Can you let a kitchen attendant know I want to surprise the king and Elzbeth with a toast during the announcement?"

"Yes, of course," the guard said before waving at a guard standing at the bottom of the stairs to take his place. Anna glanced at Dru as they ascended. She was smiling brightly. She reached for Dru's hand and squeezed it tightly. In just a moment, she was going to lose her again, hopefully only momentarily and for the last time.

They stepped onto the landing, where double glass doors let in bright sunlight. The cheers of the waiting crowd echoed up from the courtyard and through the glass. Cyndra was next to the balcony doors, holding Augustus in one arm, the other looped through Edgar's. On the other side of the doors, the king stood next to Elzbeth. She looked at them, her expression marking her displeasure at their tardiness.

Anna held herself, waiting for Dru to fall back under Elzbeth's spell. Her stomach dropped as Dru let go of her hand and shuffled quickly to Elzbeth and embraced her with a congratulations.

Anna drew in a long breath, plastered on a fake smile, and approached the wicked woman.

CHAPTER
Thirty-Seven

ELZBETH: 15 HOURS, 30 MINUTES BEFORE THE
CLOCK STRIKES 12

"Bellenda, I know you see this as an invasion of Drury's privacy. But Annalie has never been gone for three days," Elzbeth said as she stood outside Drury's bedchamber door.

Three days and not a word from her? She could've at least sent me a fire message to let me know she's still alive!

Prince Rupert at least had the courtesy to send a fire message to Edgar. It said he needed time to process the engagement—which was a plausible explanation for his absence. Things were moving fast. The mending heartbreak potion was far too strong, and she had no idea what Prince Rupert thought of his father acting like a lovesick puppy.

The king had been sending her extravagant gifts every hour, on the hour for the past three days. As excruciating as it was, it was far preferable to his physical presence, which was why she'd lied and told him she was still ill.

While the prince's explanation was believable, Elzbeth suspected it wasn't the truth. She didn't think the hidden prince really needed time to process his father's engagement. She believed he was avoiding her so he wouldn't fall under her spell. *Smart boy.*

Normally, she'd be thrilled that someone figured out how to avoid falling under her spell, but if Prince Rupert knew the truth of what they were up to, it could ruin everything they had been working towards for the past decade.

"I know," Bellenda said, pulling her from her thoughts. Elzbeth knew what Bellenda was thinking. She was aware of the line she was about to cross. It was a line she said she'd never cross because of how much she valued her own privacy. But desperate times called for desperate measures.

"I need to figure out where Annalie is," Elzbeth said after opening the door. The truth felt heavy, like it was digging deep into her bones. There were so many unknowns lingering around her, and everything was on the line. One little hiccup could destroy it all. Plus, she didn't know how much longer she could avoid the king without him becoming suspicious.

Bellenda and Will were shocked to learn about Prince Rupert's curse, and they were just as angry as she was that he'd been locked away his entire life for his parents' and Queen Lily's actions. She also informed them of Rupert's magic and how it made him the prime suspect for the threatening messages.

"Where is that damn light thingy Drury created?" Elzbeth said, fumbling around on the wall. "Ah, here it is," she said, flipping the switch. She maneuvered carefully through the chaos of Drury's room, careful to keep her skirts from knocking one of Drury's many projects over. She had no clue where to start.

Bellenda picked up a small tube, holding it toward the light as Elzbeth stared at a painting of the three girls with their father hanging by Drury's desk. She gritted her teeth. *If they only knew.*

"Elzbeth," Bellenda said, looking over her shoulder at the painting. She could hear the regret in her voice.

"I know what you're going to say. It's too late now to do anything about Drury and Annalie," Elzbeth said. "I wanted to take care of them, and we should've done that immediately after their father's death. Just like the others."

It was a low blow, almost four years too late. But Elzbeth

couldn't help herself. They should've sent Annalie and Drury to the Sanctuary and told all three girls the truth about their father.

"I know. I'm sorry I convinced you otherwise. But unfortunately, we can't change that now." Bellenda sighed heavily, shuffling through some papers and other items scattered on Drury's desk before moving to a bookshelf to search through the various items on display. "Also, I agree with Will. Marrying the king is too risky. This isn't like before, not with what we have…"

"It isn't too risky, and you know it has to be done," Elzbeth said firmly, not wanting to have this conversation again. Will said she should give the ring back after the potion had gone haywire and she'd shared what she'd discovered of Prince Rupert's magic. He thought it was too dangerous. He was worried for her—he always was. "You know there's no other way to get what I want," she added.

"What we want," Bellenda replied, but Elzbeth saw the concern etched on her face before she turned away to continue her search.

She could do this. She had to. Too many girls' lives were at stake. Her girls' lives were at stake. *Her girls.* It was the first time she'd thought of Cyndra, Drury, and Annalie as hers. Her heart pieces squeezed, and tears pricked her eyes.

"Emotions are a sign of weakness." Her father's words echoed in her mind. Elzbeth shook her head to banish the dead bastard again and focused.

"True, what we want," she replied to Bellenda. "So we need to find out where Annalie is, and we need to do it quick because my patience is running thin." She didn't know how much longer she could keep up the facade of a loving fiancée to a lovesick puppy who locked his son away because of his sins. Elzbeth worried she may break character, end him, or expose him before they even got married. And that would ruin the bigger plan of stopping the Link for good in Phannel.

"What are you looking for?" Bellenda asked as she shifted around the space.

"For any clue on where Annalie could've gone," Elzbeth replied. "I searched her entire room and found nothing."

Bellenda threw her a look. She hadn't told her that she'd searched Annalie's room the night prior because she couldn't sleep. Elzbeth blamed it on the stress of everything, but she knew what she'd done was wrong. And now she was doing it again.

"Maybe she went to see Drury? Heard the news of your engagement and left the party to tell her sister?"

She opened her mouth to ask why Annalie hadn't sent her a fire message, but the sound of horns blaring snapped her mouth shut. They hurried to the window. Six black horses pulled the king's bouncing royal carriage up the drive with alarming speed. Elzbeth sighed, tapping her silver slipper. She'd have to face him now.

"What the hell is he doing here?" she gritted out.

"Probably wanting to see his fiancée since it's been three days. But let's find out for sure what he wants," Bellenda said, putting her hand on Elzbeth's arm and giving it an encouraging squeeze. She nodded and followed her out the door, hoping that neither Drury nor Annalie would find out that she'd violated their privacy.

⊠ ⊠ ⊠ ⊠ ⊠

"My love," her fiancé said, using the nickname for the hundredth time that night. "I'm so sorry we had to cut our night short."

"It's fine, Tyson," she replied, trying to disguise her elation as dismay. The carriage ride to the nighttime picnic was unbearable on account of how much he drooled over her. Over the years, she'd endured many men falling at her feet, but this was something else. She thought by now the potion would've worn off, allowing her to put a few inches between them.

That was not the case.

He was on bended knee before her, apologizing like it was his fault a fire message had come from Edgar, beckoning him back to the castle. He explained his magic was needed in order to make a girl forget royal details she'd overheard. The irony wasn't lost on Elzbeth, who'd been just about to slip some truth serum into his drink so she could ask him about his secrets.

Alas, it wasn't meant to be, because she received a fire message from Bellenda immediately after.

Bellenda's said that Drury and Annalie were back. The engagement announcement was happening tomorrow, and the king was needed because Daffodil learned about Prince Rupert when the news was announced to Drury and Annalie at the library. The truth serum would have to wait. Time was of the essence, and she needed to check in with Bellenda and Will to finalize their plans.

"I completely understand what it means to be engaged to a king," Elzbeth cooed.

The carriage bounced down the estate drive, horns blaring to announce the king's arrival. He beamed at her mention of their engagement, finally sitting back in his seat across from her, but he kept his hand intertwined with hers.

The carriage halted before the estate steps. Elzbeth let out a breath of relief at the promise of a reprieve, small as it may be. She'd asked to be dropped off to change into something more comfortable before joining him at the castle. Truth was, she wanted to be rid of him for the night. She wanted to have time to check on Annalie and find out where she was before preparing for the next day. All she'd managed to negotiate was one hour away. She took it.

The door opened to a royal footman holding out his hand. Elzbeth tugged free of her fiancé's grasp, offering her hand to the footman and gliding out of the carriage before hurrying up the stairs.

"Elzbeth, wait!" he called after her. *So close.* She'd hoped to get away without him wanting to accompany her to the door.

The doorman held the door aloft. The king closed the gap between them, taking the stairs two at a time with a royal guard on his heels.

"Yes, darling," she said sweetly as he stood before her. "I just need to freshen up and check on my daughters, and then I'll join you at the castle." She reminded him again why she was hurrying inside, hoping it would give her more time.

He had no clue that Annalie had been missing the past three days. He thought she'd locked herself in her room, refusing to come out because Elzbeth was engaged to him, the king, who was replacing her father. He thought this because that was exactly what Elzbeth told Cyndra to pass along to him when she came to check on her ill stepmother yesterday, because Elzbeth didn't want the king also worried sick with Annalie's absence.

"Don't take too long." He took her face in his hands and kissed her so deeply that she thought she might be sick.

"I'll be an hour at the most," she said once he broke the kiss, hoping he'd give her that long before coming to look for her. "Annalie may need some time to talk," she added for good measure.

"Of course, my love. I'll take the time to freshen myself up after I use my magic on the library girl," he said, placing a quick peck on her lips. He turned, striding down the steps with his guard close behind.

Elzbeth walked inside the large entryway. The door shut behind her before she wiped the back of her hand across her mouth. "Kissing a fish would be a more pleasant experience," she murmured and moved toward the hallway that led to her bedchamber. Fire crackling filled the space as a fire message popped in front of her. She plucked it from the air and broke the seal.

Meet me at The Devil's Tavern in ten. W.

"Thank the Stars," she said. She needed a drink.

The message burned up as she moved to the window and peeked out. The royal carriage bumped down the gravel drive away from the estate. She pulled her flask from her dress pocket and took a large gulp of the energy potion, hoping it would also wash the taste of the king's kisses from her mouth. She moved her neck, stretching out the muscles she'd held taut while with him.

Elzbeth pinched her cheeks. Even with the potion energizing her, Will knew her well. And she didn't need him seeing how exhausted she truly was. He'd try to convince her to end things with the king. She took a cleansing breath before opening the front door and stepping out. "Carriage, now!" she demanded more harshly than intended. Her emotions were bubbling to the surface, even after years of practice to keep them contained.

"Yes, my lady," the doorman said before running toward the carriage house.

She drew in another cleansing breath, fighting against the waves of feelings that were trying to take over. If she just knew where Annalie was and why... If something had happened to her...

Emotions are weak! Her father's words boomed in her mind. She rolled her head again, cracking her neck, forcing everything she was feeling into a deep internal pit where it couldn't interfere. Once her feelings were locked up, she convinced herself that Bellenda was probably right. Annalie was with Drury and had come home with her when the workshop was over.

The carriage pulled to the front of the estate, slowing before her. The footman opened its door as she called to the driver, "To The Devil's Tavern."

Thirty~Eight

ELZBETH: 13 HOURS, 25 MINUTES BEFORE THE CLOCK STRIKES 12

Elzbeth waited for Will in the far corner booth of the half-destroyed empty tavern. He was late, as usual. She'd watched the tavern owner for the past twenty minutes as he swept up shattered glass and cleaned tables and overturned chairs. According to the owner, a fight had broken out earlier over a card game where one man used his magic on another, resulting in an early closing time. However, it only took one smile from her to convince the owner to let her come in and wait for her friend. She had a sneaking suspicion Will was behind the destroyed tavern, aiming to give them a private place to meet.

"Are you sure I can't get you anything while you wait?" the owner asked for the second time since she'd sat down. He smiled, showing a broken tooth.

"You know, I will take you up on your offer," she said, smiling softly, making his grin grow. "Two ales, please." He practically ran behind the bar to get her drinks. She really didn't care for ale, but it was easy to pour, and she didn't want to be more of a bother.

Several birds rustled in the trees outside, and a horse neighed from the same direction. *Finally.* She resisted the urge to thrum her fingers against the worn wooden table as she waited for Will to dismount and come in. *But seriously, can't the man be on time for once?*

The door swung open. Will entered, glancing over the empty tables and chairs until he met her eyes. He smirked, seeing where she was sitting. It was the same booth that Augustus Beck had been sitting in when she seduced him. He closed the distance between them in several long strides and stopped, staring down at her and saying nothing. Will knew the protocol: no talking until all eyes and ears were silenced around them. He sat across from her and stayed quiet as the tavern owner approached, carrying their drinks and placing them on the table.

"Need anything else?" the owner asked with a goofy smile. Elzbeth hated her manipulative beauty spell at moments like these. But Will watching, his jaw ticking because he understood the discomfort it brought her, made it bearable.

"No, thank you," she said, and Will snapped his fingers. A smokey green cloud of magic puffed onto the barkeep's face. Enchanted to sleep, the man slumped to the ground, snoring peacefully. "How long until he wakes?" Elzbeth asked.

"Ten minutes at most. I had to use a fair amount of my magic earlier to get this place to ourselves." He winked, confirming it was him behind the fight.

"Did you take care of my coachmen?" Elzbeth asked.

"Yes, they are sleeping comfortably, just like him."

She smiled, picking up her ale and taking a long drink. Will did the same.

"Thank you for coming so quickly," he said before setting his mug down.

She made the mistake of looking into his eyes. They always sucked her in. They were captivating. Elzbeth averted her gaze.

"Well, you called," she answered and flicked her eyes back to his, and damn her for doing so. She blinked, but it was too late. He stood, motioning for her to slide over so he could sit next to her. "What are you...?" She scooted all the way to the wall, trying to put distance between their bodies, but Will had different plans.

He leaned in, eyes heavy with want. Heat poured over Elzbeth's body. She lifted her hand to his chest, but he softly clasped his hand over hers. Will moved a loose strand of hair from her face, sending chills down her spine. His touch was sweet and gentle, and his gaze was warm and loving, making emotions she had promised to keep locked up until they finally finished this mission bubble out from beneath the surface.

But this was Will. Will, who knew what she truly looked like, and yet was devouring her with his eyes.

She flicked her eyes to the skylight, trying to gain control over the situation again. "I'm engaged." Her words came out breathier than intended as her eyes landed back on his.

"Don't marry him." He tapped the ruby on her engagement ring.

"Jealous?" Elzbeth teased with a small laugh.

"No, Elz," he said gruffly. "I'm not jealous." He leaned forward, putting his lips so close to hers she could feel his breath warming her face. "I'm green with envy."

His words thawed her frozen heart pieces. Elzbeth's chest tightened. She wanted him. She had wanted him for longer than she cared to admit. Finally, she gave in to what she wanted.

Elzbeth leaned in, pressing their lips together. The kiss was warm and soft. Will's lips moved against hers with instinctual rhythm. It was as if they had been doing this their entire lives. He moved his free hand around her neck, holding her like he'd never let her go as he deepened the kiss. She let herself sink into him, her hands brushing against his chest, feeling the beat of his heart against her fingertips. Their breaths mingled, sparking something magical.

A loud crash broke through the magic of their entanglement.

They broke apart. Birds burst from the trees outside the tavern, some flying through the open windows. Will and Elzbeth whipped their heads about, searching for the source of the disruption. *Is somebody here? Did they see us kissing?* Elzbeth went still as they both listened. They didn't see or hear anything.

"Stay here. I'll go check," he said, getting to his feet as the tavern owner moaned. Will turned to her and whispered, "I have to hide. He won't remember I was here. Tell him that he slipped and knocked his head." Elzbeth nodded, cursing herself for not putting her rings on to make the owner sleep for a bit longer. Will squeezed her hand quickly and darted for the back room.

The owner groaned again. She scooted from the booth and knelt next to him. He blinked several times and tried to sit up. "Hold on, take it easy. You knocked yourself out when you slipped on the wet floor from tonight's fight," Elzbeth said softly and put a hand on his arm to keep him in place. He blinked again, dazed from the lifting enchantment, and smiled goofily at her.

He opened his mouth, but horns blared, announcing the king's arrival. The barkeep shook his head again and jumped to his feet, scurrying behind the bar and bowing his head as the king entered.

"Tyson," her voice squealed an octave too loud as he strode toward her, flanked by two guards. She cleared her throat. "Now you've ruined the surprise," she added and made a pouty face. "I was going to bring you the drink I've been telling you about to toast our engagement announcement."

"I'm sorry for ruining your surprise." He put a hand to his heart, stepping closer. "Your doorman told me you'd come here, and I needed to see you." He burst into tears.

"What's wrong?" she asked, closing the gap between them. He slumped into a seat, his cries turning into sobs.

"Me, I'm what's wrong," he said, putting his hands over his face. *Shit! Is this just another side effect of the mending potion being too strong?*

"My magic! It's gone wrong," he said between cries. "It made the library girl…" He sucked in a deep breath. "It made her fall into a deep sleep. I'm a failure, and I don't deserve you." He wailed the last words, dropping his arms and head onto the table.

Daffodil! Her heart pieces squeezed for the girl. But she had to stay in character.

"You're not a failure," she said, putting a hand on his back and rubbing it slowly, just like Bellenda did when comforting someone.

"But my magic, it failed me." His words came out muffled. "Because of what I did." Elzbeth held herself. *Is he going to confess?* "It's my fault, and now the Stars are exacting their justice." An arrow rained from above, landing less than an inch from his bowed head, piercing the tabletop with a loud *twang*.

He jumped to his feet, chair falling back onto the floor. The two guards drew their swords. "It came from the skylight, Your Majesty," one of the guards said. He flung his head up, but Elzbeth's eyes stayed glued to the piece of paper that was delivered by the arrow. Footsteps thundered on the wood planks behind them as two more guards charged in.

I know what you did.

Her stomached twisted into knots at the words, which were written in the same handwriting as the back of Lord Beck's autopsy report and Prince Rupert's adoption papers.

"Your Majesty, we need to get you both back to the castle," Will said. Elzbeth looked up from the paper to find him standing next to the king dressed in a royal guard uniform.

"Yes, let's go," the king said, eyes puffy and bloodshot. He put his arm around Elzbeth as Will led them to the carriage. "Get in first, guard," he commanded. Will did as he was told, and Elzbeth scurried behind him. This wasn't normal protocol, but an arrow had been shot at his head. He was understandably shaken up. He slid next to her, grabbing her hand once he was seated. Will waved his hand, and a puff of green smoke hit the king's face, causing him to shut his eyes.

"Won't last long," Will said as the carriage began to move. "What did the note say?"

"Same as what is written on the back of the reports," Elzbeth said. She leaned into Will and whispered, "It has to be Prince Rupert."

"Probably. But we need to find out for sure."

"Do it quickly because the engagement announcement is tomorrow, and I'm beginning to think he may show up and—" Elzbeth stopped as the king groaned, waking from his enchantment.

Anna drew in a deep breath. She could do this. Just a few more minutes, and the kingdom would finally know the truth about her wicked stepmother. She'd been dreaming for so long about this moment, and it was almost here. *Finally.*

"There you are," Elzbeth scoffed as she embraced Dru awkwardly. Dru had no idea the hug was awkward. She was back under Elzbeth's spell and was currently beaming at their stepmother.

"Yes, sorry," Anna said before Dru could speak. "I overslept and wanted to check on Daff." Dru nodded along enthusiastically. Elzbeth pulled her makeup mirror from her dress pocket, ignoring Anna, totally absorbed with herself. *Big surprise,* she thought mockingly, suppressing an eye roll.

Anna glanced over her shoulder, hoping Phil was there with the ring. It was just the guards lined up on each side of the doors, one holding the pillow that cradled Elzbeth's ring. *Come on, Daff,* she begged as her stomach swirled like it was full of swarming bees.

The castle courtyard clocktower tolled. The crowd's cheers

erupted, louder with each strike in anticipation of the king's official engagement announcement. Anna knew how it would go.

The king would welcome his citizens and thank them for coming to celebrate on this joyful day… *blah blah blah*. Then the ring would be held up on a pillow floating with magic by…

No! Anna clasped a hand over her mouth. Her heart raced as blood rushed in her ears. *Fairy Godmother!*

Anna was so focused on exposing Elzbeth she'd forgotten that Fairy Godmother was part of the ceremony. It was her magic that made the pillow float. Without her there would be no floating pillow, and this ceremony was definitely happening without her on account of how she was still locked in the dungeon. *Shit.* Would this mistake get them caught? It felt like the bees had multiplied and taken flight as panic swelled inside her. Beads of sweat formed on her brow and trailed down her cheek and neck.

"What's wrong, Anna?" Cyndra asked. Her eyes were heavy with concern.

The clock tolled the twelfth time. "Fairy Godmother." Her magic had her answering. *Please don't ask me more questions! Please, Cyn, for once in your life, drop it!*

"Yes, we know," Cyndra said, cutting into Anna's spiraling thoughts. "She replied to the fire message before you and Dru arrived. She won't make it to the ceremony. Something about granting a wish." Anna's heart dropped from her chest to her stomach. *Thank you, Phil and Daff.* She knew they'd sent the fire message using Daff's magic. *Daff's magic!* Anna glanced around, looking for Phil. But he was still absent, and the ring hadn't been switched yet.

Edgar tugged on Cyndra's arm, pulling her attention back to the royal announcement. He smiled at her as two guards opened the doors and walked onto the balcony.

Dru shuffled up to Anna's side. "Our turn," she said giddily, as if they were announcing her engagement. Anna smiled back, mentally crossing her fingers that their plan would work.

She stepped onto the balcony, taking her place next to Dru. She glanced at Cyndra, who was now holding an unhappy Augustus on her hip as he covered his ears with his chubby little hands. The crowd's volume doubled as the king and Elzbeth strolled onto the balcony.

Anna peered down the six stories at the crowd assembled below. *This was how the true king died. Why Phil was cursed.* She drew in a deep breath and let it out slowly, trying to ease her nerves. They'd tackle the problem of Phil's Star Kiss curse next. Now, she needed to focus and delay the ring being placed on Elzbeth long enough for Phil to switch it out.

Anna glanced at the clocktower: 12:05 p.m. She saw the guard holding the pillow. He was out of sight from the crowd, near the balcony doors. Standing in the opposite corner was Gertrude Penny, the top reporter for *Fairytales, Facts, and Fables.* She had a quill and notebook and looked ready to write down the details of the announcement for tomorrow's paper.

The king held his hand up to silence the crowd. He then flicked his hand, and red sparks jetted about the balcony like fireflies before dissolving into thin air. He boomed his welcome to everyone with the amplified spell he placed on himself. *Oh, to be royals and have more than one magical ability.*

Anna's eyes were trained on the door, waiting for Phil. When this was over and Phil's curse was broken, would Phil's magic be stronger? Or possibly, would he gain further abilities?

"And with that," Phil's father cut into Anna's thoughts. "I would like to present my beautiful fiancée…"

"Excuse me, Your Majesty," Anna said loud enough for the crowd below to hear. She didn't realize the amplified spell was on the entire balcony, not just on the king. Cyndra and Dru scrunched their faces at Anna as Augustus clasped his ears again. The king turned to her, as did Elzbeth. She was glaring at Anna. If looks could kill, Anna would have been six feet under. She swallowed hard, trying to ignore the wicked woman, and continued. "I would like to make a toast?" Anna said, turning the proclamation into a question.

"Oh," the king said. He looked utterly delighted. Anna mentally thanked Phil for the idea. "That would be splendid. However, we don't have…" Right on cue, an attendant walked through the doors, holding a tray of fizzing flutes.

"I asked for them," Anna said, observing the king's brows scrunched with confusion.

"Well, that was kind of you, Annalie," he said, taking a glass. Elzbeth followed suit. "Wasn't that kind of her, my love?" He turned to Elzbeth. She smiled at him, then at Anna. She was getting under Elzbeth's skin. *Good.*

The rest of the party took their glasses and waited for the attendant to move off the balcony. "To King Tyson and Lady Elzbeth Beck," Anna said, holding up her glass. Her pause extended well beyond the deep breath she took. "May your love be as strong as King Tyson's rule and true as Elzbeth's beauty."

The crowd below called back: "To King Tyson and Lady Elzbeth Beck."

She brought the glass to her lips to hide her pleasure at the secret meaning of her words. The king drank, stopping halfway through his glass at the realization Elzbeth was not drinking hers, halting Anna before she took a sip.

"Sorry, dear. Nerves," Elzbeth said.

"Understandable, my love," he said, smiling at her. "As I was saying before, I would like to present…" He paused and gestured to the guard holding the ring. It was *not* the dragon's breath stone.

Anna's heart dropped to her stomach. *What about him giving a toast after me? What happened to him loving the sound of his own voice? Why won't the wicked witch drink the damn alcohol so the man will give his own speech?*

"Stop!" Anna called frantically.

"What now?" Elzbeth seethed as she stared daggers at Anna.

She quickly broke the magic-suppressing string from Dru

with her fingernail. "It's just…" *Think*, she pleaded internally. Anna had one minute to lie. "It's just that I know today is your day, but seeing Elzbeth happy with you, it just… makes me remember our father and…" She looked at Phil's father and hoped he'd fill in the pieces however he wanted. She just needed to delay. She needed to halt him putting that ring on Elzbeth's finger. She glanced at Gertrude Penny feverishly writing away.

"Yes, I miss Father too," Dru said lowly.

"We all do," Cyndra agreed. "And he is still with us now celebrating this special day. He wouldn't want you to be sad, Anna."

He wouldn't want to be dead either, Anna thought but said, "You're right." The string's effect was almost spent. She had to avoid being asked any more questions. "But could we still take a moment? To remember our father? A moment of silence to honor him and also Queen Lily?" she added, looking at the king.

"Yes, absolutely," he agreed. "In honor of our loved ones who couldn't be with us, let's take a moment of silence."

The crowd hushed, and Anna lowered her head in respect. *Come on, Phil!* she begged. After a minute the king cleared his throat. "So, without further delay, I, King Tyson Phillip…"

Anna glanced to the door, but the ring was still the original one nestled in the pillow. She collapsed onto the ground. Her flute crashed against the pavers, breaking into dozens of pieces. Cyndra gasped. Anna lay still with her hand on top of her left thigh so no one would notice the quiver beneath her skirt.

"Anna," Dru said, smacking her face lightly. She stayed still, doing what was necessary to keep delaying until Phil could get there with the ring.

"Anna!" Dru said louder, slapping her cheek harder. She winced at the sting and reluctantly opened her eyes, glancing from Dru to the ring.

It was still Elzbeth's engagement ring. *Where the hell is Phil?*

"See? She's fine," Elzbeth said. "Leave her there so we can do this." She waved her hand, coaxing Dru to stand back up. Dru obeyed like an obedient puppy, leaving Anna lying on the floor.

NO! Anna's mind screamed as she eyed the guard carrying the pillow closer to Elzbeth.

All eyes were on the ring, so she yanked up her skirt to pull her bow and an arrow from the quiver. Anna launched to her feet, notching the arrow, and aimed it at the king.

"Stop!" Anna commanded. All eyes were on her now. The swish of the guards' swords unsheathing echoed in the silence. Several of them approached her slowly.

"I said stop!" Anna said and pulled the bow string back, aiming it at the king's heart. The guards ignored her command and moved towards her. "Stop them, or I'll tell them what you did," she said to Phil's father before nodding slightly at the balcony wall.

His eyes widened, but he recovered quickly and commanded his guards, "Do as she says." They obeyed but didn't sheathe their swords. He flicked his hand, and his red sparks jetted about the balcony before he said, "What is this about?" His voice was no longer amplifying to the crowd below.

"You can't marry her!" Anna exclaimed, still frantically scanning for Phil. "She's a murderer!"

"Anna, enough with this nonsense!" Cyndra said. But Anna ignored her sister, just like Cyndra had ignored her ever since Elzbeth entered their lives.

"She marries for money and status, and then she—"

"Annalie, how dare you!" Elzbeth bellowed. "How dare you accuse me of such things!"

"Well, here's one more accusation." Anna paused for several heartbeats before continuing, "I saw Elzbeth last night at The Devil's Tavern, kissing another man." Cyndra gasped. "One of the royal guards."

"You were the one who shot the arrow at King Tyson last night?" Elzbeth blurted, putting her pea-green hand to her heart.

"It's the same arrow," the king said. Gertrude Penny's quill was scratching away, recording every detail.

"I didn't shoot at the king last night," Anna said. "If I had, I wouldn't have missed." Cyndra and Dru gasped. Anna ignored their dramatics and stared directly at the king. "Elzbeth is planning to kill you."

"How dare you," the king said, clenching his jaw.

"She marries for riches and status, then kills her husbands! She killed my father and at least half a dozen men before him," Anna spat.

"Annalie!" The wicked woman said her name like it was a curse.

"Lift your spell, witch," Anna said, turning her bow on the woman who'd stolen everything from her.

Out of the corner of her eye, Anna saw Edgar step in front of Cyndra and Augustus. Cyndra grabbed Dru's arm, pulling her closer. *Do they think I would harm them?*

"I don't know what you're talking about. You're overcome with emotion," Elzbeth said, waving her hand between herself and the king. "I understand you are grieving, but you cannot continue to act out like this."

"You're a liar!" Anna screamed with all the pent-up rage of the last four years.

"Annalie," Cyndra said. "Put your bow down. We can talk."

"I've tried talking to you, Cyn!" she bit back, not taking her eyes off Elzbeth. "You never believed me when I told you the truth about Elzbeth."

"Because it's ridiculous," Cyndra replied. "You know Elzbeth loved Father."

A guard took a step closer to Elzbeth. Was he the one she saw with Elzbeth last night? The one helping her? *Shit!* What was she going to do if Phil didn't arrive in time? Shoot the guard? Shoot Elzbeth? She didn't want to make herself a murderer. She wasn't anything like Elzbeth. And yet she wondered if it would be worth it to save her family and kingdom.

She pulled the arrow back to the release point just as she spotted Phil sliding onto the balcony. Her heart leapt. Phil stood behind the guard holding the pillow and exchanged the rings. She was the only one who noticed. All eyes were trained on her. He took a couple steps back and motioned for her to lower her bow.

"Fine," she said, lowering her weapon, hoping she looked defeated. "Go ahead. Make it official."

"Annalie!" Cyndra chided. "You don't order the king!"

"She certainly doesn't," Edgar replied. Before Anna could blink, Edgar snatched her bow and threw it at the guard's feet holding the pillow and grabbed Anna's wrists, pulling them behind her back simultaneously, making her wince.

"Edgar, wait! She didn't hurt anyone. She's unwell. She's never recovered from our father's death and is acting out now that Elzbeth is engaged," Cyndra pleaded.

"Even if that is the case," the king said as Edgar's hold tightened on Anna's wrists, "there was an assassination attempt on my life last night, and Annalie has confessed to being at the scene."

"I didn't shoot you," she said. "I left after I saw Elzbeth kissing your guard."

"Enough!" the king bellowed.

"Maybe we should discuss this inside, Father," Edgar suggested as the crowd's murmurings increased and Gertrude Penny scribbled on her notepad.

"Yes, you're right, son," he said to Edgar before turning to Elzbeth. "I'm sorry that today was ruined."

Anna struggled to loosen Edgar's hold. She had to do something, but he tightened it into a vise. The guard nearest Elzbeth bent down to pick up her bow. And when he stood, he knocked the pillow and the ring at the fake king's feet.

Please, Stars! Anna begged as her heart leapt in her chest. The king sighed heavily before plucking the ring up, holding it out to Elzbeth. She nodded, then smiled, baring her teeth like a tiger closing in on its prey. Anna kept her face blank as the ring slid onto Elzbeth's green finger.

Nothing happened. The dragon's breath stone must have failed.

A bloodcurdling scream erupted from Elzbeth, making Anna's body freeze all the way to her bones. Elzbeth's eyes rolled to the back of her head before she crumpled to the ground like a marionette whose strings had been suddenly cut. The guard who knocked the pillow turned to Anna, his honey-colored eyes blazing with fury.

"Take her to the dungeon!" Edgar commanded, handing Anna over to the closest guard.

No! Anna's mind screamed as the guard practically dragged her toward the balcony doors. Edgar and the king rushed to kneel at Elzbeth's side. Cyndra let out a broken sob.

Anna took one more look at her stepmother's lifeless body before she was dragged away, aware that her fate was now sealed. The dragon's breath stone had broken Elzbeth's spell by killing her. And now Anna truly was a murderer.

E lzbeth thought she'd experienced every kind of pain, but nothing could compare to the agony of the ring singeing a circle of fire around her finger. She looked at it, blinking as the stone changed. *Not her engagement ring.* The pain of her past was rendered to nothing as the stone's magic flayed her like a fish. Her skin peeled away from her flesh as the beauty spell fought against whatever magic this ring held.

The magic released her skin and allowed her to take one jagged breath before it zeroed in on her eyes. Pain erupted like twin daggers, boring into them. Bloody tears ran down her cheeks, blinding her instantly. Elzbeth begged the Stars to let her die.

But the Stars mocked her, watching in silence as she suffered, abandoning her once more.

The pain ebbed slowly from her eyes, winding its way to the two pieces of her torn heart. Elzbeth wondered if the spell knew what it had done to her heart, but it was taking no responsibility for that now. A scorching needle weaved right, left, and right between the two halves, stitching the pieces back together. Left, right, and left… and then finally, blessed darkness.

✄ ✄ ✄ ✄ ✄

"Elz."

A familiar voice had her opening her eyes. She blinked against the onslaught of bright light. The pain was gone, and she knew she was dead because he was kneeling next to her, taking her hand into his.

"Thomas" was all she could choke out as tears streamed like waterfalls from her eyes.

"Hey, don't cry," he said as he gently wiped a few tears with his thumb. "You did it. You figured out how to break the spell."

"I didn't break it. This ring, it broke it," she said.

"Yes, it was the ring, but it was also you. Your heart had to be ready to love again, or nothing would've broken the spell." He smiled tenderly at her.

"Wait. I… don't… understand," she said.

"I knew what the future held for you, so I created the spell to only be broken when your heart was ready to love again."

"You used the spell book!" she exclaimed and sat up. He leaned back with her quick movement. "When you were gone for so long. You used the map to see the future?"

He nodded, and her lips trembled.

"Why not change it if you knew you and your grandmother would *die*?" Elzbeth asked, barely able to utter the last of the question.

"I lied to you that day in the library." Thomas pulled his hand through his rumpled hair. He looked older. Smile lines creased his lips and eyes, marking a life full of laughter and smiling. It was how it should've been if Elzbeth's father hadn't killed him at sixteen. Tears flooded her eyes again.

"I didn't just use the *Map of the Forgotten* but also *Map of Tomorrows*. I wanted to know if you and I had a future. After I saw what your father was planning to ensure you married the evil king of Tranik, I used the book to go to the dragon's den. I'd heard a story about a powerful spell book gifted to a dragon," he explained.

Her face scrunched. "My spell. You didn't create it?"

"I did. But with some help," Thomas said. "The dragon caught me before I could search for the spell book." She blinked at him through watery eyes, remembering the tale. "I barely escaped and was going to use the map spell book again, but you were there, and, well, you know the rest."

She shook her head, because she clearly didn't.

"After you decided to run away and marry me, I used the book again—before we left your estate. I wanted to see the outcome of our decision. I saw your father come for us and kill…" His breath hitched. "My grandmother. We knew the risk." He paused as the grief of that moment washed over them both. "She loved you dearly," he added.

Elzbeth began to sob, the floodgates opened by those four simple words. Thomas and his grandmother had known they were walking into death but still did it because they loved her. Thomas wrapped his arms around her, cocooning her in his warmth. It felt nice to have him hold her again. She missed him more than words could express.

"Why?" Elzbeth asked after several moments, when her words were able to break through the tears. "Why do this when you knew all I would go through just to end up dead now?"

"Because you're not dead," Thomas said.

Elzbeth pulled back, staring at him through watery eyes. He wiped a few stray tears from her cheeks.

"Once I knew what the future held, I started working on the spell but couldn't get it right. So, I made a wish the night of the Tranik royal ball, and Fairy Godmother answered."

Her eyes widened. Jaq told her that was the night Bell's mother learned Elzbeth wasn't dead. Thomas had been gone for hours that same night. *Was what Fairy Godmother told Jaq about how she learned of my survival a lie?*

"I told her what I saw and what I had planned but asked that she grant me three things," he said, cutting into her thoughts. "First, to help me make the spell strong enough to protect you until you figured out how to break it. Second, to let me speak to you one time after you broke it."

Her mouth fell open. She could feel her heart pounding against her rib cage.

"And third, to not speak a word to anyone about our arrangement so the future I saw for you would hold and you could be free from your father."

"No one can rewrite the stars." Bell's mother's bloody words rang through her mind. She had lied to keep her deal with Thomas a secret.

"That's why the map spell book never took us to Fairy Godmother," Thomas concluded. Bell's mom knew Elzbeth would kill her in order to gain her freedom from her father. She knew and still she agreed to Thomas's wish.

"I needed you to know that none of it was your fault and that we loved you," he said, beaming at her with so much warmth. "You are loved, Elzbeth."

Her tears began to flow again. Thomas wiped them from her eyes and leaned down to press a soft kiss to her lips, barely a brush of their skin. "I will always love you. But it's time to let me go now that your heart is whole again."

"I can never let you go," she protested. His face went rigid, making her almost laugh because Stars, did she miss that too-familiar expression. "There's room for both of you," she blurted before he could argue, mustering up a smile.

"There's room for so much more, Elz." He smiled, deepening the creases around his eyes. Thomas was right. Her heart was full of so much love. For Thomas, Will, Bell, Jaq, Gray, her nieces, and her three girls.

And just then, she remembered. "Annalie!" she gasped. "Oh Stars, she threatened the king. She's in trouble!"

"Which is why it's time for you to wake up," he said, gently squeezing her hand. "Annalie needs you."

With that, Thomas faded into the light, but not before leaving Elzbeth more whole than she thought she'd ever be with his parting words.

"I promised you I'd love you until the day I died, and beyond."

Forty-One

ANNA: 2 HOURS, 45 MINUTES AFTER THE CLOCK STRUCK 12

Anna sat against the damp dungeon wall with her arms wrapped around her bent legs, resting her chin on her knees. With each breath she took, the humid, foul odors swirled up her nose, absolutely failing to distract her from her drowning thoughts. She wondered if she'd see the dawn or if the decree for her death would arrive before the sun went down. After all, she'd murdered the king's fiancée and threatened his life.

She wondered, if she had to do it all over again, would she? A tear trickled down her cheek. She didn't know. Maybe it would've been better to stay in her lonely world where no one believed her about Elzbeth. At least there she wouldn't be a murderer.

She closed her eyes and drew in a long breath, ignoring the rancid odors that assaulted her as she imagined her life ten years from now if she had just kept quiet and been the good little pawn until she was married off to some man of the court.

She shuddered at the image of her future self, trapped in a life where she hosted tea parties for other ladies and talked about things like needlework or what she should have the cooks prepare her husband for dinner. Her whole body began to tremble.

Phil's face flashed before her closed lids, his slate-grey eyes sparkling with flecks of silver. He looked at her like she was his sun, the center of his universe, as their lips touched, tasting of dreams that would never come true.

Tears flowed like water freed from a burst damn. Anna wished on the Stars for a miracle to save her from the nightmare reality she was locked in. She wished for a home where instead of hosting tea parties, she laughed with Phil because they were both free. Free of Elzbeth and free of Phil's curse. *Oh Stars! What will happen to Phil now? And to Drury and Daff? Surely, they'll be found out as accomplices?*

A sob burst from her before she could choke it back.

It's all my fault.

She should've kept her head down and her mouth shut. Another sob rattled her ribcage.

"Are you alright, Annalie?" Fairy Godmother's voice rang off the damp stones from the cell next to hers, causing Anna's heart to stop. *Shit!* She'd forgotten Phil had locked up the double-crossing woman.

She wondered why Fairy Godmother hadn't said anything this whole time. Anna had been down there for at least a few hours.

"I'm sure once you children explain…" Fairy Godmother began before the sound of boots stomping down the stone stairs cut her words short.

Anna lifted her head and winced. Her neck was sore from the hours hunched in the same position, blinking away her tears as they landed on the dungeon floor. *Is this it?* she wondered.

Wait a minute! She wiped the last of her tears away, seeing a light at the end of the tunnel. Or the cell, in her case. When Anna had to stand trial, she would expose Prince Leo.

She held her breath as the guards moved in front of her cell. But they weren't coming for her. Anna gasped, throwing a hand over her mouth. They had Elzbeth. Her head was slumped forward, the toes of her silver slippers hissing against the stones as the two guards dragged her between them. They halted at the cell directly across from Anna's.

One of the guards fumbled the key into the lock, turning it with his free hand as the other opened the cell door. The squeaking hinges pierced her ears as they laid Elzbeth on her back. Relief flooded Anna at the steady rise and fall of Elzbeth's chest. *Thank the Stars! I'm not a murderer.* Fresh tears pricked her eyes.

"Welcome to your new home, witch!" one of the guards spat, slamming the cell door as the other chuckled lowly.

Anna's eyes brightened. She wanted to shout for joy at the guard's words. The dragon's breath stone had worked! Elzbeth's spell was broken.

"What's going on?" Fairy Godmother exclaimed.

The guards turned, eyes wide behind their hooded masks.

"Fairy Godmother has been helping Elzbeth," Anna shouted quickly before the traitor of a woman spun a story for the guards.

Whack!

The guard on the left grunted before falling to the ground.

Whack!

The second guard fell, his body collapsing onto the first.

Anna blinked, not seeing a soul. Her heart jumped at the hope it was Phil. *But why would he knock the guards out?*

"Phil?"

Pink stardust sparkled above the unconscious guards, falling like snow before melting away and taking the guards with it.

Shit!

"Thank the Stars! What's going on, Will?" Fairy Godmother asked.

"Elzbeth's spell is broken," a man said. Anna recognized it as the voice of the man with Elzbeth in the tavern. A puff of emerald-green smoke, the color of Elzbeth's skin, clouded the corridor blocking Elzbeth's cell before Will materialized in a royal guard's uniform.

"How?" Fairy Godmother exclaimed.

"The ring," Anna said before Will could answer, pride replacing her guilt.

"Annalie, you broke Elzbeth's spell?" Fairy Godmother asked, sounding flustered.

"I had help," Anna replied. "But you already knew that," she added smugly.

"Really? You children broke it?" Fairy Godmother's words dripped with shock and awe. Anna wished she could've seen her expression rather than imagining it. It wasn't every day a bunch of children bested *the* Fairy Godmother.

"Yes, really!" Anna bit back at the woman who had aided her wicked stepmother with her evil deeds. "And you will be held—"

"Will, you need to take Elzbeth and Annalie to the Sanctuary." Fairy Godmother cut Anna's threat short.

"I agree," Will said as he approached Fairy Godmother's cell. "But that was the last of my stardust supply." Anna strained to hear his next words. "If you slip me your wand, I can whip up some more to…"

A familiar voice carried down into the depths, making Anna's heart leap. "You don't understand, I need to see my sister," Dru demanded, masking her panic with cool confidence.

"Lady Drury, we are under strict orders. No one goes in the dungeon but royals and guards."

"Please, Anna is innocent! She wasn't threatening the king, she was only trying… Just let me speak with her," Dru pleaded.

"Will, I need you to get my wand," Fairy Godmother said. "Lady Drury, Annalie, and Prince Rupert stole it last night before they imprisoned me." Her words rushed from her like a raging river.

"Is that so?" Will said, stepping in front of Anna's cell, his honey-colored eyes blazing. Anna took a step closer to the bars, meeting his glare. The wards' humming increased at their close proximity, several inches beyond the bars, reminding her to cross her arms in front of her chest to not reach through.

"You little liar. You were the one who shot the arrow last night," he said, seething. "Working with the hidden prince to threaten not only the king, but Elzbeth too?"

"I didn't shoot at anyone," Anna said, unblinking, willing her blue eyes to be sharp as ice. "We wouldn't be having this conversation if I'd taken the shot." Her lips quirked.

Will chuckled. "Well, aren't you a cocky one?"

Fairy Godmother clapped several times. The sound reverberated off the dungeon walls as she asked, "Annalie, where is my wand?"

"No clue," Anna lied, grateful the osmium bars were suppressing her magic.

Dru's voice suddenly echoed down. "Would you pass on a message to my sister for me then?"

"Yes. I can do that much, Lady Drury," the guard replied.

"I'll have Lady Drury tell me where your wand is and be back," Will said to Fairy Godmother, cutting Anna a parting glare.

"Dru, run!" Anna screamed at the top of her lungs. *Dru, run!* Her warning echoed down the damp dungeon corridor. "Get Phil!"

Will's wrist rotated. A puff of emerald smoke billowed like a cloud, swallowing her words and their echo before it could reach Dru. Silence dripped like moisture from the damp stone walls for several heartbeats.

"Bastard," Anna hissed, lunging forward, arms shooting through the bars, her fingers curling to wrap around the evil enchanter's throat. Lightning struck her fingertips the moment they grazed the ward's barrier, on the other side of the bars, sizzling through her entire body. The invisible force threw her like a discarded rag doll, and she crashed into the stone wall.

Blinding white pain tore her in two before the world turned black.

⧗ ⧗ ⧗ ⧗ ⧗

Drip. 1,032. *Drip.* 1,033. Anna counted to help the time pass in the silent dungeon, waiting. She wasn't sure how long she was out for, but she woke with a pounding headache and large goose egg on the back of her head. She begged the Stars that Dru had heard her warning and gotten away from Will. *Drip.* 1,034.

She lifted her eyes to Elzbeth's cell. Elzbeth lay unaffected by the dungeon's dankness, while Anna held multiple layers of her dress in place over her nose and mouth. Anna had no clue what Fairy Godmother was doing. She couldn't see her, and she hadn't made a sound in the past two hours after giving up trying to get Anna to answer her questions.

Boots scuffed on the dungeon stairs as two royal guards marched in. They stopped in front of her and Elzbeth's cells, carrying dinner plates. Wordlessly, they slid the meals through the bars. The wards crackled as if in resistance to even their inanimate meals crossing the barriers.

"Please, you need to help…" Anna crawled to the bars as the guard slid her plate in, but she froze upon seeing his glassy stare.

Shit… they're enchanted.

She stared at the plate of food as their boots pounded against the stones, leaving Anna alone again. Her stomach growled, but she refused to eat. Will probably poisoned her food or water before he enchanted the guards to bring it to them.

"So, how does *the* Fairy Godmother come to work with a murderer?" Anna finally asked.

"Annalie, there's a lot—"

"Wait, Bell," Elzbeth chimed in. Anna's head whipped to her cell. "I want to explain."

"Elzbeth!" Fairy Godmother gasped. "You're awake."

"I am," she said with a groan. "Though I feel like shit," she added, rolling to her side. Anna practically swallowed her tongue at Elzbeth's cursing.

"Take it slow. You've been unconscious for hours," Fairy Godmother suggested.

Elzbeth slowly scooted to the stone wall and leaned back. "Annalie, we need to talk."

Anna pressed the material tighter over her nose and mouth. She stared back at Elzbeth for several heartbeats. "I have nothing to say to you." In fact, she had a lot to say. She sighed, staring daggers at the woman whose fault it was that she was here now… for the lengths Anna had to go to save her family and kingdom and break Elzbeth's spell. "You're a vile woman. A monster. You're the reason my father is dead and I'm here now!" Anna had been waiting *so long* to say that to Elzbeth. Uttering the words felt like a weight lifting off her chest.

Elzbeth glanced toward Fairy Godmother's cell, then lowered her head. But not before Anna saw what she was trying to hide in the movement. A single glistening tear streaked down Elzbeth's green cheek.

Forty~Two

ELZBETH: 6 HOURS AFTER THE CLOCK
STRUCK 12

Annalie's words, like her arrows, hit the bullseye of Elzbeth's heart. It was her fault that Annalie was here now in this dungeon with her. Bell too. A tear escaped down her cheek. She bowed her head to hide it.

"May I say something?" Bellenda asked sweetly. Elzbeth wiped the tear away before raising her head.

"It's not like I can stop you," Annalie said dryly, tossing her fiery red braid over her shoulder.

"True, dear," Bellenda replied, keeping her tone sweet. "But might I suggest you read the article for tomorrow's *Fairytales, Facts, and Fables* newspaper that was left under our plates of food?"

Elzbeth pulled her plate towards herself, every muscle in her body protesting as the tin scraped against the rough stone pavers, making the same sounds as Annalie's flute during their lessons.

"I didn't get a copy," Annalie said sharply. "Apparently Will doesn't think I need to be in the know."

"Will?" Elzbeth asked, glancing from Annalie to Bellenda.

"Read the article first, Elz. Then I'll explain," Bellenda said. Elzbeth shook her head but lifted the plate and plucked the paper from beneath. She read tomorrow's date below the headline, then said aloud: "'Scheming Stepmother and Jealous Juvenile' by Gertrude Penny."

Annalie growled lowly, jumping to her feet, and wrapped her hands around the bars of her cell.

Elzbeth gingerly rose to her feet and moved to the bars so Annalie could hear her read the article better.

"Fairytales are normally told from the perspective of the one whose life has changed dramatically for the better, like Lady Annalie Beck's oldest sister, Princess Cyndra. She, like her two younger sisters and many of the girls in our kingdom, dreamed of one day becoming a princess. Her dream came true when she met our wonderful Prince Edgar at the ball, but Lady Annalie's story wouldn't even make it to the back page of *Fairytales, Facts, and Fables* on a slow day, because the truth is… Well, let me start at the beginning, dear reader, so you understand why Lady Annalie gave me this interview days before she was arrested for an attempted assassination of our dear King Tyson."

"Hold on! I didn't give Gertrude Penny an interview!" Annalie protested. "And like I've been saying, I did *not* shoot that arrow at the king!"

"Keep reading," Bellenda encouraged. "You both need to hear what you're accused of working on together."

"What?" Annalie's voice rang two octaves higher through the dungeon.

Elzbeth sighed, gently leaning against the stone wall to continue reading.

"It all started on Lady Annalie's thirteenth birthday. You could say that she was a late bloomer when it came to her magic waking. I know what you're thinking: her magic should've appeared on her tenth birthday. But Lady Annalie Beck is unique. Her words, not mine, dear reader. Her magic appeared on her thirteenth birthday, the same day her father was spelled by her now stepmother, Lady Elzbeth Beck. Lady Annalie claims that if her magic had only sprouted earlier, she could've stopped her father from marrying Lady Elzbeth and would have saved her father and our kingdom, which Lady Annalie claimed at the time of this interview 'was under Lady Elzbeth's dark spell.'"

"She took that from the letter I wrote! Well, sort of. But I lost it and…" Annalie paused. "Gertrude could've at least used my favorite line," Annalie continued. "It was, *'If I had been there, I would have called bibbidi, bobbidi, bullshit.'*"

"Oooh, I like that one." Bellenda laughed and pulled her small notebook and pencil from her dress pocket.

"Of course you do," Annalie said, rolling her eyes.

Elzbeth shook her head at them and went back to the article.

"But Lady Annalie, who claims she would've stopped the wedding, wasn't even there when her father and stepmother were joined in union by Fairy Godmother. She was at school because she had no magic—until that day, so she claims. Even her oldest sister, Princess Cyndra, was quoted saying that neither of her sisters have magic. She went on to say, 'Annalie is a good kid who has taken the sudden change in me becoming a princess and then our father's death very hard and is just lashing out in pain.'"

"Seriously, Cyndra!" Annalie squealed.

Elzbeth continued.

"I believe Princess Cyndra to be speaking truth because I was at Prince Augustus's birthday party. And while there, I overheard Lady Annalie doing just that—lashing out at our dear princess and seeming quite jealous. She complained about the lavishness of the party, saying, and I quote, 'It's just a one-year-old's birthday party!'"

"What I said at the party was taken out of context," Annalie practically growled. "What the hell, Gertrude?"

Elzbeth nodded. She knew how nosy the reporter was. Elzbeth cleared her throat and went back to the article.

"But considering all that happened during the engagement announcement of Lady Elzbeth Beck to our beloved King Tyson, I decided to write this article from the perspective of a spectator on the balcony who could see Annalie holding her bow aimed at our king's heart. I wanted you, dear reader, to be given the same opportunity as me to weigh in on Lady Annalie's motives. Is Lady Annalie, like Princess Cyndra suggested, a jealous juvenile? Or is she an angry assassin hoping to take her sister's place?"

"What? I would *never* want to take Cyndra's place!" Annalie exclaimed, her knuckles white from gripping the bars.

"Keep reading," Bellenda encouraged.

Elzbeth blew out a hard breath before continuing.

"Now, I will admit, reader, that when Lady Annalie pulled her bow and arrow on our king, I thought it was due to her heartbreak over the loss of her father and her lovely stepmother getting engaged, just as our dear Princess Cyndra told me in her interview. But when it was declared that the arrow pointed at our beloved king's heart was identical to the one shot at him the night prior, the wheels began to spin, and Lady Annalie became the target suspect (pun intended) of the attempted assassination of King Tyson. I believed Lady Annalie was trying to frame Lady Elzbeth. That was, until she put her engagement ring on. I watched as the beautiful fiancée of our king turned an ugly shade of green, and my mind cleared, like a fog lifting. That's when I realized that Lady Elzbeth and Lady Annalie Beck were working together."

"We're not working together!" Annalie gritted her teeth.

"Clearly, dear, but keep reading, Elz."

Elzbeth gripped the paper tighter and continued.

"Multiple times, Lady Annalie tried to stop the king from putting the engagement ring on Lady Elzbeth's finger. She knew the king and Fairy Godmother had caught on to their scheming and had the ring spelled to expose them."

Elzbeth's breath hitched in her throat. She looked up. "Annalie, the ring? It was you?" she asked, shock and awe swirling together at what Annalie had accomplished.

"I had help," Annalie said, gritting her teeth. "Like you, with all your murderous—"

"Stop wasting time and finish the article!" Bellenda said sharply. No one dared to breathe. The sounds of water dripping against stones filled the humid space. Bellenda cleared her throat. "Sorry, but you really do need to finish this."

Elzbeth nodded and returned to the article.

"What was their true plan, you ask, dear reader? I believe it was to poison our dear King Tyson and Prince Edgar so they could mold Prince Augustus before he took the throne. They would use Lady Elzbeth's spell the next seventeen years to manipulate Princess Cyndra to shape Prince Augustus into a puppet that they could control to fulfill their agendas."

Elzbeth took a quick breath.

"I know what you're thinking. How can I make such an accusation? How could I assume something so horrible? I couldn't. Until I was sent a fire message with a copy of Lord Beck's autopsy report. The report detailed the poison used to stop his heart. That same poison, according to my interview with Lady Drury Beck, was confirmed to have been placed in the drinks for the engagement toast. This poison works by placing the victim in a deep sleep. Minutes after Lady Elzbeth's spell lifted, the king and Prince Edgar were locked in the grips of said poison, which will slowly kill them unless an antidote can be found."

"Oh hells!" Elzbeth said lowly. *How did Annalie get her hands on that poison?* Elzbeth hadn't used it in years because it took months, rather than days, to kill her husbands.

A thought suddenly occurred to her. *I didn't use that poison on Lord Beck! Someone must've sent a fake autopsy report to—*

"You need to give them the antidote," Annalie commanded.

"There isn't one," Elzbeth replied. "And that's not what—"

"There's more," Bellenda said, cutting off Elzbeth's confession.

She drew in a breath, trying to calm the frantic beating of her heart. There was still so much unknown, like who wrote the messages on the back of the documents, their infiltration in the Link, and who had knowledge of the king's true identity. Was it the same person who had sent the reporter the false autopsy report?

"We'll figure it out, but you need to finish the article." Bellenda's voice yanked Elzbeth from her swirling thoughts.

Her hand shook, bouncing the words, making them difficult to read.

"I know what your next questions must be, dear reader. First, how do I know the autopsy report isn't a fake on account of all documentation having been burned in last month's fire? Well, I had this same thought. I had a notary take a look at the report, ensuring it was official."

That notary must be involved with the Link, Elzbeth thought.

"Second, who sent me the report and how did they have it? I have no clue. But I am working closely with authorities and hope to have more information to share in my next article. As for your last question, how do I know Lady Elzbeth and Lady Annalie were the ones to poison the king and prince? This information I got from a royal guard whom I interviewed after the engagement catastrophe. He told me that Lady Annalie asked him to have a kitchen attendant prepare a toast for the announcement. A toast that both Lady Annalie and Lady Elzbeth refused to drink."

Elzbeth took a quick breath.

"Now, what about Princess Cyndra and Lady Drury? Wouldn't they have also drunk the poison during the toast?"

"Exactly!" Annalie exclaimed. "Proof we are… I mean, *I am… innocent.*"
Elzbeth's heart pounded in her chest, but she kept reading.

"Well, I asked Princess Cyndra this same question after receiving her father's autopsy report. She was by her husband's bedside, holding his pale, limp hand. Princess Cyndra said, and I quote, '*Anna knows I'm pregnant and wouldn't drink the alcohol and that Dru hates the taste of it.*'"

Cyndra is pregnant? Augustus just turned one, and she's now going to have another baby! No wonder she's been so exhausted lately. Elzbeth drew in a long breath.

"So, there you have it, dear reader. All the facts I was able to glean. Now we wait for Fairy Godmother and our dear Prince Aaron, who replied by fire message that he would finally be returning home after two decades to oversee the trial of Lady Annalie Beck and Lady Elzbeth Beck's assassination attempts not once, but twice on our dear King Tyson and Prince Edgar as they slowly slip away to their deaths unless an antidote can be found in time."

"Why does Cyndra think I'm working with you?" Annalie asked sharply. "None of this makes sense."

Tell me about it.

"And why hasn't Dru told them that it was you two working together, not me?" Annalie said.

"Because Lady Drury isn't here, and I stopped the newspaper's fire messages from going out," Will said, his voice as smooth as his honey eyes as he emerged from the shadowy corner near the dungeon steps.

"**Y**ou bastard!" Anna screamed. "Where is Dru? I swear, if you laid a single finger on her, I'll—" Her threat was cut short as Will unsheathed his sword. The sound of steel on steel clanged through the dungeon, followed by sparks. Will pivoted, his sword moving, fighting an invisible force that only he could see.

"Phil, is that you?" Anna called.

"Yes," Phil replied. "I was hoping to sneak in but apparently her henchman can see through enchantments, illusions, and spells like you," he added sounding breathless. Will slashed down. "Not only do you have horrible taste in women," Phil continued. *Clang. Clang. Clang.* "But your form could use some work."

"How dare you, Prince Rupert!" Fairy Godmother's voice cut as sharp as the sword Will was wielding.

"It's alright, Bell," Elzbeth said. "Annalie and Prince Rupert don't know the truth, so I don't expect them to understand."

"What truth?" Anna spewed. "I highly doubt there's anything you could tell me that would make me understand what you've done!" Sparks burst in front of Will's chest.

"That I saved you," Elzbeth said, tearing her eyes away from Will to look at Anna.

"Saved me!" Anna scoffed. "You tricked me! Well, at least you tried to." Will spun and jumped. "Phil, save your magic," Anna yelled. "We need to use the book—"

"Annalie, there's lots we need to discuss." Elzbeth cut in. "I'm sorry to say, but your father, he wasn't a good man—"

Anna's blood boiled. "How dare you say that about my father!" she shouted. "You're a liar and a murderous monster!"

"I'm not a monster!" Elzbeth snapped back. She drew in a long breath and let it out slowly as sparks ignited at the edge of Will's clanging blade. "I can admit that I'm not *good*. At least by the common definition of the word," Elzbeth said more calmly. "But I did what I had to do to protect others. Women and young girls like you and Drury. I will never be sorry for that. But *I am* sorry that I never told you the truth about your father. I should've done that a long time ago."

What truth? Anna's mind screamed. She shook her head. She wouldn't fall for the witch's trap. *She's a liar and a murderer, for Stars' sake!*

Will jumped back, hitting Elzbeth's cell and rattling the door, his back pressing into the bars.

"Enough!" Fairy Godmother demanded, standing in the middle of the aisle in front of the cells and wielding her wand like a sword.

"Shit!" Anna exclaimed. Phil flashed into sight, his sword pressed to Will's heart. "Wait," she said, her mind reeling as she glanced between Phil's sword and Fairy Godmother's wand. "How did you get your wand back?"

"Me," Will answered with a smile and a wink.

Arrogant bastard. Anna rolled her eyes.

Before Anna could get out another thought, Fairy Godmother pointed her wand at her cell. She flicked it, and pale pink stardust opened the lock with a click as the wards' humming ceased. Anna didn't move. *Is this a trap?*

"Come on, dear, we don't have time to dillydally," Fairy Godmother said. Anna pushed the cell door open and took an awkward sidestep around her.

"Run, Anna!" Phil shouted. He was still holding his sword to Will's heart. Anna rushed for the stairs as quickly as she could in her heavy, layered dress. Then, she froze midstep as pale pink stardust landed on her legs and turned them solid, like blocks of ice.

"Release me!" Anna craned her head, staring daggers at Fairy Godmother.

"I told you, we don't have time for this." She waved her wand, floating Anna like a feather next to Phil. Her locked legs kept her trapped.

"Annalie, I'm sorry. This is not how I wanted any of this to happen," Elzbeth began.

"Don't speak to me, witch!" Anna's words fell from her mouth like shards of broken glass. "I don't want your voice to be the last thing I hear before you murder me like all your past stepchildren."

"Oh, Annalie…" Elzbeth's shoulders drooped like a wilting flower. "There's so much you need to know."

"Don't bother lying," Annalie said, her words landing like arrows on Elzbeth's still healing heart. "We overheard you talking when you were searching Dru's room."

Elzbeth's eyes widened. "You were in the room?" She turned to Prince Rupert. "Were you using your magic to spy on me?"

Before the prince could answer, Annalie asked softly, tears lining her eyes, "Is Dru dead?"

"She's fine," Will answered. "After I learned of the article, I took her to the Sanctuary to start working on an antidote with Grayson."

Elzbeth sighed in relief at the thought of Drury being at the Sanctuary. *She's safe.*

Will took a quick breath and continued, "She's a brilliant kid. Kept her flute laced with the poison. They estimate to have the antidote finished in the next day or two." Elzbeth watched Annalie's shoulders relax.

"Who's Grayson, and what's the Sanctuary?" Prince Rupert asked.

"We don't have time to explain," Bellenda said.

"How did you get Fairy Godmother's wand back?" Prince Rupert continued his questioning, ignoring Bellenda. He pushed his sword into Will's chest. A blotch of blood formed around the tip, staining Will's tunic.

Elzbeth flicked her eyes to Bellenda, willing her to use her magic to stop the prince from hurting Will further.

"I enchanted Drury to tell me where it was. Took me a bit to find it. Her room is something else." Will smiled broadly, completely unbothered by the sword pressed to his chest.

I love this cocky man. Elzbeth's mending heart flipped. She couldn't wait to say those words to him.

"I came back here to give Bellenda her wand, but while I was on my way, I overheard the reporter reading the article to Princess Cyndra," Will continued. "So I enchanted Gertrude to give it to me and tell me where the autopsy report was. I dropped Drury off at the Sanctuary on my way and—"

Bellenda flicked her wand. Pink stars fell on the prince's sword, pulling it from his hand and floating it to hers. "Later, William, you can tell us about your heroics. The clock is ticking."

Bellenda flicked her wand at Elzbeth's cell, releasing her. Will grabbed her and pulled her to his chest. She practically melted into his body.

"Are you alright?" he asked. He cradled her face with his hands, glancing at the ring that broke her spell. Elzbeth hadn't realized it was still on her finger.

"I'm a bit sore, but I've survived much worse," she said.

Will leaned in, his honey eyes trapping her, beckoning. Elzbeth leaned in until their lips were barely touching. She needed to tell him how she felt first. "Will, I love—"

"Sorry, but we don't have time for that either," Bellenda interrupted. *Damn you, Bells!* "We need to go now before a guard comes down here."

Will groaned, eyes blazing, and locked on Elzbeth's. They both let out a breath. *Later,* she mouthed to him. Will responded with a devilish grin.

Bellenda flicked her wand to release Annalie's legs.

"We're not going anywhere with you!" Annalie shouted as she latched onto Prince Rupert's arm. Elzbeth's eyes widened at their familiarity. The prince pulled the map spell book from his bag with his free hand. Elzbeth hadn't seen the book since Bellenda used it to show her the truth of her birth.

"Yes, dear, you are correct. I'm not going with you. I'm needed here for Prince Aaron's arrival. I also need to ensure there are no more copies of this article. If it ever got out, it would do more damage than even I could fix." She flicked her wand at the paper still clutched in Elzbeth's hand, turning it to ash.

"Good luck with that," Annalie said dryly as the book fell open in Prince Rupert's hand. "But we're taking matters into our hands now. We need to go back and stop the king and Edgar from drinking the poison."

Not a bad idea, Elzbeth thought.

"No. You need to go to the Sanctuary," Bellenda argued, pointing her wand at the book, closing it.

"Hurry up. Prince Aaron wants to interrogate Princess Cyndra's sister and stepmother before Fairy Godmother shows up," a guard's voice echoed from the top of the stairs. Heavy footsteps followed.

They really were out of time.

"I'll handle things here, but you need to go now," Bellenda said and flicked her wand at the book, opening it up in the prince's hands again. "Use it to take them home, William." She tossed the prince's sword to him and flicked her wand over her head, disappearing in a rain of pink stardust.

"No!" Annalie yelled. "We won't go with you."

"Sorry, kid, but you are," Will said, waving his free hand over Prince Rupert's face. A puff of green smoke fell on his skin and put him under an enchantment.

"Grab Annalie's hand and hold it and yours on the book," Will commanded the enchanted prince. Rupert smiled and did exactly as Will instructed. *"Map of the Known."*

"You bastard!" Annalie screamed. "You'll never be able to get away with this!" Elzbeth's heart squeezed at Annalie's anger. She wished there was another way. But there wasn't. Once at the Sanctuary, Elzbeth would tell Annalie everything. She would take as much time as she needed to help her understand.

"Sorry, no time for pleasantries," Will said, sliding the prince's sword into his sheath and putting his left hand under the book. Elzbeth inched closer and put her hand beneath his. Will gazed in her eyes. "Read the spell, Elz, and I will think of where to go." The guard's footsteps echoed louder as they approached.

Elzbeth began the spell.

"Think of a place you have been, but focus your mind not to spin—"

"Stop!" a guard yelled, running toward them with his sword drawn.

"Concentrate while closing your eyes, then open them up for a big surprise."

She finished quickly. Will's magic puffed over the book, making it glow. The guard's sword barely missed the book, which sucked them inside it just in the nick of time.

The colors swooshed past, blending in and out of each other. Elzbeth closed her eyes, drawing in her first deep breath in almost four years. She was finally taking Annalie to the Sanctuary, where she and Drury would be safe. She exhaled, her feet landing on solid ground.

"Release him," Annalie hissed the second they arrived.

Elzbeth took a moment, keeping her eyes shut to center herself.

"He should be coming out of it in a few seconds," Will said.

He took hold of Elzbeth's face, running his hands over her skin tenderly. Warmth overtook her body as she opened her eyes to peer at this man whom she loved so much. She couldn't wait to tell him how she felt—when they didn't have an audience.

"Phil, look at me," Annalie was calling to Prince Rupert. *Phil?* Elzbeth would have to explore that later. She was locked in Will's gaze.

"The spell is broken, Will, and—" she said, staring into his eyes.

Will ran a finger over her lips, stopping her words.

"Whoa," the prince said, coming out of Will's enchantment.

"Are you alright?" Annalie asked.

"I think so… but…" The prince stopped. "Where are we?"

"This is the Sanctuary," Elzbeth said. She couldn't stop smiling at Will. He blinked, breaking their connection. She turned to the prince and Annalie. "This is our…" Her words halted as she took in their surroundings. *Wait. What? Where the hell are we?* Her eyes widened at the unfamiliar throne room they stood inside. Her pulse started to race.

"I'm sorry, Elz," Will said softly, cupping a hand to her face and pulling her eyes back to him.

"Sorry?" she asked confused. "Will? Why do you know this place? What in the Stars is going on?" Her breaths suddenly felt labored.

"Believe me, Elz, I'm so sorry," Will said again and waved his free hand. A puff of green smoke blinded her. She startled back, lifting her hands to clear the magical smoke. *No, no, no!* her mind screamed in utter disbelief. Her natural green skin had been replaced with sun-kissed rosy skin that even she could see.

She lifted her eyes to his, wide wond frightened. "Why?" was all she could manage. *Why did he enchant me?* The throne room doors burst open. A half-dozen royal guards in red and black uniforms marched in. A large man followed, wearing an equally large golden crown.

"King Zegan," Prince Rupert said lowly.

"King Zegan of Lexlent?" Annalie asked.

Elzbeth raked her eyes over the man as he marched toward them, guards flanking both sides. He was tall, almost a head more than some of his guards, and just as broad. His face was set in a scowl that didn't diminish his striking attractiveness. He was almost too perfect-looking, with golden-tan skin unmarked by his sixty years.

"It's an enchantment, Elz," Will said softly. "He enchants himself to be seen as—"

"How dare you!" she spat lowly for his ears only. "You enchanted me!" The stitches on her heart tugged apart as tears lined her eyes. "Against my will!" Elzbeth choked on the last words.

"I'm not like him. *You have to know I'd never use my magic on you without your permission."* The echo of Will's promise rang in her mind like a cruel joke.

"You promised you would never!" The stitches holding her heart tugged further, allowing a trickle of blood to seep through. She was drowning in a sea of pain.

"I'm sorry, Elz, but this is the only way I can protect you."

The king stepped in front of them. Will turned, moving to her side to face him.

"What are you doing here?" the king boomed, speaking far too loud for their close proximity. A vein on his neck bulged with each word.

"No idea," Annalie said quickly.

"King Zegan, we are—" Prince Rupert began.

"May I introduce Lady Anastasia," Will interrupted and gestured to Annalie. She blinked feverishly at the fake name but recovered quickly and bowed to the king. "Lady Anastasia's cousin, Lord Phillip." He waved his hand to the prince, who followed suit and bowed.

"And this is Lady Anastasia's beautiful mother, Baroness…" He cleared his throat. "Baroness Tremaine. My fiancée."

What the hell is going on?

Elzbeth reeled at the boldness with which Will spoke to the king. Before she could ask, Will continued, freezing her heart so deeply she feared it would never thaw.

"May I introduce you all to the king of Lexlent, King Zegan William Tiberius. My father."

Afterword

Dear Reader,

Well, that was quite a cliffhanger to end on. And like Elzbeth apologizing to Annalie, I'm sorry I ended it so shockingly but also not sorry, because Will now gets to tell his side of the story.

So stay tuned for the next book in the the Virtuous Villains series, all from Will's point of view, following a similar timeline as Elzbeth in *Wonderfully Wicked*.

Thank you from the bottom of my heart for reading *Wonderfully Wicked*. If you would be so kind as to rate and review on Amazon, Goodreads and BookBub, I would appreciate it.

Also, please check out my website at www.kamylavin.com and follow me on TikTok and/or Instagram @kamy_writes to keep up-to-date with all the goings-on with me and my books.

Until next time,

Kamy M. Lavin

Acknowledgments

There are so many fingerprints on this book, so I'll go in chronological order, hopefully not missing anyone.

First, Jesus. The Author and Finisher of my faith. Thank you for making me in Your creative image.

Mom and Dad. You tie for second because without you both, I wouldn't have a love for storytelling. Thank you, Dad, for your stories and songs that not only entertained me but sparked life in me to create… but also for always dreaming big and instilling that into me. And Mom, I wouldn't have written my stories down if I didn't have my personal cheerleader encouraging me to put pen to paper from an early age; but also thanks for participating with me and my imaginary friends in whatever fun we were getting into, helping me create characters and worlds. Thank you both from the bottom of my heart. I love you dearly.

Ben. My amazing husband. You helped me see that there are men who want a partner to walk alongside them, not a damsel in distress, which sparked the idea for this book. Thank you for showing up daily to do the hard work with me so we can have OUR happily ever after.

Emma and Ella. My magical girls. I wrote this book for you. A story with heroines who are not perfect but are strong and fight for a better world. Dad and I pray daily that you're fierce and kind, helping kick down doors for women. We love you to the moon and back times infinity.

Shannon. My therapist. You listened to me read every draft of this book while helping me process. You truly are a unicorn. (You are not allowed to retire for a very long time.)

Katie W. My writing coach and developmental editor. Thank you for the countless hours of letting me verbally process and for the multiple versions you helped me tweak, rewrite, and edit for this book to be polished. Thank you for reminding me that this is a marathon… and for being on my team for life.

Jennifer Fuller. My critique partner. Your fingerprints are on every chapter of this book, and each time I see them, I smile broadly. Thank you for reading at least two dozen drafts and for the countless hours on the phone and voice texting with me. You are forever my Bellenda… bestie for life!

Jill N. Davies. My formatter, line editor, and professor. Seriously, you would've been my favorite teacher in high school—or bestie in class since we are around the same age—but I am so thankful I get you now to help me make my stories stronger.

Merri, Audrey, and Corin. My amazing beta readers. Thank you for taking the time to read *Wonderfully Wicked* and giving your feedback. I can't wait to share the next book with you three.

About the Author

Kamy Lavin started creating imaginary friends and worlds at the age of three and hasn't stopped since. She lives in Northern California with her amazing husband, two magical daughters and adorable fur babies. When she isn't writing books, she can be found reading them and cosplaying as some of her favorite characters on social media.

Visit Kamy at www.kamylavin.com

9 781963 729016